Becoming Lisette

Becoming Lisette

A Novel

Rebecca Glenn

Zinerva Publishing, LLC

ZP

For information contact:
www.zinerva.com
www.rebeccaglenn.com

Book and Cover design by EBQ Book Designs

ISBN: 978-1-941081-20-4

First Edition: April 2015

10 9 8 7 6 5 4 3 2 1

For Emma, Will and Owen

Chapter One

The nuns' busy chatter awoke Lisette as they approached her cell. Most days, she would have dreaded hearing their voices coming down the corridor. But today was different.

During her solitary confinement in the underground storeroom, Lisette had comforted herself with memories of painting with her papa. Alone with nothing but the convent's summer supply of grain, Lisette thought about returning home to her parents. After today, she would no longer have to endure these punishments. *I have more than repented this time*, she thought.

Lisette slowly opened her eyes. Was it morning? She looked over to the small crack in between the floor and the door. *It must be about seven*, she thought. For the duration that Lisette had lived at the Convent of the Trinité, the nuns had kept a tight schedule. Each day of the past five years had been the same. Days began at precisely seven in the morning with prayers, followed by a light meal and morning studies of reading, writing and counting. The afternoons were reserved for sewing, embroidery and etiquette lessons.

Lisette had spent the first six years of her life in the village of Épernon, near Chartres. Like many other bourgeois girls, she had lived with a peasant family in the care of a wet nurse. According to her mother, the peasant woman had cared for Lisette like she was her own daughter.

At the age of six, Lisette was enrolled as a student in the Convent of the Trinité, on the Rue de Charonne, in the Faubourg Saint Antoine just outside Paris. Having reached her eleventh birthday, Lisette's years of formal schooling at the convent were ending.

Today, Papa will be here to take me home, Lisette thought. *Soon, I will be painting again.*

As the nuns approached her cell, Lisette listened carefully. She recognized Mother Marie's and Sister Grace's voices. *If only it was Sister Anne and not Mother Marie,* Lisette thought. Sister Anne always brought a fresh biscuit and uplifting advice, while Mother Marie delivered stale bread and chastisement. The nuns at the Convent of the Trinité had never tolerated her drawing, especially during her lessons. When Lisette would tell them that her hands had a mind of their own, she would be punished even more severely. Mother Marie often accused Lisette of taking credit for someone else's work. She was convinced that Lisette's drawings were executed by a boy. The punishment that resulted was usually bread and water in place of her daily meals, but sometimes she received lashes and solitary confinement.

Lisette listened. The voices outside the door became quiet. A key clicked in the lock and the door creaked open.

"Time to rise." Lisette heard Mother Marie's voice before she could see her.

With the door open, Lisette was temporarily blinded by the flood of bright sunlight into the windowless cell. Her eyes burned as they adjusted.

"Look at me when I'm speaking to you," Mother Marie ordered.

"The light is very bright," Lisette said as she tilted her head up toward the voice and squinted. *Where is Sister Grace?* she wondered. Lisette saw only Mother Marie. With her large build and long, flowing robes, Mother Marie was an imposing figure. "I apologize, Mother," Lisette said cautiously. She didn't want to anger Mother Marie today of all days.

"You will repent in your morning prayers. Come off that pile of straw and kneel," said Mother Marie.

Lisette slowly maneuvered her legs underneath her body so that she could kneel. Stiff all over, Lisette's body protested as she moved. For three days, she had been lying on a makeshift bed of straw with only a thin layer of burlap protecting her from the cold stone floor.

"Move faster!" Mother Marie barked.

Lisette's eyes had adjusted and she could now see that Sister Grace stood behind Mother Marie holding a tray of food. She had been silent since entering the room. Sister Grace leaned down to set the tray on the ground. She placed her hand on Lisette's back and guided her into praying position. The nuns knelt down on either side of Lisette.

Mother Marie led the prayer. "O God, we pray for this child today. We pray that she will know the error of her ways. We pray for her to know the path of righteousness. Have mercy on her soul. In the name of the Father, the Son and the Holy Spirit, Amen." The nuns crossed themselves. Lisette did the same.

"It is time for private prayers, my child," Sister Grace said. She spoke so softly Lisette barely heard her words.

Still kneeling with her eyes closed, Lisette reached between the slits on the side of her simple, woolen dress and into the sack tied around her waist. *Papa's handkerchief is still there,* she thought. Lisette had pushed it deep into her pocket bag. Touching it, Lisette felt as if her papa was kneeling next to her, protecting her.

With her hand clutching the handkerchief, Lisette began her silent prayer: *O God, please let today be the day I see my family*

3

again. Please keep them healthy and safe. Please keep me safe. Please let me paint with my papa again. Amen.

Lisette remained kneeling on the unyielding floor waiting for the nuns to finish their prayers. She knew she should pray longer, but a few words were all Lisette could muster this morning as her stomach rumbled. More distracting were her thoughts of home. Silently waiting, Lisette thought about returning to her family. Being eleven years old, she had finished her schooling. Like other bourgeois girls, once her education was complete, she would return home to prepare for marriage. She would be expected to help her mother with domestic duties, but Lisette only thought of painting with her papa.

After what seemed like hours, the nuns finally stood. Lisette rose too.

"Lisette, my child. It is time to go," whispered Sister Grace.

Lisette peered at the tray of food on the ground near her mattress. Her stomach grumbled again.

With a gentle motion of her hand, Sister Grace urged Lisette to take the food on the tray. "You may take the bread with you," she said.

Lisette bent down, slid the bread into her pocket bag and began walking out of the storeroom.

"Wait. Stop!" Mother Marie commanded.

Lisette had passed over the threshold, but she stopped immediately. More than the words themselves, it was the tone that made Lisette pause.

"What is the meaning of this?" asked Mother Marie as she contorted her body. She turned so that her torso was facing Lisette, while her lower half faced the rear of the storeroom. Her sausage-like forefinger pointed to the back corner of the room. Mother Marie's impossible pose reminded Lisette of a statue of an ancient Greek athlete.

Neither Sister Grace nor Lisette said anything. Both stood frozen. Lisette glanced at Sister Grace who appeared confused.

"I asked you a question! Now answer me!" ordered Mother Marie as she jabbed her fat, extended finger in the direction of

4

the back corner.

"Mother, I do not understand. Could you please explain to me what you are asking?" Sister Grace's words trailed off as she spoke. She seemed as afraid of her own voice as she was of Mother Marie. Mother Marie was the most senior nun at the convent and nearly everyone was frightened of her.

"I'm not speaking to you, Sister." Mother Marie turned her entire body around to face Lisette and then slowly approached her. "Lisette, what do you have to say for yourself?"

Lisette could smell last night's turnips on the nun's breath. *I should respond, but what does she want me to say?* Lisette wondered. Her mind searched for an appropriate answer. "Mother, please. I am sorry."

"Let me help you remember why you need to explain yourself. Have you forgotten the reason you are in here in the first place?" Mother Marie said, without budging.

Lisette tried again. "I apologize for −" Lisette stopped herself. What had she done exactly? Lisette found it difficult to continue speaking.

Out of the corner of her eye, Lisette could see Sister Grace bent over to examine something on the floor. *The drawing,* Lisette realized. She now knew the cause of Mother Marie's anger. *She won't let me go home,* Lisette thought. She felt her palms moisten and her heart race.

"I know how to help you remember," Mother Marie said as she pulled out a switch from inside the folds of her robes. She raised her arm in the air.

Lisette knew the time for words was over. She closed her eyes and prepared for the blows.

"Wait! Mother Marie, we can't be sure of what this is," Sister Grace said, pointing to the drawing. "I don't believe there is any need for the switch."

Still facing Lisette, Mother Marie said, "Of course we know what it is. It is the drawing of a man's face....the bishop's face," Mother Marie said and then held her breath as she made the sign of the cross.

Lisette watched a small smile form at the edge of Sister Grace's mouth as she inspected the drawing. "Even so, it is just the doodle of a child's fingers in the dirt. No cause for alarm."

"No cause for alarm? Have we not already forbidden her from this unnatural practice? Yet she continues to defy us. She must be punished until she understands," Mother Marie said. She turned and glared at the junior nun.

Lisette watched Sister Grace back up slowly and carefully. Sister Grace dragged her feet as she moved backward into the corner.

"Sister! Watch your step. You will erase the evidence!" Mother Marie shouted. She held up her hands in protest as she rushed over to the corner where the drawing had been. "You've destroyed it!"

For a moment, Lisette feared that Mother Marie would strike Sister Grace. Lisette had seen that look of anger on Mother Marie's face many times, especially before she would dole out lashes.

Mother Marie spun toward Lisette. "You insolent girl! Hold out your right hand," Mother Marie screeched.

Lisette refused. She painted with her right hand and Mother Marie knew it. When Lisette didn't move, Mother Marie grabbed Lisette's right hand and extended it in front of her body.

Lisette closed her eyes and once again prepared herself for the lashes. Whoosh. *One.* Lisette started counting inside her head. *Two.* Counting the lashes helped her withstand the punishment. She had never received more than three. It would be over soon. *Three.* Lisette opened her eyes. *Four.* Mother Marie was not going to stop. Lisette saw the determined, twisted hatred in her face. *Five.* Lisette felt the skin on the top of her hand split open. She was too afraid to look down and see the blood. Lisette fought the urge to reach in her pocket and clutch her papa's handkerchief. *Six.*

"That's enough!" Sister Grace called out.

Her thundering voice startled Lisette and must have surprised Mother Marie, because the lashes stopped.

Sister Grace ran over to Lisette and pushed her arm down so that it rested naturally by her side. "This poor child has had enough," Sister Grace said as she stood blocking Lisette.

Mother Marie was at a loss for words.

In her years of living at the Convent of the Trinité, Lisette had never witnessed any of the nuns stand up to Mother Marie. The senior nun's authority was never questioned. Lisette feared for Sister Grace.

Lisette stared at Sister Grace, who in turn was fixated on Mother Marie. *Can I move?* she wondered. Lisette turned toward Mother Marie, but received no answer. The silence hung thickly in the air for what seemed like hours.

Finally, Mother Marie broke it. "This unholy girl requires further sanctification, but she is no longer in our charge." Mother Marie swung around and floated out of the room. As she strode away, Lisette heard her voice echoing in the corridor, "See to her release."

Sister Grace faced Lisette and gently rested her hands on Lisette's shoulders. "It is time for you to go, my child. I will see that your belongings have been loaded onto the carriage. Your father is waiting." Sister Grace retrieved a handkerchief from inside her robes and handed it to Lisette. "To stop the bleeding. You don't want to stain yours." She smiled.

Lisette saw genuine kindness in her light eyes.

"Now, be on your way. May you go with God, my child."

As Lisette walked down the corridor, away from the storeroom, she placed Sister Grace's handkerchief on the top of her right hand and held it firmly in place. It quickly soaked up the blood. Before she reached the end of the hallway, she looked down at her hand. The bleeding had stopped. Lisette took a deep breath and held it while she tried to make a fist. It hurt, but she could curl her fingers inside her hand. She slowly exhaled. Lisette would still be able to hold a paint brush. She hoped that she could paint later that day. Then she remembered, *Papa promised we would paint together again when I came home.*

Chapter Two

As Lisette picked up a knife to slice the turnips, she noticed the long, white scars that stretched across the back of her right hand. She shuddered. It had been many years since she had been punished for sketching. While her hands had long ago healed from the lashes, the memory of the degrading incidents at the Convent of the Trinité lingered. But there had been no broken bones. Mother Marie had not taken away Lisette's ability to draw or paint.

"Lisette, pay attention to what you are doing," Lisette's mother scolded.

Should I rework Venus so that she is clothed? Lisette thought as she sliced.

"Lisette! I said slice ten turnips, not twelve," her mother said, this time in a harsher voice.

With her latest painting occupying her thoughts, Lisette found it difficult to concentrate on meal preparation. She had nearly finished her latest work, but had doubts about the painting. It was only the second time she had attempted an allegory painting. Lisette was pleased to have graduated from painting the less ambitious choices of landscapes and portraits. *No, I should leave her nude,* she thought.

"You are going to cut yourself! Watch what you are doing," Lisette's mother chastised her again. Abandoning her pie crust, Jeanne Vigée marched down to Lisette's end of the long pinewood table that stood in the middle of the kitchen and snatched the knife away from her.

"Do you see what happens when you are distracted by art and not paying attention?" Jeanne said, raising Lisette's scarred hand up to her face. Her mother's hands were cold and slimy from handling the pie crust.

"Yes, Mother. I promise. I will concentrate on the cooking."

"It does you no good to be thinking about painting. It won't help you find a suitable husband and get married." Jeanne handed Lisette the knife again and returned to her pie crust.

Lisette watched her mother gracefully navigate around their kitchen. She effortlessly moved from the preparation table to the hearth, to the stove and then back again to the table. Lisette believed that her mother was one of the most beautiful women in Paris. Her papa said so often. With thick, raven black hair and ivory skin, she could still turn men's heads.

"Move on to the carrots. They need to be peeled and cut up for the soup." Jeanne gathered the sliced turnips from the table and dropped them into a medium-sized copper pot that had been warming on the stove. She moved to the open hearth and inspected the veal roasting on a spit. Her back was to Lisette.

"Mother, I have time. I'm not that old." Lately, her mother's favorite conversation topic was Lisette's future marriage, even though there were no specific suitors.

"Plenty of girls marry at your age. If you wait much

longer…" She spun toward Lisette. "You deserve your pick of suitors while there are plenty of eligible young men still available. Right now, you have many options. You are very becoming Lisette." Jeanne's eyes teared.

To Lisette, they looked like sparkling blue sapphire gemstones. Since she was very small, Lisette had wanted to trade her hazel colored eyes for the deep blue of her mother's. They seemed to possess a magical power, drawing people to her, especially men.

I should deepen the blue of Venus' eyes, Lisette thought. Questioning her previous decision, Lisette's mind returned to her dilemma. *Should I clothe Venus or leave her nude?* Lisette tried to see the painting in her mind. *Maybe if I think about it long enough the answer will come to me,* she hoped. Lisette needed her papa's advice to finish the painting.

Louis Vigée was downstairs painting in his *atelier.* Her papa's studio doubled as his exhibition space where he would showcase and sometimes sell his latest pastels and oil paintings. Their apartment, located directly above the studio, was on the most gracious floor in the building. They were fortunate to have six rooms, including four fireplaces and a separate kitchen with a charcoal stove. Lisette knew that her papa didn't earn as much money as some artists, but he did well enough for them to live like the families of merchants and lawyers.

"Mother, may I go downstairs?" Lisette asked.

"Absolutely not. Do you see servants that can help me? No. We aren't *that* prosperous," Jeanne said resigned. "Get started with the carrots." She pulled out a dozen carrots from a large wicker basket. Letting out a sigh of exasperation, Jeanne placed them in front of Lisette on the long pinewood table.

Lisette knew that her mother yearned for a more lavish life. Louis had never achieved the status or wealth of some other painters, particularly those members of the Académie Royale de Peinture et de Sculpture. Given her disappointment, she spoke of it rarely. Jeanne Vigée had long ago accepted her fate. She told Lisette they would never be wealthy, but would always have their needs met.

"But Mother, you know that I am a terrible cook. When was the last time I didn't ruin a meal when I helped you in the kitchen? I am quite possibly the worst cook in France. I'd spoil chicken broth!"

"Lisette, you're not a terrible cook. You simply need practice before you get married."

When Lisette did not reply, her mother continued, "Lisette, your future husband will want you to possess culinary skills ...not artistic skills."

"May I go downstairs and tell Papa to come up?" Lisette asked her mother.

"No. Supper won't be ready for several hours. Monsieur Vernet isn't expected for at least an hour." Then she added, "Besides, it is nearly nightfall and you know that your father has forbidden you from painting in the studio at night. Help me with the soup. Keep peeling." Jeanne pointed to the carrots on the table as she stirred the sauce for the veal dish.

Lisette peeled the carrots while her mother added more ingredients to the copper pot.

Jeanne closed her eyes as she inhaled deeply. "Smell that soup. *You* did that. Your skills are already improving. You'll be ready to cook for your husband in no time," Jeanne said. "Come here and stir."

Lisette took the ladle from her mother and leaned over the stove. The soup did smell good. Her stomach growled. *If I could only get downstairs to the studio,* she thought, shifting her mind from the minor discomfort of hunger to her art. When Lisette was busy painting, there were some days that she would forget to eat altogether.

"What's that about Lisette and her husband?" said Lisette's papa as he entered the kitchen.

Not Papa too, she thought.

"Lisette's culinary skills have improved. She is almost ready to get married and cook for *her* husband," Jeanne said proudly.

"Are you sure that is a good idea? We don't want to starve the poor man." Louis smiled at Lisette and then let out a low laugh.

Ignoring Louis' sarcasm, Jeanne asked, "How are the paintings for Monsieur Aubert coming along?"

Louis did not answer her. Instead, he moved toward the stove. "That smells delightful."

"Louis, you've been working day and night on those paintings. Aren't they finished yet?"

Louis faced Jeanne. "Almost," he said quickly and then looked toward the stove again.

"I should hope so. Hasn't Monsieur Aubert said he will pay 200 *livres* per painting? It's certainly not what Monsieur Greuze or Vernet can command, but it is money we need," Jeanne said. She continued talking as she fussed about the kitchen. "I heard that the King just paid 16,700 *livres* for a painting. 16,700 *livres*! Can you imagine? It is more than you earn in an entire year, Louis!" Jeanne said. She paused and then added, "It's more than most Parisians make in an entire year."

At a young age, Lisette had learned that the large-scale allegorical and historical paintings sold for many thousands of *livres* and were usually purchased by royals or other illustrious families to decorate their grand homes and palaces. The high prices were mandated by the Académie Royale de Peinture et de Sculpture and the King's Minister of Buildings. *If I could gain a reputation as a painter of history and allegory...*she thought. Lisette fantasized of the possibilities that would follow from such a reputation.

"Papa, weren't you just saying that Monsieur Greuze sold his painting, *The Village Bride*, to a Monsieur de Marigny? How much was the final amount?" Lisette remembered her papa talking about his friend's recent good fortune.

"It was for 3,000 *livres*," Louis muttered, barely audible. "But it was highly unexpected for a genre painting," Louis said a little louder.

"Genre painting or not, 3,000 *livres*...that money would improve our position, would it not?" Jeanne asked Louis.

He didn't respond to her, focusing instead on the simmering soup. "What is in that soup? It smells better than usual." As her papa bent over to peek in the large copper pot, he started to cough. He immediately covered his mouth. It took him several moments to compose himself.

"Louis, are you well? That is the fifth time this week you've had a fit. Should I send for the doctor?"

Lisette had noticed his coughing too. Since beginning several months ago, it seemed to worsen with each incident.

"I think that soup will cure whatever ails me."

"Are you sure, Papa? I helped with it." Lisette smiled at her papa.

"Enough of that kind of talk. Monsieur Vernet will be here in an hour," Jeanne said. "Lisette, it is time to finish the veal dish."

"Yes, Mother." As Lisette helped her mother take the heavy kettle out of the hearth, she wondered if her papa would want to go back downstairs after supper. Then she thought, *Maybe Mother and Papa will be distracted with Monsieur Vernet and I can sneak out during the meal.*

"Lisette, put the soup spoons on next," Jeanne reminded her. Lisette helped her mother place the dishes, glasses and cutlery on the dining table. Monsieur Vernet had arrived early forcing Jeanne to accelerate the preparations.

"Set them to the right of the knives," Jeanne said, pointing to the correct placement on the large table.

Lisette nodded absently as she focused on her papa's conversation with Monsieur Vernet in the next room. *Did Papa just mention the King?* she wondered.

"Please pay attention, Lisette. After you finish with the soup spoons, I need you to set out the mustard pots and sauceboats,"

13

her mother said. "Are you listening to me?"

Lisette moved the spoons to their rightful places on the table and then positioned herself at the edge of the dining room to better hear Monsieur Vernet and her papa.

"Lisette…the mustard pots and sauceboats," Jeanne said as she found the mustard pots in the tall corner cabinet that stored their serving pieces.

She took the pots from her mother and placed them on the table as Jeanne returned to the cabinet and removed their only two pieces of Sèvres porcelain. The slender, aqua-blue vases sat atop marble bases. They had decorative gilt handles attached to slightly swollen middles covered with pastel-colored flowers. Lisette watched her mother gaze adoringly at the vases as she carefully positioned them on either end of the long rectangular table.

"There. The table is set. As soon as we carry in the prepared dishes for the first service, we will eat," Jeanne said.

"May we go in and talk to Monsieur Vernet and Papa now?" Lisette asked.

"Yes, but only for a few minutes. The soup will need tending soon and the other dishes are almost ready to be served." Jeanne then walked into the drawing room to where Monsieur Vernet and Lisette's papa were sitting discussing business.

Lisette followed her mother. They stood at the edge of the room.

"But will it please the King?" Louis Vigée asked his guest.

"Most certainly. He has requested a gallant theme and nothing is more gallant than Saint Denis. The venerated saint is one of the greatest patrons of Paris *and* France," Monsieur Vernet said to Louis.

"You don't think it is overdone? Both Vien and Van Loo have executed the same theme."

"And yours shall be superior, old friend." Monsieur Vernet exuded confidence.

Louis shook his head enthusiastically. "Yes, yes. I quite

agree."

"I am anxious to see the finished paintings," Vernet said.

"I'm afraid I have much more work ahead of me before they are finished," Louis said.

"That is shrewd. You certainly don't want to rush the King's paintings," Vernet replied.

Spellbound, Lisette listened to Monsieur Vernet dispense artistic advice to her papa. Vernet was a member of the Académie Royale de Peinture et de Sculpture and had been commissioned by the King many times to create seascape series. Just months ago, her papa had received his very first commission from King Louis XV. The King had requested two paintings with a gallant theme for the upcoming Guild exhibition. It was the most important commission of Louis Vigée's career. Lisette knew that her papa didn't want to disappoint the King.

"Jeanne, Lisette, come sit with Monsieur Vernet before we begin our meal," Louis said as he waved, indicating for them to move deeper into the drawing room.

Jeanne sat down on a settee directly across from the two armchairs where Louis and Vernet were seated. Lisette took a seat next to her mother on the long upholstered sofa.

"How lovely to see you, Jeanne," Vernet said to Lisette's mother as he bowed his head to her. Saying nothing to Lisette, Vernet kept his gaze on Louis and Jeanne. Lisette had met Monsieur Vernet several years ago and she doubted that he remembered her.

"Claude-Joseph, it is good to see you out. You are looking well. How is Madame Vernet? It is a shame she couldn't make it this evening. Please give her our regards," Jeanne said.

"Virginia is slowly returning to our world. She saw nothing but blackness after Emilie passed," Vernet said.

Lisette saw his face darken at the mention of Emilie's name. Lisette had never met the Vernets' only daughter, but she remembered her parents talking about her death a few months ago. Emilie had been the same age as Lisette.

15

"It was a particularly bad bout of smallpox. Many souls were claimed in Paris. Our own Etienne was afflicted," Louis said gravely.

"But he recovered, no?" Vernet asked.

"Yes. God chose to spare him. We are very fortunate," Jeanne said quietly.

They all nodded in silence.

Vernet, who had been avoiding Lisette, looked at her for the first time since she entered the room. "Lisette, look at how you've grown." Vernet gave a slight nod of his head.

Lisette returned the nod.

He continued, "You have blossomed into a beautiful young woman. I am sure that the suitors are fighting each other to court you."

Lisette noticed a deep sadness in his eyes.

Jeanne quickly spoke up, "Monsieur Vernet, tell us about Italy. When did you return?"

Lisette watched Monsieur Vernet's demeanor change before he uttered a word. He stood up excitedly. Her mother had been right to change the subject. Like most important artists that Lisette had met at her papa's suppers, Vernet couldn't resist the invitation to talk at length about himself and his recent travels.

"The Académie in Rome is thriving. In fact, there is a young Academician there that everyone is talking about. I think we are going to see important works from him in the future," Vernet said as he paced.

"And what is this promising young man's name?" Louis asked.

Vernet stopped pacing. He faced the wall of their drawing room that displayed several paintings.

"Jacques-Louis David," Vernet said distractedly.

Lisette watched him move closer to a portrait she had painted of her younger brother, Etienne. Like most bourgeois boys his age, Etienne was away at school. He occasionally returned home, but spent most days of the month at the Collège des Quatre-Nations. Lisette's papa was enormously proud of Etienne. As one of the colleges of the University of Paris, the Collège des Quatre-Nations was attended by the most prosperous sons of Parisian merchant and bourgeois families.

"His name isn't familiar to me. Was he a member of the Guild?" Louis asked.

"No, he was not. He went straight to the Académie," Vernet said as he examined Lisette's painting.

Her mother grimaced as Vernet said the word *Académie*.

Monsieur Vernet and Louis had become friends while Vernet was still a Guild member. They had remained friends even after Vernet had been elected to the Académie and had left the Guild. Her pride wounded, Jeanne had wanted to cut their ties to Vernet, but Louis had convinced her of her shortsightedness. Being a prudent man, Louis maintained their friendship. Later, Jeanne had admitted the importance of the relationship. Had it not been for Vernet's status at the Académie, Louis would have never received the commission from the King. Her parents had often discussed how the money from the King's paintings would pay several years' tuition for Etienne.

"Is this your son, Louis?" Vernet asked pointing to Lisette's portrait.

"Yes, it is Etienne," Louis replied.

"It is a wonderfully executed portrait. I didn't know that you had begun painting portraits, Louis."

"It wasn't done by my hand," Louis said.

"It is my portrait," Lisette said proudly.

Vernet immediately turned toward Lisette. "Extraordinary. I had no idea Lisette could paint. Where does she study?"

"Here with me," Louis said in a low voice.

Lisette thought she heard a tinge of guilt in his tone. Earlier that day, he had denied her request to study with a master painter, Gabriel Briard. Master Briard was one of the few Académie members who accepted female students.

"Astounding. She has come this far with only your tutelage."

Vernet then looked embarrassed. "I didn't mean to insinuate that you are not a good teacher, my friend."

"No offense taken." Louis started to cough, but managed to control it quickly.

"I only meant that she has gone this far without proper training at the Académie. Have you considered finding her further instruction?" Vernet asked.

"It is time for supper, gentlemen." Jeanne stood and tried to guide everyone into the dining room.

"Doesn't Monsieur Briard accept female pupils at his studio at the Louvre?" Vernet asked.

"Yes, he does!" Lisette said excitedly. She hoped that Monsieur Vernet might convince her papa to allow lessons with Briard.

"Please, gentlemen, if you will make your way into the dining room. I will bring out the food," Jeanne repeated herself.

Louis stood, but Vernet remained seated as if he wanted to continue the conversation about Lisette.

"Louis, she has incredible potential. She could follow in the steps of Madame Vallayer-Coster who was admitted to the Académie two years ago."

"Monsieur Vernet, marriage is in Lisette's future, not the Académie Royale," Jeanne said quickly.

Ignoring Jeanne, Vernet said to Louis, "She could easily be accepted into the Guild first. You could help with that, Louis." Vernet stood as he spoke.

"Perhaps. But like Jeanne said, Lisette will be married soon. Besides, the Guild is about to see increased fees for its members. Hardly worth a short-term membership," Louis said as he took Vernet's arm and escorted him into the dining room. Louis was beset by another coughing fit as he walked. This time, it took him longer to recover.

"The government is raising the fees of Guild members?" Vernet asked.

Lisette lingered in the drawing room as they withdrew. Vernet quickly gave up discussing Lisette. He seemed more interested in the increased fees as both of her parents began raging against them. Lisette heard her papa coughing in between sentences.

With her parents and Monsieur Vernet engrossed in a discussion of the proposed Guild fees, Lisette took the opportunity to leave the apartment.

She picked up a candelabra sitting on a small stand next to the settee where she and her mother had been sitting. It was already burning one candle, so she would at least have some light. Lisette quietly made her way to the front door, left their apartment and went downstairs to her papa's studio.

Darkness enveloped the studio. In the cold months, there would have been a dim light coming from the fireplace, but since summer was nearing, the fireplace was blocked with a board and wasn't in use. Lisette placed the candelabra, with its single lit candle, on its designated table. *If I am going to get much done tonight, I will need more light,* she thought.

Lisette hunted around her papa's *semainier*. She knew the candles were stored somewhere in the high, narrow chest. Lisette started at the bottom, opening each of the seven drawers. By the sixth drawer, she had found a tinderbox for lighting the candles and a snuffer for extinguishing the candles, but no candles. Then she remembered how her mother frequently complained about the high price of candles. Jeanne doled them out sparingly, giving her papa only a few at a time. Sure enough, when Lisette reached into the far back of the top drawer, she felt two candles. After inserting them into the empty branches of the candelabra, she lit them with the flame from the original burning candle.

With the candles lit, she was ready to paint. Lisette stood before her easel staring at her canvas. If she worked diligently tonight, she might finish. *Should I add another layer to Venus?*

19

she wondered. Again, she had doubts.

Unsure about how much time she had to paint, Lisette decided to mix only one color – a light brown. First, she prepared a mix of raw umber pigment, linseed oil and a little turpentine. Next, she blended white pigment with linseed oil and turpentine. Using her palette knife, Lisette then transferred the brown and white paints to her palette. Finally, to complete her process, she pulled the darker paint into the lighter paint creating streaks of white within the brown. *Perfect*, she thought. After painting a few strokes on the canvas, she stood back to judge the overall effect of that particular color of brown. It was difficult to see in the flickering candlelight.

"Lisette! What are you doing in here?" It was her papa.

She hadn't heard him enter.

"You shouldn't be burning your mother's candles! She will be very upset. You know that I forbid you from painting down here at night."

"But Papa, you heard what Monsieur Vernet said about my abilities. I need to keep working. It is the only way to improve," Lisette said as she continued to paint.

"Monsieur Vernet said many things. We mustn't take stock in all of what he says."

"You don't agree that I am talented?"

"Of course I think you are very good, Lisette. That isn't what I meant. Monsieur Vernet may have inserted himself into matters that were not his business."

"Do you mean the lessons?" Lisette asked.

Her papa was silent.

"You have said yourself that Briard would accept me as a student."

"Lisette, I cannot afford to pay for lessons with Monsieur Briard. I've told you this."

"Not even after you receive the money for the King's paintings?"

"That money is for your brother's education. Lisette, I will not discuss this further. For now, my guidance will have to suffice."

Louis' cough had returned and Lisette didn't want to agitate him. She had noticed lately that once a fit began, it was difficult to control. He seemed to be getting a little sicker each day.

Louis studied her canvas. "Pull the brown from dark to light on the edges of Venus. It will make her stand out more against the blue sky." As a pastelist, her papa was especially good at blending colors. Louis then moved his easel closer to the candelabra table that stood between them.

"Papa, what are you doing?" Lisette asked.

"The candles have been lit and you've mixed paint. We might as well make use of both."

"What about your supper and Monsieur Vernet?"

"He was called away on Académie business. Your mother sent me down to check on you."

"Won't Mother be upset if we both stay here?"

"You let me handle your mother," Louis said as he started to paint.

Lisette regarded her papa. Even in the shadows she could see that he had changed. Where she had once seen a strong, vigorous artist, she now saw a haggard man who appeared much older than his age. She watched him sitting a few feet from her, working at his own easel. He could no longer stand up to paint. He couldn't even sit up straight and as a result, his back had a hump that protruded from between his shoulders. Lisette missed the days when her papa was in better health. The outside world didn't exist when she painted with him. Entire days and sometimes weeks would disappear. She missed their conversations about painting techniques, the Guild, the Académie and whatever else they wanted to discuss. Lately her papa didn't talk much at all.

Lisette turned to face her canvas. "Papa, is this enough contrast?" Lisette knew that her painting of Venus was her finest creation. She had worked diligently for months...and tonight she would finish. *My Venus,* she thought affectionately.

Before Louis could respond, he started to cough and wasn't able to stop for several minutes.

Lisette set down her brush and palette on the deep window-sill next to her easel. She poured her papa a glass of watered wine from a tall decanter. Although it was difficult to see in the dim light, she was careful to step over the half-finished canvases scattered throughout the small space.

"Here, Papa, drink this." She handed him the glass. Her papa looked especially tired and worried tonight.

He took several sips from the glass and returned it to Lisette. "Thank you." He picked up his brush and started painting again.

"Do you want me to go down and ask Mother for some Barbados water?" Lisette had seen her mother give her papa the sweet, light brown spirit to ease his coughing. Costly, it was imported from the island of Barbados. Jeanne poured it sparingly.

"No. I must return to work."

Lisette remained standing next to him. She loomed over her papa who was hunched over as he painted. "Papa, you are working too much. It is making you sicker."

"You don't need to worry about me," her papa said. Lisette noticed he held back another cough.

"You are not well. You should be resting in your bed."

"Lisette, you know I cannot rest now, not when there are so many paintings I must finish. Le Brun needs these very soon. His auction is scheduled to take place shortly."

"But I thought these paintings were commissioned by Monsieur Aubert. Why would they be going to Le Brun's auction?"

Louis said nothing and continued to paint. Lisette knew from her papa's silence that Monsieur Aubert no longer wanted the paintings. To avoid a total loss, her papa must have negotiated a contract with Le Brun.

Lisette peered around the studio. There were a dozen unfinished paintings, many barely begun. *I could finish them for him,* she thought. Tonight, she would not suggest such a plan. Lisette would wait until it was the right time.

Reticent, Lisette returned to her easel.

Her papa put down his brush. "Lisette, I know you are concerned about me…" He could barely get the words out before his cough took over his body.

Just as the fit seemed to wane, Lisette saw her papa swaying on his stool.

She leapt over to him as he lost his balance and fell. "Papa!" Supporting his body, they both collapsed. She had reached him just before his head hit the floor. Lisette sat up and supported Louis' head in her lap.

"Papa! Wake up. Can you hear me?" Lisette gently shook him, but he did not respond. She wasn't sure if he had hit his head on his easel or on the candelabra. The candelabra had been knocked off its table and laid on its side. Its branches were empty and the room had darkened. *Where are the candles?* Lisette thought.

The room did not remain dark for long. In an instant, it was light again, made bright with the flames of the liberated candles. A small fire burned in the middle of the studio.

"Fire!" Lisette quickly moved her papa's head off of her lap, stood up and reached for the nearest pail.

Lisette found a small pail sitting on the window sill. She threw its contents onto the fire and held her breath. *That should work*, she thought. But instead of putting the fire out, it grew larger.

Lisette smelled the empty pail. *I just threw turpentine onto the fire!* Lisette realized.

She then searched for a pail of water. She knew there would be at least one in the studio. Her papa kept water pails for cleaning brushes.

On the other side of her papa's easel, she found several pails of water. Lisette immediately tossed the water on the growing fire, but it didn't help. The flames were quickly spreading. The fire had begun to consume many of the paintings scattered throughout the studio.

Lisette watched it move toward her painting of Venus. If she didn't act now, the entire studio would be destroyed by the fire.

She searched the studio for something...anything that might put out the fire. *The bed linens!* she thought as she spotted the large, white sheets piled in a corner. Her papa used the bed linens to veil any unfinished works he didn't want to be seen.

Lisette grabbed the sheets and then quickly threw them onto the fire. They were just large enough to cover the biggest flames. Lisette stomped on the linens until the fire was merely smoldering.

Then there was smoke...thick, suffocating clouds of smoke. She started coughing. *Papa shouldn't be breathing this smoke,* she thought.

Her papa remained unconscious on the floor. Lisette rushed over to him. She placed her hands on his shoulders and shook him. "Papa! Wake up!"

His eyes fluttered. "What happened?" When he tried to sit up, Lisette stopped him. Instead, she supported his head on her lap.

"You fell off your chair. I think you hit your head on your easel. A fire started from the candelabra that fell over at the same time. And...I'm afraid I made it worse before I extinguished it," Lisette explained.

"Is that why you smell like turpentine?" he asked.

Lisette looked down. The front of her dress was soaked in it. As she sat on the ground, still holding her papa in her lap, she caught a whiff of the strong smell. She winced.

"I hope it dries before mother smells me."

"Lisette, she won't care. You saved both of our lives." As his eyes focused, the expression on her papa's face softened. "Thank you, my dear daughter. I was fortunate that you were here with me," Louis said as he tried to stand.

"Papa, no, you are too weak." Lisette kept him down on the

floor with her. "We can't stay in here with this smoke. We need to leave now." She smiled at her papa. "You want to get away from me because I smell like a pail of turpentine."

Louis' laughing gave way to coughing.

"Lisette? Louis?"

Lisette heard her mother's voice near the door.

"Mother!" Lisette called out to Jeanne.

Jeanne rushed over to where Lisette held her papa on the floor. "What happened? I smelled smoke from upstairs!"

Jeanne and Lisette brought Louis to his feet. He leaned on Lisette as she and her mother helped him out of the *atelier* and back up the stairs to their apartment.

As they left the studio, Lisette saw the destruction. At least half of her papa's paintings had been ruined by the fire. Then she saw her easel, cracked and in crumbled pieces. It had been under the linens that she had trampled. Lisette realized, *My Venus is gone.*

Chapter Three

The next morning, Lisette checked on her papa. As she quietly entered his bedroom, she saw his eyes were closed. *Good, he is resting*, Lisette thought. She had heard him coughing throughout the night. She knew the smoke from the fire had only worsened his condition. Lisette walked to the side of his bed, drew open the bed curtains and sat down.

"Lisette." Louis opened his eyes and looked at her with great tenderness.

"Papa, how are you feeling?"

"Like I should get back to work," he said as he coughed.

"No, Papa. You need your rest."

"That is what your mother says. But you don't know Le Brun. He will cut my share in half for being late. And now, because of the fire, I am further behind. How many paintings were destroyed?"

Lisette didn't want to tell him that well over half of his paintings were gone.

"I can tell by the look on your face that the news is bad. Please tell me."

"Most were destroyed."

Lisette saw tears welling up in his eyes as he considered his predicament. Louis looked away from her.

"Papa...I can help you. Le Brun *will* get his paintings for the auction."

He turned to face her. His eyes were red and swollen, but he was no longer crying. "Lisette, you are a girl. Your place is helping your mother. You are needed in the kitchen," he said, suppressing a cough.

"I can finish them for you," Lisette blurted out.

"Lisette, no. That is not a good idea."

"No one will know it was me. You told me the other day that I have already exceeded your abilities," Lisette said.

"I am not selling my paintings executed by your hand. That is fraudulent," her papa said adamantly.

"Then I could sell *my* paintings...ones that I painted."

"That is preposterous," Louis said.

"Many of my paintings survived. I had been safekeeping them in my room. Papa, I could sell my *Death of Caesar*." Lisette believed that her painting of Caesar Augustus was her best painting now that the Venus canvas had been lost to the fire. As a scene from Rome, it was a *de rigeur* theme in high demand by Parisians.

Her papa said nothing.

"Papa, I think my *Death of Caesar* would sell. You told me that Parisians are buying any painting with a Classical theme. If only you would consider..."

"Not that one, Lisette."

"What is wrong with it?" Mulling the details in her mind, she thought, *The proportions were right, the composition was*

27

balanced, the placement of the horizon line was correct...what could it be?

"Lisette, that is an historical canvas. You know as well as I do that it won't sell," her papa said plainly.

"But it isn't too big. It is cabinet-sized and is the perfect addition to any gentleman's salon or gallery."

He looked her in the eye. "Lisette, only *men* paint those kinds of paintings. You are very skilled, yes. But it does not change the fact that you are a girl. I promise you that Le Brun won't sell that painting. A portrait or landscape, perhaps."

"Am I not talented enough?" Without allowing him to answer she continued, "I can improve, Papa. If you would only agree to lessons, I could improve."

"We have been over this too many times. I will not discuss it further."

Lisette glanced down at the floor. She remained at the side of her papa's bed without saying anything.

Her papa broke the quiet first. "Lisette, you are an adept painter. Why can't you put history painting aside...focus on what is open to you...as a female painter. I've seen you compose wonderful portraits." His voice was soft and gentle.

He only means well, but I am not a simple portrait painter, she thought. There was nothing left to say to her papa. Lisette kissed him on the cheek.

"Rest, Papa," Lisette said and walked out.

Chapter Four

*L*isette peered out of the side of the carriage. The route from their home on the Rue Coquillière to the Palais du Louvre was a familiar one to her. From a young age, she had accompanied her papa to art salons at the Louvre. Today was no different.

Monsieur Vernet had invited them to his latest exhibition. It was taking place in his *atelier*, which adjoined his living quarters at the Louvre. Her papa had many friends who were members of the Académie Royale de Peinture et de Sculpture, most of whom lived and worked at the Louvre. Still the nominal seat of the French government, it had long ago ceased to function as the royal residence. She had heard her papa talk about how it was not only the home of the Académie Royale de Peinture et de Sculpture, but all of the royal academies, including the Académie des Sciences and the Académie des Inscriptions et Belles-Lettres. Her papa often told Lisette that one had an equal chance of encountering an artist, a scientist or a writer when inside the Palais du Louvre.

"Papa, who do you expect will attend?" Lisette asked.

"Many people. Monsieur Vernet hasn't held a private exhibition of his paintings in at least a year. His recent seascapes that were commissioned by the King will be on display. I'm sure he will draw a crowd. We'll be some of the first people to view them."

"Why did he insist on my presence?" Lisette asked.

"He was very impressed with your portrait of Etienne. He has taken a special interest in you, Lisette. Your mother and I believe that you remind him of his daughter, Emilie."

Lisette thought about all the people she knew that had died in the most recent outbreak of smallpox. She shuddered when she remembered Etienne's brush with death. During his illness, there had been rumblings of an inoculation against smallpox, but Lisette's parents hadn't trusted it for their son. The Dauphine, Marie-Antoinette, believed in inoculation because she had survived a mild case of the smallpox as a young girl. She had spread speculation that inoculation might spare lives. But most Frenchmen, including King Louis XV, did not believe in it. The Dauphine could not convince her husband's grandfather to be inoculated.

"Be sure to thank Monsieur Vernet for inviting you, Lisette," her papa said.

Lisette nodded. She was with her papa today because Monsieur Vernet had requested that Lisette attend. Jeanne had resisted, arguing that Lisette's time was now better spent preparing for marriage. Not wanting to offend Vernet, Louis had placated his wife by suggesting that eligible suitors would be present. If the excursion's purpose was to attract a potential husband, Jeanne Vigée was happy to consent. She had spent all that morning dressing and primping her daughter.

Lisette was wearing one of her best dresses, a pale blue taffeta gown and matching petticoat. Her mother had insisted that Lisette wear a corset as well. At first, Lisette refused, arguing that some women were giving up their corsets. Jeanne would hear none of it.

Now, sitting in the carriage with her papa, Lisette considered how much freer she would feel without the corset. Lisette shifted in her seat, searching for an agreeable position. She realized it was futile. The whalebone stay precluded comfort.

"Lisette, please stop fidgeting," her papa said, his voice tinged with irritation. "This carriage isn't big enough for it." To attend Vernet's exhibition today, Louis had hired a small, one-horse, two-wheeled carriage. It barely held the two of them, but the *cabriolet* was the least expensive. Her papa smiled at her. "I don't mean to be cross. Next time, we will hire a *fiacre* and enjoy plenty of space. I'm certain I'll have been paid in full for the King's paintings by then."

Lisette tried to distract herself with the sights and sounds of the streets. She watched as they passed slowly through the Palais-Royal neighborhood. Their carriage carefully maneuvered around the multitude of vendors, entertainers and pedestrians. Lisette noticed the *cabriolet* begin to slow down until it was creeping along. Then it came to a complete stop.

She peered out and saw two people standing in the middle of the road quarreling. Covered in a sheet of white flour, a wig merchant was violently shaking his wares in another man's face. The carriage driver demanded that the men clear the road. After a few moments, the carriage lurched forward. From what Lisette could make out as they drove past, a wigmaker was trying to collect what he was owed from a customer who thought he was being overcharged.

People weren't the only impediments. Other carriages retarded their progress too. The general disorder and chaos of the streets made travel anywhere within the city slow and dangerous. Sometimes, traveling via carriage was no faster than walking. But when you arrived, you were clean and not covered in layers of dust and mud. You were also less likely to be hurt. Without dedicated passageways for pedestrians, people were forced to walk in the street alongside carriages. Not all drivers were patient and careful. Some tried to be responsible by having footmen or greyhounds running ahead of the carriage yelling *make way*, but most were impatient and charged ahead like a *capitaine* leading his regiment into battle. Lisette's mother had always told her to remain close to the buildings, thereby reducing the chances of colliding with a carriage and losing limbs. Like most women whose husbands' livings depended on the use of their arms, Jeanne was most afraid that Louis would lose his. Accident victims were awarded set amounts of money for lost appendages, but Jeanne said receiving a few *livres* would never be fair recompense for the loss of their livelihood.

As the *cabriolet* rolled forward, Lisette watched the street vendors plying their wares shamelessly, their individual cries drowned in a sea of collective voices. It was difficult to distinguish the calls of the knife grinders from the wood cutters. She saw a woman remove a large wicker basket from her back and take out a stone bowl. As the woman traded her goods for money, Lisette noticed her disfigurement. The weight of the stoneware had taken its toll on the woman's body, preventing her from standing completely upright. Next to the stoneware peddler was a rat-catcher. Lisette followed his movements as he meandered from one side of the street to the other, with little regard for pedestrians or carriages. He quickly disappeared from her sight. Then, without any notice, they came to a sudden stop.

"Watch yourself!" the driver of the carriage yelled out.

Lisette turned her head and saw the same rat-catcher jump out of their path. Their *cabriolet* had narrowly missed hitting him.

The man came right up to the carriage and yelled back at the driver, "You watch where you are driving." The man, who was now very close to the carriage on Lisette's side, started shaking his fist at the driver. In his other hand, he held a spear. Tied to the top of his tall, wooden stick were over a dozen dead rats. Lisette considered the rats. She knew that some rat-catchers collected only the tail rather than the entire creature. Paid per tail, many rat-catchers simply cut off the rats' tails rather than fully perform their duties of ridding the streets of the vermin.

The driver was about to descend, probably to confront the rat-catcher, when Louis caught his attention. "Driver, please continue toward the Palais du Louvre," Louis said politely, but forcefully.

The driver nodded and coaxed the horse moving again, but Lisette heard him talking to himself as they drove off, "No good rat-catchers. He likely bred those rats himself to collect more money."

"We've arrived," Louis said as the *cabriolet* drove into the Cour Carrée. Looping around the large courtyard in front of the Louvre was a long line of carriages waiting to unload their passengers. Lisette surveyed the royal palace. She looked up toward the arm of the building that was nearest to their carriage.

"Papa, is that where Monsieur Vernet's *atelier* is?" Lisette asked. She had been to the Palais du Louvre many times with her papa, but only to the Grand Galerie, which displayed the royal collection of paintings.

"Yes. It is up there in the northeast pavilion...not very close to the Grand Galerie. I know what you are thinking, Lisette. Remember, we promised your mother," Louis said pleadingly.

"Papa, I remember. I won't get into trouble," Lisette said.

"More than that, Lisette, I need to be sure that you won't wander off by yourself. I know how curious you can be. No matter how much you want to see the King's paintings in the

Grand Galerie, please stay by my side, even if you are bored of waiting for me. I need to discuss the Guild fees with Monsieur Vernet. He indicated that he has some ideas to prevent their increase. I am anxious to hear them." Louis paused and then leaned in closer. "Lisette?"

She nodded slightly as she continued to study the building. *I'm sure there is a painting of Venus in the collection,* she thought. She wanted to see how the Italian painters rendered Venus. Lisette would take this opportunity to gain inspiration from the Old Masters in the royal collection.

"We are agreed then," her papa said.

Lisette said nothing more and before her papa could question her again, their carriage had reached the front of the queue. It was their turn to disembark.

Lisette linked her arm through her papa's and they went inside the palace.

When they had reached Vernet's studio, they encountered another line. Lisette and her papa took their place at the end of the queue. Her papa had been right. Many people wanted to see Vernet's seascapes. They waited patiently until they were inside the studio and it was their turn to greet Monsieur Vernet.

"Louis, it is wonderful you could make it today," Vernet said to her papa. "And you brought Lisette." Vernet bowed slightly.

"I would never miss this important reception, Claude-Joseph. I recall you told me once, 'Guild membership is forever.' We support each other for life," Louis said.

"Yes, Louis, I remember well," Vernet said.

"Where is Madame Vernet? I should like to say hello." Louis was interrupted by his coughing. It took him several moments to regain his composure.

"My dear friend, are you well?" A concerned look came over Vernet.

"Yes," Louis responded as he kept coughing.

"You don't appear to be so. Come. Let me take you into my private study to rest. I can fetch my private physician…or better yet my surgeon. When was the last time you had a bleeding?"

"Not necessary, but I would like to sit down. I'd like to talk about your ideas to prevent the Guild fee increases." Her papa had managed to compose himself.

"Of course, old friend." Vernet took Louis by the arm and escorted him out of the room.

Lisette started to follow them and then stopped herself. *Should I go now? If I hurry, I can see the Old Masters and be back before Papa is finished discussing the Guild fees with Vernet,* she thought. Lisette decided that this was her opportunity. Stepping out of Vernet's studio, Lisette realized she would have to walk quickly to cover the distance to the Grand Galerie.

Moving as fast as she could without drawing unnecessary attention to herself, Lisette made her way through the pavilions of the Cour Carrée and toward the Grand Galerie. As she approached the wide hallway of the Grand Galerie, her attention was diverted. *The Salon Carré*, she realized. It had been just over a year since she had been there last. She stepped inside the large room. During the biennial Salon de Paris, the room had been filled with paintings hung floor to ceiling. But today, there were only a few paintings displayed. She noticed one in particular and walked up to it. It was a self-portrait by Rembrandt completed toward the end of his life. Lisette was drawn to Rembrandt's expressive eyes.

"Such sad eyes," a man's voice said.

Lisette quickly turned and saw a tall, broad-shouldered man standing next to her. She had thought she was alone. The man was wearing a royal blue waistcoat trimmed with red collars and cuffs and red *culottes* with white leggings. *Is he an officer?* Lisette wondered.

Agreeing that Rembrandt's eyes were sad, Lisette nodded.

"Capitaine Amante Fabien de Chaumont, of the Armée

Royale Française and the Gardes Françaises, at your service."
He reached out to take her hand.

Lisette wasn't sure if she wanted to extend it to him. She
glanced around. They were alone together in the room.

He smiled warmly and said, "I assure you, Mademoiselle,
you are quite safe with me. I intend you no harm. What is your
name?" He kept his hand out to take hers and kiss it.

His gentle voice competed with his imposing stature. Lisette
decided to trust his kind eyes. "My name is Élisabeth Louise
Vigée," she said reluctantly as she extended her hand.

He kissed it politely and then promptly returned it.

"The daughter of Louis Vigée, the Guild painter?"

Lisette nodded.

"I saw you waiting in line with him at Vernet's *atelier*. He
did not appear to be well. I believe Vernet called for his surgeon."

Lisette stood up to leave. Her papa needed her.

"I can take you to him," he said.

"Thank you, but I can find my own way, Capitaine de Chaumont," Lisette said.

"Please call me Amante." He offered her his arm. "I won't
take no for an answer."

"Really Capitaine – "

"Please, I insist." He drew close to Lisette and extended his
arm again. "Call me Amante."

Lisette knew that her mother would disapprove, but she
somehow trusted this man.

"Shall we go?" Amante asked her.

Lisette took his arm. They walked out of the Salon Carré
and started down the corridor back toward Vernet's rooms.

"Do you have a favorite Rembrandt?" He spoke as if they had
known each other for ages.

Lisette said nothing. She couldn't allow herself to be that
relaxed. Her mother had lectured her time and again about the
need for chaperones when in the presence of men. *Your rep-*

utation as an honorable and virtuous woman depends on it. Never let yourself be alone with a man until you are married. Lisette could hear her mother's words.

"Mine is the self-portrait that you were examining when I found you. There is something about his eyes."

"I like how he uses so many layers of paint in his paintings. I have tried to replicate it," Lisette blurted out. She found it so easy to talk to him. It seemed natural. *What am I doing?* she wondered. Lisette could not let down her guard.

"Ah, you are an artist. Do you study here at the palace?"

"No, but I have seen many paintings here...from the King's collection and from the Salons."

"Have you approached Master Briard for lessons? He takes female pupils."

Lisette looked down at the floor. "No."

"Would you like me to speak to him? After he returns from Italy, of course."

Puzzled, Lisette studied him. *Why would this man help me?* she wondered.

"My papa would not allow it." Lisette wanted to explain that there were so many obstacles, not the least of which was her papa.

"What if you were to have a patron?" he asked.

Lisette looked at him like he was speaking a foreign tongue.

"A patron," he repeated. "Someone who takes an artist under their care and protection...pays for training, supplies, and more...in exchange for paintings whenever they ask."

Lisette had a vague notion of what a patron was, but she wasn't sure exactly how the relationship worked. Her mother had often mentioned her disdain for wealthy patrons. Jeanne would criticize Louis' friends for being beholden and obsequious to their patrons. Lisette had heard her papa talk about them more favorably, but she never considered that she could have one.

"Who would want to be my patron? I've not yet sold any

paintings."

"I am certain you will attract a patron...and sell many paintings."

"But how? You have never seen my work."

"I have a feeling." His eyes danced as he looked at her.

Aside from his great height, his dark eyes set him apart from other men. They were mysterious and yet familiar at the same time. They drew her in, much like his lips which were full and appeared soft. She watched them as he spoke.

"You have become quiet," he said to her.

Lisette dropped her eyes. "I should return to my papa."

Amante stopped. They stood in front of a closed door in the desolate hallway. Amante came close to Lisette, placed his fingers on her chin and gently raised her head.

"Monsieur Vernet's surgeon is one of the best in Paris. I'm sure he's already bleeding your father. He is in good hands, Mademoiselle Vigée."

Lisette found it difficult to speak. She knew that this behavior wasn't proper. They were alone in a dark hallway.

"May I kiss you?" he asked, still caressing her face.

Lisette took a step backward. "Capitaine de Chaumont!" She had heard the tales of how many French army officers behaved badly, taking advantage of women wherever they went. He had committed a gross violation of etiquette by touching her so boldly *and* asking for a kiss. "Please take me to my papa, Capitaine de Chaumont," Lisette said, standing a good distance away from him.

"Your father is right around this corner." Amante held out his arm again, but she refused to take it. Lisette would not continue to give him the wrong impression.

They started down the hall. Lisette looked over at him and immediately noticed a fluttering in her stomach. *What is wrong with my insides?* she wondered. Lisette had never felt such a sensation. It was like a small creature was rolling around inside her.

They continued down the hall. Once they had turned the corner, Amante stopped and pointed to the nearest door. Lisette approached and pressed her ear against the door to listen. The voices were muffled, but her papa's voice was distinct. When she heard coughing, Lisette had no doubt that he was behind the door.

"I will leave you here, Mademoiselle." Amante came up to her and tilted his head like he was going to kiss her. His breath was warm on her face.

Her heart raced and her chest rose and fell quickly with each breath. *What is happening to me?* she wondered.

Amante didn't kiss her, instead he touched her face again, this time caressing her cheek longingly as a lover might do.

"Capitaine, what are you doing?" Lisette's mind told her to move away from him, but deep inside a feeling of pleasure welled up at his touch and she found herself unable to move.

"Simply admiring beauty," he said.

Stepping back, Lisette managed to gain control of herself. Her mind had won this battle.

"I apologize, Mademoiselle. I did not mean to offend you."

Then, in muffled tones, Lisette heard someone say, "Good bye." She suspected it was the surgeon. She also noticed her papa trying to speak through his coughing.

"*Ma chérie*, I must take my leave," Amante said quietly and then strode away.

Lisette had never heard a man speak to a woman with such a gentle tongue. She wasn't sure if she wanted to see him again and yet at this moment she didn't want to leave him. She couldn't help but watch him walk away. Never before bewildered by a man, Lisette didn't like feeling so flustered and out of control.

When Amante was out of sight, she inhaled deeply. *That's better*, she thought. Lisette was herself again. Then she felt her stomach flip.

Chapter Five

"Lisette, help me bring out more dishes for the first service. Only a few remain in the kitchen," Jeanne said as she placed several covered serving dishes on the dining room table. "We must put out every dish for the first service before your father and his guests are ready to sit down and eat." Now empty-handed, Jeanne walked back toward the kitchen.

Instead of following her mother, Lisette moved to the doorway to better hear her papa and his friends. The usual dinner guests were in attendance: Jean-Baptiste Greuze, Claude-Joseph Vernet, Hubert Robert and Gabriel François Doyen. Besides these familiar men, there was also a newcomer, Denis Diderot. His bold statements captured Lisette's attention as she kept watch from her unique vantage point.

Careful to remain inconspicuous, Lisette had wedged herself

in between a decorative column and the doorway that led from the drawing room to the dining room. Her papa had insisted on including the stately columns when the dining room had been installed, which was also at his insistence. At first, Jeanne had not understood the need for a room dedicated to eating meals. But after only a few weeks of use, Lisette's mother found herself unable to imagine life without a dining room. Her mother had said, *Louis, you were right. Eating in a dining room is more civilized than eating in the drawing room. It is so goût moderne!* Lisette hadn't seen many other homes, but she had heard her parents' friends declare their dining room to be very much in the modern style.

"Stop eavesdropping, Lisette. Help me finish setting up the dinner." Jeanne had returned from the kitchen.

Lisette turned away from the drawing room and examined the table. A variety of round, oval and square dishes, some with covers and some without, sat on stands. Each dish was perfectly arranged according to the prescribed pattern. Her mother knew exactly how to serve a meal *á la Française*. The dinner would include four services with at least six dishes for each service.

Jeanne quickly noted each dish for the first service. "Cucumber soup, green pea soup with croutons, fried mutton feet, veal roast in pastry, small *pâtés* and melons." Satisfied that she hadn't forgotten any dishes in the kitchen, Jeanne placed the last few on the table. She put a pair of oval *terrines* containing soup and a pair of round *pots à ouille* full of stew in the center of the table. Jeanne mumbled to herself, "These will suffice. No one will notice that I do not have a silver *surtout de table* as a centerpiece."

Jeanne spun toward Lisette. "Lisette! You haven't moved. At least set the places at the table while you listen to the men. Set six places." Her mother went to the corner of the room and lifted the plate bucket. She had brought it in earlier in the day from the kitchen. Being made of solid wood and full of twelve matching dinner plates, she struggled to carry it closer to the dining table. "I'll come back with the cutlery, decanters and glasses," Jeanne said as she walked away again. Lisette thought she heard her add, "And the wine tasters, I must not forget them."

Lisette returned her attention to the men.

"Monsieur Robert, are you saying that you do not agree with Rousseau?" Monsieur Diderot asked.

"Not on that point, no. I do not believe that everyone should be equal," Monsieur Robert said.

Diderot leaned forward in his chair. "So, you don't believe that all men should be granted equal rights?"

Lisette couldn't believe what her papa's friends were saying. She had never heard such blasphemy nor such radical ideas. Her mother seemed to be oblivious to the men's conversation.

"You are twisting my words, Diderot. I never said that. What I said was that *women* have been squawking for equal treatment, which I cannot support. Of course I believe that *men* should have equal rights," Monsieur Robert said.

"But Rousseau has never advocated for the equality of women. He firmly touts patriarchy," Diderot retorted.

"That may be, but women seem to be hearing a different message. His novel, *Julie, or the New Héloïse,* has allowed some women to lose all moral judgment. Just look at how many unmarried women there are now. They are shirking their duties and avoiding their responsibilities of marriage and childbearing," Robert replied.

"Monsieur Robert, we must not be too harsh on the fairer sex. You cannot blame them for their weak-mindedness and susceptibility to strong emotions and desires," Monsieur Vernet said.

As Lisette listened, she thought, *I suppose some women are putting off marriage, but not me. I'm simply busy with my painting.* Lisette freely admitted that her desire to create art was a force that was beyond her control at times, but she was not weak-minded. Other women, maybe, but not her. Lisette wondered what Rousseau and her papa's friends would think about her art. *If only there was an opportunity tonight to show them my painting,* she thought.

"Diderot, how are the final volumes coming along?" Louis asked.

Thinking about her art, Lisette realized that she must have missed the change of topic. They were now discussing Diderot's *Encyclopédie.*

"They are nearly complete," Diderot said.

"But how can you trust Le Breton after his earlier actions?" Louis asked.

Monsieur Diderot didn't hesitate responding. "I don't see that I have a choice. I need him. There is no one else who will publish it. It is too dangerous."

"But he censored many of the articles and illustrations in each volume of the *Encyclopédie,*" Monsieur Robert said.

"Yes, but because Le Breton removed so much of the objectionable material, he also kept Diderot out of jail," Monsieur Greuze said to Monsieur Robert.

"It wasn't objectionable to me," said Monsieur Doyen.

"Tell that to the King and the Church. It is ridiculous that they want to keep the people in the dark. I blame them more than Le Breton. He was only acting in his own self-interest," Diderot said.

"And yours…you didn't go to jail," Greuze said.

"This time at least." Diderot smiled.

"Yes, I remember a few years back you became well acquainted with the jailer…you host his family for Sunday dinner every week, no?" Monsieur Doyen asked grinning.

The room exploded in laughter. *He must be jesting,* Lisette thought. *But how could they joke about jail?* she wondered.

"Lisette, check on the dishes for the second and third services, they should be nearly finished," her mother said. Frazzled, Jeanne furiously darted back and forth between the kitchen and dining room.

Lisette didn't want to miss any of the men's conversation. She hoped they would discuss art soon. The last time Monsieur Robert had attended one of her papa's dinners, he had talked about convincing the King to transfer more of his royal collection to the Louvre. Monsieur Robert wanted to transform the Louvre into a national museum, one where all of France could see the King's paintings and sculptures. Lisette wondered if Monsieur Robert had made any progress with the King.

"Lisette!" her mother chirped.

Not wanting to fray Jeanne's patience further, Lisette obeyed her mother. She dashed to the kitchen and peeked in the copper pots sitting on the stove. The boiled leg of mutton, duckling with peas, rabbit steaks with cucumbers and chickens with white onions were finished cooking, so Lisette removed them from the burners. Then, she checked the third service fowl roasting on spits in the hearth. The turkey, capon, partridges and squabs needed more time. Lisette noticed that her mother had already prepared the fourth and final service, dessert. The fresh fruit, various compotes, cheeses and pastries were arranged in their dishes on the long pinewood table in the center of the kitchen. *Mother has outdone herself*, Lisette thought. She hurried back to the dining room.

"Well?" Jeanne asked.

"The second service dishes are ready, but the roasting fowl could use more time in the hearth," Lisette answered.

"We are ready," her mother said as she smoothed out the front of her dress and stood up straight. She moved to the doorway and announced, "Messieurs, dinner is served."

The men filtered into the dining room and took their places at the table.

Monsieur Vernet came over to Jeanne. "This is the most elegant table, fit for a prince of the blood. The food smells marvelous. Well done," he said and gave her a slight bow. The other men nodded their heads toward Jeanne.

Lisette watched her mother's face light up.

"Enjoy, messieurs," Jeanne said and then headed out of the room. Her mother motioned for Lisette to follow, but she remained in the hallway just outside the dining room so that she could see and hear the men.

Lisette watched Monsieur Vernet's valet pour his wine. Vernet authorized him to pour wine for everyone. He was the only one fortunate enough to employ a valet.

When Doyen put his hand over his glass, Vernet objected. "Monsieur Doyen, you are turning down Bordeaux?"

"Yes. I do not want to be part of illegal activity. I know that you did not pay taxes on this wine. If the *fermier généraux* discovered it traveled into Paris tax-free, we would all be in great trouble."

"The taxes on wine brought into Paris are disgraceful. I remember when the tax on a barrel coming into the city via land was only a few *livres*...not the nearly 50 *livres* a barrel it is now. One could rent a room on the Île Saint-Louis for an entire year for that much money. I don't know why the people stand for it," Diderot said indignantly.

"I'll drink his!" Louis held out his glass and they all broke out in applause.

Lisette noticed Louis start to cough. The fit lasted more than a few moments before it subsided.

"Speaking of nefarious activities...does anyone know who is robbing the grand houses in the Marais district?" Doyen asked.

"I heard that in the past six months, four houses have been robbed of their finest jewels," Greuze added.

"I'm sure it is an Englishman, or a Prussian," Vernet said confidently. "You cannot trust foreigners."

"This thief you are speaking of should steal from the Church. They have plenty of jewels," Diderot blurted out.

Several of the other men concurred.

Lisette was astonished at what she was hearing. She had never heard anyone publicly speak out against the Church. Her papa looked uncomfortable.

"How is everyone enjoying the food? I hope you are finding it agreeable," Louis said, trying to change the subject.

There was a low roar of voices.

"Very agreeable, yes. Although I do prefer my fried mutton feet warm," Monsieur Doyen said.

"I have heard that the Russians have found a solution to that problem. Their meals are served differently from ours in France," Diderot said.

"Please go on..." Doyen said, listening attentively.

"Individual plates are served as they become ready. The food is brought out when it is hot, directly from the kitchen," Diderot explained.

"But then you don't have several choices for each course." Monsieur Vernet pointed out.

"No, but you never have the problem of cold food with service *á la Russe*," Diderot said.

Lisette was glad that her mother was in the kitchen. Not only would Jeanne be offended if she heard the men disparaging the Church, but she would never forgive them complaining about her food being served cold.

"Diderot, tell us how you managed to go forward even in the face of the arrest warrants," Louis said, changing the subject again.

Lisette suspected that he wasn't comfortable with Jeanne's service being criticized.

"I don't see that I had a choice. The people must have knowledge...of everything and not only what the King or the Church wants to allow them." Diderot's voice rose with each word.

Lisette saw her mother coming toward her. "Are they ready for the second service?" she asked.

Lisette shrugged her shoulders.

Jeanne rolled her eyes and went into the dining room. She returned almost immediately.

"They are," Jeanne said and disappeared again.

When she reappeared moments later, she held two large,

round dishes containing duckling with peas and boiled leg of mutton. She handed Lisette a dish and they both stepped into the dining room. Lisette set the food on the table, but didn't leave the room. Instead, she lingered.

Lisette felt her arm being pinched. Her mother whispered, "Go in the kitchen and bring out the salads for the third service," Jeanne said as she passed by her.

Lisette nodded to her mother, but was fixated on Diderot.

"We need to give the people more knowledge! Then, they will possess the power to change the old ways of thinking," Diderot said with a resounding voice and animated countenance.

Lisette could watch him speak for hours.

"Impossible. We are not allowed to think or say whatever we please. The King and the Church will always place restrictions on the people," said Doyen.

"Precisely why the people need *all* knowledge, not simply the subjects served by the Académies, but every branch of human knowledge," said Diderot.

"I agree with you on that point, yes, but your ideas on religious tolerance and the value you place on science...those will never be accepted," said Doyen.

"I refuse to believe that. If you are correct, then my life's work will have been for naught. I will fight until the day I die trying to reverse that kind of thinking," Diderot insisted.

Lisette's papa appeared distressed again. He shifted in his seat, like he wanted to get up and leave the room. He had been trying to interrupt the conversation for several minutes. "Messieurs, what is the consensus on the Salon de Paris? Success or not a success?" Louis asked.

Again, Diderot glowed.

To Lisette, this man was conversant on every subject.

"Monsieur Pierre's entries were abhorrent...such dismal renderings of the Dauphin and his sisters. I don't think I have seen a more mediocre painter at a recent Salon than Pierre," Diderot said.

47

All of the men agreed, but Monsieur Greuze was noticeably silent.

"Jean-Baptiste, you can't hold out forever," Monsieur Vernet said to Monsieur Greuze.

"And why not? Hambert did," Greuze replied.

"And look what happened to him," Monsieur Robert interjected.

"Those pretentious asses at the Académie. They can't tell me what to do. The public loves me."

"But they are fickle. You know that," Doyen said.

"That's why I'm appealing to them directly. I've written a letter to be published in next week's issue of L'Avant-Coureur asking for the public's support of my history painting."

"And you believe they'll convince the Académie to accept you as a painter of history and not of genre?"

"Yes," Greuze said simply.

"Lest you forget, it was your genre paintings, particularly *The Village Bride*, that won the hearts of the public," Vernet said.

"And so now they will also love my history paintings," replied Greuze.

"That doesn't change the fact that the Académie yet requires a reception piece. I don't understand why you don't give them what they want," said Diderot. Then he added, "Once you do, I will be able to praise you in *my* writings," Diderot said, grinning at Greuze.

Lisette felt a poke on her back.

"Take these salads in," Jeanne said as she handed Lisette two dishes. "I'll fetch the rest of the third service." Jeanne turned back toward the kitchen while Lisette walked slowly into the dining room.

Lisette watched Greuze's face contort as if he was about to say something but stopped himself. Everyone waited, watching him until he finally spoke. "I do have something in mind...I'm working on a picture of the death of Caesar," Greuze said.

As soon as Lisette heard, *death of Caesar*, she spilled the salads onto Monsieur Vernet's lap.

"Lisette! You apologize! How could you be so clumsy?" Louis Vigée scolded her, coughing as he spoke.

"There has been no harm, Louis," Vernet said, picking the salad off of himself. "My daughter used to drop dishes too." He glanced at Lisette, gave her a faint smile and then looked away.

Before Lisette could apologize or say anything else, she blurted out, "I've created a painting on the death of Caesar."

Lisette heard cutlery fall onto plates and the room fell silent. Everyone gaped at her.

"Please excuse her, messieurs, Lisette was just leaving," Jeanne said. Her mother's face had turned a shade of dark pink like a turnip.

"Tell us about your painting, Lisette." Monsieur Vernet seemed genuinely interested. Greuze and Doyen nodded while Diderot and Robert appeared skeptical. Only her papa shook his head *no*.

Lisette ran to her bedroom. Her painting was just where she had left it, in the back corner of the room. Spared from the fire, she was thankful that it hadn't been left in the studio. Lisette quickly returned to the dining room. She stood beside her papa at the head of the table and proudly displayed her painting.

"It is quite good for a girl," Diderot said in a restrained manner.

"Indeed. I have rarely seen such execution among female painters," Robert said. He continued, "It is quite unusual for a woman to paint subjects of history or allegory. Wouldn't she fare better painting portraits or still lifes?" Robert asked as if Lisette was not in the room.

"I don't think the Académie would accept history paintings from a woman. They believe, as do most Parisians, that it is the domain of men...and not even all men," Greuze said bitterly.

"They would never sell. Connoisseurs are only interested in paintings by women if they are sentimental portraits," Diderot said authoritatively.

"Don't forget still lifes," Doyen added.

"Still, it displays a certain virtuosity. I would pay 100 *livres* for it," Monsieur Doyen exclaimed.

Monsieur Vernet stood and motioned to his valet who was standing in the back of the room. "I'll give her 150 *livres*."

Is this a dream? Lisette wondered. Just weeks ago, her papa had refused to sell the painting. *150 livres is more money than many people earn in a month. How could this be happening?* she asked herself.

Finally, Louis spoke up, "Lisette, you have made your point." He took the painting from her. "I will take your painting to Le Brun in the morning."

Lisette threw her arms around Louis. "Thank you, Papa!"

Jeanne shot her a disapproving glare and then motioned for Lisette to leave.

Lisette resumed her position in the hallway just outside the dining room.

"If that scoundrel Le Brun can't sell it for 150 *livres*, you come to me, Louis. I will take it off your hands," Vernet said.

"I'm sure he'll get that much, at least. He may be a scoundrel, but the man can sell art...better than anyone else in this city," Doyen said.

All of the men agreed but Vernet.

"I don't trust him. I prefer Monsieur Paillet, even if it means a few less *livres*. He is more forthright and the percentage he takes for himself is significantly less," Vernet said.

"If the Académie Royale had its way, there would be no dealers in Paris," Robert chimed in.

"Their strictures against commerce are ridiculous. The Académie could enforce such outmoded rules while Louis XIV lived, but not now," Doyen said. "Le Brun and his ilk are here to stay," he added with a nod of his head.

With all of the commotion over her painting and disagreement over Le Brun, Lisette did not see the messenger arrive.

She watched her mother accept a small note. Jeanne handed it to Louis. Lisette squinted to make out the name on the back of the note. Sprawled across its envelope in large letters was *J.-B.-P. Le Brun*. As her papa read the note, Jeanne peered over his shoulder to see its message too. Once they had both read it, her parents exchanged looks of despair. The note was clearly upsetting both of them, but particularly Louis. *It must be about the auction*, Lisette thought.

As the men continued their conversation, Louis started to cough. His cough became progressively more violent until it finally brought him out of his chair and onto the floor. His coughing ceased. Louis lay motionless.

Lisette rushed over to him. "Papa!"

Chapter Six

*L*ooking around the apartment, Lisette saw only black. Her papa's friends and acquaintances had come to say their final goodbyes to Louis before his funeral and burial. Jeanne had mindfully followed each ritual. They had stopped the clocks at the hour of Louis' death, at four the previous afternoon, and Jeanne had immediately alerted the Guild of his passing. They were quick to have his body washed, wrapped in a burial shroud and placed in a coffin in their drawing room. A basin of holy water rested on a small table next to the coffin for visitors to sprinkle on Louis' body and on themselves.

From the other side of the room, Lisette watched as Louis' friends gathered around him. With the coffin open, Lisette couldn't bring herself any closer to it. She did not want to see her papa's lifeless body. As she glanced toward the wooden box, her breath drew short. *Breathe*, she told herself.

She reached through the side slits in her dress, into the pocket bag that was tied to her waist and clutched her papa's handkerchief. Lisette let out a deep exhale. She considered Monsieur Greuze, Monsieur Robert, Monsieur Doyen and Monsieur Vernet. It had been just yesterday when they were seated around the dining table with her papa eating, drinking and conversing. Huddled around their friend's expired body and speaking in hushed tones, the group of men appeared nearly as lifeless. Their subdued conversation seemed all the quieter when Lisette recalled the boisterous dinner the previous afternoon.

"Where is Mother?"

Lisette's fog was interrupted by her younger brother Etienne.

"She told us to stay near the casket," Etienne said.

"Etienne, I want you to remain here with me. Don't go over there." Lisette pointed toward their papa's body. She thought it best for her younger brother to keep his distance from the casket too. Etienne was at school when their papa had died and Lisette didn't want his final memory of Louis to be such a morbid one.

"I'm going over there." Etienne moved away from Lisette and walked across the room.

Lisette tried to stop him, but he insisted on following their mother's directions. Not wanting to cause a scene, Lisette let him go.

Etienne never disobeyed or questioned their mother. In turn, Etienne could do no wrong in Jeanne Vigée's eyes. Lisette watched Etienne until he had found their mother. There were so many people in the drawing room, Lisette wanted to be certain he was safe. Jeanne embraced her son and seemed content that he was now by her side.

Lisette turned away from them and scanned the room to make sure it was in order. Earlier that morning, they had flipped the mirrors to face the walls and had draped black cloth over the paintings. Lisette noticed one painting had lost its black cloth. It was a portrait that Lisette had painted of her papa. She headed toward the painting to replace the drape.

When she reached the painting, there was a man standing directly in front of it. He was the only man in the room not wearing black.

"He could have portrayed the eyes with more realism, but not a bad attempt," the man said. He appeared to be in his middle twenties and was dressed in the sort of fine clothes worn by men of rank. Never meeting Lisette's eyes, he focused on the portrait.

"I don't know what you mean. The eyes look perfectly realistic to me," Lisette said.

"No, they aren't. Louis had a difficult time with eyes," the man insisted.

"It isn't a self-portrait, Monsieur," Lisette said, admiring her papa's joyous expression. She had wanted to capture his proudest hour: the King had just commissioned her papa to create several paintings for the Guild exhibition. Lisette felt that his eyes especially revealed his happiness in that moment.

The man cackled. "Of course it is. This is the home of Louis Vigée and these are his paintings."

"Yes, but this one isn't. This one is mine," Lisette said, never once taking her eyes off of the painting.

The man snickered again, but this time louder. His laughter disrupted the stillness in the room. Everyone stared at him.

Whoever he is, he doesn't know much about art, she thought. Lisette would not allow him to dampen this memory of her papa. She continued to enjoy Louis' ebullient face.

No longer laughing, the man said, "You are being genuine."

Lisette ignored him. She bent down, picked up the black cloth that had fallen on the floor and draped it over the painting.

"Is this man bothering you, Mademoiselle Vigée?" Monsieur Vernet was now standing in front of the portrait with them.

"Mademoiselle Vigée?" For the first time since he had begun insulting her portrait, the man looked directly at Lisette. "Jean-

Baptiste Pierre Le Brun, pleased to make your acquaintance," he said as he bowed to Lisette.

She gave a slight nod of her head to acknowledge the polite introduction, but she was still annoyed with his initial haughtiness.

"Lisette, I can make him leave," Vernet said forcefully.

"I was merely discussing Mademoiselle Vigée's talent. This portrait of Louis behind the black cloth is quite remarkable," Le Brun said, pointing to the now covered painting.

Lisette watched as Le Brun became a completely different person. Did he not remember his insults from moments ago? Lisette could see right through his newfound charm. This man was a chameleon and his sudden complimentary tone sickened her.

"Le Brun, it is time you left," Vernet said sternly.

"Not just yet, Vernet. I have business to discuss with Jeanne. Louis owed me paintings for the auction next week. He has an unfulfilled contract with me. There are half a dozen canvases outstanding."

"I hardly think he can fulfill that order now, Le Brun."

"Well someone has to! Or I need the money back. I gave him an advance of 200 *livres*. I am owed."

Lisette noticed Le Brun transform again. The chameleon was changing colors. The charm was gone, quickly replaced with ruthlessness.

"Not here. Not now, Le Brun," Vernet told him.

Lisette saw Vernet wave to his fellow artists. Like a pack of wolves defending one of its young against a panther, they swiftly moved across the room and descended upon Le Brun.

Le Brun understood that he had worn out his welcome. "I'm leaving." He turned to Lisette, "Mademoiselle, tell your mother that I need my money returned *or* the finished canvases."

They did not have the money to pay back her papa's advance. Lisette also knew that there weren't any finished paintings for Le Brun to take. *I could finish them,* she thought. But it would take her days, perhaps weeks to finish her papa's paintings. She knew that Le Brun needed them now. As Le Brun stood waiting for her to respond, Lisette realized that she had to say something.

"Monsieur Le Brun, I will make sure you receive your finished canvases," Lisette said. She would have to give Le Brun *her* paintings. There were six completed canvases sitting in her papa's *atelier*. Lisette estimated that her *Death of Caesar* painting alone would satisfy more than half of the debt. After all, Monsieur Vernet had been willing to pay 150 *livres* for it the day before.

"Very well. My agent will come by the studio after the funeral to collect them." He bowed slightly to her and walked toward the front door of the apartment.

Over Vernet's shoulder, Lisette watched Le Brun leave. Vernet would not allow her to chase after him and Lisette didn't want to disrupt her papa's funeral further. She wanted to discuss details with Le Brun, but not with Vernet looming. She would find a way to talk to Le Brun at a later time.

As soon as Le Brun left, her papa's friends scattered, but Vernet remained. "That man is trouble. What do you want with him?" he asked.

"That is between Monsieur Le Brun and me."

"Lisette, there are other dealers in Paris." Vernet had the look of a dog who refused to release a bone.

Lisette knew that Monsieur Vernet was right about the other dealers, but she had overheard her papa and his friends talking about how none of them were as good as Le Brun. He alone fetched the highest prices for paintings.

"If you'll excuse me Monsieur Vernet, I must find my mother," Lisette said. She needed to inform Jeanne that Le Brun intended to collect on his debt and that his agent would be retrieving paintings after the funeral.

"I believe she is near Louis' casket." Vernet bowed to her and smiled.

Lisette looked toward her papa's casket, but didn't see her

mother. The apartment grew more crowded by the moment. Lisette continued to search. As everyone was wearing black, it was difficult to distinguish men from women. Usually, the bright colors of women's dresses stood out, but not in this room. Her mother's black widow's dress looked just like the other women's dark dresses.

Reluctantly, Lisette stepped to the opposite side of the room, closer to where her papa's casket stood. She spotted her mother. With one hand she clutched a linen handkerchief and with the other, a rosary. Even in mourning, her mother was a vision. The darkness of her black dress contrasted sharply with her luminously white skin. Her deep blue eyes glistened with tears. Lisette had always admired her mother's great beauty. Her papa had told Lisette that she had inherited her pretty face from her mother. Louis Vigée had delighted in calling Jeanne and Lisette his *beautiful girls*, as he would pull them close in a group embrace. Lisette half expected her papa to stroll in through the front door and squeeze his *beautiful girls*, just like he would do each evening when he had returned to their apartment from his *atelier* below.

As Lisette marveled at her mother's loveliness, she also noticed the man standing next to Jeanne. He was a tall, well-dressed man who appeared to be about the same age as her papa. When Lisette's mother began to weep, the man offered his handkerchief and Jeanne accepted it. Lisette watched as the man continued to offer her mother comfort, first with his handkerchief and then with a supportive, strong arm. Jeanne took the man's arm and leaned against him while she cried. *Who is this man?* Lisette wondered. *I've met all of Papa's colleagues and friends*, she thought.

Lisette felt a tug on her wrist, "Lisette, where is Mother?" Etienne asked. Wearing an expression of panic, he appeared lost.

"Etienne, Mother is over there," Lisette said, pointing to where she was standing.

He didn't seem relieved. "Lisette, Mother is not paying attention to me. I want to leave," Etienne said.

Lisette smiled at him. "Me too."

Conveying Le Brun's message to her mother had lost its urgency. Lisette took her younger brother's hand and escorted him out of the crowd to his bedroom at the rear of the apartment.

"It is much quieter in here," Lisette said as she noticed a man's handkerchief in Etienne's hand.

"Where did you get that?" she asked him.

Etienne shook his head, unwilling to answer.

"Etienne, you can tell me. I won't say anything to Mother." Lisette tried to reassure him. "Where did you get it? It looks like one of Papa's."

"It is. I took it from him...in there." Etienne gestured toward the drawing room.

Lisette hugged her brother tightly. "I miss him too. Don't ever forget that he loved you. He loved both of us very much. But now we have to be brave. Can you be brave for me?"

Etienne squeezed Lisette. She felt his head moving up and down as he answered affirmatively.

Lisette needed to say one final goodbye to her papa. She released Etienne. "I'll be back later to check on you."

She returned to the drawing room and headed straight to her papa's open casket. Lisette peered down at his pale face and wished she could look into his eyes one last time. *Papa, I miss you,* she thought. Her eyes filled with tears. She pushed them back, not wanting to shed them in front of so many people. Earlier, Jeanne had made a spectacle of herself by crying hysterically. Lisette had heard her mother say that women were expected to show emotion, but Lisette felt otherwise. She had never been comfortable displaying her private feelings.

Lisette reached into her pocket bag and removed the handkerchief that she had carried with her for over a decade. She placed it next to her papa in the casket. *He shouldn't be without a handkerchief. He always had one with him,* she thought. As she tucked it neatly into his jacket pocket, she felt his pocket watch. Lisette took out the watch. She observed it for a few moments and instead of returning it to her papa, she slipped it inside her pocket bag. She glanced down at him one final time.

"Goodbye, Papa," she said.

As Lisette backed away from the casket, she collided into a group of men. *Is the room shrinking?* she wondered. Lisette found it difficult to breathe again. *I have to leave,* she thought.

Talking to no one, she removed herself from the drawing room and then the apartment. She ran down the stairs, into her papa's studio and shut the door behind her. She slumped to the floor, pulled out her papa's pocket watch and studied the small face with its black roman numerals and gold background. She had seen her papa with the watch for as long as she could remember. Being very valuable, it was one of his most prized possessions.

Alone, Lisette sat staring at the watch in the dark and would not permit herself to cry. But as she thought about her papa and the time they had spent together in this studio, she allowed a tear to escape. Then another...and another. Soon they were coming too quickly for Lisette to stop them. The tears were now gushing out of her. *Papa...*

Chapter Seven

*L*isette sat on her bed looking at her papa's watch. She didn't care what time it was, she wanted to remember him. Imagining him holding the watch made Lisette feel a little less sad. As the months had passed, it had become more difficult to see and hear him in her mind. She never wanted to forget the sound of his voice or the way he smiled at her.

"Are you ready? Lisette!" Jeanne called out from the other side of Lisette's closed bedroom door.

Lisette looked down at her shoes sitting on the floor next to her bed. She did not want to wear them again. They were her best pair and perfectly matched her finest dress, a buttercup yellow silk gown trimmed with spotted gauze. Only worn on Sundays and feast days, her shoes were a similar yellow shade of damask silk with buckle closures and a low heel. Her papa had called them a splurge for his *beautiful girl*. Originally delicate shoes, their soles were now so worn they were practically non-existent. Her mother still insisted that she wear them to Mass and then promenading, even though Lisette could feel every pebble and sharp object on the street when she walked.

Today, Lisette had removed her shoes as soon as they had returned home from Sunday Mass at the church of Saint-Eustache. The blisters on her feet had only recently stopped aching. Finished with their mid-day meal, it was now time for Lisette and her family to take their Sunday afternoon walk. She would have to put her shoes back on her blistered feet.

"Hurry along, Lisette! We are going to be late. Come out of your room!" She heard her mother holler again.

Lisette glanced at her shoes once more before giving in to her mother. *When will Mother take me to the shoemaker for a new pair?* she wondered. Her papa had bought Lisette and Etienne new shoes well before they needed them. New shoes weren't the only thing that had become unavailable. In the several months since her papa had died, Etienne had forsaken his schooling and even their meals had grown simpler. Gone were the expensive, roasted meats and fowl dishes. Instead, they ate bland soups and stews with one or two vegetables, mostly onions. They always managed to buy bread, but some days it was stale. Even though her mother refused to discuss it, Lisette knew that her papa had left them in dire financial straits.

"Lisette!" Her mother's raised voice was also unfamiliar. Jeanne had been much less patient with both Lisette and Etienne. Before Louis' death, Jeanne had very rarely lost her temper. Now, it was a daily occurrence.

"We can't be late. Come out of there at once," Jeanne repeated.

Why is she in such a hurry? We are only going promenading in the Tuileries, Lisette thought.

Like most of Paris, they took their weekly Sunday afternoon walk in the gardens behind the Palais des Tuileries. Over the past months, her mother had continued the family tradition. Lisette suspected it was on purpose, to help them become accustomed to life without Louis. But today seemed different. This afternoon, Jeanne Vigée was in a great rush.

Lisette slipped on her shoes. It wouldn't take too many steps before her feet would hurt again. She wasn't sure how she would get through the afternoon. "Coming, Mother," Lisette said as she walked out of her room.

"There you are. Put on your cloak. There is a chill in the air," Jeanne said as she inspected Lisette from head to toe. She said nothing, just handed Lisette her cloak.

She must not disapprove, Lisette thought.

Then Jeanne moved on to Lisette's brother. "Look at you, my handsome Etienne."

Lisette regarded her brother. She agreed, he was charming in his navy blue, embroidered waistcoat and matching *culottes* with white silk stockings, but the pained look on his face tainted his appearance. Lisette glanced down at his shoes. The worn leather was stretched beyond its capacity.

"Look at Etienne's shoes, they are at least two sizes too small for his feet. Mother, when can we go to the shoemaker?" Lisette asked.

Etienne appeared hopeful as he waited for his mother's reply.

"I don't know, but not now," Jeanne said.

Lisette watched her brother's scowl return. He looked like he was about to cry.

Jeanne bent down to Etienne's eye level and said, "Soon, very soon. Our life is going to change very soon." Her voice was soft.

"When is that? When exactly can we get new shoes?" Lisette pressed her mother.

Jeanne stood and glared at Lisette. "Soon is all I can say. We can't waste any more time. We must go," Jeanne said in an abrasive voice as she held open the door.

"Mother, do we have to go to the Tuileries gardens today? Can we visit the Saint-Laurent Fair instead? It won't be open for much longer, the feast day of Saint Michel is almost here," Etienne said.

"Yes! Can we, Mother? There is a play by Monsigny being performed that I'd like to see, *La belle Arsène*. The troupe is performing the second act. We saw the first act last spring at the Saint-Germain Fair," Lisette said.

"Yes, I remember. It was a clever play. Another day perhaps. We are going to the Tuileries today." Her mother had a tone of finality. She gestured toward the stairs in the hall.

Lisette stepped out first, followed by her younger brother and finally their mother who locked the door behind them. When they reached the street, Lisette stopped to wait for a carriage.

Her mother continued walking.

"Aren't we hailing a carriage?" Lisette asked her mother.

"We are walking. It will do us good to take in the air," Jeanne replied.

Lisette suspected otherwise. Like everything else related to their finances, her mother was too embarrassed to be honest with her.

They walked briskly down the Rue de Coquillière toward the Rue Saint-Honoré, which would lead them to the Palais des Tuileries. Lisette's feet seared with pain as she navigated the stones, mud and refuse in the road. They had to cross many more streets before reaching the Tuileries. Then they would walk some more. Lisette wanted to slow down.

"Mother, can't we slow our pace? Why are we walking so fast?"

Jeanne didn't answer her. She continued at the same clip. Her mother appeared animal-like in her determination to reach the gardens.

"Mother, look at poor Etienne. He can't keep up." Lisette thought that if her mother wouldn't slow down for her, maybe she would for her favorite.

"We can't be late," Jeanne said, refusing to reduce her break-neck pace. Lisette had guessed wrong.

As they turned onto the Rue Saint-Nicaise and the Tuileries came into view, Jeanne moved faster.

Are we meeting somebody? Lisette wondered. *Who could be this important?* she thought.

Once they entered the grounds of the palace, Jeanne turned in the direction opposite the gardens. They were now headed toward the Place du Carrousel, the courtyard in front of the palace entrance. Lisette watched her mother scan the immediate area.

"I hope he shows. He said to meet over there." Jeanne pointed toward a small, temporary pavilion erected in the corner of the courtyard. "Let's go," Jeanne said as she darted off toward the building.

Lisette and Etienne followed, but they couldn't catch up to their mother. The blisters on Lisette's feet made it very difficult for her to walk at all, let alone quickly. Etienne complained to Lisette about his cramped toes. Lisette feared that they might spasm if he didn't sit and rest.

"Mother, please wait for us," Lisette called out to Jeanne. Her mother continued marching toward the pavilion, never looking back at her children.

They tried to reach her, but Etienne soon tripped and fell to the ground.

"Mother! Etienne has fallen!" Lisette yelled.

Jeanne stopped and turned around. She walked back and held out her hand to Etienne.

"Mother, my knee hurts," Etienne said as he clutched his right knee. He had torn his silk stockings and his *culottes* were scuffed at the knee.

"Get up," Jeanne said. She turned toward the pavilion.

"I can't," Etienne groaned.

Lisette gingerly pushed up his right *culottes* to inspect the injury. She saw a bump on his knee that was beginning to swell. "Mother, I think he has hurt himself badly. We should go home,"

Lisette said.

"I have to meet someone very important in the pavilion and I can't be late. You two make your way there. Lisette, you stay behind and help him." Jeanne rushed off.

By the time Lisette had raised her brother off of the ground, their mother was nowhere in sight. Lisette scanned the crowd. She didn't see her mother, but a strange couple caught her attention. An unusually tall, well-dressed man was talking to a servant woman. Their interaction somehow seemed nefarious to Lisette. They were partially hidden behind a large oak tree, but Lisette could see most of their bodies and faces. *I have seen that man before*, she thought. *But where?* she wondered.

Lisette carefully watched the man and the woman. After exchanging a few words, she saw the woman put her hand in the man's waistcoat pocket, slipping a bundle of cloth into it. Lisette couldn't be sure what she had seen. The man glanced up to see if anyone was watching and Lisette quickly looked down at the ground. When she raised her head again, they were both gone. *How strange,* she thought.

"We should find Mother," Etienne said as he tried to walk on his own.

"You can lean on me and we can take our time," Lisette said.

With Etienne holding onto Lisette's arm, they started walking in the direction of the pavilion. As they approached the temporary structure, the crowds in the Place du Carrousel grew thicker. There were vendors renting chairs and selling a variety of treats including lemonade, brandy, ices, pastries and fruit. Lisette surveyed the mix of people. She spotted noble men and women, merchants and their wives, laborers and apprentices, all relaxing on a Sunday afternoon. The air was fragrant with the smell of fashionable women's nosegays and perfumed hair powders. Lisette knew that this *mélange* of people also included prostitutes and thieves. She had heard many tales of how pickpockets and harlots were attracted to crowded public spaces like the Palais Royal, the food market at Les Halles and the Tuileries. Lisette held Etienne a little tighter.

"Lisette, you are hurting me," Etienne yelped.

She loosened her hold on him. "I'm sorry. I only want to keep you safe."

Lisette remained vigilant as they walked. Like she had promised her brother, they kept a very leisurely pace. Etienne never once complained as they slowly made their way to the pavilion.

"We are nearly there," Lisette said as she gently squeezed her brother's hand to comfort him.

Lisette and Etienne continued walking until they were just outside the pavilion.

She stooped to check Etienne's leg. "How is your knee?" she asked him.

"It hurts, but it will mend," he said bravely.

Lisette noticed that the swelling had increased. Etienne needed to sit down and rest his leg.

"Let's find Mother, get a few *sous* from her and hail a *cabriolet* home. You have no business promenading today."

Still leaning on Lisette, Etienne hobbled the last few steps into the pavilion. Once inside, Lisette saw ladies and gentlemen dressed in their finery. The women displayed elaborate *coiffures* and gowns while the men showcased expensive waistcoats and mahogany, gold-knobbed canes. Some women carried bejeweled fans, while others held little dogs.

"Lisette, look over by the Duchesse, there is Mother," Etienne said.

Lisette recognized the Duchesse de Chartres too. She could be found promenading in the Tuileries most afternoons and always on Sunday. She was married to the Duc de Chartres, who was a near cousin of the King. All of Paris wanted to be near her. Being married to a prince of royal lineage, she was usually the highest born aristocrat at the Tuileries. She was also the most fashionable. All of the women wanted to look like her and often did. No one in Lisette's family had ever been included in a conversation with the Duchesse. They were not important enough. *Why is Mother talking with her now?* Lisette wondered.

She looked closer. Her mother was deeply engaged with the Duchesse de Chartres and....the tall man that Lisette had just seen with the servant woman. Each time the man spoke, Lisette's mother and the Duchesse threw their heads back and laughed. Both of the women seemed to be captivated by this man and whatever he was saying to them. Lisette studied the man's face. *I've seen him before today*, she thought. Then she remembered. Lisette recognized him as not only the same man that had acted strangely with the female servant behind the oak tree moments earlier, but he was also the man that had been comforting her mother at her papa's funeral. Lisette felt like she was completing a puzzle, but only a few of the pieces were falling into place.

Leaving Etienne resting on a chair, Lisette walked over to where they stood. Her mother appeared happy to see her. "Lisette, come meet the Duchesse and Monsieur Le Sèvre."

The Duchesse scanned Lisette from head to toe, pausing at her shoes. Saying nothing to Lisette, the Duchesse seemed uninterested in meeting a bourgeois girl with worn-out shoes. Lisette knew that nobles were within their right to behave in that manner with those who were lower born, but she didn't like it. Lisette felt that she deserved respect no matter how tattered her shoes.

Monsieur Le Sèvre spoke up, "Pleased to meet you."

Lisette held out her hand and allowed him to kiss it. He wasn't a bad-looking man. His face was pleasant with steel gray eyes that imbued a sense of confidence and strength. His clothes contributed to his distinguished air. He wore a long coat of pale blue with prominent silver buttons, an embroidered silk vest of the same blue and burgundy-colored *culottes*. He was not wearing a wig, but his hair was powdered white, pulled back and tied at the nape of his neck with a black ribbon. Lisette thought he could have passed for a nobleman in his fashionable costume.

She often saw highborn men dressed similarly every Sunday when they promenaded in the Tuileries.

"You are as lovely as your mother described you, Lisette." He looked over to Jeanne as he said this.

"Le Sèvre, when will you have the Turkish jewels ready for me to view?" the Duchesse asked him, continuing to ignore Lisette.

Le Sèvre immediately turned away from Lisette and addressed the Duchesse. "I suspect in three days. I will send a messenger in advance of my arrival."

"I will want to examine them in my salon in the late morning. That is when the light is best," she said.

Le Sèvre nodded and the Duchesse walked away. Before Le Sèvre could return his attention to Lisette and Jeanne, another noblewoman approached him.

"Good afternoon, Marquise," Le Sèvre said as he bowed to the highborn woman.

"Le Sèvre, I heard that you have a new shipment of jewels coming from the Ottoman Empire...is that true?" the Marquise asked.

Lisette regarded the woman. She wore a dusty rose-colored silk gown with an apron of embroidered muslin and held a bamboo walking cane. Peeking out from underneath the Marquise's skirts, Lisette noticed the tips of her silk shoes perfectly matched the pink of her dress. The Marquise smelled beautiful too. She was a walking garden of blooming spring flowers and ripe oranges.

Le Sèvre responded, "Only for you, Marquise. You know you are my foremost client...I save the best for my favorites," he said, kissing her hand.

The Marquise blushed as he flattered her.

As soon as she had walked away Le Sèvre turned to Jeanne and Lisette. "Shall we walk around the gardens? Their natural beauty will edify us." He held out his arm for Jeanne to take. Then he leaned in close to Jeanne and whispered loudly, "But nothing compares to your magnificence, my darling. I could gaze upon your exquisite face forever."

Jeanne was beaming.

"Mother, Etienne and I are going home. He needs to rest." Lisette could finally get a word with her mother.

"You two can leave. I am going to walk in the gardens with Monsieur Le Sèvre. I will be home by dusk," Jeanne said. Then she muttered a few words in Le Sèvre's ear. He moved a few steps away, giving Lisette and her mother privacy.

Jeanne faced Lisette. "Did you see that I was talking to the Duchesse de Chartres?" Jeanne asked. Her mother was giddy like a young girl.

Lisette nodded. Jeanne seemed to have overlooked the Duchesse's dismissive behavior.

"She is one of Le Sèvre's best clients. He has known her for years. He has many noble clients, just like her. You'll see, Lisette, he is going to introduce us to many important people. We are rising in the world."

Lisette was confused. Why were they suddenly going to be spending so much time with Le Sèvre and his noble clients?

Her mother looked at Le Sèvre and smiled broadly. It was the kind of smile that Lisette hadn't seen on her mother's face since before her papa died.

Never taking her eyes off of Le Sèvre, Jeanne said, "Lisette, Monsieur Le Sèvre has asked me to marry him...and I've accepted."

Chapter Eight

*L*isette held her cloak tight around her shoulders with her free hand. The other was carrying her canvas, *The Death of Caesar.* As she walked, Lisette thought about her mother. It had been weeks since Jeanne had announced her wedding. Lisette was still reeling from the news. *How could Mother get married?* Lisette wondered. Her papa had only left this world months ago. *She can't,* Lisette thought. *I cannot accept it.*

Carefully, Lisette made her way down her street, the Rue de Coquillière. She moved quickly, skillfully dodging the many piles of black muck scattered throughout the streets. The dark filth was a foul mixture of animal dung and particles of iron that had flaked off carriage wheels. Lisette knew that if the bottom of her skirts grazed the muck, they would be forever stained pitch black. As she turned onto the Rue du Four, toward Les Halles, she tried not to breathe too deeply. The water flowing onto the street from the domestic kitchens was enough to induce nausea, if not vomit. She navigated around the puddles created by this putrid water.

Lisette then followed the Rue Saint-Honoré, one of the widest streets in Paris, until she had crossed over the Rue Saint Denis and was on Rue des Lombards. As she made her way past the Cimetière des Innocents, she held her breath for as long as she was able. Lisette had heard that the fumes emanating from the decomposing bodies were dangerous. The cemetery had been over-crowded with too many souls for many years. The overwhelming number of dead bodies had created an uneven landscape with prominent bulges of corpses that had been buried beneath a too-thin layer of earth.

When Lisette reached the Rue Saint Martin, she turned toward the river Seine and the Pont Notre-Dame, where Le Brun's shop was located. As she drew closer to the Quai Pelletier and the Pont Notre-Dame, her progress was abruptly slowed. *What is happening?* she thought. Then she heard the bells of St-Gervais-et-St-Protais Church tolling.

Only a few streets over, Lisette realized that she was passing near the Place de Grève. People had filled the square and were spilling out onto the street. *There must be an execution today*, she thought, *or at least a public flogging*. Deeming them unnecessarily cruel, Lisette had never desired to watch public punishments or executions. She continued toward the Quai as there was no need to enter the Place de Grève.

As Lisette walked past the people milling around waiting for the execution to begin, she overheard two women talking. Lisette determined from their appearance that they were servants of a great house. The young women both wore fine cotton dresses, aprons and linen caps. The dresses had a worn look, as if they had been passed down to the servants from their mistress. It was well-known that loyal and obedient servants often received their masters' old clothes when they no longer had use for them.

"Dreadful business about the mistress' daughter," one of the women said. She spoke with an accent that betrayed her provincial origins.

"I heard that she is innocent...set up by her betrothed," her companion said. She held a basket full of vegetables.

"He was the one who had her arrested?"

"Yes, and now she'll be flogged, branded and then banished from France."

"What were the charges?"

"Heresy. The betrothed would not stand for having a wife that outshone him in any way. He never approved of her writings or of her associations with the *philosophes*. I heard our mistress declare her daughter's innocence with my own ears."

"So then she didn't commit heresy?"

The woman holding the vegetables shook her head. "Not according to what I overheard. Our mistress plead with the Lieutenant Général de Police, Antoine de Sartine, to spare her daughter but he would not budge. Apparently the betrothed's father had already intervened."

"Such a shame. Now she will never become a wife or be the mistress of her own house."

The woman with the basket clucked in agreement.

A woman punished for writing? Betrayed by her betrothed? Lisette suddenly had an interest in public punishment. She pushed her way through the masses until she caught a glimpse of the center of the square. Lisette stopped moving and looked up to get a better view of the pillory. The pillory in the Place de Grève was placed high enough for everyone in the square to see the criminals confined to its platform.

Lisette saw a man and a woman, each standing with their hands and heads poking out of the holes in the wooden boards that held them. The condemned were both wearing placards that hung around their necks. The large board hanging around the man's neck said, "Distribution of Counterfeit Coins" while the one around the woman's neck read, "Heresy." Lisette caught a glimpse of the accused woman's face. She looked defeated and tired, undoubtedly from the multitude of floggings she had already received. *Has her spirit been broken?* Lisette wondered. She wanted to walk away and push this condemned woman far from her mind, but she couldn't avert her gaze. The woman's anguish somehow felt familiar to her. As Lisette stood watching, she heard a man next to her talking.

"They'll be starting the whipping in a few minutes," the man said.

"That's not even the best part. Me, I like the branding," his friend said.

"Who is that next to the counterfeiter? What was her crime?" the first man asked. Evidently he couldn't read. He had a head full of blond hair and a dirty face, like he hadn't washed himself in months. He didn't look much older than Lisette.

His companion said, "She is a heretic, convicted of going against the Church." Lisette noticed that this man spoke with a lisp because he was missing most of his teeth.

"I bet she'll squeal like a pig when they brand her." The blond-haired man rubbed his hands together in anticipation.

"What about that man there?" the toothless one asked, pointing to a third criminal on the far edge of the square. For some reason he had been separated from the others. He wasn't wearing a placard, so Lisette was unsure of his crime.

"Burglar. After they whip and brand him, he'll be put to death – broken on the wheel. See over there?"

Lisette looked in the direction that the blond-haired man was pointing toward. She saw a wheel at the far edge of the square. She knew that the burglar must have committed a violent burglary if he was going to be killed on the wheel. Lisette had to leave. She had no interest in watching them break his legs, arms and back on the sinister device.

"Ooh, I can't wait to see that. We'll be here a while," the toothless man said. The two men went on discussing their other favorite forms of punishment and torture.

Lisette left the square. It took some force, but she was able to make her way back out and away from the Place de Grève. Once she was past the crowd, she picked up her pace. She wanted to leave the branding, whipping and especially the wheel safely behind her.

Lisette shivered. Snow had not yet fallen, but the low temperatures signaled that winter was coming soon. A new season was beginning, yet another reminder of how long her papa had been gone.

Today, Lisette was headed toward Le Brun's shop. Le Brun's agent had visited her papa's studio just days after the funeral, but Lisette had heard nothing from Le Brun. Out on an errand for her mother, Lisette had missed the agent. When she had returned, everything was gone from the studio. To Lisette's immense pleasure, Le Brun's agent had taken every canvas, both hers and her papa's. Her only regret was that she had been safekeeping her *Death of Caesar* painting in her bedroom. It hadn't been taken along with the others.

This afternoon, she would ask Le Brun to sell her painting of Caesar's death. She was also expecting to receive some money from the paintings that Le Brun's agent had taken. Le Brun had held his auction weeks ago, more than enough time for him to have collected on the sales. *Mother won't have to get married,* Lisette thought. If her mother needed money for their family, then Lisette would provide it. She knew her paintings could support them. She hoped to convince her mother to call off the engagement. The wedding was to take place in three weeks. *It will be enough,* she reassured herself.

It felt right to Lisette to be thinking about painting again. In the months after her papa had died, Lisette couldn't bring herself to paint. The studio had felt too empty without him. Several of her papa's friends had come to visit her and had shared encouraging words.

Lisette could hear Monsieur Doyen's advice: *Lisette, return*

*to your drawing and painting. It will bring you solace and help
you to get through life's greatest misfortunes, including this one
you are experiencing right now. Your papa would want you to
continue to paint. He was so proud of you.*

After Jeanne had made her announcement about marrying
Le Sèvre, Lisette knew it was time to paint again. Besides her
Death of Caesar, Lisette had no other finished paintings to give
Le Brun, but she would collect what was owed to her. At the
very least, she could give her mother *some* money.

Lisette turned onto the Pont Notre-Dame. Like many of the
bridges in Paris, it was crowded with houses and merchants'
shops. She thought of her mother's words as she entered the
bridge, *One can never be too careful on the Pont Notre-Dame.*
Jeanne didn't like using the Pont Notre-Dame to cross the Seine,
for fear that it would collapse as it had in the past under the
weight of all of the houses built on it. Lisette thought that her
mother's fear was unfounded. The last time the bridge had collapsed was over 200 years before and since then the bridge had
been rebuilt with stone to replace the wood. Recently, a number
of houses had been demolished to preserve the structural inte-
grity of the bridge.

Lisette made her way down the bridge. *I must be close now,*
she thought, *surely Le Brun's shop can't be far.* Lisette had heard
her papa's friends talk about how the picture-dealers' shops were
clustered on the Pont Notre-Dame. *I'll simply ask until someone
directs me,* Lisette decided.

She stood in front of the first shop on the street. Lisette
searched for a sign, but couldn't find one. She noticed the
wrought iron brackets protruding from the façade that had once
held a hanging sign, but were now empty. Hanging shop signs
had been banned by the city more than ten years ago, but some
merchants had not replaced them with any other signage.

When Lisette walked inside, she saw a stocky, well-dressed
older man standing behind a long oak counter. He was returning
a drawer to its place along the back wall of the shop. The counter

was L-shaped, running parallel to the side and back walls. There was a small gap, just big enough for a person to pass through, at the end of the front portion of the counter where it neared the left wall. The drawers covered the back wall, from floor to ceiling. Lisette approached the counter. There were several drawers sitting on the counter, all full of ribbons. Each drawer held a different fabric or different color of ribbon.

The man greeted her. "Bonjour, Mademoiselle." He was friendly and welcoming. "Can I take out some ribbons to show you?"

"Monsieur, can you tell me where I can find Monsieur Le Brun?"

Immediately, the man's demeanor changed. He squinted at Lisette and said, "I am a respectable *marchand de rubans*. I do not have anything to do with that man." He came close to Lisette. "And you shouldn't either."

Lisette bowed politely to him and abruptly left. She walked a short distance to the next shop and went inside. She was in such a hurry to get away from the *marchand de rubans*, Lisette didn't look for a sign outside, but the moment she entered the shop, she knew it was a grocer-druggist. She was immediately struck by the powerful, strange mix of smells found only in this type of shop.

Lisette often frequented their grocer-druggist, Monsieur Goban, to buy her art supplies and foodstuffs for her mother. This shop looked very similar to Monsieur Goban's, but was gaudier. The mahogany *boiserie* had a tulipwood veneer and decorative arabesque inlay designs. The carved wood paneling in her local grocer-druggist was not as elaborate or made out of such expensive wood. An enormous, silver-framed mirror covered the side wall. On either side of the mirror were gilt-bronze *bras de lumières* large enough to hold three candles each. The wall sconces in Monsieur Goban's were of a simple, pewter, two-candle design. All along the back wall were shelves lined with bottles full of cinnamon, oil, pigments, sugar, arsenic, brandy, jam and cheese. As she looked at the jam and cheese, Lisette felt her stomach grumble. *When was the last time I ate?* she wondered.

A stocky woman wearing an apron peered up from behind the counter. "What would you like?" she asked curtly.

"Madame, can you tell me where I might find Monsieur Le Brun's shop?"

The woman scrunched up her face and pointed her finger wildly at Lisette. "Get out! I will not have that scoundrel's name uttered in here!"

Lisette quickly ran out of the grocer-druggist. *Le Brun must be close,* she thought. If all of these shopkeepers knew who he was, his shop couldn't be far.

Before she had moved away from the grocer-druggist's storefront, a young girl came out of the store.

"Mademoiselle, I apologize for my mother. I believe the proprietor you are seeking is farther down, toward the middle of the bridge," the girl said and scurried back inside the shop.

Lisette started walking again. Her search for Le Brun was taking much longer than she had expected. She tightened her cloak once more.

When she had reached the middle of the bridge, Lisette stopped and searched the buildings for Le Brun's shop sign. Not seeing it, she decided to look in the windows of each building. She began with the one in front of her. Lisette peered through the shop's front windows and saw that it was crammed floor to ceiling with paintings. *This must be it,* she thought.

Lisette went inside. She was immediately struck by the grandness of the space. The ceilings were very high and the walls were covered with intricate *boiserie*, which was difficult to see because the profusion of paintings covered the beautiful wood paneling. It reminded her of the galleries inside the Louvre. Lisette craned her neck to see the paintings hung at the intersection of the ceiling and the wall. As she looked up, she noticed how the paintings were illuminated from above. *Re-*

markable, she thought. In all of the artists' exhibitions she had frequented at the Louvre, she had never seen paintings displayed in this manner. There was a narrow wooden shelf just below the ceiling that surrounded the room. The light coming off of the candles on the shelf lit each painting. It was incredible.

This must be where Le Brun displays the works in his collection, she thought. Lisette knew that individuals could buy paintings from Le Brun at any time, but the majority of his sales took place during his bi-annual auctions. Lisette tried to examine all of the paintings, but there was too much to see. As she scanned the paintings high up on the walls, she found herself drawn to a series of four small portraits whose sitters looked famliar to her. She squinted to see their faces better.

"Mademoiselle, how can I help you?" a man's voice said from behind her.

Lisette jumped. She had been so busy looking at the portraits that she hadn't noticed anyone walk into the front room. She turned to look at the man. He was very short and carried himself with a distinct pompousness.

"I need to speak with Monsieur Le Brun." Lisette stood up as straight and tall as she could.

"He is indisposed at the moment," the man said, barely looking at her.

Lisette continued undeterred. "I will speak only with Monsieur Le Brun. When will he be available?"

The man's eyes darted around. "Mademoiselle, where is your escort? Are you here with your husband or father?"

"Will Monsieur Le Brun be available soon?" Lisette asked again.

Before the little man had a chance to reply, Le Brun emerged from the back. Lisette could see there was a heavy, dark red curtain separating the front of the gallery from the back area. *He must have been watching, or at least listening*, Lisette thought. She suspected Le Brun's usual business practice was to screen his visitors before he made himself known to them.

"Ah, Mademoiselle Vigée," Le Brun said. He approached Lisette and kissed her hand. "It is always a pleasure to have such a beautiful young woman in my gallery."

Lisette was confused by his use of the word *gallery*. She had never heard a picture-dealer call his shop a *gallery*. Galleries were the spaces in grand houses and palaces like the Louvre where a nobleman's paintings were displayed. They weren't places for commerce.

When she didn't say anything to him, he spoke again, "How can I help you?"

Lisette bowed politely. "Monsieur Le Brun, I'm here for the money owed to my mother from the sale of the paintings your agent collected from my papa's studio."

A knowing look came over Le Brun's face. "Yes, of course."

Le Brun went into the back again, but only briefly. When he returned, he had a wide grin on his face. He handed Lisette a large sack of coins. Being much heavier than she expected, her arm dropped from the weight of it.

"You are a clever girl." Le Brun smiled at her. "Slipping your own canvases in with those of your father...you knew I would take notice of the superior works."

To Lisette, it was bittersweet for Le Brun to describe her works as superior to her papa's. She didn't like hearing that her papa was an inferior painter, but at the same time she couldn't believe that she had actually sold a painting.

"You've sold my work at auction?" she asked.

"No, not at auction. I sold them to one of my most discerning collectors."

"What about my papa's paintings?"

"Many were unfinished, so they were worthless. But the ones that he managed to finish were presented at auction, as Louis and I had agreed upon before his death. I'm afraid they did not sell."

Papa would be very upset, Lisette thought. He had worked tirelessly on the paintings before he had died. Lisette pictured her papa hunched over his easel, coughing while he painted.

"But yours did sell." Le Brun gestured toward the sack Lisette held in her hand.

She gently shook the bag of coins. Lisette tried to guess the coins' worth. She moved her arm up and down to better judge.

"It is 700 *livres*," Le Brun said.

Lisette considered this number. She remembered that her papa's friends had been willing to pay her at least 150 *livres* for her painting, *The Death of Caesar*. Le Brun's agent had taken exactly six of Lisette's paintings from her papa's studio. She quickly computed the amounts in her head.

"I think my canvases are worth more than that, Monsieur Le Brun."

"I do too. I sold them for 300 *livres* each," Le Brun said plainly.

"300 *livres* each?" Lisette knew that her papa had rarely commanded that great of a sum for a single canvas. She wasn't sure she heard him correctly.

"Yes," Le Brun said.

Once Lisette let herself accept this fact, she did some more computations. She could feel her face get hot. "How much did you take for yourself?"

"Fifty percent, plus the 200 *livres* that I advanced your father before he died."

"Fifty percent?" Lisette was stunned.

"It is standard," Le Brun said flatly.

Lisette didn't know what was "standard," but she strongly suspected that it wasn't half. She would never be able to support her family if Le Brun continued to take half of her earnings. Lisette put the sack of coins into her pocket bag beneath her dress. She narrowed her eyes at him.

"That is what your father and I settled on. He agreed to fifty percent," Le Brun said.

Lisette thought about her papa working furiously to finish the paintings right up until he died. *Papa must have been des-*

perate, she realized. Lisette wasn't eager to follow in her papa's footsteps.

Le Brun glanced over to the canvas in her hand.

"Do you have another canvas for me to sell?" he asked her.

Not at a fifty percent commission, she thought. Lisette put it behind her back.

She moved two steps closer to Le Brun. "Monsieur Le Brun, if we are going to do business together you will take ten percent for yourself, not fifty."

Monsieur Faucher snickered. Le Brun looked like he wanted to laugh too, but managed to stop himself. Then he tapped Faucher on the arm to urge him to gain control.

"Ten percent, you say?" Le Brun asked. His tone indicated that he was mocking her.

"Yes," Lisette replied firmly.

Monsieur Faucher interrupted before Le Brun could speak again, "Monsieur, we have a very busy afternoon. We don't have time for this...this girl. I hardly think she is worth our time. We need to get back to business. Our next appointment is in a few minutes. Come."

Ignoring Faucher, Le Brun grinned at Lisette. "I see you aren't afraid to speak your mind...very unusual for a girl. Of course I would expect it from a man." Le Brun seemed pleased at her boldness.

Lisette stood tall. She didn't know if she could remain dauntless for very much longer. She wanted to crumble inside. *Please agree,* she thought.

"Confidence is very becoming. It is the mark of every great artist." Le Brun's face became serious again. "Forty percent."

Lisette was tempted to agree, but she wasn't sure. She had never negotiated anything before. Her intuition told her not to give in too quickly. Besides, she knew that earning sixty percent would not be enough to stop her mother's marriage.

"Twenty percent and that is my final offer," Lisette said. *Why won't he just agree?* she thought.

Le Brun replied without hesitation. "Mademoiselle, I am out of time. I have an appointment elsewhere. I must leave."

Monsieur Le Brun turned to go. Lisette didn't want to lose this opportunity. She might not get it again.

"Twenty-five percent," she said hastily.

"If you will excuse me." Le Brun started toward the back of the shop.

Before he could disappear behind the curtain, Lisette moved to block his path. "Monsieur Le Brun, please, can't we agree on a number today?"

"Mademoiselle Vigée, you are charming. You are also a very talented painter whose paintings I would be happy to sell. But at a forty percent commission. I would be pleased to meet with you again, but I do not have time for this today. Good afternoon." Le Brun motioned to Faucher. "Monsieur Faucher will show you out."

Monsieur Faucher held open the front door. "Good day," he said to Lisette as he glared at her. Faucher looked like he wanted to push her out with both hands. Lisette moved slowly out of the door. Saying nothing, she met his eyes and walked out.

As she left Le Brun's and started walking back home, she wondered if she had missed her only chance to establish a business relationship with Le Brun. She gripped her *Death of Caesar* painting, still in her possession. She couldn't give it to Le Brun to sell if they couldn't reach an agreement on his commission.

She reached into her pocket bag and felt the heavy sack of coins safely hidden from any prying eyes. Although it was more than she had anticipated, now that the money was in her possession, she instinctively knew it was not enough to prevent the impending nuptials. Lisette's stomach cramped as she thought of her mother marrying Le Sèvre.

Chapter Nine

A few days after her disappointing meeting with Le Brun, Lisette sat in her room thinking about his refusal to accept her terms. *How can I get him to agree to less than forty percent?* she thought. *Should I simply concede so that I can sell my paintings?* Lisette went back and forth in her mind. *No, I will wait until he accepts a lower commission,* she decided. But then she would consider how much she needed the money. With more money, there would be no need for her mother to remarry. Lisette stood up and paced.

She was lost in thought when she heard a knock on her bedroom door. "Lisette! Are you in there?" Jeanne asked. The knocking grew louder and more forceful.

Lisette opened the door for her mother.

"Are you ill?"

"No, Mother."

"Good. I have some wonderful news. Please come out for dinner. We have a guest," Jeanne said and walked out of Lisette's room.

A guest for dinner? But what would we serve them? Stale bread and apples? she wondered. Lisette thought back to when her papa was alive and he would host his dinners. She never thought those days would be numbered. Lisette missed her papa terribly.

Her mother came back to her room. "Lisette, I mean now. You need to greet our guest." As Lisette watched her mother walk away again, she had the urge to close her door and lock it. She didn't feel like talking to a dinner guest, she wanted to stay in her room and find a solution to her dilemma with Le Brun. She hated that he had put her in such a difficult position.

As Lisette stood in the doorway and considered remaining in her room, her mother's laughter filled the hall. She hadn't heard her mother carry on so jubilantly since before her papa had died. Then she heard a man's voice. It was booming and carried throughout the apartment. He said, "I am beside myself with joy, my darling."

Lisette hoped that she had heard the man wrong. *Who would be calling Mother darling?* she wondered. Lisette dreaded the answer, but she had to see what was happening in the other room.

She wandered down the hall and into the drawing room. Lisette stopped short when she saw Le Sèvre sitting comfortably in her papa's arm chair. Then she looked closer. *Is he wearing Papa's jacket?* she wondered.

Not only was he sitting in her papa's chair, but Le Sèvre was also wearing her papa's finest piece of clothing, a dark green, satin coat with embroidered trim. Lisette suddenly felt dizzy with anger.

"Lisette, come, sit down." Le Sèvre motioned for her to sit in the armchair opposite him. When she hesitated, he repeated himself. "Please, sit. Your mother and I have some important news to share."

Jeanne came in from the other room and stood close to the chair. Le Sèvre reached up and put his hand on her back.

What is Mother doing? This isn't appropriate behavior for an unmarried woman, she thought. Lisette stared at them in disbelief.

"Your mother and I are now married." Le Sèvre puckered his lips and kissed her mother.

Jeanne looked at Lisette. She said nothing but her eyes begged for Lisette's approval.

Lisette would not give it. She could never accept another man taking her papa's place beside her mother.

"But I thought the wedding wasn't until next month," Lisette said. She was stupefied.

"We decided that we couldn't wait," Le Sèvre said as he beheld Jeanne.

She flashed a smile at her new husband and said to Lisette, "Le Sèvre was anxious to have a family again. You know he lost his daughters and wife to the smallpox." Jeanne then turned to Le Sèvre. "We have both suffered so much loss."

Lisette watched Le Sèvre. She could see a hint of despair in his steel gray eyes, but he quickly dismissed it and stood.

"Enough talk of sad times. It is time to eat." Le Sèvre held out his hand and her mother took it.

"Yes, I am famished. Let's sit!" Jeanne said happily as they sauntered arm in arm into the dining room.

That is all the explanation I get? Lisette thought. They were both acting as if they had only decided to attend a performance at the Opéra on the spur of the moment. Lisette watched Le Sèvre enter the dining room and sit at her papa's place at the table. The storm raging inside her gave way to nausea and the queasiness caused her to sway. Lisette felt unsteady on her feet.

"If you'll excuse me, I don't feel well. I need to go to my room and rest." Lisette didn't wait for an answer. She turned and started toward her room.

"Lisette! No, you need to come sit with us," Jeanne said urgently.

"Jeanne, I'll take care of this. This is my job now. You go sit, my lovely wife," Le Sèvre said to Jeanne. His voice was low and soft.

Lisette turned around to face them, but remained in the doorway leading out of the dining room. She saw her mother do exactly as he asked without any hesitation.

Le Sèvre approached Lisette and gently laid his hand on her back. "I know this is difficult for you. We have just given you very big news, but it would mean so much to your mother and to me if you would join us for dinner. I want to begin our new life together with a pleasant meal. Look at your mother's face. Don't you want to make her happy?"

Lisette studied her mother. Jeanne was about to cry. Lisette didn't want to upset her mother, but she also didn't want to be near a usurper like Le Sèvre. She felt an obligation to honor her papa's memory.

"I have brought in some of your favorite dishes, Lisette. Your mother has told me about your preferences. Doesn't that partridge smell savory?" Le Sèvre asked her.

Lisette regarded the table laden with food. Her mother had prepared an elaborate meal, just like her papa's dinner parties. There were at least eight covered dishes, not counting the soup tureen and the *pots à ouille* loaded with stew. Jeanne had covered the table with their finest linen damask tablecloth and set three places, complete with wine goblets and cutlery for all four services. Lisette hadn't seen any of these serving pieces on the table since before her papa had passed.

"Lisette, meals like this one will be ours to enjoy every day. Monsieur Le Sèvre will be providing a better life for us. You'll see. My dear, please join us," Jeanne said pleadingly.

Not wanting to disappoint her mother, Lisette walked slowly back into the dining room and sat down. She watched Le Sèvre take her papa's place, next to her mother. He extended his hand to Jeanne and squeezed it. Lisette looked away, toward her brother's seat. She noticed it was empty.

"Mother, where is Etienne?" she asked.

Before Jeanne could reply Le Sèvre said, "I have sent him back to school. That is where he belongs."

Jeanne nodded approvingly.

"Enough talk. It is time to partake of this marvelous food," Le Sèvre said, waving his arm toward the food.

Lisette looked at the many prepared dishes carefully displayed on the table. She hadn't seen meat or fowl and heavy cream sauces at their table since before her papa died. The sight and smells of the rich food should have made her mouth water. Instead, she had no appetite.

As Le Sèvre handed her the platter of her favorite dish, the one that her papa used to buy especially for her, she shook her head declining it. Lisette was sure that the roast partridge would never appeal to her again.

Chapter Ten

L isette wondered who Le Sèvre would have her paint to-day. *I will keep working on my new painting of Venus until the noblewoman arrives, whoever she is,* Lisette thought. She was recreating the Venus painting that had been started many months ago in her papa's studio. Lisette was determined to re-place the painting that had been lost in the fire. She worked on it whenever she wasn't painting portraits for Le Sèvre.

After seeing Lisette's portrait of Louis, the one that had caught Le Brun's attention, Le Sèvre had declared that she would paint portraits for him and thereby help him grow his jewelry business. Le Sèvre bought Lisette the highest quality painting supplies, but hadn't given her a dedicated studio in his home. He had said that her bedroom would suffice.

Despite her desire to finish her Venus canvas, Lisette found it difficult to concentrate on her painting. Instead, she stared out of her bedroom window. It was nearly mid-day and the street below was at its busiest. Noble ladies and gentlemen were on their way to the *cafés*, gardens and other amusements at the Palais-Royal, while customers and clients of the luxury merchants of the Rue Saint-Honoré were scurrying to the shops.

Le Sèvre had left their house hours ago, to ready his own shop on the Rue Saint-Honoré for today's clients. Le Sèvre's jewelry shop was located a few buildings down from their house and was only one of many exclusive stores on the illustrious street. Besides jewelers, the Rue Saint-Honoré was home to drapers, furriers, goldsmiths, ribbon manufacturers and wine merchants.

The Rue Saint-Honoré also boasted the entrance to the Palais-Royal. Le Sèvre had transported Lisette's family to one of the most fashionable districts in Paris, where Parisians were willing to pay a premium to be close to the royal Orléans family who resided in the Palais-Royal. Lisette's mother loved discussing the Orléans dynasty. She was only too happy to explain their lineage to Etienne, who could never remember how many cousins the Duc d'Orléans was removed from the throne. Jeanne had often reminded him that the current Dauphin and his two brothers would have to die before the Duc d'Orléans and his heirs could reign.

Lisette smiled as she thought about Etienne. Lisette wondered how he was getting along at school. He wrote letters home to both Lisette and her mother, but they were sporadic at best. Etienne's latest reports were that he was settled and content at the Collège des Quatre-Nations. Lisette was a little jealous of his contentment. He seemed to have finished grieving for their papa quicker than she had. Since their papa had died, Lisette had wanted to visit her brother at school, but her mother had made excuses. Now, as the new wife of a wealthy jeweler, Jeanne was far too busy. Lisette missed her brother, but she was accustomed to him living away from her.

Still looking out of her bedroom window, Lisette thought, *I'll watch for the carriage.* Today, Lisette allowed herself to be distracted by the goings-on outside her window. If Le Sèvre had allowed her to have her pick of bedrooms within his house, she would have selected a different one, but she *was* pleased with the view this room offered.

Le Sèvre's house looked out onto the terrace of the Palais-Royal. Each day, Lisette observed fashionable ladies headed toward the gardens of the Palais-Royal to promenade. Her mother also enjoyed watching the noble ladies. Le Sèvre had given Jeanne a small Galilean telescope as a gift when they had first moved to his home. For the first few weeks they lived on the Rue Saint-Honoré, the monocular device seemed permanently affixed to her mother's eye as she peered into the lives of the privileged.

Now that they had been in Le Sèvre's house for three months, Lisette saw the telescope less frequently. Her mother's new preoccupation was running the household and managing the servants. Jeanne regularly told Lisette that they were very fortunate to be living in such a splendid home complete with fine furnishings, the best food, views of the Palais-Royal and servants.

While her mother had immediately settled into their new life, Lisette remained uncomfortable. She hadn't wanted her mother to remarry at all. No one could replace her papa, but after witnessing her mother's recent joy, Lisette was determined to give Le Sèvre the opportunity to continue to make her mother happy.

That must be her, Lisette thought as she watched a noblewoman exit a carriage in front of the house. *I should prepare,* she thought. Lisette put away her painting of Venus and brought out a new canvas that she had stretched and prepared the day before. She placed the blank canvas on her easel and took inventory of her supplies. Le Sèvre had bought her the most expensive pigments and brushes. As she looked at the kingwood *commode* in the corner of her bedroom that held all of her new art supplies, she thought about her papa. Louis could never have afforded the chest of drawers *or* the supplies. Lisette struggled with the guilt.

"Mademoiselle Lisette? Are you there?"

Lisette heard the faintest tapping at her door and an even fainter voice accompanying it. She recognized the voice as belonging to Henri, a young servant boy in Le Sèvre's household. Henri had been serving in Le Sèvre's house since before he could walk. His mother had been Le Sèvre's chambermaid and had died shortly after giving birth to Henri. Knowing she was about to die and that she was unwed, she had begged Le Sèvre to house and employ her son. *Better a servant than an orphaned street urchin,* Henri had said to Lisette quoting Le Sèvre's former wife. According to the older servants, who had told Henri of his early years, it had been Le Sèvre's first wife that had convinced Le Sèvre to allow Henri to stay.

Henri was the same age as Etienne, but already looked much older. Lisette had been drawn to his tired, sad eyes and immediately befriended him. Henri was a constant presence in Le Sèvre's house. He was the first one to wake in the morning and the last one to retire at night.

Lisette went to the door and opened it a crack. Henri pushed the door open just enough so that he could be heard. As he held the door, Lisette noticed his hand was covered in callouses.

"Mademoiselle Lisette, they are downstairs. They'll be up shortly."

"Thank you, Henri," Lisette said.

Henri quickly returned downstairs.

Lisette regarded the blank canvas sitting on her easel. Soon it would be filled with another pretty face. Le Sèvre was bringing her a new sitter today, another noblewoman. *This will be the third*, she thought.

Le Sèvre had been trying to accommodate his best clients from his jewelry shop. If he could at the same time provide a worthy portraitist to paint their beauty *and* sell them jewels to enhance that beauty, then all the better, or so Le Sèvre claimed.

He had made it clear that Lisette was free to paint anything else she wanted, as long as it didn't interfere with the portraits for his clients. Le Sèvre had been initially skeptical of Lisette's wish to paint allegories, but he had said that he would allow it as long as she remembered her priorities and never neglected his clients. Lisette had agreed, considering the bargain fair.

Within moments, Le Sèvre was outside her door. She could hear him speaking loudly. Without giving any advance notice, Le Sèvre opened the door and came into her room. Standing next to him was the Duchesse de Chartres.

Lisette took a step back. *The Duchesse de Chartres? Why would she be here?* Lisette wondered. *Does Mother know?* Jeanne would be beside herself. One of the wealthiest and most important women in all of France, the wife of the Duc de Chartres of the royal Orléans family, was in their house. Chatting with the Duchesse in the Tuileries was a noteworthy event, but hosting the Duchesse in one's home was an extraordinary occasion.

Lisette inspected the Duchesse. She was dressed in a mint green *robe à polonaise*, with trimmings of embroidered silk. Her hair was arranged *à la marmotte*. It was piled high on her head, bound with a ribbon and covered with a linen headdress. The Duchesse appeared just as fashionable as she had the last time Lisette had seen her. She wondered if the Duchesse would deign herself to speak to Lisette this time.

Le Sèvre stepped to the *commode* in the corner of the room. Lisette stored not only her supplies in the chest of drawers, but also the small portrait of her papa. Le Sèvre found it in the top drawer.

"You wanted to see for yourself, Duchesse," Le Sèvre said as he took hold of Lisette's easel and dragged it to where the Duchesse stood. He removed the blank canvas from the easel and replaced it with the portrait. Le Sèvre had not yet acknowledged Lisette. He was focused solely on his business with the Duchesse.

The Duchesse carefully examined the portrait and then

looked over to Lisette. "My, my, the rumors are true. There is a pretty young girl living on the Rue Saint-Honoré who paints like a man." The Duchesse studied the portrait further. She had a puzzled look on her face. "This is a most unusual circumstance. She is so young to be able to paint so well."

"Then we are agreed. Shall we retire to the drawing room to discuss the terms for the completion of your portrait?"

The Duchesse toggled back and forth between Lisette and the portrait. She hesitated, but then said, "I am not sure what my husband would say."

Lisette watched the Duchesse's eyes narrow.

"She could paint you wearing some of my newest precious gems...I've recently received a shipment from Persia that you must see. They are most rare. You would be the only woman at court wearing them and the first one to have your portrait painted with them."

Lisette noticed that Le Sèvre was making inroads with the Duchesse. Her face softened and her eyes widened. Saying nothing to Lisette, the Duchesse brushed past Le Sèvre and headed out of the room. "I will have my first sitting a week from this Tuesday at one in the afternoon." She continued walking without looking back at either of them. The mere mention of being the first woman at court to do anything was more than enough for the Duchesse to agree.

"Wait, Duchesse. May I show you the gems?" Le Sèvre called out, trying to catch up to her.

Lisette watched both of them quickly disappear from sight. *She is an unpleasant woman*, Lisette thought. Tuesday afternoon could not come and then go quickly enough for Lisette. The sooner she was finished with the Duchesse, the better. At least she wouldn't have to paint her portrait this afternoon. She could work on her allegory of Venus.

Lisette stared at the empty hallway and then back at her easel where Le Sèvre had placed the portrait of her papa. She looked at her papa's radiant face. *It worked again,* she thought.

Each time Le Sèvre brought a new client to determine Lisette's worthiness, he showed that portrait. To Lisette, it seemed like a violation of her papa's memory. Instead of making her feel better, for the first time since he had died, looking at the portrait of her papa made her feel worse.

Chapter Eleven

Three days after the Duchesse de Chartres' visit, Lisette took stock of her supplies. She noticed that several vials of her pigment powders were nearly empty. She looked at her painting of Venus sitting on her easel which was only partially finished. Lisette realized that if she was going to complete this painting *and* the portraits for Le Sèvre, she would need more pigments. She would have to speak with Le Sèvre, but didn't want to wait until he returned home for the evening. *I will visit his shop today*, she decided.

Lisette left the house and walked the short distance down the Rue Saint-Honoré to Le Sèvre's shop. She passed by several upscale merchants whose shops were just opening for the day. In between Le Sèvre's house and his shop was a milliner, a dressmaker and a perfumer. Through large storefront windows, Lisette could see that they were all preparing for their customers to descend upon them. The street was bustling with noble ladies and gentlemen on their way to see the merchants. Many of them were hurrying because of a perceived fashion emergency or hair problem that needed to be solved before the dinner hour later in the afternoon, when they would be judged by hosts and guests alike.

Lisette watched one noble lady screeching at her servant girl who was trailing behind, unable to move as quickly. The woman shouted, "Hurry, we must reach Monsieur Léonard before the Baronne de Blaise. I must have *my* hair done first."

Lisette had recently learned that Léonard Autié was the most fashionable hairdresser in France. He had created the elaborate *poufs* of the Dauphine, Marie-Antoinette. All of the Paris noble ladies had followed suit, each one trying to outdo the others with hair of greater height and complication. From her bedroom window, Lisette had seen some *coiffures* reaching as high as three feet and adorned with such spectacles as mechanical birds and miniature ships.

As the noblewoman disappeared from the street, Lisette reached Le Sèvre's shop. She looked at the shop sign nailed to the façade. It was a representation of Le Sèvre standing on a pier examining a bright gold, jeweled tiara in a Turkish Empire port on the Mediterranean Sea. On the bottom of the sign were the words: *Jean-François Le Sèvre, Marchand.* Lisette recognized the hand of Monsieur Vernet. Le Sèvre's sign very nearly matched another one farther down the street that Vernet had painted for Monsieur Granchez's *Magasin Anglais*. Lisette had been disappointed when she had recently learned that Vernet had been the one to introduce Le Sèvre to her mother.

Lisette lingered for a few moments studying the shop sign before she went inside. She wondered if Le Sèvre had actually traveled to far-off Mediterranean ports. *Does he really buy his jewels from the Turkish Empire?* Lisette thought.

She then examined the display of jewels in the front window.

There were two long, horizontal windows on either side of a central, arched doorway. Le Sèvre had arranged elaborate necklaces, tiaras and aigrettes on each of the windows' four shelves. The displays were eye-catching. Lisette would have stared at the jewels in the front windows longer if she hadn't been interrupted by a couple fighting as they left the store.

"But Monsieur Le Sèvre said we could leave with the necklace today," said a woman, wearing a dark violet silk dress with a white linen *fichu* to cover the gown's low neckline.

"I want to pay him first. I do not like owing anyone, my dear," replied a man wearing a simple black coat and sober gray *culottes*. From the couple's expensive, yet modest dress, Lisette surmised that they were not noble, but were of the merchant or robed class, probably a successful lawyer and his wife.

Lisette waited until they had cleared the doorway before she proceeded inside. She was immediately struck by its opulence. There were at least one hundred pieces of mirrored glass covering the ceiling and the back walls of the shop. Two large columns of mahogany framed the interior space and were decorated with gilt and more mirrored glass. In the corners were two mahogany display cabinets that appeared to be specifically designed to fit the space. Two large wooden counters with built-in drawers stood perpendicular to each other in the center of the room. Four lanterns and ten globes provided lighting while the entire shop was heated by a stove. The stovepipe was disguised inside a large Grecian column extending to the very top of the ceiling.

Once she had absorbed the grandiose interior, Lisette searched for Le Sèvre. He was talking to a noble man and woman.

"Comte, Comtesse, these are a wonderful value. You will not be disappointed with them. Let me show you some of the ways they can be arranged...in a necklace, a bracelet or a tiara." Le Sèvre beckoned his assistant. He rattled off a list of items for the assistant to retrieve and the young man ran off.

"But Monsieur Le Sèvre, I thought I saw the Duchesse du Pessin wearing these pieces last week at Versailles."

Le Sèvre quickly responded, "Oh no, I assure you that you haven't. I received them from Turkey yesterday. They were most difficult to procure. Jewelers in the Ottoman Empire are quite the negotiators."

"Are they?" asked the Comte. He no longer appeared bored.

Undeterred, Le Sèvre continued his sales speech, "They are most exotic and would look so lovely against your skin, Comtesse."

The Comtesse lowered her head in false modesty. Lisette knew that she was merely following etiquette by pretending to be embarrassed at Le Sèvre's adulation. "Oh, Monsieur Le Sèvre, you are too complimentary."

Le Sèvre held the largest stone next to her face. "Your thoughts, Comte? Do you not agree?"

The Comte nodded. "Monsieur Le Sèvre is absolutely correct."

"They would be a most sound investment, Comte. The Duc de Clerc just bought several of a lesser clarity from me last week."

"These are of a higher clarity than the Duc de Clerc's?" the Comte asked.

"Yes."

"Then we will take them…all of them."

"Superb! I will have them wrapped and delivered first thing tomorrow morning."

"Could you send them sooner? I would like to wear them this evening to the Opéra," the Comtesse implored.

"For you, Comtesse, of course. You can expect them this afternoon," Le Sèvre said as he bowed to her.

Lisette enjoyed watching Le Sèvre with the nobles. Their interactions appeared effortless. Le Sèvre gracefully appealed to both the women who wore his jewelry and the men who paid for the jewels. Lisette remained quiet until they had concluded their business and the Comte and Comtesse departed.

Le Sèvre had acknowledged Lisette's presence with a slight nod of his head when she had first entered the store, but they had not yet talked. As soon as the Comte and Comtesse were gone, Le Sèvre came over to her.

"Lisette, how lovely to see you this morning. To what do I owe this surprise visit?" Le Sèvre said, smiling warmly at her.

"I am running low on pigments and other supplies. I'm afraid I won't have enough to complete all of my paintings," Lisette said plainly.

"You have sufficient pigments to finish the portraits. I do not believe that you need more right now," Le Sèvre said as he turned to talk to his assistant again.

"But I do think that I require more," Lisette said.

He turned to face her. "Lisette, I am not buying more supplies and that is the end of it. I am not discussing this further with you. I am very busy and I must get back to work."

Le Sèvre disappeared behind the side counter and into a back room. Lisette remained standing in the middle of his shop. She had not expected him to say *no*. She had not considered that he would ration her pigments and other painting supplies.

She slowly turned toward the door and made her way out. As Lisette trudged home, she wondered, *How am I going to finish everything*?

Chapter Twelve

*I*t had been a week since Le Sèvre had refused to buy Lisette more pigments. With her dwindling supplies, she had been forced to make a choice, but she wasn't sure if she had made the right one. Every day for the past week, Lisette had risen early to work on her allegory painting of Venus. Each day, she had doubted her decision. This morning was no different.

Lisette stood at her easel and looked at her canvas, but could see little with her thick curtains still drawn. She went to the windows and pulled open the heavy damask curtains. The early morning light came streaming into her room. It was especially bright this morning and created a glare on her canvas.

She moved her easel out of the direct sunlight so that she could see her painting better. *This Venus will be far superior to the earlier one*, she thought. Her new painting was more focused.

This version was an allegory of love with not only Venus, but also Cupid, Venus' son, and Mars, the Roman god of war. The painting would depict love conquering war. Lisette's plan was to perfect it on a smaller canvas and then later transfer it to a bigger one, more appropriate given the theme. Grand themes involving the Roman gods deserved a grand canvas to match.

Lisette had not yet been convinced to abandon history and allegorical paintings. Several of her papa's friends had encouraged her to concentrate exclusively on portraiture, claiming that she could not only make a small fortune, but she could also apply for membership in the Académie Royale de Peinture et de Sculpture. Lisette disagreed. She knew that she would make her mark as a history painter, as all the great painters had. If she became a member of the Académie Royale, it would be as a history painter, the highest and most esteemed rank of painter – certainly much higher than portraitist.

For now, she needed to replenish her supplies. Lisette had decided that the best way to ensure a steady supply of pigments was to sell her allegory paintings. Such paintings always sold for more money than portraits.

Lisette looked closer at her main figure, Venus. *The goddess of love needs more depth,* Lisette thought. Over the past week, Lisette had nearly completed this smaller-sized canvas. She knew that she had to finish and sell this allegory to Le Brun. She could then replace the pigments that she would need to complete portraits for Le Sèvre's clients. Time was running short.

In the past week, Lisette had also considered how to approach Le Brun. The last time she had spoken with him, they had reached a stalemate. She had not been willing to accept his offer of a forty percent commission. In the hopes of getting some answers, Lisette had written to Monsieur Doyen. She had asked his advice for how to proceed with Le Brun and whether she should accept his offer of forty percent.

Doyen had told Lisette that Le Brun had tried to take advantage of her. Le Brun was known to take thirty percent from all of his other artists. Doyen also counseled Lisette to be discreet about any business arrangements with Le Brun, and to especially keep Le Sèvre in the dark. As her new male guardian, Le Sèvre was entitled to collect and keep all of her earnings for himself. After considering Doyen's words, Lisette concluded that Le Brun would be so impressed with her painting of Venus, that he would agree to take his standard thirty percent commission.

As Lisette began mixing her colors for the day, the door to her room suddenly opened. It was Le Sèvre. He never knocked or asked for her permission to enter.

"Is it finished?" he asked.

Lisette swallowed hard. She had been dreading this question.

"Well? Where is the painting of the Baronne de Lande?" Le Sèvre asked.

It wasn't finished. Lisette had been working on her painting of Venus. There hadn't been enough paint for both.

When she remained silent, he walked around to her side of the easel and looked at the painting.

"What is this?" he asked.

"A painting of Venus," Lisette said flatly, but inside she was panicking. She told herself to remain calm. Something about his demeanor unnerved her.

"I can see that. This is an allegory. Our arrangement was that my clients' portraits come first, before any allegories. Where is the painting of the Baronne? She has asked for it."

"It isn't finished."

"That is unacceptable, Lisette. I will not allow you to embarrass me."

"I will finish it," Lisette said.

"You most certainly will. And no more allegories. You are to paint only portraits of my clients. If you want unrestricted access to the pigments and other supplies, you will obey my rules." He studied her waiting for a confirmation.

Lisette shook her head affirmatively.

"I need to hear you say that you understand."

"Yes, I understand," Lisette said. She uttered the words, but she knew they weren't true. She didn't understand. Lisette didn't see why she couldn't paint both allegories and Le Sèvre's portraits.

He stared at her as if he wanted something more. Lisette didn't know what else to say to him.

There was silence for a few moments until he finally said, "You'll need to prepare a fresh canvas. The Duchesse de Chartres will be here this afternoon."

It is Tuesday already? she thought. Lisette had lost all track of time while she had been working on her new painting of Venus.

"Mix your paints and ready the canvas now. She expects her first sitting to be productive." He hesitated, then added, "And pleasant." Le Sèvre turned and headed for the hall.

Lisette remained behind her easel, still gripping her sable brush. *As soon as he leaves, I can go back to Venus,* she decided. Lisette was so close to finishing it, every moment counted. She would work on her allegory painting until the Duchesse entered her room.

Le Sèvre sauntered toward the door. When he reached the threshold he paused and faced Lisette. "Why aren't you stretching the canvas?" he asked as he approached her. He drew close and said, "You *will* paint the Duchesse's portrait today." Lisette could smell his rose water facial wash.

The Duchesse wasn't expected for hours. *Why do I need to begin preparing now?* Lisette thought.

"If you are unprepared for the Duchesse, you will be sorry, Lisette." Le Sèvre fixed his gaze on her.

She was motionless, her feet refusing to move.

As Lisette and Le Sèvre considered each other, she knew he was contemplating his next steps.

After only moments, his eyes told Lisette that he was resolved. They appeared confident and decided.

"You will do as I say," Le Sèvre said in a low, calm voice. It wasn't the same soft tone that he used with her mother. This voice was cold and detached. "I give you this house. I give you pigments and oil. I decide how they will be used. Just as easily as I provide you with supplies, I can take them away." He walked toward the door again. Without turning to look at her, he said, "The Duchesse's sitting *must* proceed smoothly," he said and swiftly left the room.

Lisette stood gaping at the empty doorway thinking about Le Sèvre. She had not seen this side of him before. He had changed. Le Sèvre's charm was gone. Lisette realized that he could not only ration her supplies, but he could also take them a-way completely. Suddenly, she felt a greater urgency to finish and sell her allegory painting.

Lisette returned to her easel to resume painting. Before she loaded her brush with paint, she glanced at her papa's watch. *The Duchesse will be arriving soon*, she realized. *Too soon.*

Chapter Thirteen

*L*isette awoke and immediately left her bed. *This is the day,* she thought. She had furiously painted for the past few days and nights. The Duchesse de Chartres had cancelled her sitting at the last minute, leaving Lisette more time to finish her allegory of Venus.

She carefully inspected the painting. *It is ready*, she thought. Lisette had allowed a day and a half for the painting to dry. *This will work*, Lisette told herself. It had to work. Lisette had finished her allegory just in time. She had depleted nearly all of her pigments, including the two most expensive colors, red Lac and ultramarine blue. She was unable to mix enough paint in the needed hues for the Duchesse's portrait. Lisette did not want to tell Le Sèvre about the situation, but had instead decided to rely on herself to obtain more supplies. He never needed to know. *My plan will work*, she reassured herself.

Lisette stepped over to her window and peered out. It was her favorite time of the day. Dawn had broken several hours ago, yet the morning was still fresh. The bakers had come in from the outskirts of the city carrying their enormous quantities of loaves. The gardeners had already emptied their carts and driven away. This was the time of the morning when the bustle really began. Barbers, hairdressers, coachmen and *café* waiters were scurrying in every direction. Lisette especially enjoyed watching the panicked barbers and hairdressers who were late to meet their demanding clients. They were usually covered from head to foot with white flour and could be seen carrying wigs in one hand and tongs in the other. The sight never failed to amuse her.

I don't have much time, she realized as she glanced at her pocket watch. The Duchesse had rescheduled her appointment for that afternoon and it was already mid-morning. Lisette was planning to sell Le Brun two paintings, buy more pigments *and* return home in time for the Duchesse's sitting. *There won't be any time to spare,* Lisette thought. She needed to get dressed.

Lisette stood before her *armoire.* The delicate patterns of flowers decorating its walnut veneer doors were repeated in the floral designs of the silk dresses inside. Before her papa had died, Lisette had only owned one silk gown. Now, Lisette possessed several embroidered silk gowns and coordinating petticoats. Her mother had spent great sums of Le Sèvre's money on a new *coterie* of dresses for both herself and Lisette. Wearing the gowns required not only a corset, but also a female servant's assistance.

Eschewing formality for comfort, she threw on a lavender flared jacket and matching skirt, which she had owned for years. Her mother had tried to expunge Lisette's wardrobe of these vestiges of their previous life. Lisette had resisted, claiming that jackets and skirts were no longer the clothing of peasants and working women, but were now becoming quite fashionable. Eventually, Jeanne had relented, but not before she had the

106

jackets and skirts altered. They were now trimmed in delicate lace and gauze.

Lisette regarded her appearance in the looking glass. *I'm ready*, she thought.

Lisette had to time her departure carefully so that no one stopped her. Her mother would not be a problem. Jeanne remained at her *toilette* for hours, indulging in her beauty rituals. Since living at Le Sèvre's home, Jeanne had taken up many aristocratic habits, including wearing rouge on her cheeks and piling her hair high like the noble ladies of Versailles. Jeanne had said to her many times, *Lisette, never interrupt me during my toilette. That is my time to become youthful and radiant.*

Le Sèvre was another matter. Lisette patiently remained in her room until Le Sèvre had left for the day. She kept watch for Le Sèvre's departure from her bedroom window. Once she saw him walking away from the house, she knew it was safe for her to leave.

She put on her heaviest mantle and went over to her easel. Lisette picked up her small *Venus, Cupid and Mars* canvas and wrapped it in a linen sheet. She did the same with her *Death of Caesar* canvas. Then she tucked both paintings securely under her arm, safely hidden under her cloak. Still attached to the stretcher bars, neither was heavy, but they were awkward to carry. *My plan has to work. I have to convince Le Brun to sell both paintings,* she thought.

Lisette slowly opened her bedroom door and moved cautiously down the stairs and toward the front door of the house. She didn't want to take any chances. She had to avoid all of the servants too.

Lisette made her way out of the house and then onto the Rue Saint-Honoré. She scanned the street for anyone she might recognize. *Henri!* she realized. He was coming straight toward her carrying a basket of vegetables from the market. She quickly spotted an open *porte-cochère*, ducked inside and waited until he passed. Lisette held her breath and prayed that no carriages would drive through the open gate while she was hiding there. She waited a few extra moments just to be sure he was gone. Lisette covered her head with her hood and then headed out again.

Just as she stepped away from the *porte-cochère*, a fast-moving carriage came speeding toward her. Quickly darting out of the way, she dropped one of the paintings. Her heart stopped as she saw the canvas lying exposed in the middle of the street. It had slipped out of the linen sheet. *My Venus!* she panicked. It had just missed falling into a long puddle of filth in the gutter running down the street.

Without any thought to her own safety, Lisette ran into the street and scooped up the painting. Before she could move back closer to the buildings, a lanky Auvergnat boy came up to her.

"Mademoiselle, allow me to offer you my plank." He placed the wooden board down over the puddle and extended his hand to help her across.

"No, thank you." Lisette walked around the board, careful not to step in the murky water.

"I insist, Mademoiselle." He followed closely behind Lisette.

She ignored him and continued walking.

"Only three *sous* for my plank. It will keep the bottom of your dress free from filth," the young provincial boy said, still following her.

I cannot walk to Le Brun's. This Auvergnat might follow me the entire way, she thought. Lisette hailed a carriage.

Once safely inside the *cabriolet* and away from the Auvergnat and rogue carriages, Lisette exhaled. She knew that today she had been very lucky. With nowhere to walk but the road, pedestrians were forced into dangerous situations. Lisette rewrapped her painting of *Venus, Cupid and Mars* in the linen sheet and placed it under her arm once again, next to *The Death of Caesar*. The carriage ride was uneventful and within half of an hour she had arrived on the Pont Notre-Dame.

When Lisette entered Le Brun's shop, she was immediately

greeted by Monsieur Faucher. "Good morning, Mademoiselle. How can I help you?" Monsieur Faucher wore a welcoming expression until she removed her hood. He scowled. "You. Monsieur Le Brun is busy. Come back later."

"Monsieur Faucher, tell him I am here. He will want to see me." Lisette wasn't going away that easily.

"He is busy. Return later." Monsieur Faucher spoke with his nose in the air.

"I don't think he is too busy to make some money....would he be interested in 1,000 *livres?*" Lisette raised her voice knowing that Le Brun was probably in the back weighing whether or not to show himself.

Almost immediately, Le Brun emerged from behind the curtain that separated the back from the front of the shop. "Mademoiselle Vigée. What a pleasant surprise. What do I hear about 1,000 *livres?*"

Lisette removed the canvases from the sheets and displayed them proudly in front of Le Brun. Then she watched him and waited.

He moved closer to the paintings as if he was carefully studying them. His expression was neutral. He was very good at hiding his authentic feelings and thoughts. Finally, after several agonizing moments of silence, a smile formed in the corner of his mouth.

"I can sell this one for about 600 *livres*, I am sure of it," he said, pointing to the allegory of Venus, Cupid and Mars. "This one of Caesar's death, for 500 *livres*. Excellent. I'll take them now."

Lisette wasn't quite ready to hand over her paintings. They had not yet discussed Le Brun's commission. "Your commission...we never settled on it."

"Yes, we did. My commission is the customary forty percent." Le Brun was no longer smiling. His face was grave.

"No, we didn't. You will take your usual thirty percent." Lisette was firm.

"Forty percent and no less," Le Brun said again. "Take it or leave it."

"Monsieur Le Brun, I know for a fact that you accept thirty percent for all of your other artists. I will only accept the same," Lisette said flatly. She desperately wanted to make an arrangement with him, but she didn't want to show it. She hoped that her face wasn't betraying her thoughts.

"Forty percent." Le Brun was unyielding.

"Then I will have to take my business elsewhere...perhaps to Monsieur Paillet." Lisette started walking toward the door.

"Thirty percent," he said. When she turned around, she saw his smile re-emerge. "Clever girl." He held out his hand to shake hers.

She reached out and they shook like Englishmen.

"It is agreed then. Now, there is one small thing that I would like to suggest," Le Brun said.

"About our business arrangement?" Lisette asked.

"No, about your drawing. It is very good, but it could be better. I want you to take lessons." Le Brun said this as if she was a child who had never considered how to become a better artist.

"I am well aware of how to improve my drawing, but lest you forget I am not male. There is only one artist at the moment who accepts female pupils and he is in Italy."

"Ah, yes. Briard is in Italy. True."

Lisette looked at him. *When will he give me the sack of coins?* she wondered.

"You don't get your money now," he told her.

"When?"

"After I sell the paintings."

"Can I get an advance? Like my papa?" She had to leave Le Brun's with at least some money.

"No. That is not my usual practice. I have no idea when these paintings will sell. I do not have any auctions scheduled and private collectors can be very selective."

"But you just said it shouldn't take long."

"I said I was sure I could sell the one for **600** *livres*, and the other for **500**, not that either would necessarily sell quickly. Come back next week. I have a certain collector in mind. He might like them."

"But I'm here now. Isn't there something we can arrange?"

Lisette could see he was becoming irritated. His face hardened.

"I have to return to work," Le Brun said brusquely. He turned to go but then added, "Practice your drawing of faces and figures by painting portraits." He paused. "Besides, they sell better. Bring me portraits to sell."

Lisette felt like she had been dealt not just one, but two blows. She knew that as long as she lived in Le Sèvre's house she would be painting portraits for him. She wasn't going to paint them for Le Brun too. Lisette had no interest in painting portraits for money. She only wanted to sell her allegories.

"If it is money you want, Lisette, bring me portraits. You'll have money in no time. Good day." His voice was much softer, but resolute. Le Brun disappeared behind the curtain.

Lisette slowly moved toward the door and left the shop. *I can't go home now*, she realized. She had no money, no pigments and no way to buy more in the next few hours. She couldn't face the Duchesse or Le Sèvre empty-handed. When Le Sèvre returned home, there would be repercussions. But she couldn't think of that now. Lisette took her time walking back.

That evening, Lisette sat in front of her easel. She stared at the largely blank canvas. Without any money to buy the enormous canvas required for the larger version of her allegory of Venus, Cupid and Mars, Lisette had opted for the next best choice – another cabinet picture.

She had decided to paint a copy of Botticelli's *Mary with Christ Child and John the Baptist*. She had seen it in the King's royal collection and had been touched by Botticelli's expressiveness. Lisette wanted to emulate the sentimental mother-child bond that Botticelli articulated so well. She had no pigments, but she could at least begin sketching the figures in charcoal. Lisette found it difficult to concentrate. She knew Le Sèvre would be home any moment and that she would have to face his ire. The Baronne de Lande's portrait remained unfinished *and* she had missed the Duchesse de Chartres' sitting.

Lisette stepped to the window to watch for him. Before she reached it, her bedroom door swung open.

Le Sèvre strode in, immediately shutting it behind him.

Odd, she thought. Le Sèvre had never closed her door.

Lisette walked back to her stool and sat in front of her easel. Placing a small barrier between her and Le Sèvre somehow made her feel more comfortable.

"What do you have to say to me?" Le Sèvre's voice was low and steady. His steel gray eyes were fixed on her.

Lisette wanted to avert her gaze, but she forced herself to look directly at him. She remained behind her easel, but could see him clearly. "I had to go out this afternoon," Lisette replied.

"To go where? You are a girl. You have caused me considerable problems with the Duchesse by missing her sitting today. You have also embarrassed me. What kind of man cannot control his own daughter?"

"I am sorry," Lisette said, trying to sound sincere. She realized that she had egregiously miscalculated her plan's chance of success. Now, with Le Sèvre looming over her like a hawk about to devour its prey, her decision to use her remaining pigments on her allegory of Venus felt like an enormous mistake.

"That is all you have to say for yourself? That you are sorry? I want to know where you were and what possible reason you could have for missing the session." Le Sèvre came closer to Lisette.

She felt a strong urge to step off her stool and escape the room, but instead she ordered her feet to plant themselves on the floor. She didn't move.

"I did not mean to offend anyone, *father*," Lisette said. She had never called him father to his face. It was all she could think to say. Lisette would never tell him about her dealings with Le Brun. She tried to focus on Le Sèvre's face, but her eyes were drawn to her canvas...to her sketch of the Madonna. She couldn't help herself.

"What are you looking at?" he asked her, scowling.

Lisette noticed irritation in his voice.

"Tell me now." He marched around to her side of the easel. When Le Sèvre was directly in front of the canvas, he said, "This is unacceptable. I have already forbade you from painting anything but portraits. What is the meaning of this?" He immediately snatched the canvas off of the easel.

"No, please don't take it!"

Le Sèvre looked at her and then stopped. "You're right. I will leave it. I want you to see its unfinished form. It will serve as a reminder of what you've done...how you've disobeyed me." He glared at Lisette as he returned the canvas to the easel. Then he walked over to her remaining supplies and collected them.

She watched Le Sèvre as he carefully arranged all of the canvases, brushes, buckets and pails so that they would fit in his arms.

"You can't take my supplies." Lisette ran over to him. "Please, no!"

Le Sèvre cocked his hand back and slapped Lisette across the face. She stumbled backward from the force of the blow. She nearly lost her balance, but managed to remain upright.

"You mean *my* supplies. Don't ever forget that this is *my* house...*my* supplies...and most importantly *my* rules. Until you are ready to obey me, I will be keeping these." He walked away, pausing as he reached the doorway. "The Duchesse is returning in three weeks for her sitting. I expect that you will not disappoint me again," Le Sèvre said. Then he added, "I will bring you a ration of pigments and other needed supplies for the Duchesse's portrait, but not until the hour that she arrives for her sitting." Le Sèvre turned on his heel and swiftly left the room.

Lisette didn't have to stand before the looking glass to know that her face was red and beginning to swell. She could feel the stinging worsening.

Lisette stepped to the window and opened it. She poked her head out into the cold night air. The biting winter wind came rushing toward her, swirling around her head. It was a welcome relief. When the passers-by began pointing at her, she pulled herself back inside and closed the window. She didn't want to give Le Sèvre another reason to punish her.

Lisette went back to her easel and regarded the faint figure of Botticelli's Madonna. For the foreseeable future, the half-sketched Madonna would remain the only figure in the painting. Not only was Lisette without pigments, she no longer had her charcoal, pencils or any other supplies. Le Sèvre had taken them all.

Lisette felt her swollen cheek and thought, *I never want my Madonna to be handled by Le Sèvre again*. With his rough hand, he had intended to hurt her canvas. Lisette determined that she could not allow that to happen again.

Chapter Fourteen

The next morning, after the swelling in her face had subsided, Lisette returned to her easel. She sat and stared at her canvas. She knew exactly what needed to be done, but without pigments, she was unable to mix more paint. She didn't even have a brush. *Maybe Mother can convince Le Sèvre to change his mind*, she hoped.

Lisette headed downstairs to look for Jeanne. Before she had reached the bottom of the stairs, she could hear Le Sèvre's voice. He sounded like he was berating a child. Then she heard her mother speaking. Lisette stopped on the stairs to listen. They were talking in the drawing room, which was directly behind the center staircase. From this position, she was well hidden. She couldn't see them, but they couldn't see her either.

"Etienne is now a pupil at the Lycée Louis-le-Grand," Le

Sèvre said.

"But he has been attending the Collège des Quatre-Nations for years. How could you move him to Lycée Louis-le-Grand without notifying me, his mother?" Jeanne sounded helpless.

"Because it is a more prestigious school. He will be in the company of the country's elite," Le Sèvre said.

"But I am his mother, you should have consulted me," Jeanne retorted.

"He is under my care now. I was unaware of any need to consult a woman," Le Sèvre quipped.

"He has been in my care much longer than yours," Jeanne replied.

"As your husband, I make the decisions for you. There is nothing else to say."

"But you must consult me where Etienne and Lisette are concerned."

"No, I do not. I make the decisions for all of you — even that insolent daughter of yours."

"She is not insolent, François. She has a strong mind and spirit. She can be fiercely loyal. You'll see. Give her more time and you will see," Jeanne said, defending Lisette.

"She has already tested my patience. I have confiscated her art supplies until she can learn to obey me in my house."

Her mother said nothing in response. There was silence for several moments.

"Don't look so morose, Jeanne. Of course I will return them to her in three weeks when she is scheduled to paint the Duchesse for me."

"I find that to be very harsh, François...taking away the poor girl's painting provisions."

"I am finished discussing this matter. Now leave me," Le Sèvre ordered Jeanne, just as he commanded the servants.

Lisette knew it would be of no use to speak to her mother. She realized that her mother's relationship with her new husband was very different than her marriage to Lisette's papa.

When Lisette didn't hear her mother's heels clicking against the sleek marble floor of the drawing room, she realized that her mother was refusing to leave.

"Did you not hear me, Wife?" Le Sèvre asked her.

"Yes, François, I heard you. But I am not finished discussing this matter," Jeanne said.

"Etienne and Lisette are now my children. I am their father and I will make the decisions for this family. That is final," Le Sèvre said.

Then Jeanne uttered something that Lisette couldn't quite hear. She was speaking very softly, perhaps under her breath.

"What? I cannot hear you Jeanne, speak up if you have something to say to me." Le Sèvre seemed to be taunting her.

"It is nothing," Jeanne said. Her voice sounded defeated to Lisette.

"I don't think so. What is it that you want to say to me?" Le Sèvre insisted.

There was silence for several more moments before Lisette heard Le Sèvre's heavy footsteps thudding across the floor. Then her mother let out a squeal.

"You are hurting me, François. Please remove your hand from my arm." Jeanne sounded distressed. Her voice was much louder than usual.

"Only when you tell me what you said. And be mindful of the servants. Keep your voice down, Wife," Le Sèvre said in a low and controlled tone.

"You will..." Jeanne hesitated. "You will *never* be their father."

Lisette moved down the stairs and around the corner so that she could see what was happening. She knew she was risking being spotted, but she wanted to be able to help her mother if the need arose.

Before Lisette could see anything, she heard Le Sèvre brutally strike Jeanne.

As soon as Lisette peeked into the room, she saw Le Sèvre

117

shove her mother down to the floor like a disobedient dog. *Mother!* she screamed inside her head. Her mother slumped down to the floor and remained there while Le Sèvre continued to bark at her.

"You are my wife and you will not disrespect me," he said. Lisette desperately wanted to run to her mother, but she knew it would only worsen the situation for both of them.

"I will not discuss this further, Jeanne. I do not need to consult you on anything that concerns this family. I will not say this again — I make the decisions for you, Etienne and that willful daughter of yours," Le Sèvre said and strode out of the room.

Quickly, Lisette stepped back around the corner and up the stairs to her bedroom. Once she was safely behind her bedroom's locked door, the ugly incident replayed over and over in her head. She took a deep breath and then exhaled slowly. It didn't help. Lisette couldn't catch her breath.

Chapter Fifteen

It was Thursday and Lisette knew that Le Sèvre would be leaving the house well before the noon hour. She had been tracking Le Sèvre's comings and goings, taking notice of the patterns. With Le Sèvre gone, Lisette would have time to see Le Brun this morning. A week had passed since she had seen him last. Le Brun had said that a private collector was interested in her allegory paintings. *They should have sold by now*, Lisette hoped. She was out of time.

Lisette heard Le Sèvre hollering at a servant in the front vestibule. She looked down at her papa's pocket watch. *Right on schedule*, Lisette thought. She opened her bedroom door just enough to better hear what was going on downstairs. Le Sèvre was snarling orders at Camille, the chambermaid. After a brief exchange, she heard the heavy front door close. To be sure he was truly gone, Lisette waited a few extra minutes before leaving the house.

On foot, Lisette headed straight for Le Brun's shop. *Surely they've sold,* she thought. *If Le Brun can fetch 1100 livres like he claimed, I can easily replenish my provisions.* She calculated in her head how many vials of pigment powder and how many canvases 770 *livres* would purchase. She could buy herself the highest quality supplies, even the most costly pigments, and still have plenty of money left over.

Lisette was so distracted tallying up the cost of her new supplies that she ran headfirst into a man. When they collided, the case he was carrying fell to the ground. Lisette managed to stay on her feet. Clad in a black gown and wig of white curled and powdered hair, Lisette recognized the man as a lawyer. He had been screeching at a defendant...or plaintiff...Lisette could not distinguish between the two, who had been walking several paces behind him, unable to keep up with the fast-moving advocate.

"Stupid girl! Watch where you are walking!" The lawyer picked up his case, turned to his companion and rushed off.

Lisette set off again too. She had been walking down the Rue Saint Denis, where the street neared the Pont du Change and the Île de la Cité. This area teemed with lawyers, especially in the middle of the day. *It must be nearing noon,* she thought.

She watched as all of the lawyers scurried toward the Châtelet and the other courts. Even though it had been entirely rebuilt by Louis XIV, the Châtelet retained its imposing castle-like appearance. Besides housing the criminal courts, it also held a police headquarters and several prisons. She had heard tales of prisoners languishing in the underground dungeons of the Châtelet. Lisette hurried past the ominous building.

When Lisette entered Le Brun's, it felt empty. Monsieur Faucher had not immediately emerged to greet her. She walked back toward the curtain that divided the front area from the more private back space of the shop.

"Monsieur Le Brun?" Lisette called out.

She was about to turn and go, when she heard a woman giggling. Then she heard someone try to shush the woman. It sounded like a man was with her. *Le Brun,* she thought.

"Monsieur Le Brun, I'm not leaving until you come out and talk to me." Lisette was determined.

She heard the woman snigger again just before Le Brun appeared. He was unkempt with his linen *chemise* partially hanging out of his silk *culottes*. His hair fell loosely onto his shoulders. It was not pulled back and tied at the nape of his neck with a black ribbon as usual. Lisette wasn't sure, but she thought she saw a faint hint of red rouge smeared on his face. It looked like he might have tried to rub it off with the palm of his hand. Lisette knew that only noblewomen and wealthy merchants' wives wore rouge of that deep red color.

"What do you want? I am a very busy man," Le Brun said earnestly.

Lisette heard a faint giggle from behind the curtain again.

Le Brun maintained a serious face.

"Have my paintings sold?" Lisette asked him.

"No. Now good day." Le Brun turned away from her.

Lisette quickly spoke again, "But it has been a week. You said to come back in a week."

Le Brun spun around to face her. Lisette suspected that he didn't like being proven wrong. "They will sell, I'm sure of it. But I don't know when."

"Then can you advance me a portion of the sales proceeds?" Lisette asked him.

Le Brun immediately replied, "I can't give you an advance. That is not the way I conduct business." He turned again to go.

Lisette didn't want to give up that easily. She had learned in her interactions with Le Brun that everything was negotiable.

"What about a partial advance?"

"Good day, Mademoiselle Vigée. I have urgent business that requires my attention." He started back toward the curtain.

As he parted the heavy drape, he turned to Lisette and said, "In the meantime, remember what I said before – bring me portraits. They sell quickly, faster than allegories."

Lisette watched as a woman's hands pulled him into the back. The muffled giggling resumed.

Part of Lisette had a mind to march behind the curtain and haggle with him some more. If he would agree to a small advance, anything really, she could buy her own supplies. But Lisette knew the woman's laughter meant that Le Brun wasn't going to re-emerge and give her any money today. He was otherwise occupied.

Why didn't they sell? Lisette wondered. She had been so sure that her allegories would have sold already. She slumped her shoulders and hung her head low. Lisette couldn't believe she was once again leaving Le Brun's empty-handed.

She reluctantly walked out of the shop. Not sure of her next steps, she stood outside Le Brun's for a good while. She watched the passers-by. The swiftly moving carriages and harried pedestrians seemed out of place to her. Her world had just come to a halt. Lisette had no urgent business. There were no buyers for her finished paintings and she couldn't complete the paintings she had begun. Lisette had no supplies and no way of buying more.

Then another thought occurred to her. Even if she had the money to buy new canvases, Lisette was unsure of how she could hide her paintings, especially while they dried. Le Sèvre routinely came into her room unannounced. Her allegories required several days for the many layers of paint to dry. Lisette realized that she had not thoroughly considered this plan. She needed to go home and think, but she dreaded the idea of going back to Le Sèvre's house and to her empty room.

Lisette remembered Le Brun's advice: *Bring me portraits. They sell quickly.* His words reverberated in her head.

Lisette decided not to dismiss Le Brun's idea. The Duchesse de Chartres' sitting was less than two weeks away. Maybe portraits were the key to moving forward.

Chapter Sixteen

ou are quite the storyteller, Mademoiselle Vigée," the Duchesse de Chartres complimented Lisette.

"The most amusing part of the incident was that no matter how hard he tried, he couldn't return his wig to its original position. With every readjustment, it looked worse!" Lisette said.

The Duchesse tossed her head back and laughed out loud at Lisette's story of the Duc de Choiseul. Lisette had seen this man, who was normally a fixture at Versailles, promenading in the Tuileries last week. She had been privy to an extremely embarrassing incident involving high winds, a loose wig and a very self-conscious, bald-headed Duc.

"Please, Duchesse, try to keep your head and face still," Lisette said.

"Then I beg you to stop entertaining me with your wit," the

Duchesse responded.

Lisette noticed that she was suppressing a smile.

"I promise," Lisette said warmly. Much to her surprise, Lisette had been enjoying their time together. She had dreaded the portrait session for many reasons, not the least of which was the Duchesse's earlier ill-treatment of Lisette.

After the Duchesse's haughty behavior in their previous encounters, Lisette had anticipated the session to be excruciatingly difficult to endure. But as the afternoon wore on, Lisette found the Duchesse to be charming, with an enchanting face to match. The Duchesse had also graciously forgiven Lisette for missing their first sitting.

All through today's session, they had found more to discuss than Lisette would have imagined. From the latest play on the Boulevard du Temple to Rousseau's novel, there had not been a single lull in their conversation. Lisette had to admit that she was enjoying herself.

Lisette focused on the Duchesse's facial features. The Duchesse's large, dark blue eyes and pale pink cheeks offset her prominent aquiline nose. Lisette painted her chestnut brown hair in loose curls that fell to her shoulders. She preferred the natural look over the formal *poufs* that had become so popular. She was surprised that the Duchesse had agreed to have her hair portrayed in such an informal fashion, but Lisette had flattered her by saying that her shiny brown hair complimented her pale violet and white striped satin gown.

After Lisette had completed the Duchesse's head, she moved to her neck and bust. The Duchesse had removed her *fichu*, exposing the milky-white skin of her chest and neck. Her small bust protruded out of her deep neckline just above a narrow, violet bow. Lisette decided to include the bow in the painting at the bottom edge of the portrait.

"We are nearly done for today, Duchesse," Lisette told her.

The Duchesse gave a slight nod of her head.

They sat in silence while Lisette finished. As Lisette looked down at her dwindling provisions, she was glad they had lasted for the session. True to his word, Le Sèvre had provided her with a small ration of pigments just minutes before the Duchesse had arrived. It would not be enough for more than today's sitting. Le Sèvre had made sure of that.

The quiet in the room was short-lived. Without any warning, the door flew open and Le Sèvre entered the room. *He must feel the need to check up on me,* Lisette thought.

"Does the sitting meet with your expectations, Duchesse?" he asked. Le Sèvre's voice was less steady than normal. He glanced over at Lisette as he asked the question.

Is he nervous? Lisette wondered. The Duchesse de Chartres was his most important client. Losing her support would devastate his business, since other noblewomen would follow her lead.

Lisette saw him out of the corner of her eye, but did not return his gaze. She continued working on the portrait.

"It has exceeded them, in fact. Mademoiselle Vigée is exceptional, both at painting and at conversation," the Duchesse said to him.

"If she is bothering you with too much chatter, please do tell me. I am more than willing to accommodate you in every way," Le Sèvre said.

Le Sèvre stood watching Lisette.

He is afraid that I'll bungle his good relationship with the Duchesse, Lisette realized. She concentrated hard on the portrait, never acknowledging Le Sèvre.

"Thank you, Monsieur Le Sèvre. You may leave us now," the Duchesse said with an air of finality. As a person of much lower birth and social rank, Le Sèvre was compelled to obey the Duchesse. Besides, Lisette knew that he would never dare disregard her wishes. He profited too much from the jewels that he sold to her and to her friends.

Le Sèvre bowed to the Duchesse and added, "If you would like to have a fitting after you are done here, I have some splendid new jewels to show you."

"No, not today. The sitting has been more than enough activity for one day. I must return home as soon as Mademoiselle Vigée is finished."

"Yes, of course, Duchesse. I will leave you." Le Sèvre bowed again to the Duchesse and then narrowed his eyes at Lisette, as if somehow it was her fault the Duchesse had not agreed to see his new jewels.

Lisette saw the Duchesse take notice of his disdain.

The Duchesse furrowed her brow.

As soon as he had left the room and shut the door, the Duchesse spoke, "Never mind that man. I tolerate him because he has the most beautiful jewels to sell to me. I don't know who his supplier is, but he always has a varied selection, the best in all of Paris." She paused and then continued, "He was foul to you because I will not be buying jewels from him today." The Duchesse smiled at Lisette. "There will be another day for me to look at his newest collection."

Lisette returned the smile as she finished the afternoon's work. She had completed as much of the portrait as she could with her limited pigments. Lisette needed more of several colors.

"We are finished with today's sitting, Duchesse. I believe we should only require one or two more to complete the portrait."

"How wonderful. Do you think we could finish it later this week?"

"I think so, yes," Lisette said. She had agreed, but Lisette knew it depended on Le Sèvre and how quickly he would replenish her pigments. She didn't want to disappoint the Duchesse.

"I should like to bring the portraits to my father-in-law and present them as a gift for their newly renovated *château*. The masked ball in honor of the completion is next week." The Duchesse stood and arranged herself.

"So you will want several copies then?" Lisette asked.

The Duchesse nodded.

"Please, come see our progress," Lisette said, inviting her to examine the portrait.

As soon as the Duchesse saw her portrait, she let out a high-pitched shriek. "Oh my!"

"You are pleased then?"

"Very much so, Mademoiselle Vigée," she said.

Quickly Lisette saw the Duchesse's satisfaction transform to puzzlement.

"Duchesse?" Lisette asked her.

"It is magnificent...but why does the bow on my dress appear faded when the rest of the dress is brilliant?"

"Because I have run out of Madder pigment and am unable to mix the violet color," Lisette said.

"Doesn't Le Sèvre keep you well supplied? It won't be difficult to acquire more of that color will it? I absolutely adore this dress, which is why I wore it to the sitting."

Lisette wondered if she should tell the Duchesse of her predicament. They had shared a pleasant afternoon, but Lisette didn't know if candor was appropriate.

"What is it? Mademoiselle Vigée?" The Duchesse returned to her chair facing Lisette and leaned forward as if she was preparing to hear a secret.

Lisette looked at the Duchesse and then at her portrait. *It would be a shame if it remained unfinished*, she thought. "Monsieur Le Sèvre rations my supplies. I never know when I will be getting more," Lisette blurted out.

"I have a husband who once tried to ration my spending allowance. Imagine that! Me, the heiress of the largest fortune in France."

The Duchesse laughed about it now, but Lisette saw in her eyes that the insult had hurt her deeply.

The Duchesse moved close to Lisette and whispered in her ear, "When you have finished, be sure to make an extra copy for yourself."

Searching for understanding, Lisette studied the Duchesse.

"For you to do with what you like...perhaps to sell." The

Duchesse stood and slipped on her embroidered, silk gloves.

Lisette didn't want to question the Duchesse, but she knew that if Le Sèvre discovered this extra copy, he would not be happy.

"I can see that you are worried...don't be. Simply don't tell him. It will be our secret. You have painted me beautifully...and you have been the most pleasing company." The Duchesse smiled warmly at Lisette and swept out of the room.

As Lisette watched her leave, she thought, *Maybe I won't have to rely on Le Sèvre after all.*

Chapter Seventeen

As Lisette made her way to Le Brun's, she could think of nothing but her portraits of the Duchesse de Chartres and the Duchesse's friends. *Have they sold?* she wondered. *It has been over three weeks.*

Lisette had intended on seeing Le Brun earlier, but Le Sèvre had escorted Lisette and her mother to Longchamp to celebrate the end of Holy Week. Lisette's mother wanted to attend the Tenebrae service on Good Friday. The village church at Longchamp was known for its choir. Lisette suspected that Le Sèvre had less interest in the religious service. Like many nobles and merchants, Le Sèvre wanted to be seen in his new carriage. Those who traveled to the outskirts of Paris to Longchamp announced their privilege and wealth with their expensive horses and elaborate carriages. Not wanting to miss any opportunity to display his success, Le Sèvre insisted on driving out several days before Good Friday with all of the other important Parisian families. They had been in good company as they drove along the crowded, muddy paths of the Bois de Boulogne to and from Longchamp.

As soon as Lisette entered Le Brun's shop, Monsieur Faucher approached her. He held out his hand to stop her from moving any farther into the gallery.

"Monsieur Le Brun doesn't have time for *you* today. Come back later." Monsieur Faucher appeared neat and flawlessly groomed, as usual. He was dressed in an embroidered coat and matching *culottes* with a silk *cravat* around his neck. Lisette knew his clothing was much too expensive for a picture dealer's assistant.

"Good, so he is here," Lisette said, sweeping past Faucher. She moved as fast as she could with the two paintings under her arm. She hurried toward the back. Lisette was anxious to see if any of her recent portraits of the Duchesse or the Duchesse's friends had yet sold.

Over the past few weeks, Lisette had dropped off portraits and collected money from Le Brun several times. At each visit, Monsieur Faucher treated her with disdain and each time Lisette ignored him. Monsieur Faucher fancied himself Le Brun's gatekeeper. He perpetually claimed that Le Brun had no interest in seeing Lisette, but Le Brun was always happy to see her and take her portraits.

Lisette stopped at the curtain and called out, "Le Brun, I don't care who is back there with you. We need to discuss business."

In the past several weeks, Lisette had found herself flooded with portrait requests from the Duchesse de Chartres' friends. These friends had followed the Duchesse's example and had also permitted Lisette to paint additional copies of their portraits. Lisette had already completed many of these portraits and would very quickly have more for Le Brun to sell...and Le Sèvre was none the wiser. She had been able to hide both her new supplies and the extra portraits. Le Sèvre never asked her exactly how many copies the noblewomen requested.

"Mademoiselle Vigée, you cannot go back there!" Monsieur Faucher ran after her.

Lisette continued to ignore Faucher and remained near the curtain. "I have more portraits for you," she said loudly.

Within moments, Le Brun emerged from behind the curtain. Bedraggled, with tousled hair and smeared rouge on his cheeks, he smiled at Lisette. "Mademoiselle Vigée. I'm glad you are here. I have something for you."

Lisette saw that he held a small sack, just like the one Le Brun had first given her, except it was fuller. She reached out to take it from him. Instead of giving it to her, Le Brun immediately pulled his hand away, removing the sack from her reach.

"Not just yet. Let me see those paintings you said you have for me. Portraits, I hope."

"No, first I need what is owed to me from the sale of my two paintings." Lisette glanced at the bag of coins.

He handed over the sack.

As she accepted it, Lisette thought, *It is heavier than last time!*

"840 *livres*. You can count it if you aren't sure. I took my thirty percent."

Lisette let the numbers seep into her head. *My paintings sold for 600 livres each!* Lisette realized. She suddenly found it difficult to move or speak.

Le Brun smiled. "And they sold quickly." He looked at the paintings under her arm. "Do you have more portraits for me?"

"What about my allegories? Have they sold?" Lisette asked.

"No," Le Brun responded curtly.

"Even the newest one?" Lisette asked. She had been disappointed that neither her *Death of Caesar* nor her *Venus, Cupid and Mars* canvases had sold. Lisette had continued to create allegories and Le Brun had continued to reluctantly accept them, as long as they were accompanied by portraits.

"They aren't going to sell," Le Brun said plainly.

"But the newest one is after Rubens' painting, *The Council of the Gods*. It is a faithful copy. I went to the Luxembourg Palace many times to view it, sketch it...understand it."

"I've asked around and contacted all of my usual buyers and even some dabblers. No one is interested in buying an allegorical painting done by a woman, especially not one copied from Rubens' *Marie de' Medici Cycle*...too ambitious."

"Is it too small?" Lisette thought she had judged the size correctly. It was an easel painting that easily could be displayed, along with tens of other paintings of its size, on a wall of a gentleman's drawing room or in the gallery of a grand house.

"No, the size is appropriate. There are far too many male nudes, which you have not studied from life. Now, bring me as many portraits as you can. I can sell them."

Lisette was convinced that he wasn't working hard enough to sell her allegories. Le Brun only wanted a quick sale from portraits.

"I don't believe it," she said.

"Believe what you will, but don't bring me any more allegories...just portraits. You have a singular talent for them." He glanced again at the paintings she held.

"Yes, these are two more portraits...the Baronne d'Esthal and the Comtesse de la Vieuville." Lisette handed him the portraits.

He greedily snatched them and then disappeared behind the curtain. When he reappeared a moment later, he no longer had the portraits, but instead held another, smaller sack of coins. He handed it to Lisette. "A partial advance...on these next two portraits. Come back in a few days, I'm sure they will have sold by then." He paused. "Mademoiselle," Le Brun said as he bowed slightly to her.

She was taken aback. In the time she had known him, Le Brun had neither given her an advance nor had he bowed to her so respectfully.

"Monsieur," Lisette said as she nodded her head in acknowledgment and left.

Chapter Eighteen

Lisette pulled her stool over to her window and waited for Le Sèvre to leave the house. Over the past few months, this had become a regular occurrence. Most nights he was gone for at least a few hours. Her mother had said earlier in the day that tonight he was attending a supper. Lisette expected him to be gone until well past midnight.

It was already dark, but the street lamps had been lit, so Lisette could see outside, below her window. There were two lamps that illuminated the street in front of Le Sèvre's house, but only one burned brightly. The other flickered weakly. The lamp oil was replenished daily, but it rarely lasted past nine in the evening.

There he goes, Lisette thought as she watched him leave the house. Once he had disappeared down the street, Lisette quickly moved away from the window. *I can get it out now,* she thought.

Lisette scurried to the corner of her room and knelt. She pulled up the small Savonnerie carpet that covered this corner of her bedroom floor. Lisette was careful not to bend the expensive carpet. Her mother would notice if it was damaged. She bent over and searched for the floorboard that she had marked with a small *x*. With the end of her palette knife, she pried open the marked board and several on either side of it. She had removed the floorboards so many times, they were now loose and easy to remove. Before Lisette reached in to retrieve her latest allegory painting, she noticed the money bag that was also hidden beneath her bedroom floor.

Her sack of coins had grown and shrunk over the past three months. With the majority of her earnings from portrait sales, Lisette had been paid nearly 3,000 *livres*. Even though she had sold many portraits of the Duchesse de Chartres and the Duchesse's friends, Lisette was most proud of the sale of her allegory paintings: *The Death of Caesar* and *Venus, Cupid and Mars.* Le Brun had finally sold them. At 200 *livres* each, they hadn't fetched quite the sums that she had hoped for, but their sales meant more to Lisette than any of her portrait earnings.

Her reputation as an artist was growing, but it wasn't as a painter of history and allegory. It was as a portraitist. Lisette tried not to be discouraged. She knew that in time she would be accepted as a history painter. For now, she had worked out an efficient system of painting extra portraits for noblewomen and selling them with Le Brun's help.

Even though Lisette's portraits were commanding great sums, she was not accumulating any real wealth. Lisette was spending the money as fast as she was earning it. Afraid that she would have to rely on Le Sèvre, Lisette continually replenished her supplies, buying only the finest provisions. She believed that great artists used only the highest quality brushes and pigments. She picked up the money bag and looked inside. Her sack now held 200 *livres*.

Lisette set aside the sack of coins and carefully pulled out a canvas. After replacing the floorboards, she placed the canvas on the easel. While she hadn't been able to complete the large versions of her allegory paintings, she had painted many cabinet-sized allegories like the one before her now. Lisette had realized that there was no possible way to hide a floor-to-ceiling painting in her bedroom. When she thought about her earlier, grandiose visions, she felt foolish.

Lisette lit several candles. It was more difficult to paint at night, but she had no other choice. She couldn't risk working on this painting or any other allegory during the day. Lisette regarded her figure of Helen of Troy. She had decided not to copy a great masterpiece, but instead to create her own version of the Greek myth. She had titled her painting, *The Abduction of Helen of Troy*. Over the past few months she had nearly finished it. Under normal circumstances, this painting would have been completed in a matter of weeks, not months. In order to make sure Le Sèvre didn't find it, Lisette had worked on small portions at a time and only at night. Le Sèvre never entered her room in the evenings, so she had decided that it was safe to allow those small portions to dry while she slept. Then in the early morning, she returned the canvases to their hiding place beneath the floor.

As Lisette searched through her brushes, she thought she heard Le Sèvre's voice in the front vestibule. *Impossible,* she decided. *I saw him leave.* Lisette looked out of the window. There was no sign of Le Sèvre or his carriage. Only the gleaming street lamps lining the gardens of the Palais-Royal were visible. Their flickering reminded Lisette of twinkling stars. *I ought to paint this scene at night*, she thought. Lisette searched among her brushes for just the right one. She needed the brush with the fine tip, for the details of Helen's face. As soon as she found it, the door opened. Lisette dropped the brush. Le Sèvre stood in the doorway. Lisette froze.

"I knew it! When I saw the candles shining in your window,

I knew you were painting. And right now we are in between portraits. I knew you were disobeying me." He walked over to where she stored her brushes and other supplies. "How is it that you have so many pigments? I remember only giving you a few." He pointed to a much smaller box containing half a dozen vials of pigment powder.

Lisette remained silent. She didn't want to jeopardize her relationships with Le Brun or the Duchesse.

"Don't want to talk?" he asked as if taunting her. Le Sèvre seemed like he already knew the answer. He had a wry smile on his face as he picked up her newest supplies leaving only the few vials of pigment he had provided.

Lisette felt her stomach churn as she watched him gather her provisions. She had spent almost all of her earnings on these brushes and pigments.

Lisette glanced over to the door which Le Sèvre had left open. She started moving toward it, but Le Sèvre intercepted, blocking her path.

Not being able to move, Lisette said in a loud voice, "You will want Henri's help collecting everything." Lisette hoped Henri had heard her. She and Henri had worked out an arrangement that whenever Le Sèvre was home, Henri would remain close by. In exchange, Lisette brought Henri extra food whenever she could filch it from the dining room after their meals. Le Sèvre had never been violent with her when there was someone else in the room.

"That is a good idea. Henri can help," he said. Then he scowled at Lisette. "I know about your relationship with Le Brun. That has ended. I saw Le Brun this afternoon and he has agreed to comply with my wishes. *I* will be the only one who communicates with Le Brun. *I* will be the one who collects all of your money from sales. All of your portrait commissions will go through me and only me. Do you understand?"

Lisette was dumbfounded. She wanted to scream *no* at him and then run out of the room, but her body prevented her from moving.

"If you don't comply, I will be forced to resort to drastic measures, Lisette. Actions that I'm sure will break your mother's heart, but in the end she will agree with my decisions. She has been a good wife, gladly accepting the choices I make for this family."

Lisette knew he was speaking the truth. She had seen how easily Le Sèvre was willing to hurt her mother. He wouldn't think twice about breaking her heart. Lisette glanced at the door. *Where is Henri?* she wondered.

"Well?" Le Sèvre was waiting for an answer.

Lisette thought of her mother and nodded. "I understand, Monsieur."

"Very good...just one more thing. No more historicals or allegories. I thought I had made that clear." Le Sèvre marched over to her easel and grabbed the canvas. He put it under his arm. Lisette hadn't expected him to take her canvas too.

"No! You will destroy all that I've done for months." Lisette took a step forward. She wanted to wrestle it out of Le Sèvre's hands, but she stopped herself. She knew what he could do to her. Instead, she called out for Henri again. This time Henri came rushing into the room.

Henri looked at Lisette before he turned to Le Sèvre. "How can I be of service?"

"Henri, I need you to take this painting and have Mademoiselle Tothier place it into the wood fires in the kitchen," Le Sèvre ordered him as he held out Lisette's canvas.

Henri took the painting into his arms but didn't budge. He stared at Lisette as if he was unsure what to do next.

"Go on, boy, do as I told you," Le Sèvre said in a stern voice. "You don't want to disobey me. I do not tolerate insubordinate servants. You *will* get the switch."

Lisette didn't want Henri beaten. If Le Sèvre could so easily hurt his wife and step-daughter, Lisette could only imagine the horrible punishments he would inflict on a disobedient servant.

Lisette nodded to Henri and he left the room.

Le Sèvre drew close to Lisette. "Do not go to see Le Brun...he cannot help you." He narrowed his eyes and lowered his voice adding, "You have only me now." Le Sèvre sauntered toward the door, taking his time leaving Lisette's room.

Le Sèvre snapped orders at Henri all the way down the front stairs. His voice faded as they descended into the lower level of the house, toward the kitchen. Lisette waited five minutes before retrieving a few *sous* from her money bag hidden beneath the floor. She had to see Le Brun, even if Le Sèvre had forbade it.

Lisette left her room, carefully shutting the door behind her. As she went down the stairs she heard Le Sèvre in the drawing room talking to her mother. Once in the front vestibule, she hurried toward the back stairs. She would exit the house through the servants' entrance on the lowest level, near the kitchen. It was her best chance of avoiding detection.

Lisette didn't like to go out after dark. It was dangerous for anyone on the streets of Paris in the evenings, but especially for a young woman by herself. At night, Paris transformed into a perilous place. Thieves, scoundrels and worse lurked in dark alleys and in the shadows. Respectable people only moved on its streets protected by a carriage. *Fiacres* were more expensive to hire than the smaller *cabriolets*, but they were also more substantial and safer. She had brought enough money to hail a *fiacre*.

As she reached the bottom of the servants' staircase, Henri stopped her.

"Henri, I can't talk now. Please don't tell Monsieur Le Sèvre that I have left."

"Mademoiselle, come with me to the kitchen. Mademoiselle Tothier has something for you," he said and motioned for Lisette to follow him through the narrow passageway. Lisette walked closely behind him.

Once they were in the kitchen, Mademoiselle Tothier immediately came up to Lisette. She grinned widely while she held up Lisette's canvas.

"You saved it!" Lisette wanted to hug the kitchen maid.

"Yes, Mademoiselle. I never put it in the fire. I knew that wasn't the right thing to do...even if Monsieur Le Sèvre ordered it." Lisette noticed that the maid had several front teeth missing and many others that were decayed.

"But you could get into serious trouble." Lisette didn't want the servants punished for helping her.

She smirked and once again exposed a mouth of half-rotted teeth as she said, "I put an old woolen sack and some thin strips of wood into the fire and burned it instead of your painting. The ashes look similar enough."

Lisette eschewed etiquette and squeezed the young maid. "I am in your debt. Thank you."

Awkwardly, Mademoiselle Tothier broke away from the embrace, curtsied to Lisette and resumed her kitchen duties.

Clutching her canvas, Lisette swiftly returned to her room. Henri followed on her heels.

"Henri, can you stand outside the door and watch for Monsieur Le Sèvre?" Lisette asked him in a muted tone.

"Yes, Mademoiselle," Henri said.

Lisette knew that she had a friend in Henri. Lisette had never mistreated Henri or any of the other servants. She was the only one in the house who was fair and respectful to them. When Le Sèvre wasn't actually abusing the servants, he was threatening them with punishment. Over the past few months, even her mother had become verbally abusive, especially to Henri and Camille.

Lisette rushed into her room and quickly hid the canvas underneath her floor, carefully replacing the floorboards and the carpet. *At least Le Sèvre hasn't found my hiding place,* she thought. After tonight, Lisette would have to be more careful when she brought out her allegory paintings. She didn't want to discover what Le Sèvre's idea of "drastic measures" were. Lisette would forever regret breaking her mother's heart.

After Lisette had smoothed out the Savonnerie carpet, she left her room and gingerly pulled the door closed. She nodded to Henri to let him know he was no longer needed. He gave a slight bow to her and departed down the hall.

Lisette followed him. When she had reached the bottom of the front stairs, she heard Le Sèvre arguing with someone in the drawing room...a woman. She didn't recognize the woman's voice. It wasn't her mother's or one of the female servants. Lisette stopped to listen.

"I told you never to come to my house. You have to leave now," Le Sèvre said in a voice that he was trying to keep hushed, but not succeeding. Lisette clearly heard every word.

"But it is urgent. I had to tell you that Jacques was arrested," the woman said in a loud whisper.

"Keep your voice down, Madame Gervais. You did not need to come to my house to tell me this news. We can discuss it tomorrow morning at the store."

"But the inspector is going to send him away without a trial unless he gives them information tonight. You need to come with me now," Madame Gervais insisted. There was an urgent desperation in her voice.

Le Sèvre was silent. Then Lisette heard him say, "I am going out, Henri. I don't know when I will return. Fetch my coat."

Lisette tip-toed back up the stairs so that she wouldn't be seen when Le Sèvre came into the foyer. She crouched down behind one of the large banisters at the top of the staircase. From that position, she could see down to the foyer, but it would be difficult for her to be spotted, especially if she was quiet.

Lisette watched the pair head for the front door. When Madame Gervais turned toward the staircase, Lisette scrutinized her face. She recognized the woman. But where had she seen her? Le Sèvre went out first with Madame Gervais following. Lisette remained hidden behind the banister until she was sure that enough time had passed. *Where have I seen Madame Gervais?* she wondered. Then it came to her. Madame Gervais had been the servant woman who had met with Le Sèvre in the Tuileries gardens that day many months ago, before her mother had married Le Sèvre.

Lisette thought back and remembered seeing the servant woman slip something into Le Sèvre's pocket. It had all seemed so clandestine, but Lisette had not been able to explain it. She didn't know what Le Sèvre had been doing with the woman then and she didn't know what they were doing together now. Lisette couldn't explain their relationship. Was she Le Sèvre's lover?

Lisette waited until the servants cleared the foyer and it was quiet. Detained long enough, she headed for the front door. *I need to see Le Brun tonight*, she thought.

Hastily, Lisette made her way out of the house and onto the Rue Saint-Honoré. She immediately tried to hail a carriage. She noticed there were very few that passed. She looked at her papa's pocket watch. She had been delayed too long. Everyone was now hurrying to the evening's performances. Lisette was out at one of the busiest times of the night. She decided to walk a little farther down the Rue Saint-Honoré. *Maybe I will have better luck here,* she hoped. Lisette raised her hand again. Then again and again. Not a single carriage stopped for her. She looked at her watch once more. *Le Brun will be leaving his shop soon*, she realized. *I am going to have to walk.* Lisette would have to move swiftly if she was going to arrive at Le Brun's safely on foot.

At least the main streets are still well lit, she thought. Only sporadic lamps had exhausted their oil supplies. There would be no shortcuts tonight. Lisette would stay on the main thoroughfares. She moved as fast as she could, while remaining alert for approaching threats. She avoided getting too close to anyone who appeared suspicious. When she could see Le Brun's shop, she quickened her pace.

"Why you are a lovely little thing. Let me see your face." Out of nowhere, a large, burly man approached her. The man had a low, raspy voice. He was dressed in rags and smelled of Sulphur, like the filth on the streets. His face was sullied with mud.

Lisette lowered her head and ran.

The man pursued her.

Please have your front door unlocked. Please be there. Please..., Lisette thought as she raced away.

Lisette reached Le Brun's shop and immediately tugged at the door, but it was locked. She whipped around. The brutish man was nearly upon her. Lisette pounded on the door with her fist. "Le Brun, open the door!"

She turned again but didn't see anyone. He was gone. Lisette released her breath.

Then she felt a hand on her arm.

"You are quick for a girl. Come here, my pretty one!" The man gripped her arm trying to lead her away.

Before she knew what was happening, the door opened and Lisette felt herself being pulled with a stronger force into the shop.

"Le Brun!" Lisette had never been so happy to see him.

Le Brun shooed the man with his hand. "Get out of here! Or else I'll summon the *sergent*...there's a watch house just around the corner," Le Brun said to the scoundrel.

Lisette didn't recognize the harshness in Le Brun's voice. She watched the man dash away and Le Brun promptly locked the door.

"Mademoiselle Vigée! Why would you risk coming here at night?" Le Brun looked genuinely concerned.

"To talk about Monsieur Le Sèvre." Lisette needed answers tonight.

Le Brun's expression immediately changed. He now looked irritated. "I'm sorry, but there is nothing I can do about him."

"Nothing you can do?"

"Monsieur Le Sèvre is your legal guardian. Under the law, he has the right to collect all of your earnings. He can do as he pleases with your money. It is his right. I cannot do anything to

144

change the law."

"But you didn't seem terribly concerned about the law before."

Le Brun looked past her as he spoke. "It is out of my hands. From now on, I can't sell your paintings. Don't come here again."

Lisette hadn't expected Le Brun to give her such an unsatisfactory explanation. Once again, her step-father had inserted himself into her world...into a place where he didn't belong.

She met Le Brun's eyes. "There is nothing else to say. Good night."

Lisette headed toward the door. She wasn't eager to go back out into the night alone. *I'll find a lantern man,* Lisette thought. She reached into her pocket bag to ensure she had sufficient coins to pay their modest fee for escorting her safely home. With the path well lit by the lanterns they carried, Lisette felt confident she could avoid harm.

"Wait." Le Brun came after her.

Has he changed his mind? Lisette hoped. For a brief moment, Lisette wondered if he might still want to help her, regardless of Le Sèvre.

"You cannot walk home. It is too dangerous."

"I will hire a lantern man," she replied.

"No, let me find you a carriage," said Le Brun avoiding her gaze.

Chapter Nineteen

*L*isette had stayed awake for most of the night considering Le Brun's words, *From now on, I can't sell your paintings. Don't come here again.* Le Sèvre was gradually taking everything that mattered away from her. Still in bed, she glanced over to her easel. *I'd be taking too much of a risk,* she thought. *Le Sèvre will find out.*

Lisette remained in bed until she heard Le Sèvre leave for the day.

She rose and dressed herself. She put on a simple, pale pink satin dress that closed in the front and was edged with delicate white lace. Lisette put her sketchpad and some money in her pocket bag that was safely hidden beneath her dress. She hadn't yet decided where she would go today. *As long as it isn't here,* she thought. Lisette needed a distraction.

She was on her way out of the house when her mother cornered her in the front vestibule. "Lisette, you look lovely today. It is nice to see you wearing one of your newer ensembles. Although if you will be out tonight, you will want to change to a formal gown."

Lisette nodded.

Now aware of the fashion "rules," her mother was keen to enforce them. This morning, Jeanne was dressed more like a courtier than the wife of a wealthy *marchand*. She donned a striped emerald and ivory silk *robe à l'anglaise* and a matching silk gauze kerchief which crossed at her breasts and then tied at the back of her waist. The newer open gown design was worn by the most fashionable women at Versailles. Jeanne's hair was swept up revealing large emerald drop earrings.

"You look fetching today as well, Mother. Are those new earrings?"

"Yes, a gift from Le Sèvre," her mother said, lowering her eyes and hiding her arms behind her back. Jeanne always seemed to be wearing new jewelry whenever she had fresh bruises. She looked back up at Lisette, "Where are you going? You are never home lately. I would like to spend the morning with you."

Lisette regarded her mother. Jeanne was right, they hadn't spent much time together since her mother's marriage to Le Sèvre. When her papa was alive, Lisette had often enjoyed the company of both her papa and her mother. With her brother away at school, the three of them would visit the Luxembourg Palace and gardens. They also went to the fairs together – the Saint-Germain Fair in the winter and the Saint-Laurent Fair and Saint-Ovide Fair in the summer. Lisette hoped that she and her mother might continue their traditions even without her papa.

"Shall we go to the Saint-Ovide Fair? I overheard some ladies in the gardens discussing how enchanting the fair's *cafés* are this year, especially Le Chat Café," Lisette said. Being respectable places for well-born ladies, she knew her mother would agree to visit a *café* at the Saint-Ovide Fair. Both men and women frequented fair *cafés*, unlike the permanent *cafés* in Paris, which only men patronized.

"Let's go. It sounds very fashionable," her mother said.

Lisette shook her head in agreement. She knew her mother could not resist following the advice of the noble ladies from the Palais-Royal gardens.

Then Jeanne added, "I will buy you a hot chocolate."

Lisette had never tasted the expensive drink. "Mother, are you sure?"

"Of course. Today, we will be well-dressed ladies sipping what the court ladies drink every day." Her mother smiled at her.

Eager to begin their outing, Lisette linked arms with her mother. Jeanne winced at Lisette's touch.

"Mother, are you hurt?" Lisette asked her.

Jeanne pulled her arm out of Lisette's and took several steps back into the room. "Let's wait for Le Sèvre to return. He won't be long. We can all go as a family, like we used to do with Louis."

Since their marriage, Jeanne wanted to include Le Sèvre in everything. Lisette wanted to be with her mother, but only her. Lisette had no intention of spending time with Le Sèvre today. He would never take her papa's place. She had to think quickly to get out of this excursion that was now going to include him.

Lisette hastened toward the front door. "Mother, I forgot! I have to meet with the Duchesse de Chartres to discuss her next portrait sitting. I must go. We will visit the fair another day." Lisette didn't wait for her mother's response. She hurriedly left the house.

As Lisette traversed the Rue Saint-Honoré, her thoughts returned to Le Brun's words: *Under the law he has the right to collect all of your earnings...It is out of my hands.* She stopped herself. *I don't want to think about Le Sèvre or Le Brun today.*

Lisette decided to go to the fair by herself. The Saint-Ovide

Fair was a reasonable distance from Le Sèvre's house. Located in the Place Louis-XV, west of the Tuileries gardens, it was much closer than the Saint-Laurent Fair, which was outside the old city walls and just beyond the Porte Saint-Martin.

Lisette strolled down the Rue Saint-Honoré, toward the Saint-Ovide Fair.

Lisette reached the Saint-Ovide Fair in well under thirty minutes. She heard the raucous noises of the fair before she saw any of it. Lisette entered a new world as she walked past the fair attractions and booths. The sights alone were enough to stimulate the senses: a monkey playing a hurdy-gurdy, tight-rope walkers on ropes overhead, acrobats leaping all around, puppeteers manipulating marionettes, and dwarfs and clowns mingling among the crowd.

Lisette noticed the fair was smaller than the previous year. There were fewer shops in the bazaar. She saw a smattering of vendors in their wooden stalls selling perfumes, Venetian mirrors, gloves, paintings, Moroccan leather and knives. There were also fewer pavilions offering games of chance. Lisette spied one billiard hall and two enclosures where cards and dice games were played.

She walked deeper into the narrow passageways in between the booths. Lisette hadn't yet seen any *cafés*. There were plenty of vendors roaming the crowds selling all manner of drinks and treats to eat, but she couldn't find any *cafés* or taverns.

She was approached by several women who were selling spiced breads, fruit, hard cider and *eau-de-vie*. She wasn't interested in losing her senses to spirits like hard cider or *eau-de-vie*. Lisette wanted to sit in a *café* and sip a hot drink. She lowered her head to dodge the vendors. They were relentless and would follow fair patrons until they had been acknowledged. She was also careful to avoid any contact with the young boys, whom everyone knew were pickpockets. They often staged an accidental encounter to steal items from unsuspecting fairgoers.

The fairs were notorious for illicit activity. There were not only simple pickpockets, but dangerous thieves, hucksters and prostitutes. The taverns and cabarets were frequently in trouble with the police and *commissaires* charged with keeping order. Still, the fairs in Paris generally remained a respectable place for everyone to enjoy, even nobles and princes.

After a few more minutes of searching, Lisette found the *cafés*. She peered up and read a small rectangular sign nailed to the front of a temporary wooden structure: *Le Chat Café*. There was a large silhouette of a black cat underneath the words. Lisette had never been to a *café* without her mother or her papa. Together, they had frequented the *cafés* during their visits to the fairs. Her mother had always pointed out the inappropriateness of unescorted women. *If I go inside, I'll be one of those women,* she realized. Then she remembered that her mother had insisted on including Le Sèvre. Lisette went inside.

As soon as she walked in, her nose was overwhelmed by the smell of coffee. After a few minutes of breathing in the strong aroma, it became less jarring and more pleasing. The smell was energizing and yet comforting at the same time.

She scanned the *café*. The front tables were packed with people, so Lisette headed toward the back where it was emptier. She sat at an open table. A young serving girl handed her a sheet of the available drinks. It listed the different ways the coffee was served, including with or without milk. The *café* also offered cups of hot chocolate and even drinks that mixed chocolate with coffee. Lisette then noticed the prices. The hot chocolate was the most expensive item on the list. Her mother had wanted to buy her a cup with Le Sèvre's money. Lisette dug around her pocket bag. She felt a few dozen copper *sous* coins. *More than enough,* she thought.

"I'll have a cup of the hot chocolate."

"Yes, Mademoiselle. You will like it. It is the Dauphine's drink of choice. I haven't yet heard of a Parisian who hasn't liked it," the girl said and then rushed away.

Lisette imagined the Dauphine sitting in Versailles sipping hot chocolate. She had heard the ladies in the gardens discussing the Dauphine often. They were skeptical of her. Being a foreigner, and one from a country that had recently been at war with France, Marie-Antoinette had not been readily accepted by the French people. Lisette had never met an Austrian before, or a Dauphine. She was hesitant to rely on the opinion of garden gossip and decided to reserve judgment on the Dauphine. She certainly wouldn't avoid hot chocolate because particular well-born ladies disapproved of Marie-Antoinette. *If the future Queen of France enjoys hot chocolate, and she can have any drink she pleases, then I'll probably like it too,* Lisette decided.

Waiting for her drink, she surveyed the crowded *café*. There were men animatedly discussing politics, laborers enjoying their day off, merchants' wives gossiping about Guild business and, to Lisette's surprise, another young woman sitting by herself. The woman was reading a book. Lisette looked closer. The book was *Julie, or the New Héloïse,* by Rousseau. Lisette smiled as she remembered Monsieur Robert's opinion on it. He would be disgusted. A story about a woman who had freely chosen her lover, the novel enjoyed the most scandalous reputation. Lisette considered approaching the woman to ask where she had purchased her copy of the novel. Being very popular, it was hard to find. Lisette had heard the ladies in the garden saying that the publishers couldn't print it fast enough for the high demand, so they rented the book by the day and even by the hour.

On the other side of the woman with the novel was a young couple talking quietly. To Lisette, the woman resembled Helen of Troy. *I'll sketch her likeness,* she decided. Always searching for ways to master the faces in her allegory and history paintings, Lisette took out her sketchbook and pencil. As she began to sketch, the woman's lover glared at Lisette. She needed to be less conspicuous, so she used the mirror on the wall to watch them. Even though it was a temporary structure, the proprietors had taken great pains to replicate the permanent coffee houses sprinkled throughout the city. There were mirrors on each side of the pavilion, which made the space seem much bigger. *That's better*, she thought. Lisette could now stare at the woman and sketch her without being impolite.

She was half-finished with the sketch when the serving girl returned with her order. Lisette set down her sketch book and inspected the drink. It was an unsavory brown color, but the aroma emanating from it was sweet and pleasant. Lisette brought the cup to her lips. Because of the hot steam escaping from the drink, she slowly tipped it, taking a small sip. Lisette felt the warm, sweet liquid hit her tongue and then easily slide down her throat. It was like nothing else she had ever tasted. *Delicious!* she thought. She immediately took another sip, and then another. Lisette wondered if it tasted so delightful because she had bought it with her own money.

"Is it proper for a young woman such as yourself to be sitting alone in this *café*?" Lisette heard a deep male voice. She was so engrossed in her drink that she hadn't noticed a man approach her table.

She glanced up. It was Capitaine Amante Fabien de Chaumont. Lisette hadn't seen him since their encounter at Vernet's exhibition at the Louvre, nearly a year ago. He appeared the same. As the year had passed, Lisette had thought about him less frequently. Still, her throat tightened and she didn't know what to say to him. She had not expected to see him there. Lisette felt unprepared.

"I think it is exciting that you are here by yourself. You are not like most young ladies." He smiled at her and sat down.

"Capitaine de Chaumont, I have not invited you to sit." Lisette found her voice. She was rattled in his presence and didn't like the feeling.

"Please, call me Amante." He remained sitting as if he had every right to be there.

"Does your mother approve of you being here by yourself,

conversing with strange men?"

"No, she would not approve of me being here alone. I'm not sure about talking to you."

"Don't worry, I'm not going to bite you." He grinned mischievously. "I only want to be your friend, Mademoiselle Vigée. I find you infinitely interesting." Then he leaned in close. His breath smelled as inviting as the hot chocolate.

Lisette had never been flattered by such a handsome man before. She wasn't sure how she should act.

"Thank you." At least she could be polite. Part of Lisette wanted to tell him to leave so she could enjoy her new drink alone, but another part wanted him to remain.

When she didn't object further, he motioned to the serving girl. "I'll have what she is having." Then he looked at Lisette. "What is it that you are drinking?"

"Hot chocolate," Lisette said.

"I have heard it is quite popular. What does it taste like?"

"Capitaine, what —"

"Amante. Call me Amante," he interrupted her.

"Amante, what is it that you want with me?" Lisette knew that he hadn't sat down with her to discuss the attributes of hot chocolate.

"Right down to business." He smiled at her. "Do you still desire lessons with Monsieur Briard?"

"He is in Italy."

"What if I told you that he has returned early?"

"Briard is back in Paris?" Lisette tried to maintain a neutral face and not allow her emotions to betray her. She could feel her heart beat faster.

"Yes," Amante replied.

Lisette's mind raced as she thought, *I could show Briard my canvas of Helen of Troy and then I could ask him for help with her proportions and then I could...*

"Lisette?"

His voice brought her back to the present moment.

"So you are interested in becoming his student?"

Lisette was about to say *yes* when she remembered Le Sèvre. If it wasn't his idea and he wasn't controlling all aspects of it, he would never allow it.

Amante eagerly awaited an answer. She saw it in his face.

"No...I mean yes...but no...," Lisette said, wavering. Her voice trailed off, fading away as she thought about Le Sèvre.

"Which is it?" Amante looked confused.

Lisette didn't know how to explain it to him.

They sat in silence. For the next several moments, Amante studied Lisette as if he was carefully calculating what he would say next. Then he glanced at her sketchbook sitting on the table.

"May I?" he asked.

Lisette nodded.

Amante picked up her sketchbook and quickly, but carefully flipped through it. He paused at about its halfway point. Amante held it high in the air and displayed the open page.

Lisette immediately recognized the sketch. It was a young woman she had seen in the gardens at the Palais-Royal.

"Look at what you can do. You have a talent that should be cultivated."

Lisette remained silent. She wanted to scream out, *of course I want lessons*, but she knew it was futile. Le Sèvre would never consent.

Amante closed the sketchbook and returned it to the table. "I have an offer for you. Please hear me out." He paused and moved in closer. "I would like to pay for your lessons."

"But what about my step −," Lisette immediately protested.

Amante gently put his forefinger on her mouth. "We don't have to tell anyone. It would be our secret."

Lisette pulled back at his touch. It was highly unusual for a man, especially a near-stranger, to touch a young woman in public. Lisette's lips tingled as she tried her best to focus on his words.

"I don't think it is a good idea." Lisette couldn't accept his offer. Since living in Le Sèvre's house, she had kept too many secrets. First Le Brun, then the Duchesse, now Amante. She was skeptical. Le Sèvre had a way of discovering her secrets.

"You are afraid of what I want in return," he said. Amante regarded her like he had solved a mystery.

He has no understanding of my situation, she thought. Lisette wasn't going to explain it to him. She would let him believe what he wanted.

"I only ask to be your patron...and your friend." He drew closer.

Lisette focused on his dark eyes. *My patron?* she wondered. They had talked of patrons when they first met, during Vernet's exhibition at the Louvre. Today, she hadn't expected him to offer his patronage. Lisette didn't know how to respond, so she said nothing.

"Let me explain. As your patron, I would expect that you create art for me when I ask for it. This is in exchange for my financial support, which would include the lessons and any supplies you would need."

Lessons and supplies, she repeated to herself. Lisette's head was spinning. She had dearly wanted unrestricted access to both for as long as she could remember.

"That is all? You don't want anything else in return?" she asked him. *How can I trust this man?* she asked herself.

"No...well yes, there is one thing I want in return...," he said.

Lisette felt a lump form in her throat. Then she saw a smile come over his face.

"I ask that you accompany me to the best salon in all of Paris."

"Salon?" Lisette asked. *Why would he want to go to the Salon with me?* she wondered.

"Have you been to a salon?" Amante asked.

"Of course, many times, since I was a child. My papa and I never missed the Salon de Paris."

Amante let out a low laugh.

"What is so amusing?" Lisette didn't like that he was laughing at her.

"I'm not speaking of the art Salon at the Palais du Louvre...I'm talking about the private salons where only the most intriguing Parisians can be found discussing everything from music and art to the King's ministers...like Madame de Tougereau's salon."

Lisette understood the difference. "I have heard they are dangerous." Her mother had talked about how they were places of ill-repute.

"Nonsense. They are where talented men *and* women can freely express themselves. Artists, musicians, writers, poets and diplomats. I think you would fit in wonderfully." Amante moved his chair closer to Lisette's.

She had to control her breathing as she watched him move toward her. "My mother always told me that they aren't for respectable women."

Amante's chair was now so close, his leg pressed against hers. "Oh, *ma chérie*, quite the opposite. They are magnificent affairs where only the most accomplished and clever women gather. There are married women, widowed women, single women...all types of women. I assure you, you would be most welcome. Madame de Tougereau is well-known for her support of artists. Not only is she an avid collector, but she is highly astute. Last year she sold a pair of paintings by Van Loo to Catherine the Great. The rumor is that she sold them for 30,000 *livres* when she only paid 12,000 *livres* on commission just ten years ago. She is well-connected and can no doubt help you. She reserves Wednesday evenings for artists to gather. I would be honored to have you accompany me."

Lisette could not concentrate with Amante being so near. His eyes penetrated her, as he waited for her to agree. Lisette wanted to say *yes* to all of it, but at the same time she wasn't sure she should. Lisette had to consider Le Sèvre. She wavered in her head.

How can I turn away from this? she thought. "Yes," she answered. Lisette couldn't say *no* to the things she had always wanted. She was willing to accept the risks.

"Marvelous!" He leaned over like he was about to kiss her and Lisette quickly pulled herself away from the table.

What is he doing? Lisette thought. This was the second time he had tried to kiss her. She had not given him permission at the Louvre or just now.

As she moved away from him, she glanced in the mirror directly opposite their table. On the far side of the pavilion her mother and Le Sèvre were sitting down at a table. She saw her mother looking around the *café*. Lisette stood and carefully turned around so that they could not recognize her.

"I have to leave." Lisette barely glimpsed at Amante as she rushed out of the *café*.

She heard Amante call after her, "I'll send word when the lessons are arranged."

Lisette quickly walked home. She wanted to be there when her mother and Le Sèvre returned. As she hurried back, she thought about her conversation with Amante. She was going to start lessons with Briard soon. Her pulse quickened. *What will Briard have me paint first?* she asked herself. She also wondered when the lessons would begin. Amante had said that he would send word.

Then her thoughts moved from her lessons to Amante. There were so many questions running through her head about him. What would it mean if he was her patron? What did he really want from her? Why had he tried to kiss her without her permission – again? Her stomach flipped when she remembered his face, especially his dark eyes and full lips. Then she wondered what those full lips would feel like on hers.

Chapter Twenty

Today was Lisette's first lesson with Briard. The message had arrived from Amante the day before. He had been true to his word. Moving quickly, Amante had arranged Lisette's lessons in just a week. Lisette was ready. She had been dressed for an hour. She wore a short, fitted icy-blue jacket with a coordinating petticoat, both made of cotton and trimmed with white gauze. Her mother had insisted on cotton, the most fashionable material, for Lisette's new clothes. Lisette liked how the soft fabric allowed for flexibility when painting. It was also much lighter than her older woolen clothes. Now that summer had arrived, Lisette was happy to wear the thinner fabric. As she inspected herself in the looking glass, Lisette felt carefree like a little girl.

She was so distracted thinking about her lesson, Lisette barely heard the knock at her door. "Come in," she called out.

Her mother opened the door and came into her room. "Lisette, your father and I are leaving. We will return at a late hour," Jeanne said.

Lisette cringed at the word *father*. Why did her mother insist on calling Le Sèvre her father?

Jeanne beheld Lisette. "You look especially becoming today. Are you expecting a sitter? I thought everyone wanted to see the Joyous Entry. Even peasants from the countryside will have walked throughout the night to see the Dauphin and Dauphine."

Her mother was right that the streets would be full of people waiting to see the royal procession, but Lisette would not be one of them. Today, she would be occupied with painting and attending her first lesson with Briard at the Louvre.

"No, I don't have any sittings scheduled. I need to add the finishing touches on a painting today," Lisette said, leaving out her plans to see Master Briard. When her mother frowned, she added, "I might try to catch a glimpse of the Dauphin and Dauphine later when their carriage enters the Tuileries."

"But that won't be for hours, not until after they are finished with Mass at the cathedral. They are to dine later in the day at the Tuileries."

"It will give me time to paint, Mother."

"Would you like to accompany your father and me? We could watch the royal couple's entrance as a family," Jeanne implored as she fidgeted with her dress.

As usual, Lisette's mother donned her finest apparel. She was wearing one of her best silk gowns and matching silk shoes. Both the sack-back dress and coordinating petticoat were patterned with tiny flowers set against a lemon yellow background. The yellow and white stomacher that laid against her chest was embroidered with Le Sèvre's best jewels. Lisette noticed more jewels embedded in her *coiffure*. Jeanne Vigée was stunning with her dark hair piled up high on her head and held together by a yellow silk ribbon.

"No, thank you, Mother. I plan to watch from our terrace,"

Lisette replied.

She and her mother had been playing this game for months now. Jeanne would ask her to join them on an outing and she would decline. Her mother never pushed it further. Sometimes, Lisette stretched the truth in order to satisfy her mother, which she didn't like, but playing this charade seemed to suit both of them, so Lisette participated.

"You should have a good view from there." Jeanne turned to leave. "I will see you later tonight."

As she watched her mother withdraw, Lisette realized she was fortunate that her first lesson with Master Briard coincided with the Joyous Entry. Being such a momentous event, it had seemed odd that Briard had agreed to a lesson on this day, but Lisette had determined that Briard must be the most serious of artists if he would not allow a royal parade to interfere with his work, even if it was Marie-Antoinette's first official visit to Paris since her arrival in France over three years ago. Lisette agreed with Briard wholeheartedly.

Her mother, on the other hand, had been talking about to-day's parade for weeks. She and Le Sèvre were going to join the masses and try to spot the Dauphine and Dauphin in their royal carriage as it processed through the streets of Paris.

Today, Lisette could easily sneak out of the house, go to her lesson and return home without Le Sèvre knowing. Lisette had heard her mother and Le Sèvre discussing which dinners and suppers to attend after the ceremonial parade. They would be gone for many hours.

Lisette checked her appearance in the looking glass one last time and picked up her satchel of supplies. Then she made her way out of her bedroom.

Before leaving, she made a quick detour down to the kitchen. Mademoiselle Tothier had gathered a small meal of bread, cheese and apples. To express her gratitude, Lisette gave Mademoiselle Tothier a few *sous*. Lisette wrapped the food in a small linen cloth and tucked it in her satchel.

When she went back upstairs to the front vestibule, she made sure that her mother and Le Sèvre had already gone. Lisette then left the house and went onto the street.

Looking in both directions, Lisette saw that the Rue Saint-Honoré was already starting to fill. She noticed many changes to the streets. From what her mother had said, city officials had been busy for weeks preparing for the Joyous Entry. Thousands of beggars, prostitutes and cattle had been cleared from the royal path. Vendors had been prohibited from opening along the parade route and most shops had been closed, bringing commerce to a halt in one of the busiest cities in the world. But what struck Lisette most, were the millions of flower petals covering the path that the royal carriage would follow.

Wasting no time, Lisette made her way down to the end of the Rue Saint-Honoré. She had decided on a route that would take her away from the crowds. It would be less direct, but she would be sure to arrive on time. Lisette planned to walk all the way around to the Cour Carrée, the far eastern courtyard of the Palais du Louvre.

She would take the Rue Saint-Honoré to where it intersected with Rue de L'Arbre Sec, travel down that street to the Rue des Fossés-Saint-Germain-l'Auxerrois, then around the houses in front of the Church of Saint-Germain-l'Auxerrois and into the Cour Carrée.

Lisette could find the Louvre in her sleep, she had been there so many times with her papa. She also knew the inside of the palace, or at least where the large exhibition galleries were located. Less familiar were the residential areas of the palace where artists lived and worked. She had visited an artist's lodgings in the Palais du Louvre only once before, when she had accompanied her papa to see Vernet's exhibition.

Lisette made rapid progress and after only a quarter of an hour had passed, she had walked down the length of the Rue de L'Arbre Sec. Her longer route through familiar streets had actually saved her time because she had avoided the quickly gathering masses.

As soon as Lisette turned the corner onto the Rue des Fossés-Saint-Germain-l'Auxerrois, she immediately stopped. It seemed as if every Parisian was outside lining both sides of the street waiting for the royal procession. People were simply standing still, anticipating the Dauphin and Dauphine's arrival. Lisette could barely move forward. *I have to get there*, she thought.

Lisette began pushing until she was on the other side of the street. She decided to abandon the Rue des Fossés-Saint-Germain-l'Auxerrois and find a less congested access point to the Louvre. Lisette spotted a narrow alleyway and headed toward it.

"Watch out! Where are you going? Why are you walking in that direction? The Dauphin and Dauphine will be coming down *this* street. You are going the wrong way you stupid girl!" a fishmonger woman squawked at Lisette. The woman wore a gray dress covered with a long white apron and smelled of rotting fish.

Saying nothing, Lisette stepped around her. *She's right about the parade route*, Lisette thought. The four royal carriages would be traveling toward the Pont Neuf to make their way to the Cathédrale Notre-Dame de Paris. Lisette had no choice. Being this close to the Louvre, it might be impossible to avoid the crowds. *I must keep walking*, she realized.

Lisette continued to forge her way through the people and toward the alleyway. She had nearly finished crossing the street when she tripped and her art supplies tumbled out of her satchel and scattered everywhere. No one noticed. The crowd was caught up in the excitement of the royal couple's impending arrival. People trampled her supplies without realizing it. "Stop! Let me pick up my belongings!" Lisette shouted, but no one paid her any attention. When she bent to collect her brushes and tools, she felt her body being pushed down. The collective weight of the crowd then tipped her off balance and onto the ground. She knew that if she didn't stand up soon, she might be crushed to death.

"Mademoiselle, let me help you." Before she could see who was speaking to her, she felt her body being pulled up so that she was standing again. It was Henri.

"I saw you leave the house and thought you might need some help today. Mademoiselle Tothier told me where you were headed."

Lisette smiled at him. Although she was dubious about his ability to navigate through so many people, she was grateful for the assistance.

"Thank you, Henri," Lisette said.

Henri gathered her remaining art supplies. Once he had collected everything, he turned to Lisette and said, "Follow me, Mademoiselle Lisette." Henri pushed his way through the crowd, parting the people in front of them like he was clearing tall jungle weeds with a machete.

Lisette watched in amazement as he easily maneuvered through the throng. She no longer doubted his ability to help her.

He looked back at her and smiled. "We'll be there in no time."

"Why don't we travel down that passageway over there?" Lisette asked as she pointed toward the alley where she had been headed before she fell.

"No. It doesn't lead anywhere. Unfortunately we must force our way through this crowd. The entrance to the Cour Carrée is on the other side of this street," Henri said confidently.

Henri led the way, creating a path for them through the people. They hadn't made much progress when the fanfare began.

Lisette heard cannons fired at the Invalides, the Bastille and the Hôtel de Ville announcing the arrival of the royal couple, just as her mother had described to her.

"The royal couple has entered the city gate!" Lisette heard a woman exclaim.

"They will pass by here shortly!" she heard another woman say.

Lisette listened to the blaring trumpets at the head of the royal procession. Even though the trumpets grew louder as the carriages approached, they were quickly drowned out by the cheering and singing of the crowds. Although not everyone was engrossed in the merriment. Many pushed and elbowed each other. Lisette witnessed several fights erupt over precious street space that offered unobstructed views of the parade. The onlookers who appeared satisfied with their viewpoint craned their necks to see the Dauphin and Dauphine.

Lisette then heard the clappity-clop of the horses' hooves on the cobblestones and the creaking of the wheels. *The royal carriages,* Lisette thought. *They are almost here.* Lisette found herself swept up in the excitement. The collective energy of the crowd was contagious. She felt her heart beat faster. She had never seen the Dauphine or Dauphin.

Lisette motioned for Henri to stop. Like everyone else on the street, Lisette and Henri waited for the carriages to pass. *I will never be able to see the carriages through all of these people,* she thought.

Then, through a tiny space in between heads in the crowd, Lisette saw it. The carriage that held the Dauphine and Dauphin moved so slowly that for several moments she had a clear view of Marie-Antoinette. Lisette saw a young woman exquisitely dressed in the finest silks with an elaborate *coiffure* complete with embedded jewels and feathers. A lovely shade of soft yellow, her hair was much paler than Lisette had imagined. Marie-Antoinette waved at the onlookers with her bejeweled, white gloved hand. *She is breathtaking,* Lisette thought. She was unable to look away.

No sooner had the carriage passed, when Lisette remembered her lesson. She turned to Henri who held her satchel. He pointed in the direction of the Louvre. It was well within eyesight, just a few hundred paces away. Satisfied, the crowd simmered down. The onlookers stopped pushing and fighting each other. For the most part, everyone stood still. Lisette and Henri took advantage of the collective calm and easily maneuvered in between the people.

"Thank you, Henri, but I can make it from here on my own," Lisette told him.

"I can escort you to the door."

Lisette shook her head *no*. "Thank you again for your help." She reached out for her satchel and Henri handed it to her.

"Your secret is safe with me, Mademoiselle Lisette. Monsieur Le Sèvre won't find out." Henri bowed slightly to her and then started off in the direction of the house.

Lisette quickly moved toward the Louvre. She had to prevent her legs from skipping like a school girl's. *I wonder if Briard will have me copy a statue or a painting first,* she wondered.

Lisette stood in front of the doors to the Louvre, waiting a few moments before going inside. It felt strange to enter the Louvre without her papa. The noises from the massive crowds behind her in the Cour Carrée disappeared as she thought about him. She remembered his words, *You will be a painter, my child!*

She knew it was time to go inside. Before Lisette could take two steps toward the door, she was nearly knocked over by several young men running into the building. Shouting and laughing, they swept past Lisette and swung open the large door in front of her. One of the young men whacked her with his satchel as he ran past. The force was so strong Lisette lost her grip on her own satchel and it dropped to the ground.

Lisette picked up her bag and took a moment to compose herself. Just as she was ready to go inside, another group of boys ran past her and into the building again. This time she was prepared and stepped aside to let them pass. They didn't seem to notice her at all. *This must be the door that the students use,* she thought.

But then Lisette had another thought, *What am I doing here with all of these boys?* She stood watching the heavy door slowly close after the boys had gone inside.

Then a boy by himself, obviously a straggler, came up next to her.

"Are you going in? Could you open the door?" The boy was carrying a satchel like hers in one hand and in the other he held a folded easel. Lisette looked at him. She wasn't sure he was talking to her. "Well? Aren't you going inside? To Master Briard's *atelier*?" the boy asked her.

She looked at him again, puzzled. *How did he know?* she wondered.

"Don't look so confused. You are a girl *and* you are holding a satchel meant for carrying art supplies *and* you are standing in front of the entrance for students. You must be a pupil of Master Briard. He is the only one that teaches girls. Are you going to stand there or are you going to help me?"

Lisette opened the door for him.

"Thank you. Monsieur Briard's *atelier* is in the southwest pavilion, down the fourth corridor on the left, after the Salon Carré," the boy said and ran off.

Lisette went inside. She immediately turned south and west toward the correct pavilion. Then she walked down the hall looking for the fourth corridor the boy had mentioned. There were so many rooms and hallways that led away from the hall, it was difficult to keep track of how many she had already passed. Lisette stopped walking and looked right, left and then right again. As she looked to her right for the second time, she noticed a grand room just a few feet away. *The Salon Carré*, she thought.

She instantly recognized the room. Lisette had been there many times before with her papa. The last time she had stood in this room, she had met Amante. She thought about that day. Her papa had fallen ill with a bad coughing spell. It was just weeks before he would be dead.

Lisette entered the room. The academicians were preparing for the upcoming Salon de Paris. There were paintings hung on every available space on each wall. Some were hung so high Lisette could barely see them. She had to squint to see even the largest figures in those paintings. Lisette focused instead on the ones that were lower on the wall.

One in particular caught her attention, a painting by Chardin. It depicted a scullery maid drawing water from a copper cistern. She recognized Chardin's hand because she had seen his work in previous years' Salons at the Louvre. Chardin's paintings had grown immensely popular with the Parisian crowds. His genre paintings conveyed a sentimentalism and simplicity about everyday life to which Salon viewers had responded favorably.

Because her papa had wanted Lisette to see what current artists were creating, he had insisted Lisette accompany him. *Papa*, she thought. She missed him tremendously. Lisette reached into her pocket bag and pulled out her papa's watch. As she looked at it, she expected herself to cry, but instead she felt a warm sensation come over her body. To Lisette, it was as if he was standing next to her. She could hear her papa explaining the paintings and answering all of her questions. Hearing his voice inside her head imparted a calmness.

She returned the watch to her pocket and stood tall. *I belong here,* she thought. *Even with all of the boys.*

Lisette scanned the wall again and noticed another familiar artist, Vernet. His large canvas was hung high, near the ceiling.

As she stood on her tip-toes to get a better view of Vernet's painting, someone tapped her on the shoulder. Lisette let out a shriek. She turned around and saw a young woman, who appeared the same age, standing right behind her.

"Chardin has successfully captured the simple nature of a scullery maid's life, hasn't he?" the young woman asked with an air of familiarity, as if they had been friends for years.

"Yes, he has —" Lisette stopped herself from completing her

thought. "Why did you tap me?" Lisette asked.

"Oh, I apologize. I thought if I touched you first, you would be less alarmed when I spoke. You seemed so engrossed in the painting."

"I must be −" Lisette had been distracted by the paintings and by the memories of attending the art exhibitions with her papa, but she needed to get to her lesson.

The girl spoke over Lisette. "My mother says I am like a savage from the wilderness of the New World. I'm much too quiet when I approach someone who is unsuspecting."

"I must be going..." Once again, Lisette tried to leave, but the girl continued to talk.

"She has told me that I better not sneak up on my betrothed and especially not after he is my husband. I am marrying Monsieur Jacques Coupé next spring. He is a clerk in a notary's office and hopes to one day succeed the notary." The girl stood taller as she said the word *marrying*.

"I really must leave. Good day," Lisette finally managed to say. She didn't have time to chat. She couldn't be late for her first lesson.

Lisette left the grand room. She counted four corridors and then turned left, not sure if it led to Briard's or not. Lisette quickened her pace. *Good. I've left that girl behind,* Lisette thought.

"You are going the wrong way. You should be headed down that hallway back there," the girl said confidently. She pointed in back of them to a hall on the other side of the Salon Carré. The girl had caught up to Lisette and was now beside her.

"How do you know where I am going?" Lisette stopped walking and turned to face this irritating girl. "Who are you? Do you know who I am?"

"My name is Rosalie Bocquet. And I believe you are Mademoiselle Élisabeth Vigée, daughter of the Guild painter Louis Vigée. Everyone calls you Lisette. You are not yet married or betrothed."

How did the girl know who she was? How did she know so much about her? Lisette didn't know how to respond.

"We are both here to learn from Master Briard."

"You are too?" Lisette asked.

"Yes, I began my lessons a few weeks ago. He told me at our last lesson that you would be joining us."

"You mean we don't each have private lessons?"

"No. But I don't mind in the least. Now there will be three of us: you, Adélaïde and me. I enjoy talking while we work, but Master Briard does not allow it when he is present. Luckily, Master Briard often leaves the studio for minutes at a time and we are free to chat then. Mother says that I have a great ability to talk to anyone and everyone."

Lisette felt her heart sink. She didn't want to share the precious time she would have with her new master instructor with anyone...and from what she had seen of Rosalie so far, especially not her. Like Briard, Lisette wasn't fond of talking while she painted, unless it was required during a portrait sitting. When she worked on her own, she preferred quiet. How would Lisette concentrate on her work with Rosalie's incessant chatter?

Until then, Lisette and Rosalie had been alone in the hall. Out of nowhere, a small band of boys approached them. Lisette recognized two of the boys. They had run past her at the entrance to the Louvre.

"Oh, Nicolas, look what we have here. A couple of pretty girls." The boy who spoke was at least a head taller than the rest and seemed to Lisette to be their leader. "How about a kiss?" The boy's face nearly touched Rosalie's as he puckered his lips.

Lisette immediately moved in between Rosalie and the boy. "Leave her alone. Now let us pass," Lisette ordered him. She found her most serious voice.

The boy appeared to be younger than Lisette, but he was much taller and stronger. She knew that she could not win a physical confrontation, but she hoped that she could convince him to go away.

The boy turned to his friends. "Did you hear that? This one wants me to let them pass." He let out a low, sinister laugh. "What is that smell?" He came up close to Lisette and sniffed her. "You have an awful stench! You smell like one of us," he said with contempt.

"There is absolutely nothing wrong with the way I smell. Now let us pass," Lisette repeated herself.

The boy then sniffed Rosalie. "You should smell more like her. She smells the way a girl should smell. Ahh...lavender perfume."

Lisette took advantage of the boy's distraction with the lavender perfume and grabbed Rosalie's hand, leading her away from the group of bullies.

One of the other boys yelled after them, "We'll finish this later!"

Lisette darted toward the hall that Rosalie had pointed to just before they were interrupted. The boys must have decided that it wasn't worth the trouble, because instead of following Lisette and Rosalie, they headed in the opposite direction.

Rosalie looked back, let out a sigh and stopped. She dropped Lisette's hand. "Thank you. I don't know what I would have done if you hadn't been there with me." She was out of breath and seemed to be having a difficult time calming herself.

"I don't think it is safe for a girl to be alone in these halls," Lisette said.

Rosalie jerked her head up and down in quick movements. "Yes...yes...absolutely." She struggled to catch her breath. "Lisette, why did they say you smell awful?" Rosalie asked her. She came up to Lisette and inhaled deeply. "Oh...turpentine. You smell of turpentine."

"I was using it earlier this morning. Why does it matter?" Lisette didn't expect an answer. She didn't care about smelling like turpentine. She was more concerned about the boys. Lisette couldn't escape the feeling that the boys wanted to hurt them and to take away their honor, especially if either of them had been alone. "Rosalie, why don't we meet somewhere in between our houses and walk here together?"

"Yes, I would very much like that," Rosalie replied.

"Are you too shaken to work today?" Lisette asked her. Before Rosalie could answer, Lisette saw a man with red and gray hair that was streaked with white paint poke his head out of a nearby door.

"There you two are. I see Rosalie found you, Lisette," he said.

This is Master Briard? Lisette wondered. He looked more like a street performer than a master painter.

Briard had a concerned look on his face. "I thought maybe the two of you were swept up in all this Joyous Entry fanfare and commotion."

"Master Briard." Lisette politely curtsied to introduce herself.

"Come inside. We have a lot of work to do today."

Lisette looked Briard directly in the eye as she went toward the door. "Master Briard, I am ready to work diligently for you."

"So I have heard. Capitaine de Chaumont speaks very highly of you. I don't usually accept pupils based solely on the recommendation of a patron. However, I hold the *capitiane* in the highest regard. I trust his judgment." Briard was serious, but kind at the same time.

He turned to Rosalie. "Come in and get settled. Adélaïde is already here."

Then he turned back to Lisette, "We must get started. We are going to begin by copying this statue by Giambologna, *The Seduction of the Sabine Women.*"

Lisette was beside herself. She stood in the doorway gaping at the Florentine sculpture. She couldn't take her eyes off of it. Was she really allowed to copy this statue? All three figures were nude, including two men.

Briard came over to the door. "You look worried, Lisette. Don't be. Not only are you allowed to copy these nude figures,

171

but I fully expect you to make strides in your ability to accurately capture the musculature and bone structure. Rosalie will show you where to store your belongings."

Rosalie went in first and Lisette followed her. She watched Rosalie carefully remove her cap and gently place her lunch basket on the floor next to the window. Then Lisette saw another young woman standing at an easel.

"Lisette, this is Adélaïde de La Valette," Briard said.

Adélaïde turned and regarded Lisette. She smiled briefly. Lisette returned the smile.

Then Rosalie whispered to Lisette, "She is from the La Valette family. You must curtsy to her."

Lisette did as Rosalie said.

The girl smiled again, this time at both of them, but said nothing.

"Good. Introductions are over. Let's begin, girls. Get to your easels and start copying," Brird said, pointing to the statue in the middle of the room.

Once again, Lisette gaped in amazement at the statue. It was magnificent. She had never copied full nude figures from life-size sculptures. She had only reproduced the human figure from paintings and drawings. While this wasn't a live nude to draw from, it was better than a two-dimensional painting. It would have to suffice, because female students were not permitted to learn from live nudes, neither male nor female models.

Lisette allowed her excitement to take over and she ran to her easel. She dropped her satchel on the floor and immediately picked up the charcoal sitting on the easel's ledge. *Now which figure should I sketch first...*

Chapter Twenty-One

This carriage looks taken too, Lisette thought. She watched in frustration as another carriage passed without stopping for her. That had been the fifth one in a row. Lisette had been standing on the Rue Saint-Honoré, just down from her house, for nearly a quarter of an hour. She was trying to hail a *fiacre*. At this time of night, there were many of the four-wheeled carriages out on the streets. It was the hour before theater performances began. It seemed to Lisette as if all of Paris was already in a carriage.

Lisette shivered. The cool, damp air sent a chill that went straight through her. She pulled her cloak tighter around her body. As she waited for an empty carriage, she thought, *Why did I agree to this?* Lisette wished she was back in her warm room working on the new techniques Briard had recently demonstrated.

I wouldn't have the lessons without Amante's help, she reminded herself. During the past five months, Lisette had learned many new methods from Briard. She couldn't lose Amante's support now. It was time for Lisette to fulfill her end of their bargain. Tonight, she would meet Amante at the Salonnière's house for the Wednesday evening salon.

At least I'm not standing out here in the dark, she thought. Lisette noticed that the many street lamps had just been lit for the night. Their flickering mimicked the people's movements as they hurried to their destinations. It always amazed Lisette that the streets were nearly as busy in the evening as in the early morning hours when servants scurried to fetch their daily foodstuffs and supplies.

Lisette swiftly raised her arm when she saw what looked like an empty *fiacre* coming toward her. The carriage stopped and Lisette climbed inside. She told the driver to take her to 976 Rue du Faubourg Saint-Honoré. Although the Salonnière's home was on the same street as Le Sèvre's house, it was located on the opposite end, in the Marais du Faubourg Saint-Honoré, near the Champs-Élysées. Lisette prepared herself to be impressed. The Marais du Faubourg Saint-Honoré was home to some of Paris' most illustrious and wealthiest denizens. It was less congested than where Lisette lived and where one could find grandiose homes on spacious plots of land.

The carriage started moving and Lisette immediately felt the uneven road. The wooden wheels never easily navigated the irregular Paris streets, but tonight, the ride seemed bumpier than usual. Lisette's stomach churned. *Maybe if I close my eyes, I won't notice,* she thought.

After what seemed like hours, Lisette heard the driver shout, "976 Rue du Faubourg Saint-Honoré, Mademoiselle." Lisette's carriage had arrived behind several others, so she could not immediately disembark. While waiting in the queue of carriages, Lisette surveyed the Salonnière's home. Just as she had suspected, everything about it was grand. The deep forecourt was large enough to accommodate a six-horse royal coach and the semi-circular façade was intimidating with its enormously tall, broad columns. It took Lisette a few moments to take in the entire building. The house was the size of at least ten apartments like the one she had lived in with her papa on the Rue de Coquillière.

After several minutes, Lisette's carriage pulled up to the head of the line. She paid the driver and descended from the carriage. Lisette then searched for Amante in the forecourt where he had said he would be waiting for her. Although she would have preferred to enter on her own, Lisette had reluctantly a-greed to go inside with him. Amante had been willing to arrive in separate carriages, which she knew was a significant concession for any man.

As she stood waiting for him, Lisette wondered what she would encounter once inside the grand house. She only knew what her mother had said about salons. Amante had told Lisette that her mother's notions were misguided and that salons were places where intelligent, artistic women could freely speak their minds, especially on important issues of the day. Lisette did not have much knowledge of state policies or foreign affairs, but she was eager to discuss painting. Amante had also said that the men who attended respectfully listened to each woman's opinions. Lisette was doubtful. She would have to see for herself.

Lisette watched half a dozen men and women enter the Salonnière's house. *Where is he?* she wondered. It was cold and Lisette wanted to go inside where it was warm. She surveyed each carriage that approached, hoping Amante would appear. After several more carriages let out salon-goers, Lisette considered going in by herself. She turned and faced the front door. Just as she was about to take her first step toward it, she heard a deep male voice call out to her, "Lisette!"

Amante stepped out of his carriage and approached her. Immediately, her stomach fluttered. He wore his officer's uniform

175

of the royal blue waistcoat adorned with red collars and cuffs. His dark hair was not covered with a wig or white powder, but was pulled back and tied together at the nape of his neck. It smelled of apples and almonds and looked shiny, like it had been smoothed out with a pomade. She also noticed he was freshly shaven. Her hand wanted to reach up and touch his smooth cheek.

"Lisette, you are gorgeous this evening," he said. Amante quickly kissed her hand, but took his time releasing it. He allowed his gaze to linger too.

Lisette looked away and turned toward the front door. "Shall we go in?"

"Yes, but first I need to tell you what you'll encounter and how you'll be expected to behave."

"What do you mean? I've been to the Palais Royal, to the Tuileries —"

He interrupted her, "This is somewhat the same, but a little different from those places. You should watch your manners and be sure to defer to nobility, but there is more."

Lisette listened, but she was sure she already knew how to behave. She had paid attention to the etiquette lectures given at the Convent of the Trinité and those from her mother. To Lisette, this felt similar.

"They will expect that you already know their names. More importantly, they will be looking for your witty responses during conversation, so be prepared to offer clever banter. Try to always have the last word and to leave the group laughing, but never laugh at your own repartee. That is the mark of a good *salonnière*."

"But I don't want to be a *salonnière*. I am an artist."

"Tonight you will be both. Many important artists will be in attendance, along with musicians and poets. They utilize these salons as places to showcase their cleverness and their talent. You should seize this opportunity as well. If you show them how amusing and bright you are, you will attract more commissions.

I promise."

"But I don't want to act like some child who only makes people laugh. I take my work seriously."

"And you should convey your earnestness, but you should also demonstrate that you can be witty and enchanting. You'll see you don't have to act like a child at all. Quite the opposite. Salons are the domain of serious women...women who want to be known as writers, artists, musicians and intellectuals." His eyes danced as he looked at her.

"I think you are going to enjoy this, now let's go inside." Amante extended his arm, Lisette took it and they walked in together.

After entering the house, they waited for a servant to announce their presence in the front vestibule. As they waited, Lisette inspected the entryway. She saw more *objects d'art* than she could count. The foyer was full of marble busts, gold candelabras and crystal vases. Lisette noticed a particular pair of tall crystal vases with delicate flowers etched on either side. Le Sèvre owned a similar pair, but these were much larger. If these vases were also from the glassworks in Baccarat, Lisette could only imagine their worth. Based on the sumptuousness of this front room, Lisette expected the rest of the home to be equally luxurious.

As they handed their outer coats to the footman, a grand-looking woman approached them. She appeared just as lavish as her house. Lisette had never seen such a woman before. Her very presence was enrapturing. She floated toward them.

"Ah, Amante! How delightful it is to see you. And this must be the young Venus that you said you would bring to me. You are right. She is quite a goddess." She and Amante embraced.

I'm a Venus? Lisette thought. She had never heard anyone describe her that way. Lisette wasn't sure how she felt about being labeled the goddess of love.

"Marguerite, you look absolutely stunning, as always." Amante kissed her hand and then turned toward Lisette. "Yes, this is Mademoiselle Élisabeth Vigée."

Lisette curtsied slightly to Marguerite. "I am pleased to meet you, Madame."

"May I present, Madame de Tougereau." Amante finished the formal introductions.

Marguerite proceeded to scan Lisette's body from head to toe and then nodded with approval. "You have discovered quite a beauty....and you say she can paint too?"

"Very well," Amante replied.

The Salonnière took Lisette's hands and placed them in her own. This woman had the supplest skin Lisette had ever touched. Lisette was sure Marguerite would be put off by her hands. She looked down at them. They were rough with nails that had dark paint embedded underneath, but the large, white scars across their backs embarrassed Lisette most. She pulled her hands out of Marguerite's.

The Salonnière picked them up again. "My dear, don't ever be ashamed of any part of your body. And don't be embarrassed about what your hands might reveal about you. Embrace these extraordinary tools." Marguerite slowly released Lisette's hands.

Lisette didn't know what to say to this woman. No one had ever told her to be proud of any part of her body, let alone a part that had been forever scarred. The Salonnière's words were strangely comforting.

Marguerite placed her hands on Lisette's shoulders and slid them slowly down her arms, her eyes following her hands' every movement. To Lisette, Marguerite seemed to be inspecting a fine piece of porcelain. "Exquisite. Just exquisite. My dear, you could be the next sensation in Paris. Are you ready for that?"

Lisette didn't know how to respond, so she remained silent.

Marguerite continued, "Of course we will have to improve your fashion choices." She grabbed a handful of fabric from Lisette's gown and shook her head disapprovingly. "This gown is merely adequate."

Lisette wore a simple red and white striped silk gown that

closed in the front and had a matching petticoat. It was one of the new gowns that her mother had bought with Le Sèvre's money. *Aren't stripes fashionable?* she thought.

Marguerite then studied Lisette's face. "You need a dress that better compliments your coloring. Stripes are very fashionable, but not red. Red does not bring out your eyes." Then she looked at Lisette's white *fichu*. It was covering the bare skin that her gown's low neckline exposed. Her mother insisted that all modest women wore them. "Please, no false modesty here. No need for a *fichu*." Marguerite's eyes continued making their way down Lisette's body. Next, she examined Lisette's waist. "What is this?" Marguerite pulled out her papa's watch that had been carefully tucked into her dress. The Salonnière held it up. "Is this yours? What are you doing with a man's pocket watch?"

"It was my papa's." Lisette held out her hand.

"Marguerite! Stop harassing her. You've only just met. Wait at least five minutes before you try to transform her." Amante's voice had a playful tone, but his eyes were serious.

"My dear, it is so masculine. That won't do at all." She shook her head in disapproval.

Lisette didn't care if this woman approved or not. She would never stop wearing her papa's watch. It was all she had left of him. Lisette kept her hand extended waiting for Marguerite to return the watch.

Marguerite looked at Amante who nodded and then she reluctantly handed it back to Lisette.

"Thank you, Madame de Tougereau," Lisette said as she quickly tucked the watch into the waist of her dress.

"Marguerite! Call me Marguerite. And never Madame, it will forever be Mademoiselle. I answer to no man." Then she leaned in and whispered, "But plenty of men answer to me!" She gently squeezed Lisette's hand. Her eyes revealed a special kind of confidence that Lisette had never seen in another woman before.

"Yes, Marguerite, you are a legendary enchantress," Amante said.

"Well, my dear Amante, you are also a notorious flirt. Although I have yet to hear a single complaint from any of your women friends."

Lisette couldn't help but wonder exactly what Marguerite meant by "women friends."

Marguerite shooed them away with her hands. "Mingle and have a wonderful evening!"

As they walked out of the entry hall and into the large drawing room, Amante said in a low voice, "Marguerite can be overwhelming at first, but she means well. She has a generous heart. I think the two of you can be good friends."

When they entered the drawing room, Lisette was immediately impressed. It was a circular space with a high ceiling topped by a cupola. The elaborateness of the interior *décor* matched the extravagant design of the architecture. Lisette first noticed the window hangings. The green and pink striped silk curtains ended in a profusion of tassels tied together with pink silk ribbons. The upholstery on the *canapé* and *bergère* chairs was of the same patterned silk. Made of rosewood, the tables and desks were similar to those Lisette had seen at the Tuileries Palace. Everywhere she looked there was bronze ornament: at the corners of the ceiling, on the door handles and running up the table legs. *It is all so exquisite,* she thought.

Lisette turned her attention to the other guests. She had never seen so many women gathered together for the sole purpose of discussing art, music, philosophy and politics. The men in the room were hanging on their every word. Lisette witnessed no improprieties, only people conversing and laughing. Her mother could not have been more wrong about salons.

"I think you would enjoy talking with these artists, *ma chérie.*" Amante pointed to a group of men in the corner of the room and then turned as if he was going to leave her.

"Are you not coming with me?" Lisette asked. She wasn't sure she was ready to be on her own. She didn't know what she would say to them.

"*Ma chérie*, you don't need me. Talk about your painting. I will find you soon," Amante said as he walked away.

Lisette watched Amante confidently stride across the room and approach three very beautiful women. She noticed that they were all responding to him, leaning over just enough to display their deep *décolletage*. Their low-cut dresses pushed their bosoms together so that they nearly spilled out of their plunging neck-lines. They were also noticeably missing *fichus*. Lisette considered removing hers. *Would Amante be by my side if I wasn't wearing one? But I want to be heard, not ogled for my bust*, she thought.

Lisette saw Amante playfully touch their arms. He even went as far as placing his hand on the small of one woman's back. Lisette couldn't watch anymore.

As she turned toward the group of artists and considered whether or not to approach them, Marguerite came up to her.

"I can introduce you. Come." Marguerite grabbed Lisette's arm and escorted her over to the group. The men stopped talking when she approached. They all looked at Marguerite waiting for her to speak.

"Messieurs, may I present Mademoiselle Vigée. She is an artist," Marguerite said.

Lisette addressed the group, acknowledging each one. As they introduced themselves, she recognized many of their names. She had heard her papa talk about them. Several were members of the Académie Royale.

When Marguerite had finished introductions, she left. She headed toward another group huddled on the opposite side of the room. As Lisette watched her float away, she wondered why Marguerite would want to help her.

"Is your father Louis Vigée?" one of the older men asked. He had introduced himself as Monsieur Beauvais. His voice was welcoming.

"Yes, he was. He passed away last year." Lisette fingered the pocket watch as she spoke.

"I am very sorry to hear that. Your father attended many suppers at my home. He was a good man. I didn't know he had a daughter who painted," Beauvais said.

Lisette felt a twinge of pain in her side. *Why wouldn't Papa have mentioned to Monsieur Beauvais that I painted?* she wondered.

"What are you painting right now?" Monsieur Beauvais asked her eagerly.

Lisette wanted to discuss her allegories, but she didn't know if it was safe. She'd be openly admitting her defiance to Le Sèvre's orders. Lisette clenched her hand into a fist as she thought of Le Sèvre. *But how would he find out?* she asked herself. Lisette inhaled deeply, relaxed her hand and carefully considered her reply. "I am currently working on an allegory of the abduction of Helen of Troy."

Each and every one of their faces glowed. "Splendid! What a tremendous challenge and what a timely topic," another artist in the conversation said.

Monsieur Beauvais asked her, "Have you considered submitting it to the Académie?"

Lisette was flattered that Monsieur Beauvais thought her worthy of Académie membership, but it was the furthest thing from her mind.

One of the artists who had been silent spoke up, "But she is a woman! Is membership even possible?" The unattractive man had a large, hooked nose that he stuck up in the air when he talked. The others had been referring to him as Monsieur Cochin.

Monsieur Beauvais replied, "It is. But there are only four slots available to women at any given time. Right now, there is only one open position."

As she listened to them discuss Académie membership, Lisette knew that she could not concern herself with the Académie...not now and maybe not ever. Le Sèvre would never allow it.

Monsieur Cochin jerked his head up to speak again, when several others approached their group.

One of the newcomers abruptly interrupted, "You artists! You look far too serious! We are here to insert some levity into your sober conversation," said a rotund, jovial-looking man. He turned to Lisette, "My, my and who is this lovely young thing?"

Lisette introduced herself, "Élisabeth Louise Vigée."

"Well, aren't you an apricot *tartelette*! I'm sure every man here, well except for me, wants to eat you up!" He smiled at her cheerily and winked at Monsieur Cochin who threw him a disdainful look, stood and walked away.

"Oh, stop, Papille! You will scare her off. Why don't we talk about something else?" suggested Monsieur Beauvais.

Monsieur Papille lowered his head in what appeared to be false embarrassment, paused in silence for a moment and then said to the group, "Have you heard the latest..." Papille whispered loudly "...about the Dauphin's member?"

Lisette was shocked at hearing those words together in the same sentence, but she was intrigued. She moved in closer to hear him.

The rotund Monsieur Papille continued, "Well, apparently he has been unable to properly insert it into the Dauphine!"

There was a roar of laughter. "Impotent! The Dauphin is impotent!" Monsieur Papille's voice grew louder with every word. His careful exaggeration of every syllable added to the dramatic effect.

To Lisette, he seemed to be performing for them like an actor at the Comédie-Française. Papille's claim made Lisette wonder, *Was the Dauphin really impotent?* Lisette thought back to the beautiful Dauphine she had seen in the Joyous Entry procession months ago. *How could the Dauphin be impotent with such an alluring wife?* she thought.

Another man clamored, "That is why after three years of marriage there have been no children. Who thinks that the Dauphin doesn't enjoy copulation?"

There was a show of hands and then they exploded with laughter again.

Lisette thought back to her papa's dinner with Diderot. It had been the only other time she had heard such irreverence toward the royal family. She glanced around, afraid that they might be punished for their slanderous words, but no one stopped them. Lisette relaxed and allowed herself to enjoy the humorous banter.

A woman spoke up, "Monsieur Honet, whatever are you saying? A man not liking copulation? That is like a woman not liking diamonds!"

"True! Madame Genoux is quite right!" another wailed.

"But what about the King's diamond necklace for Madame du Barry?" Monsieur Papille asked.

"Yes, Monsieur Boehmer is supposedly collecting the diamonds for it now. When it is finished, it will be worth several million *livres*, enough to feed all of France for many, many years," Monsieur Honet explained.

"Absolutely disgraceful...the King depleting the treasury of France on a gift for *her*," Madame Genoux spoke with disdain.

"Agreed. Who is to say she will remain his whore? What if he loses interest?" another woman asked.

Lisette had heard her mother speak of Madame du Barry. She had only terrible things to say about the woman. Lisette never gave her much thought until now. She eagerly listened to what everyone said about the King's official mistress.

"You are quite right, Madame Jachet. I heard that du Barry is causing trouble again. The Dauphine refuses to acknowledge her and so du Barry is scheming against the Dauphine...using her influence with the King to turn him against Marie-Antoinette," Madame Genoux offered.

"Some say the Dauphine is being duped by the King's sisters," Monsieur Papille said.

"Those spinsters? Befriending them would make anyone miserable!" Madame Jachet said.

"Yes, but the rumor is they are telling Marie-Antoinette to snub du Barry," said Madame Genoux.

"A dangerous move...the Dauphine could easily lose favor with the King," Monsieur Beauvais added.

"Regardless, I can't blame her. I would not want to have anything to do with a prostitute either!" Madame Jachet hooted.

Lisette had heard her mother talk of Madame du Barry's life before the King. After a brief spell working as a shop girl, she had become a courtesan. She had learned from a young age how to please a gentleman.

"Well said!" Monsieur Papille yelped.

Several of the women clapped.

"I think the King should present such a necklace to his new granddaughter-in-law, the Dauphine, to welcome her to the royal family," said Madame Jachet.

"You are alone in that sentiment. If we are going to spout absurd statements, maybe the King should give it to one of his homely sisters...it might help attract a suitor," Madame Genoux said.

"There is no amount of jewelry in all of France that would help them," chimed Madame Jachet.

"I've heard the royal dogs are even scared off at the sight of their faces!" said Monsieur Papille with a serious expression.

The group erupted again, cackling and howling at Monsieur Papille's cleverness.

He had a twinkle in his eye as he added, "Maybe the Dauphin should give it to his mistress..."

"He doesn't have a mistress. He doesn't even have a properly working member!" Marguerite said.

Lisette noticed that Marguerite had only recently re-entered the conversation.

Everyone applauded once again.

"Ooh, speaking of scandals, did you hear the latest rumor about Marie-Antoinette?" Madame Jachet asked the group.

"You mean one of her ladies, Sophie Dufour...the one who is

with child?" asked Madame Genoux.

The name sounded familiar to Lisette, but she wasn't sure who they were talking about. She continued listening.

Monsieur Papille asked, "Whose child?"

"I heard a rumor that the father is the Comte d'Artois," Monsieur Cochin said as he rejoined the group.

The crowd collectively oohed. Lisette could not believe the number of court scandals. It seemed as if this conversation could go on forever. They would never run out of rumors, gossip and stories.

"No, I heard it is the King's other brother, the Comte de Provence," Monsieur Beauvais said.

"Never, he is too fat to even see his own member!" Monsieur Papille exclaimed.

Everyone giggled.

"No one knows the father's identity," Madame Genoux said confidently.

"Well, we all know it wasn't the Dauphin! He keeps his member under lock and key!" Monsieur Papille jibed.

The group burst into jubilant cries again. The reference to the Dauphin's obsession with locks was well received. Lisette had heard her mother talk about how the Dauphin was known for tinkering with keys and locks. She had said that most of France thought it bespoke of his disinterest in state affairs. He would rather be playing with his locking mechanisms than helping his grandfather rule the country.

Lisette was laughing alongside everyone else when Amante re-entered the room, walking arm in arm with a fetching woman. He sat down next to the woman and several others that were flirting excessively with him. Amante was whispering in the ear of the prettiest. Lisette wanted to stop watching, but she couldn't. Only after someone tapped on her shoulder, did she look away. Lisette peered up. It was the Salonnière.

"You're not sure what to think about Amante, are you?" Marguerite breathed in Lisette's ear.

The Salonnière's voice interrupted Lisette's stupor. She found it difficult not to watch Amante with the other women.

"Follow me," Marguerite said as she stood and motioned for Lisette to walk with her out of the room.

Monsieur Beauvais was the only one who took notice of her departure. He waved at Lisette.

Marguerite hooked Lisette's arm in hers and led her toward a more remote part of the house, down a long hall. They entered a room at the end of it. After Marguerite closed the door, she offered Lisette a seat on a luxurious velvet couch. Lisette had never seen such a room before. It was a private chamber with intimate furniture including a curtained bed tucked away in a wall alcove. She didn't know if it was its cozy location in the wall niche, or the buttercup silk linens and bright blue taffeta eider-down covering it that made the bed appear so inviting. The bed curtains were of the same yellow and blue colors and were top-ped with wispy, white feathers.

Lisette studied the room. Not only was the bed covered in yellow and blue stripes, but the decoration of the entire room fol-lowed a similar color scheme. She saw it on the windows, on the upholstered furniture and even on the floor carpets.

Lisette sank down on the couch. *What is that smell?* she wondered. She inhaled deeply. *Jasmine and oranges,* Lisette realized. In each corner of the room, sitting on small tables, were pairs of tall silver perfume burners. Lisette felt like she was in-toxicated, but had not sipped any spirits. It was as if she had en-tered another realm.

"Do you like it?" Marguerite wore an impish look, as if she was greatly enjoying Lisette's wonderment. She sat on a plush chaise-lounge opposite Lisette. Marguerite extended her legs on the long chair and reclined.

Lisette nodded her head. "What is this room?"

"This is one of my boudoirs, my private boudoir, in fact.

Scandalous isn't it!"

Lisette agreed. It did seem scandalous, but intriguing at the same time.

"I know. You have never seen a boudoir and you are wondering what takes place in such a room."

Lisette nodded, but she had a good idea of what Marguerite did here.

The Salonnière continued, "Many things go on in this room, like talking and flirting."

"But isn't that what happens in the outer rooms?" Lisette asked.

"Yes, but in this room you can become even better acquainted. You can get to know the other person much more...intimately. If the talking leads to touching and that leads to lovemaking, then so be it. You are free to explore in the boudoir."

"I see." Lisette could think of nothing else to say in response. She had never given flirting and lovemaking all that much thought. It seemed as if the Salonnière had elevated those activities to an art form. Lisette supposed that conversation and flirting could be a serious occupation for the Salonnière, like painting was for her.

"But that is not why I brought you back here. I want to tell you about Amante. Do you know what you are doing with him?" Marguerite said.

"He has agreed to be my patron. He has paid for lessons and supplies. In exchange, I am expected to paint for him. We have a business arrangement, an understanding. That is all," Lisette said plainly.

"You think that is all?"

"Yes. That is all we desire from each other."

Marguerite smiled as if she knew something that Lisette didn't. "My dear, are you sure that is all you want from him? Because I am quite sure that isn't all that he wants from you."

"Yes. I only wish to paint."

"But you are also a woman...a beautiful woman...and Amante can see that. He desires you, my dear, and I think you desire him too."

"Nothing could be further from the truth." Lisette thought about how Amante was flirting with the women in the other room.

"My dear, I have known Amante a long time. In my years of knowing many men, I've never met one quite like him. He is a special kind of man...the kind of man that can make a woman feel magnificent. He can bring you such pleasure...the sort that you have only dreamed about."

"You mean in the bedroom?"

"Yes, that kind of pleasure for certain, but another kind too. He loves all women and always wants to make women feel good ...good about who they are and about their place in this world. He truly believes women should be free to be whomever they want to be. He doesn't think they are the lesser or weaker sex ...not at all. He will bring you up so high, you'll float toward the heavens."

Lisette didn't know what to say. She sat and listened as the Salonnière continued.

"But you must also know that he doesn't remain floating with you. He always leaves. He can't be with one woman for-ever."

Lisette nodded to show that she was listening. Logically, she knew she should stay away from this man, but Marguerite's talk of pleasure echoed in her mind. She felt a faint stirring in her groin as she considered it.

The Salonnière leaned forward and said, "Be with him. En-joy him. He will change your world, but be sure you know exact-ly who you are getting into bed with and who you are allowing into your heart. He will not marry you and he won't be with you every day. But when he is there, he will give you the greatest ecstasy you have known...and probably will ever know. You will feel like each day is anew, like Venus the day she was born on the conch shell in the sea foam."

There was something in the Salonnière's tone that made Lisette think that she was speaking from experience. She guessed that Marguerite and Amante had been paramours at some point and for whatever reason were no longer lovers, but had remained close friends.

"My dear, if you want to be with Amante, be with him. If you want to be with other men, be with other men. That is your prerogative as an alluring, talented woman!"

Lisette considered Marguerite's words. No one had ever explained love or men in this way to Lisette, certainly not her mother. Marguerite spoke with such conviction, as if she was speaking from the priest's pulpit during High Mass. She seemed to believe what she was saying with all of her being. Nonetheless, Lisette knew that she was not ready to enter Amante's world.

"I simply want to be an artist," she repeated.

"If that is the case, then I can offer you some advice."

Lisette was about to say *no thank you* when Marguerite kept talking.

"You need to embrace your femininity more. Dispense with the *fichu* and reveal more of your breasts. Flirt more with men. It can only help you."

Help my career as an artist? she thought. Lisette had her doubts.

"Trust me, heeding my advice will only benefit your career. Parisians have little depth. They will line up to have you paint their portrait simply because they consider you to be a pretty, fashionable woman. They will send their friends to you because you are skilled. But be careful, they can be fickle. You remember Madame Partin."

Lisette knew what Marguerite said was true. She was keenly aware that the Duchesse and her friends could abandon her at any moment. No one knew noblewomen's fickle nature better than the merchants they frequented and particularly the milliner, Madame Partin. The year before, in the month of April,

Madame Partin could barely meet the demand for her specialty hats. Then, after the Comtesse Deblois was swept up in a scandal wearing one of Madame Partin's hats, her business quickly dwindled. By the summer of the same year, Madame Partin was forced to close her doors.

Before Lisette could say anything in response, there was a knock on the door.

"Excuse me, my dear. I had hoped we wouldn't be interrupted," said Marguerite as she rose to answer it.

Monsieur Beauvais stepped into the room. "Apologies, Marguerite, but I wanted to see Mademoiselle Vigée before I left."

"Please, come in, Monsieur Beauvais," the Salonnière said, smiling at Lisette.

"Mademoiselle Vigée, I greatly enjoyed your company this evening. If I can ever be of assistance, please do not hesitate to visit my studio." He bowed and kissed her hand.

Lisette glanced over at the Salonnière who was nodding with approval. She was also pointing to her mouth while exaggerating her smile.

"Thank you, Monsieur Beauvais," Lisette said. She forced herself to smile wider than she normally did, although she wasn't sure it was necessary. Lisette sensed that Monsieur Beauvais' offer to help her was sincere and offered without the expectation of anything in return.

Monsieur Beauvais bowed again and then left them.

"See, my dear, being more feminine helps. Flirt a little more, smile a little bigger. You will see men falling all over themselves to help you with whatever you desire."

Lisette remained skeptical.

Marguerite continued, "You need to dress in tighter gowns with exposed, low necklines. Put a little rouge on your cheeks and..."

Lisette's mind wandered as she thought about what Amante was doing in the next room.

Marguerite continued, "...Throw your head back and expose

191

your neck and bosom more when you talk. And of course, don't forget the lavender perfume behind —" She stopped talking and came over to Lisette. "I know this is all new. Don't worry, I can be patient. Someone once helped me. I was hesitant to accept her advice too. Now, let's go back out to the drawing room and tear Amante away from those women. Leave with him in his carriage tonight and let him kiss you. I promise you won't regret it."

Marguerite had made a convincing argument on Amante's behalf, but Lisette suspected that he would only bring her trouble. Lisette decided that she would be polite to Marguerite, but that she wouldn't pursue Amante. She would say good night to him and then leave on her own.

The Salonnière smiled warmly and then escorted Lisette out of her boudoir. "I want to see you at my salon every week. We can talk more when I see you next." She gave Lisette a gentle push toward the drawing room. Marguerite stayed behind, almost as if she wanted to watch Lisette from a distance.

Lisette returned to the drawing room where she found Amante flirting with the same women. They seemed to be hanging on him even more. Lisette approached him and quickly said, "Good night." She turned and made her way out of the room before he could respond.

Lisette had reached the main hall when she heard footsteps behind her.

"Lisette! Wait!"

She turned around. Amante was dashing toward her.

"Lisette, there is more I want to say to you this evening. You rushed out."

As soon as she looked at him, her resoluteness faded. She felt her legs become weak, like they weren't going to take another step on their own.

Without saying anything, Amante gently led her into a dark corner of the hallway. He pulled her close to him and leaned in to kiss her. Lisette fought to maintain control of her senses, but found it difficult. At first he kissed her gently and then as her body responded to his touch, his kiss became stronger, more forceful and more passionate. Without thinking, she put her arms around his neck and returned his kiss with equal fervor. Unable to control her body, her mind surrendered. *Amante.*

Chapter Twenty-Two

October 28, 1773

The next morning, the light woke Lisette. She had stumbled into bed with her head in a fog, unable to think of anything but Amante.

In her stupor, she had forgotten to draw her bed curtains and shut her windows' drapes. Still in bed, Lisette turned her head and looked out of her window. From this angle she could only see the sky. It was a beautiful, clear blue sky with a few clouds, not the amorphous thin-looking ones, but the fluffy, pure white clouds.

Lisette had been lingering in bed, not wanting to begin the day. She was afraid that if she started her day, she would forget last night. *Amante,* she thought. Lisette touched her lips. She could still feel his soft, full lips pressing against hers. Lisette had taken the Salonnière's advice. She had shared a carriage with Amante and allowed him to kiss her for the duration of the ride.

Even now, she could hear Marguerite's voice: *He doesn't think women are the lesser or weaker sex...not at all. He will bring you up so high, you'll float toward the heavens.* Lisette watched the clouds forming high in the sky outside her window. She didn't want to come down.

"Lisette, are you still in bed?"

She heard her mother's voice outside her door.

"No, Mother." Lisette quickly rose and pulled off her linen night shift. "Come in."

Lisette stood naked as her mother came into her room.

"You're just now getting dressed?" Her mother walked over to the *armoire* and selected a dress and matching petticoat. "This one is my favorite. You look lovely in it."

It was one of Lisette's most formal gowns, one that required a corset. She didn't want to wear it to her lesson today with Briard. It would restrict her movement, but she couldn't explain her reasons to her mother. Lisette sighed.

Jeanne brought the gown over to the bed and then helped Lisette with her corset.

As her mother laced it, Lisette glanced out of the window. The billowy, white clouds had disappeared. The sky had turned dark and it had started to rain.

"Your father tells me that you have missed sittings these past few days. You are causing him trouble," Jeanne said.

Lisette defended herself, "I have been busy, Mother."

"Not too busy to obey your father." Her mother tugged hard at the corset's strings, pulling them tight.

Lisette cringed. It was the second time her mother had used the word, *father*. Lisette jerked herself away from her mother. "He is not my father."

Jeanne took several steps toward Lisette. She resumed lacing Lisette's corset and said, "I will not hear you say that. He is your father now. You need to obey him. This is his house and we must abide by his rules." Jeanne finished lacing the corset. She picked up the gown and held it for Lisette. "He provides us with so many fine things. Like this very dress."

"But, Mother, he is cruel."

"Nonsense. He loves and cares for us." Jeanne helped Lisette slip into her petticoat and then fit the open gown onto her torso.

Lisette noticed her mother's forearms. There were new bruises, although the new ones were difficult to distinguish from the older ones. They blended so well together in one big, purple, green and red jumble.

"How did you get those bruises, Mother?"

Jeanne ignored Lisette's question.

Her mother began pinning the embroidered stomacher onto the front of the bodice as she talked. "He always apologizes...and gives me tokens of his affection. Just yesterday he gave me this beautiful bracelet." The bracelet had a wide gold band encrusted with rubies and diamonds. The diamonds dazzled in the morning light.

Lisette said nothing, neither acknowledging her mother's comments nor the bracelet.

There was silence between them while Jeanne finished grooming Lisette. She turned Lisette so that she could smooth out the pleats on the back of the dress.

Once Jeanne was satisfied with Lisette's appearance, she spoke, "He is only trying to help us...help you. Look at how your career has blossomed under his guidance."

"Mother, he is only using me...to keep his customers happy so they continue to buy his jewels."

Jeanne dismissed Lisette's comments and began searching the *armoire*. "Lisette where is your linen *fichu?*" She rifled through several drawers. "We must find it. A young woman's honor is directly tied to her modesty."

"Mother, are you listening to me?" Lisette asked.

Jeanne stepped over to Lisette's *commode* and began searching there. "Where is that *fichu?*"

"Mother, please listen to me."

Jeanne stopped searching and walked back over to Lisette. She held Lisette by both shoulders and faced her. "Look around you, this house, this neighborhood... We would have none of it without him. Louis certainly never gave us anything like this." Her voice exposed her agitation.

Lisette felt her heart beat faster. She had heard enough. Lisette couldn't listen to her mother disparage her papa like that. Her ensemble wasn't complete without a *fichu*, but Lisette didn't care. Without looking at her mother or saying anything else, she slipped on her shoes, grabbed her cloak and satchel and ran out of the room.

Her mother called after her, "Lisette! Where are you going? You aren't wearing a *fichu*!"

Lisette didn't answer her mother. She started down the stairs toward the front vestibule.

"You can't walk away from me, Lisette." Her mother ran after her. "Your father will want to know where you are going."

Lisette did not look back or answer her mother. Just before she reached the front door, she saw Henri. He looked down at her satchel and they briefly exchanged glances. Lisette knew she could trust Henri to keep her secret.

She had crossed the threshold of the front door when she heard her mother's voice. It was much louder than usual. "Henri, Monsieur Le Sèvre will want to know where Lisette is going. He *will* get it out of you."

Henri waved Lisette on with his hand and smiled at her reassuringly. "Go, Mademoiselle. Go." Then he closed the heavy door.

Later that day, Lisette was careful not to make much noise as she came through the front door of Le Sèvre's house. It was already dark and supper would be served soon. She had timed her return just right. As long as she was back in time for the late evening meal, no one would care that she had been out.

Lisette was exhausted. She had stayed at Briard's studio long after her formal lesson had concluded. The other girls had left, but Lisette had wanted to master eludoric painting before she went home. The new technique used water and oil in a way to prevent the deterioration of the oil long after it was dry. Briard was a big proponent of this innovative method. He, like other artists, was excited with the advancement in oil painting. The new method would better preserve paintings so that the paint would not flake off with time. Lisette smiled as she thought about how well her lessons were progressing. It was the one aspect of her life that Le Sèvre couldn't control.

Lisette started up the stairs toward her room. The rain hadn't stopped all day and the water falling off of her cloak made the marble stairs especially slick. Before going to the dining room, Lisette would make sure that she looked presentable. She had to safeguard her secret from Le Sèvre and her mother as long as she could.

She needed to dry off and stash her satchel, but more importantly, she had to be certain that all traces of paint were removed from her hands. Lisette had been careful to wear an apron to protect her mother's favorite gown. She had also worn a cap, but that didn't always prevent paint from getting in her hair. Lisette felt her head for any hair that had stiffened from splattered paint. *Good,* she thought. Lisette hadn't spilled paint on her hair, but it did feel unkempt. She tucked her loose hairs behind her ears. As she did this, she discovered a small paint brush behind her left ear. She pulled it out and continued up the stairs. Lisette was halfway up the staircase when she heard someone come up behind her.

"Where have you been?" Le Sèvre was suddenly with her on the stairs. His voice was booming.

Lisette paused, then turned around. "I went out for a walk in the Tuileries."

"With that satchel? And in the rain?" he asked, looking at

the paint brush in her hand that she had just removed from behind her ear.

Lisette shook her head *yes*.

"I don't believe you." Le Sèvre moved to a higher stair so that he towered over Lisette.

"May I put my bag down? I will join you and Mother for supper."

"You can hand it over to me. You won't be needing it anymore."

Lisette was stunned and unable to move.

"You heard me. No more lessons. If I find out that you continue to see Briard, there will be dire consequences. Now hand over your satchel." Le Sèvre stood with his arm out-stretched.

How did he find out? she wondered. *Had Le Sèvre talked to Amante?* She stared at him in disbelief.

"You'll need to tell Capitaine de Chaumont that he can stop payments to Briard. You will no longer be going to the Louvre for lessons," Le Sèvre explained. His voice was thundering, but somehow he maintained a calm and even timbre.

"No! You can't do this!" Lisette screeched. She had never raised her voice to him.

"What did you say to me?"

Lisette immediately realized she had made an unforgivable mistake.

Le Sèvre slapped her across the face.

The impact was so strong she fell backward, tumbling down the marble stairs. When she landed at the bottom, she was still gripping her satchel tightly. Lisette opened her eyes.

Le Sèvre loomed over her.

He grabbed the satchel out of her hands. "Go to your room. You can join us for supper after you've composed yourself." He turned and marched away.

Where is Mother? Lisette thought. Had her mother not heard her fall? Lisette remained at the base of the staircase for several moments. She wasn't sure what had just happened. Lisette surveyed her body for damage. Her head throbbed and a bump was starting to swell from her plunge down the stairs, but she was otherwise unharmed.

Satisfied that nothing was broken, Lisette's mind turned to Briard. Her heart sank as she accepted the reality of the loss of her lessons. She knew that in time her head would recover, but she was unsure how she would manage without Briard's instruction. *Le Sèvre can't do this. He can't prevent me from taking lessons,* she thought.

Lisette slowly collected herself and deliberately climbed the stairs to her room. Before she arrived at her bedroom door, she saw Henri lurking in the shadows.

"I'm sorry, Mademoiselle Lisette. I didn't want to tell him." He stepped forward and Lisette saw Henri's hands. They were wrapped in white linen bandages which were now pink from the blood they had absorbed.

"I know, Henri. Please don't worry about me. Go take care of your hands." Lisette smiled at him holding back tears as she considered the pain he had suffered in an attempt to keep her secret. Her head was beginning to ache terribly.

"Let me assist you, Mademoiselle Lisette. You should lie down." Henri took Lisette's arm and helped her walk up the stairs.

Once they were in her room, Lisette said, "Thank you, Henri. You must go downstairs to the dining room before you are missed." Lisette didn't want him punished again. She added, "Have Camille change your bandages before you retire tonight."

Lisette collapsed on her bed. She didn't care that she was still wearing her wet cloak. She gently laid her head on her pillow. In the quiet, the pain from her injury became more pronounced. Lisette closed her eyes. *Amante doesn't know. I must tell him,* she thought. Picturing Amante in her mind helped to ease the pounding in her head. Lying in the dark, Lisette made a decision.

She slowly rose from her bed, stepped over to the door and

waited until the servants were gathered in the dining room. She felt her forehead and noticed that the lump had grown. The pain was intensifying. Lisette listened at the door for several moments. When she was certain no one was in her path, Lisette made her way downstairs and out of the house.

As she stood in the foyer of the Salonnière's, Lisette felt her head. Although it was still painful, the lump had stopped swelling. *It could have been worse*, she thought. The footman had just left her to find Amante. Lisette hoped that he was there tonight.

"Here to see Amante?" Marguerite reached out to embrace her.

Lisette gave her a kiss on both cheeks.

Marguerite surveyed Lisette's body starting with her shoes and ending at her head, where the lump had formed.

"I need to speak to him and him only. I am not staying for the evening's festivities."

"No, my dear, I am not worried about your attire. I am looking at a bump on your head. Are you well?"

"I will be, after I see Amante. I won't stay long," Lisette said again.

"Pity. I have had several of my regular guests ask after you. I hate to disappoint." Marguerite gingerly spun Lisette around, not unlike the way her mother often did. "Next time I hope to see you in one of the new gowns I sent."

Lisette nodded but said nothing about the gifts. She did not have time to explain why she could never wear Marguerite's dresses as long as she lived with Le Sèvre. Safely tucked away under her bedroom floor, the dresses would remain hidden from her mother and Le Sèvre.

"Do you know where he is?" Lisette asked anxiously. She had to speak to Amante and then return home before Le Sèvre realized she was missing again. Lisette didn't want Henri beaten further.

"He is in there." Marguerite pointed to one of the smaller drawing rooms off the foyer.

Lisette hesitated. *Why were the doors closed?* she wondered. Marguerite usually insisted that they remain open.

"Go right in." Marguerite smiled strangely at Lisette. She had an odd expression on her face, one that Lisette had seen before. Lisette had noticed it when Marguerite had talked about the pleasure Amante could offer her.

Lisette headed toward the doors. Pleasure was the last thing on her mind. She needed to find a way to keep her lessons with Briard. On the carriage ride to the Salonnière's, Lisette had considered what she would say to Amante. She struggled with the best way to explain how Le Sèvre had inserted himself into their business. She wasn't sure how he would accept the news. As a *capitaine*, Amante was the one who gave orders, not received them.

Lisette opened the doors and entered the small room. She immediately saw Amante. Her stomach briefly fluttered when he looked at her. Then she saw the other women. The fluttering in her stomach was suddenly replaced with a horrible twisting. She felt her insides churning. Amante sat on a long couch in between two young women. They were giggling and playfully touching each other. *Why did I come here tonight? Amante doesn't want to hear about my lessons,* she thought. Lisette turned to leave.

"What a marvelous surprise!" Amante called after her.

Lisette pivoted to face him.

Abandoning the women on the couch, Amante approached her.

"You weren't leaving were you? How long have you been here?" Amante asked.

Lisette peered over at the women as she said, "It looks like you are otherwise occupied. We can talk at a later time...one that is more convenient for you."

Amante glanced over at the women. "Them? Nonsense. I am yours. You have my complete attention. Come, let's move to a more intimate setting. I know just the place."

Amante took Lisette's hand, gently led her down the hall and into a room that Lisette had never seen. They went inside and Amante shut the door behind them.

Lisette peered around the space. It was a smaller version of Marguerite's boudoir. Marguerite's house seemed to have many boudoirs.

Amante invited Lisette to sit beside him on a short silk upholstered sofa, just big enough for two people.

Her heart raced. Lisette's body moved without her mind's approval. She knew that she shouldn't be alone with him on this sofa or in this room, but she couldn't control herself. She sat down.

"At last. We are alone. *Ma chérie.*" He softly brushed her cheek. Then his hand moved from her cheek to her forehead. "My dear, what is this on your head?"

"Le Sèvre —"

He interrupted her, "Le Sèvre did this to you? I am going over there right now." Amante stood up with a jolt.

She saw his face redden as his chest protruded like a ferocious animal. Lisette had never seen Amante so angry.

"Wait. Let me explain. There is more," Lisette said as she urged him to sit again.

"There's more?" he said, slowly lowering himself onto the sofa.

"It is about Briard."

"I don't understand. How is Briard involved?" Amante was sitting on the sofa's edge.

"It is the lessons. Le Sèvre has cut me off. I can no longer see Master Briard," Lisette blurted out.

Amante frowned. "What do you mean? I am the one who is paying. He has no say in the matter."

"But he does. He is my guardian."

Amante bolted up again and paced in front of her. "He has no business interfering with our relationship. That is between

203

you and me."

Lisette hadn't wanted to lose control of her emotions. She felt tears building up behind her eyes. Seeing Amante become defensive of their relationship made it difficult for Lisette to hold them at bay. A tear fell down her cheek. Then another.

Amante regarded her. "Ah, *chérie*, all will be well." He sat down next to her and leaned in close. He beheld her like no man had before.

Lisette suddenly wanted him to kiss her. She closed her eyes. The instant his lips met hers, she felt her stomach dancing and the little hairs on her arms stiffen. He slowly inserted his tongue into her mouth. She pushed her body against his and o-pened her mouth wider, allowing his tongue to invade deeper. A-mante placed one hand on her thigh while the other reached up to lightly touch her cheek. As he caressed her cheek, his hand brushed her ear.

He jerked back, letting out a low laugh as he held up a small paint brush. "Are you planning to paint my portrait tonight?"

She grabbed the brush out of his hand. "I must have put it there while Briard was showing me..." She looked down at the floor.

"Lisette, I will make sure you continue with your lessons." His voice became agitated again.

"I don't see how."

"Because I am the one who has arranged and paid for them, not Le Sèvre. He has no say in the matter." Amante left the sofa and began pacing again.

"But −"

He abruptly interrupted Lisette, "You *will* continue to attend your lessons." His voice had completely changed. Lisette had never heard him use that tone with her before. He was giving orders like she was one of the soldiers under his command.

"I am not one of your soldiers," Lisette said.

"But you *will* continue with the lessons!" Amante was now

shouting at her. His voice was threatening as he gestured with his hand, similar to the way an army commander would issue an order to a subordinate. Lisette did not want to leave herself vulnerable. She had already felt exposed earlier in the night.

Lisette stood. "I've already told you that is no longer possible." She turned to leave. "Good night, Capitaine de Chaumont."

His expression immediately softened as if he had just realized what he had done. He came up close to her. "Lisette, I didn't mean to upset you." His voice was soft and gentle again. "I only want what is best for you, *ma chérie*." He pointed to the couch where they had been sitting. "Come back and sit with me."

"I must go," Lisette said as she quickly walked out of the room. She moved swiftly to make sure he couldn't come after her. She quickened her pace as she approached the foyer. She didn't want to be stopped by anyone, least of all Marguerite. Lisette wasn't eager to explain her abrupt departure.

Lisette left the Salonnière's and hailed a *fiacre*. She boarded the carriage and closed her eyes. She had hoped to calm her mind, but she couldn't stop thinking about how Amante had spoken to her like she was under his command. Her head pulsated with pain. As Lisette pictured Amante's face, the pain worsened.

Chapter Twenty-Three

The next day, Lisette's head felt better. The throbbing had subsided and the lump had nearly disappeared. She hadn't received any help from Amante, so she knew she had no choice other than to obey Le Sèvre. Lisette would stop attending lessons, but not until she told Briard herself. She would go one final time.

Today, Lisette didn't want to be delayed. *Where is she? It is nearly noon*, Lisette thought. Rosalie was always late. Lisette saw people scurrying in every direction and wondered, *Why can't Rosalie hurry?* Lisette was about to give up and walk to the Louvre by herself when she saw Rosalie sauntering down the street, her head hung low.

"I am sorry for my lateness. I have a very good reason." Rosalie barely looked at Lisette while she spoke.

When Rosalie finally did meet her gaze, Lisette could see that her eyes were red and swollen, as if she had been crying.

"Aren't you going to guess my reason?"

"Just tell me." Lisette never liked playing this game. The week before, Rosalie had hounded Lisette until she had guessed the type of flowers Rosalie would carry at her wedding. Lisette wasn't in the mood to play it today.

"Please, just guess," Rosalie insisted.

Lisette knew that Rosalie would not stop until Lisette relented and participated. She realized it was the price of peace and quiet. "Because you were meeting with your betrothed?" Lisette guessed. They started down the street.

"No, but close." Rosalie was crestfallen, like she was going to burst into tears at any moment.

"You were meeting with your dressmaker?"

"Wrong again. I know you'll get it this time."

"I give up, Rosalie. You know I have never been engaged or married."

"The hairdresser. I was supposed to have an appointment with the best hairdresser in all of Paris." Rosalie paused as her eyes filled with tears, then she slowly continued, "But he canceled saying that he had more important clients to serve."

"I'm sure you'll be able to find another hairdresser." Lisette couldn't think of anything else to say to her.

Rosalie had begun to cry. In between sobs she said, "But there is no one as good as Léonard!" Rosalie cried harder.

Léonard...Lisette thought. She knew that name. But where had she heard it? "Marguerite!" Lisette bellowed.

"What? I said Léonard, not Marguerite," blubbered Rosalie.

"Marguerite de Tougereau knows Léonard...very well. And I know Marguerite. I could get an introduction for you." Lisette waited for Rosalie's reaction.

Rosalie immediately stopped crying. "You would do that for me?"

She appeared so sad to Lisette. "Of course," Lisette said as she took Rosalie's arm in hers.

They walked with their arms locked the rest of the way. Rosalie's spirits had lifted. She had returned to her old self and was prattling on about every detail of her wedding hairstyle. As she listened to Rosalie blather on, Lisette realized she was going to miss her friend.

They made their way to the Louvre and into the building without any trouble from the male art students. As they walked toward Briard's studio, Lisette was relieved not to encounter the boys. Briard was out in the hall waiting for them.

"Rosalie, go in and begin preparing a canvas. I have some business to which I must attend. I will be back soon," he said.

When Lisette followed Rosalie, Briard stopped her. "Lisette, I need to speak with you, alone."

He already knows. He is going to tell me to go home now, Lisette thought. *I won't have a final lesson.*

Briard regarded her carefully. "After today, I cannot teach you anymore. Your step-father has been clear on that matter. Since he is your guardian, I must respect his wishes. He has made it very plain that if I don't, he can make my life extremely unpleasant. You cannot come back to see me here at the Louvre again."

Lisette looked at him without saying anything. She held back her tears.

His expression was kind. "But that doesn't mean we can't continue with today's lesson. You are here. Go in and get to work. I need to take care of some Académie business. I'll return shortly." He smiled at her.

Lisette watched him walk away, unsure of whether she wanted to go inside at all.

She peeked in and saw Adélaïde preparing her canvas while Rosalie chatted. Then she noticed the statue in the middle of the room. *Milo of Crotona, Eaten by a Lion.* Lisette recognized the statue that had been completed one hundred years earlier by the French sculptor Pierre Puget. Puget had skillfully captured the tragedy of the celebrated Olympian athlete who had met a terrible death at the end of his life. Lisette's throat tightened and her legs felt heavy, but she went into the studio.

"Briard is attending to urgent business. We are to prepare our canvases. He expects to return shortly," Adélaïde said flatly.

"Yes. He told me. I spoke to him in the hall," Lisette responded.

Rosalie was explaining her wedding day *pouf* to Adélaïde. Lisette watched Adélaïde listen respectfully, but it was obvious to Lisette that Adélaïde only wanted to work. In the past months of their lessons, Lisette had grown to admire Adélaïde. Despite hailing from the wealthy, powerful and noble La Valette family that accorded her an effortless existence, Adélaïde had impressed Lisette with her earnestness. When in Briard's studio, Adélaïde was a conscientious art student. Besides her interest in painting, Lisette knew little else of this young woman. She almost never discussed personal matters. She would politely respond with brief answers to Rosalie's questions and then promptly return to work. Lisette knew that Rosalie was bothered by Adélaïde's curtness. However, as her social superior, Adélaïde wasn't obligated to say anything to Rosalie. Of course, it didn't stop Rosalie from talking about herself, whether or not anyone else was listening. Rosalie had not begun preparing her canvas. Instead, she had taken out a sketchpad and was drawing her wedding hairstyle.

Lisette hurriedly stashed her belongings in the corner of the *atelier* and then began stretching her canvas. She would be ready to sketch when Briard returned. Lisette had tuned out Rosalie's voice and was thinking about the Puget statue. Then she heard Rosalie say the words, "last lesson."

Gaping at Rosalie, Lisette asked, "What did you say?"

"That today is my final lesson. I need to make wedding preparations...and my affianced doesn't want me distracted by the lessons. Isn't it wonderful?" Rosalie resumed sketching her wedding *coiffure*.

Lisette felt like Rosalie had punched her in the stomach. *I would give anything to keep going,* Lisette thought.

Suddenly, Lisette had an urge to run out of the studio. *I can't do this,* she realized.

Lisette stepped over to the corner, gathered her belongings and headed for the door. Rosalie was babbling and Adélaïde was focused on her canvas. Neither of them said anything to Lisette as she quickly left the studio.

Chapter Twenty-Four

"Lisette, stop fidgeting with that necklace!" Jeanne reached across the carriage, grabbed both of Lisette's hands and placed them in her lap. "Your father went to much trouble for you to wear that necklace today," Jeanne said as she tapped the top of Lisette's hands, as if to remind them to stay put.

She was not accustomed to wearing necklaces and this one was particularly bulky. On loan from Le Sèvre's shop, its thick gold chain held alternating emeralds and diamonds. Le Sèvre had wanted both Lisette and Jeanne to wear his latest jewels, so that nobles could picture how they would look on beautiful women.

Lisette hadn't noticed that she was touching the necklace until her mother had scolded her. Lisette's hands had always had a mind of their own, even from the time she was small. She didn't want to look down at her scarred hands, but she was keen-ly aware of them now. They felt heavy on her lap as she fought the urge to touch Le Sèvre's necklace again. Lisette wanted to reach up and remove it. The necklace felt tight around her neck, like a snake coiling around its prey.

She glanced across the carriage at Le Sèvre who sat next to her mother. He stared at the passing landscape, lost in thought. Lisette supposed that he was thinking of the business he was hoping to conduct today at Versailles.

She turned her head to look out too. They were on the Avenue de Paris approaching the palace. Lisette had never visit-ed Versailles before, so she did not know what to expect. It was the first event in weeks that had excited her.

For the past eight months, indifference had slowly crept into her life and nearly consumed her. Week after week, Lisette had spent all of her hours painting portraits of Le Sèvre's clients. There had been no more punishments, but there had also been no lessons, no allegory paintings and no outings to Le Brun's or to the Salonnière's. Every day for the past eight months, Lisette had been living entirely under Le Sèvre's control and each of those days she felt less like herself.

Lisette saw her reflection in the carriage window. She barely recognized the young woman looking back at her.

"Stop that! I spent an hour arranging your *coiffure*. Leave it alone!" Jeanne reached over again and pulled Lisette's hands a-way from her hair.

Lisette realized that her hands had crept up to her head and her fingers were twirling the little wisps of hair at the base of her neck.

For today's visit to Versailles, Le Sèvre had insisted on both Lisette and her mother wearing a headdress *a tapé* with two single curls. Their hair was piled up on top of their heads and embellished with accessories. Her mother had jewels and feath-ers embedded in hers, while Lisette wore a single ribbon of taf-feta that matched her gown. Le Sèvre had also selected both of their dresses, shoes and jewelry. When Lisette had complained to her mother, Jeanne had told her to accept the circumstances. Lisette remembered their conversation exactly as it happened:

"Husbands often choose their wives' clothing and accessories. I for one am grateful that I have a husband who cares enough about me to choose my gowns," Jeanne said.

"But Papa never chose your dresses, Mother," Lisette said.

"He never gave me jewels either. In exchange for my agreeable nature, François selects beautiful jewels for me to wear."

"But he is only using you to exhibit his jewelry, Mother. How long do you keep any of the pieces?"

Lisette had ended their conversation shortly after making this last point, realizing that she would not convince her mother of anything.

Lisette regarded her mother. She was stunning in her plum silk gown.

Then Lisette watched Le Sèvre inspect her mother. He was fixated on her forearms. Jeanne's gloves weren't quiet covering the bruises. They weren't particularly noticeable to someone who wasn't looking for them, but nonetheless, the purple-green splotches were still visible.

"Jeanne, I thought you were going to wear the longer gloves today….the ones that I selected for you," Le Sèvre said.

"I was. But just as we were leaving the house I noticed a large brown stain on the thumb of the right hand. I didn't think you would want me wearing tarnished gloves," Jeanne replied.

Le Sèvre grumbled, but dropped the issue. He shifted his attention to Lisette. "We are nearly there. You will behave yourself today, Lisette," Le Sèvre commanded her.

Lisette said nothing and peered out of the carriage. They had passed through the outermost gate and were slowing down to go through the first of the inner gates. There was so much to see. Lisette wanted to set up her easel and capture the scene.

The outer courtyard was full of vendors of every variety. Lisette saw men and women selling flowers, fruit, and many other wares. Some talked, some shouted and others laughed. There were people walking in every direction, while noble ladies and gentlemen were being carried in bright yellow sedan chairs. *That is strange, the sedan chairs in Paris are never that color,* Lisette thought.

Le Sèvre repeated himself, "Lisette, are you listening to me? I worked tirelessly for approval to sell my jewels today from the Bâtiments du Roi. It took months to get my license approved by the Marquis de Marigny. I will not have you embarrass me."

Jeanne turned to her. "Lisette, respond to your father."

As Jeanne said the word *father*, Lisette felt the necklace constrict her air again. It grew tighter around her neck. Lisette managed to shake her head up and down. "Yes." Lisette could barely speak.

Jeanne glanced at Lisette and then at Le Sèvre and back to Lisette again. Jeanne's nervousness was apparent. "It is a good day to be outside the city. Paris is a flurry of activity with everyone making preparations for Corpus Christi." Lisette's mother tried to ease the tension inside the carriage.

When neither Lisette nor Le Sèvre responded, she continued talking. "The streets are being cleared today for the holy priests to carry the Blessed Sacrament tomorrow. It will be truly miraculous." Jeanne went on about how much she was looking forward to watching the procession that would honor the Eucharist.

Lisette was only half-listening. She was much more interested in seeing the palace of Versailles as it came into view.

After entering the Minister's Courtyard, their carriage stopped. Not being noble, they could not travel by carriage any farther. They could either walk or be carried by sedan chair to the entrance of the palace. There were two more courtyards to pass through, the Royal Courtyard and then the Marble Courtyard. Once inside the innermost courtyard, they would have to pass inspection by the palace guards before being allowed inside.

Le Sèvre descended the carriage first, followed by Jeanne and then Lisette. Jeanne pointed to the men waiting with yellow sedan chairs. "François, there are three chairs," she said.

One of the vendors approached Le Sèvre. "Monsieur, for you and your lovely women, I give you the price of six *livres* for three chairs."

Le Sèvre ignored the man. "We will walk," Le Sèvre said as he moved toward the entrance.

Jeanne and Lisette followed him to where they would need to pass inspection. As they waited in line for the guards to evaluate those who had arrived before them, Lisette observed a variety of people entering the palace. She saw courtiers, noble ladies and gentlemen, merchants and even craftsmen. The palace guards seemed to allow anyone to pass through if they were properly attired, ladies in gowns and men with swords.

Le Sèvre and her mother had been discussing the inspection for days. Lisette and Jeanne would have to wear suitable dresses. Le Sèvre had bought them both new gowns for the occasion. He had also bought himself a sword. Not being a nobleman, Le Sèvre had not previously needed a sword. He was unwilling to rent one at the palace gate, saying that it was important to create a strong first impression with anyone he might encounter at Versailles, customer or not.

When it was their turn to be inspected, a guard in a long, dark blue coat with red trim and red *culottes* with white stockings motioned for them to move closer. Lisette and her mother went ahead of Le Sèvre. The guard quickly looked at them and nodded. "You may pass," he said briskly.

The guard then looked at Le Sèvre's sword hanging against his hip. "Go ahead," the guard said to him.

The three of them entered through the main doors and into the front foyer. Le Sèvre and Jeanne walked quickly toward the staircase that lead to the merchant's room on the upper floor.

Lisette lagged behind.

"Stop dragging, Lisette! We must not keep them waiting," Le Sèvre snarled.

Lisette surveyed the hall. She was struck by the dark green, purple and brown marble on the floor, on the wall columns and on the door frames. As they ascended the stairs, Lisette noticed the gilding on the wrought-iron and bronze banister. She saw it again in the gilt-lead sculptures that were neatly tucked into a niche on the landing of the first floor.

They entered the small merchant room and Le Sèvre rushed over to one of the few remaining empty stalls. The other luxury *marchands* had already claimed their spaces. Lisette noticed merchants selling books, lace, gloves, fans and jewels. Le Sèvre wasn't the only jeweler at Versailles today.

As Le Sèvre was nearly finished organizing his display of jewels, a page approached them. "Monsieur and Madame Le Sèvre?" The page appeared no older than Lisette. He held his breath while he stood waiting for a reply. Lisette watched his face redden.

Le Sèvre replied cautiously, "Yes."

The page exhaled loudly and the redness of his face gave way to a healthy pink. "The Baron and Baronne Fontaine have a message for you. They are attending morning Mass with the King and Queen. You are to wait in the Helvetia Salon for them."

Lisette regarded Le Sèvre. He pursed his lips tightly together and squinted his eyes. Le Sèvre had said that he wasn't satisfied to simply wait for customers in his stall in the merchant's room. Going out of his way to arrange a special session with the Baron and Baronne Fontaine, he expected results for his efforts. Lisette thought that he might holler at the page, but Le Sèvre was polite and merely responded, "Very well. Thank you."

After the page had left them, Le Sèvre turned to Jeanne. "We are going to find them in the chapel. The more time with the Baron and Baronne, the better my chances are of convincing them to buy. Let's go."

"But the chapel is on the other side of the palace in the south wing, François. We are not close," Jeanne said.

Le Sèvre ignored his wife. Instead, he shot Lisette a stern look and said, "You are coming too. I know that the Baronne will be especially enamored with the necklace you are wearing."

They left the north wing and went back down the stairs. After entering the south wing, Lisette heard an organ playing and voices singing. Le Sèvre darted ahead as if called by a Siren. Both Jeanne and Lisette struggled to keep up with him. Jeanne pleaded with him to slow down, but instead he picked up his pace and moved faster down the hall.

They arrived at the chapel and Le Sèvre marched in, waiting for neither Jeanne nor Lisette. He disappeared into the crowd.

Jeanne stopped and grabbed Lisette's hand. "We should stay here. He'll come back for us. We are wearing his goods."

Lisette slipped her hand out of her mother's grip. Standing in the rear of the crowded chapel, Lisette examined the long, narrow, oval-shaped room. It was impressive in every way imaginable. Light streamed in from all angles. The tall windows spanned the great height of the chapel, allowing natural sunlight to flood the space and imbue it with an other-worldly feel.

Soaring columns with elaborately decorated capitals defined the second level of the royal gallery, where the King and Queen attended Mass. Lisette peered up. The ceiling was covered with paintings, divided into three compartments. In each compartment a bright, light-filled sky figured prominently. She also saw angels, a dove and cherubs carrying a cross.

"There is the new King! And the Queen is standing next to him!" Her mother was awestruck.

Lisette looked to where her mother was pointing. She saw a young man wearing a blue sash with a white star on it standing in the gallery above them. He appeared not much older than Lisette. Next to him was a young woman. *Marie-Antoinette,* she thought. Lisette recognized her from the Joyous Entry. She was

217

even more enchanting than she had been a year ago when Lisette saw her waving from her carriage.

Lisette felt someone pinch her arm. It was her mother motioning for Lisette to follow.

Jeanne pointed to Le Sèvre.

Lisette saw that he was in full showman mode, charming and flattering a noble couple. As she watched Le Sèvre talk, Lisette felt the necklace tighten.

Her mother tugged at her wrist. "Come, Lisette, we are needed by his side." Jeanne was so eager to reach Le Sèvre that she left Lisette standing by herself, still near the rear of the chapel.

Lisette didn't follow her mother. Instead, she turned and searched for the exit. She noticed a set of enormous double doors. They weren't the same doors that she had come through to enter the chapel, but Lisette suspected that they led back into the main corridor.

She backed up slowly, carefully keeping track of Le Sèvre and her mother as she made her way to the doors. They never once turned around to see Lisette leaving. When she had reached the doors, she didn't hesitate. Lisette dashed out of the chapel. She had been right. She was now back in the main hallway.

Lisette moved quickly down the wide corridor, trying to get away from the chapel. She couldn't move as swiftly as she would have liked because the marble floors beneath her feet were slippery. To make matters worse, her new shoes were too big for her feet. Even though they were ill-fitting, Le Sèvre had insisted that she wear them today.

As Lisette made her way to the end of the hall, she saw a staircase. She thought it was best to climb to a different floor. The more distance she put between herself and Le Sèvre, the less time she would have to spend doing his bidding. Lisette was not excited to act as Le Sèvre's pawn today.

He was there to sell jewels for the upcoming coronation to as many noble ladies as possible. He was one of the few people in Paris who, instead of mourning King Louis XV's recent death, celebrated it. Le Sèvre knew that with the death of the old king, a new king would have to be crowned. Coronations were always elaborate affairs with all who attended wearing their finest and newest clothing and jewels. Le Sèvre knew that the coming months would be some of his most profitable ever. Lisette had heard her step-father and her mother discussing it often, but Lisette wasn't interested in jewels today.

She wanted to see the palace's renowned paintings. Lisette had heard her papa talk about the multitude of remarkable paintings displayed at Versailles. Her papa had been especially enamored with a particular Veronese painting, *Feast in the House of Simon*. Lisette hoped to find it.

As she advanced to the next floor, once again her new shoes impeded her progress, causing her to slip with each step. She considered removing them, but then decided against it when she noticed the piles of feces and pools of urine in the corners of the staircase. Lisette covered her nose and mouth with her hand to avoid breathing in the fetid odors. It smelled like the alleyway behind her house where chamber pots were emptied. Lisette decided to take her time ascending the stairs. As she dodged a particularly large, yellow puddle, she nearly collided with a servant coming down the stairs carrying a large water pail. Their shoulders brushed.

"Watch out! Pay attention to where you are going!" the young boy shouted as he balanced his pail with both hands to prevent the water from spilling over the side of it. After he said this to Lisette, he stopped to look at her. He scanned her dress and then said, "What are *you* doing using the servants' staircase? It belongs to us. You shouldn't be here. Move along." He reached out, like he was going to shove her.

Lisette moved quickly out of his reach and continued up the

stairs.

Immediately after leaving the stairwell and entering the corridor on an upper floor, Lisette heard loud voices. She couldn't determine their location because the voices were muffled, but she thought she heard a girl crying out from a room in the hall.

As Lisette peered down the hallway, she noticed that most of the doors were closed. Lisette also observed that this higher floor seemed different from the one directly below. It appeared grander. There were fewer doors and they were spaced farther apart from each other than those on the lower floor. She continued in the direction of the voices.

As she moved down the hall, the voices grew louder. About halfway down the corridor, she noticed a door that was slightly ajar. *Are they coming from this room?* she wondered. Lisette carefully pushed the door open and peeked inside. She had taken no more than two steps into the room when she jumped up. Lisette was immediately taken aback by a large, gray animal that had been stuffed and placed on a platform in the middle of the room. It had a single horn coming out of its head and was like nothing Lisette had ever seen. *What is that?* she thought.

As she surveyed the room, she noticed more bizarre objects, each one strange in its own way. The room was filled to the brim with paintings, animals and other items that were very unfamiliar to Lisette. Several walls were covered with canvases hung so closely together that the wall was no longer visible. On other walls there were more animal carcasses. Some were stuffed heads, while others were entire specimens. There were also creatures that Lisette determined must be counterfeit. They were tacked and mounted directly onto the wall.

Lisette walked closer to the far wall to more carefully inspect a skeleton that appeared to have a human torso and a long fish's tail instead of legs. *What is that?* she wondered. Next to the skeleton, she noticed tiny human heads, as if they had been shrunk. *What is this room?* she thought. Lisette's eyes moved from object to object, each one more disarming than the next. She might have stayed in the room all morning, getting lost in its strange world, but she was brought back to the present moment when she heard the girl's cries again.

Lisette left the room with the oddities and went back into the hall. It seemed as if the voices were coming from the next room down. As she approached the door, she could see it was open a crack. She went up to the door and listened. Lisette heard two voices: an older woman's and a young girl's.

"Stop! Please stop, Mother! Let me go!" The girl's voice was rife with fear. Before Lisette could peek inside, she heard a loud thump. It sounded like a body hitting the floor.

The girl continued to protest vehemently, "You can't keep me here!"

Then Lisette heard the older woman's voice reply in a loud whisper. "Lower your voice. I don't want to keep you in here, but you are giving me no choice." The woman sounded determined, but also eerily calm as she uttered the threat.

Lisette's curiosity got the better of her. She moved so that her body was concealed behind the door and then craned her neck so that she could see inside the room. A young woman was collapsed on the floor and a tall, thin woman loomed over her with a raised hand.

"Oh!" Lisette let out a gasp and then immediately put her hand over her mouth. Lisette thought that she recognized the girl, so she looked closer. It wasn't Adélaïde de La Valette, but the girl bore a striking resemblance to her. They could almost be twins.

Lisette swiftly turned to leave. *I shouldn't be here,* she realized. After she had only taken a few steps, she felt a bony hand clamp down on her wrist. Suddenly, she was jerked around. It was the older woman she had glimpsed from the doorway...the woman who had been threatening the girl.

She pulled Lisette into the room and hastily shut the door. "What are you doing in this corridor, my child?" The woman tightened her grip on Lisette's arm as she stared directly at her. She towered over Lisette and had to lower her head to meet Lisette's gaze.

"I am no child." Lisette's leg shook uncontrollably beneath her dress, but she held her voice steady. She thought it was best not to show any fear.

"You appear to be a child...you couldn't be much older than the new Queen." This woman's tone caused Lisette's leg to shake more. She had not released Lisette's wrist.

Lisette said nothing in response, but held her gaze. She didn't want to look away.

The woman scoffed at Lisette. "You haven't answered my question. What are you doing here?"

Out of the corner of her eye, Lisette saw the girl running toward the door.

The woman immediately let go of Lisette and went after the girl. "No you don't!" She grabbed the girl with both arms, shoved her down into a nearby chair and then slowly pushed the heavy armchair to the farthest corner of the room. The woman seemed to have the strength of three men. As the armchair moved along the floor it made a loud screeching noise that hurt Lisette's ears. "You stay put," the woman said.

The girl looked too scared to move again. She began to quietly sob.

Before the older woman turned back around, Lisette made a run for the door herself.

She had one foot over the threshold when the woman pulled her back into the room. "I wasn't finished with you. What are you doing here?"

As she leaned in closer, Lisette noticed that the woman had a large scar on her left cheek. A shiver shot down her back. "I was lost." Lisette hoped the woman would accept her explanation.

"Have it your way. Because you insist on acting like an insolent child and refuse to answer my questions, I will answer them for you. You will leave this wing of the palace immediately. You will mind your own business and say nothing about what you've seen here to anyone." She slid her hand to Lisette's upper arm and squeezed harder than she had earlier.

Again, Lisette was surprised by this woman's strength. The terrible pain in Lisette's arm was quickly giving way to numbness.

"Do you understand?" the woman asked her. She looked like she was about to say something else, but paused. The woman sniffed Lisette and then appeared confused. "What is that smell on you? I know it..." She inhaled deeply again and a knowing smile came across her face. "Ah yes, I know it well. It is turpentine! You smell like my older daughter. But why would you smell like a painter? Who are you?" She stared at Lisette like she was an oddity that belonged with the shrunken heads in the room next door. Then the look morphed into one of disapproval.

Despite the woman's hold on her, Lisette stood tall and said, "If you will release me, I will be on my way, Madame."

The woman's countenance returned to her initial menacing expression. Her eyes bored into Lisette. "Remember, you are to say nothing about what you think you've seen here." She quickly glanced at the girl in the armchair, probably to ensure she hadn't moved. She looked back at Lisette and added, "Or I will find you and silence you myself. You do not want to cross me, young mistress. I can hurt you and your entire family if I please."

Lisette heard the girl let out a low squeal as the woman said these words.

The older woman twisted toward the girl. "You be quiet. I will deal with you in a moment."

Then she faced Lisette again. "Weren't you leaving?"

Lisette simply nodded.

The woman seemed to be satisfied because she opened the door, pushed Lisette into the hall and returned to the room, shutting and locking the door behind her.

Lisette stood in front of the closed door considering what had just transpired. She had to tell someone what she had witnessed. *Could that woman really come after me?* she thought. As Lisette considered her predicament, she was unsure that this woman would be able to follow through on her threat. *How can she hurt me or my family if she doesn't even know my name?* Lisette wondered.

Lisette hadn't yet moved when a palace guard came by. Like the guard who had inspected them at the entrance, his waistcoat was the color of a deep blue sky and was trimmed with a red collar and cuffs. Lisette noticed that his red *culottes* and white leggings offered a striking contrast with the deep blue coat. The vivid reds and blues reminded her of the Rubens' paintings that she had seen so many times in the Luxembourg Palace.

"Mademoiselle, you shouldn't be lingering in this hall. I need to escort you to another room." This guard was just as brusque as the entrance guard.

Lisette considered telling him what was going on behind the closed door in front of them, but the guard didn't look like he wanted to listen to her.

"I must clear this hall now." He reached out to take her arm when she swiftly stepped back.

She didn't want to be held captive again. She thought quickly, trying to remember the name of the room where Le Sèvre was to meet with the nobles. "Can you take me to the Hercules Salon? I am expected there. I'm afraid I have lost my way."

He grunted and started walking.

Lisette stood frozen, still unsure of what the guard might do to her.

After a few paces, he turned around. He must have realized he was walking by himself. "Follow me," he said and waited for Li-sette to move before he proceeded.

Lisette slowly followed, careful to stay several paces behind him.

He muttered under his breath as he strutted down the hall.

All Lisette could make out was "stupid girl."

As they walked down the corridor, Lisette remained behind the guard. He would look back from time to time to ensure that she was still following him. He never said a word to Lisette, but continued talking quietly to himself. He seemed resentful of his current duty.

After they had covered the entire length of the long hall, they came to a room with an imposing set of open doors. The guard led Lisette inside the room. "The Hercules Salon," he said.

Lisette knew instantly she was not in the right place. This room was empty. She didn't see Le Sèvre or her mother.

The guard looked at her briefly and said, "I do not want to find you lingering in the halls again." He turned and left, closing the doors behind him.

Lisette released a long sigh when she didn't hear the door lock. She glanced around the room. It was magnificent. The windows stretched from floor to ceiling and were each framed by marble arches. She couldn't help but follow the marble pilasters placed in between the windows from the floor all the way up to their gold-covered capitals. As her eyes moved closer to the ceiling she noticed the golden crown molding. It was thick and framed the entire room.

She looked directly above her. *What is that painting?* she wondered. The painting covered the whole ceiling. Lisette had never seen anything like it before. It was glorious. She began to count the figures, but soon stopped when she realized that there were too many. She was already losing track. *There must be over one hundred people in this painting!* she thought.

As she lowered her gaze, she saw the Veronese, *Feast in the House of Simon*. Her papa had created a copy of this painting and hung it in their drawing room. She had grown up seeing it every day. The real painting was much bigger than she imagined. It took up most of the wall. The balance of figures, objects and space was perfect. Lisette marveled at how Veronese had divided the groupings of people evenly in between the massive Corinthian columns, with Christ in the center. She considered every element carefully: the pristine, white classical buildings in the background, the brilliant colors depicting the smallest details, the several dozen human figures, and the atmosphere of pageantry. *I must sketch this,* she thought.

Lisette pulled out a small sketchpad that she had hidden in the pocket bag underneath her dress. Before long, she had already sketched the background and middle ground. Her pencil moved rapidly across the paper. It was as if her hand was acting on its own and she had no control over it.

Lisette stepped back for an overall view of the enormous painting. She looked down at her sketch and then back up at the painting. *How does Veronese make them look so real?* she wondered. She thought about it for a few moments and then decided it was his brushstrokes. *Of course,* Lisette realized.

She raised up her right hand and pretended she had a paint brush in it. Lisette tried to recreate Veronese's brushstrokes in the air with her imaginary paintbrush. She moved her hand in small semi-circular motions, retracing the tiniest swirls of color used for the women's dresses and the men's togas.

"Lovely mural, isn't it?" a female voice said. It came from behind Lisette. "The women wearing the Venetian gowns are my favorite."

Lisette had been so absorbed in her imaginary painting that the voice took her by surprise. Startled, Lisette spun around too quickly and she nearly toppled over. She caught herself just before she fell to the floor.

"Do you require assistance?" the young woman asked her.

When Lisette had regained her composure and stood squarely on both feet, she looked up. It was the Queen. Lisette tried to find her voice.

"Your Majesty." Lisette bowed and curtsied deeply to her.

"I didn't mean to startle you," Marie-Antoinette said.

"Your Majesty, I thought I was alone," Lisette replied.

"That is the curious thing about Versailles. One can be very alone at Versailles and yet one is never alone here." She had a sad look on her face as she spoke.

Lisette had never been this close to the Queen. Marie-Antoinette appeared to be no older than Lisette, yet she was already married and a Queen. To Lisette, Marie-Antoinette had already experienced ten lifetimes.

Before either of them had the chance to speak again, they were interrupted by a servant who came rushing into the room with an armful of candles. As soon as the servant realized that he was not alone in the room, he apologized profusely and then abruptly left.

"Did you leave morning Mass early? I am supposed to stay for the entirety, but I needed a few minutes by myself, before the Grand Couvert," the Queen said.

Le Sèvre and Mother, Lisette suddenly remembered. She was sure her mother was panicking by now. She could see Le Sèvre's disapproval and hear her mother's voice saying, *Where were you?* Her heart began to race.

"I apologize your Majesty, but if you will excuse me, I must be going." Lisette turned to leave so quickly that she dropped her sketchpad right at the Queen's feet.

The Queen retrieved it and began flipping through its pages. Her face lit up. "You are a superb artist. Do you paint people too?"

Lisette wanted to say, *Yes, but only because of Le Sèvre,* but she knew candor was inappropriate. Lisette simply shook her head affirmatively.

The Queen clapped. "Splendid!"

Lisette knew what the Queen would ask next.

"Will you sketch my likeness?"

Lisette realized that she did not have time to sketch the Queen. She had to return to her mother and Le Sèvre, but it was not possible to deny the Queen either.

Marie-Antoinette did not wait for an answer, instead she

handed Lisette her sketchpad and sat on the embroidered sofa. She turned her body as if she was posing for a portrait. "Should I sit like this?"

Just as Lisette was about to plead with the Queen to allow her to leave, an older woman flew into the room like an upset hen.

"There you are. Madame, where have you been? I have been looking all over for you." The woman seemed to be holding back, as if she wanted to be harsher and reprimand the Queen more, but couldn't.

The Queen quickly defended herself to the frenzied woman, "I needed some air. I was feeling faint, Madame de Noailles." The Queen looked over at Lisette pleadingly.

Madame de Noailles shot Marie-Antoinette a stern look of disapproval. The grim older woman retorted, "It is not proper etiquette for Madame to just...wander the palace! You are Queen now." The woman was losing her previous control. "As Dame d'Honneur, it falls to me to ensure court rules are always followed...and that you behave like a proper Queen of France. To perform my duties properly, I must know where you are at all times."

The Queen defended herself, "Madame de Noailles, there is no cause for concern. I haven't been engaging in activities of ill repute. I've just met the most magnificent artist..." A slight frown came over the Queen's face. "We have not been introduced," the Queen said.

There was an awkward silence until Lisette realized that she should introduce herself first. "Élisabeth Louise Vigée," Lisette curtsied deeply as she gave her full name.

The Queen continued addressing her Mistress of the Household, "Mademoiselle Vigée has most graciously agreed to sketch my likeness, a quick portrait on paper, if you will." She looked over and waited for Lisette to confirm her statement.

Lisette had not yet agreed to anything, but the Queen appeared so desperate, she decided to go along with her. "Yes, it is true. I was about to begin a sketch of her Majesty," Lisette said.

The Queen smiled at her thankfully, like Lisette had just spared her from a terrible punishment. "Madame de Noailles, please leave us alone so that Mademoiselle Vigée can give my sketch her full attention. I want you to fetch Monsieur Pierre and bring him here in exactly twenty minutes. As the Premier Peintre du Roi, I will require his opinion of Mademoiselle Vigée's work." The Queen was now speaking with a new sense of confidence to her lady-in-waiting.

"Yes, Madame." Madame de Noailles curtsied and then left the room.

First Painter to the King, Lisette thought. Lisette had never met such an important artist of the court before. When she was sure they were alone, Lisette asked the Queen, "The Premier Peintre will be here to look at my work?"

"Yes. From what I saw in your sketchbook, you are quite skilled. If I can secure Monsieur Pierre's approval of your work, then I will encounter less resistance when I ask you back to paint me."

Paint the Queen? she thought. Lisette couldn't believe her ears. She bit her lip as she tried to control her excitement. Lisette knew it was impolite to express too much emotion, but she wanted to jump up and down.

The Queen smiled and continued, "I enjoy your presence, Mademoiselle Vigée. I believe it would be positively amusing to sit for you. None of the court painters want to talk with me. They want me to remain silent for the duration of the sitting." She paused before she finished explaining. "I have few friends here at court." The same sad look she had expressed earlier came over her face again.

Lisette was surprised at the Queen's honesty. She was also alarmed to hear that the Queen wanted for friends. Lisette had always heard that court life was busy and full. It was difficult for Lisette to imagine being lonely amid so many courtiers bustling around the palace. Nonetheless, the Queen seemed to carry a great burden.

"You may begin," the Queen said.

Lisette studied her. She emanated a deep sadness. *Perhaps this sketch will bring her some joy,* Lisette thought as she began sketching.

Lisette concentrated intensely as she drew the Queen. To Lisette, Marie-Antoinette was striking. She possessed a narrow oval face and small blue eyes. Her nose was slender and her mouth didn't appear to be too large for her face, although her lips were full. But what struck Lisette most, was her complexion. It was so creamy white that it seemed almost transparent. Her skin tone looked as fresh as the ground after a newly fallen snow.

Lisette then surveyed her neck and torso. The Queen's neck was the same creamy white as her face. Her gown had a low neckline that revealed her pristine skin. It was similar in style to Lisette's own dress, but the Queen's dress was trimmed in much more lace than Lisette's and was made of a pale blue silk instead of taffeta. She looked down at the Queen's shoes. They were the exact color of her dress and were also made of silk. Lisette thought that Marie-Antoinette was flawless.

There was silence while Lisette sketched. Her hand moved the pencil furiously across the page. Lisette was glad that today she was working with pencil. Oil would be another matter. Lisette wasn't certain of how she would paint the Queen's translucent flesh tones in oil.

After just a few minutes, the Queen said, "That is an exquisite necklace."

"Thank you, your Majesty," Lisette said. She didn't want to answer questions about it or talk about Le Sèvre, so she quickly changed the subject. "Would you like me to sketch your bust in addition to your face?"

"Today, we only have time for my face. Are you nearly finished?" the Queen asked Lisette.

"No, not quite."

"We don't have much time. Once my lady-in-waiting returns and the First Painter gives his official opinion of your work, I will be expected to dress for the mid-day meal and rejoin my husband. How I dread the Grand Couvert. I much prefer to dine in private." Lisette watched the Queen's face fall as she spoke. She looked despondent.

"May I ask you what is wrong?" Immediately after Lisette asked this question, she realized that she should not address the Queen so informally.

"You are sweet and kind for asking. Even in four years, no one here has made me feel especially welcome. I still miss my mother, my home and my country. I miss Austria."

Lisette was relieved that instead of being offended, the Queen was touched that someone would inquire after her well-being. Lisette genuinely felt sympathy for Marie-Antoinette. Her melancholy expression made her seem less like a Queen of France from one of the most prominent royal families in Europe and more like a scared girl who was lonely, homesick and looking for a friend.

"But doesn't your husband, Louis, keep you company and offer you comfort?" Lisette asked.

This question brought the Queen to the brink of tears. Lisette felt like she had made the situation worse.

"He offers me no comfort. He won't even allow me to perform my duty as a wife and share his bed. He barely touches me. I am lonelier than ever. I don't belong here." The Queen started to weep as she answered Lisette.

Lisette took the Queen's hand. She briefly considered that she was violating court protocol again, but the Queen was so distraught, Lisette felt compelled to help her. "I often feel the same way. I don't share the same interests as other girls. I have no desire to discuss suitors, marriage or the latest gossip on recent engagements. I only want to paint. Yet painting is the domain of men. I am not wholly welcome there either. I don't belong anywhere."

The Queen was silent for a moment and then giggled. "We are a pair, aren't we! Each of us a misfit, in our own way. Oh, Élisabeth, it is marvelous to talk to you."

Lisette returned the kind words, "It is wonderful to talk to you, Madame, and please call me Lisette. All of my friends do."

"Please, call me Antoinette." The Queen smiled at Lisette. "Let's finish this sketch." Antoinette's voice was exuberant.

It seemed to Lisette that their conversation had lifted the Queen's spirits.

Lisette returned to her drawing. She knew that Mass had ended and that her mother and Le Sèvre would be upset with her. But she couldn't leave the Queen just yet. Lisette hoped that she would be forgiven.

Lisette was nearly finished with the sketch of the Queen when her lady-in-waiting returned.

Madame de Noailles entered the room in such a rush that she narrowly avoided stumbling over a stool. She quickly glanced at Lisette and appeared to be on the brink of embarrassment. This matriarch of manners was exhibiting significantly less grace than earlier.

Lisette looked away.

Breathless, she addressed the Queen. "Madame, I am sorry to report that I was not able to locate Monsieur Pierre," Madame de Noailles said as she smoothed out her dress.

"What do you mean?" the Queen seemed irritated at Madame de Noailles. "I must speak with him."

Madame de Noailles replied, "I left word with his assistant." She hovered over the Queen as if she wasn't finished speaking.

"Is there more?" the Queen asked.

"Your Majesty, I want to remind you that you are expected in the Salon of the Grand Couvert shortly. We don't have time to wait for Monsieur Pierre."

Lisette noticed that Madame de Noailles had recovered her

composure. Her haughtiness had returned.

"Madame de Noailles, we *will* wait for Monsieur Pierre and I *will* hear his official opinion," said the Queen.

Lisette wondered if their time alone together hadn't given the Queen a fresh attitude. Antoinette was acting less like a frightened girl and more like the Queen of France.

"Madame, I feel that I need to repeat myself. We do not have time to indulge your interest in amateur painters. You are the Queen and your time is best spent in the presence of serious artists who can create portraits worthy of a queen. Do not forget that your mother, the Empress, is waiting for a portrait of you that satisfies her," Madame de Noailles said, undeterred.

It became clear to Lisette that even though Antoinette was no longer Dauphine, Madame de Noailles still felt that her duty was to guide Antoinette in the ways of the court. It was also obvious that Madame de Noailles did not accept orders blindly, even from the Queen.

"But Madame de Noailles, I believe I have found such a serious artist in Mademoiselle Vigée. I want her to paint my next portrait...one that we send to Mother."

"That is preposterous. I am not going along with any such charade."

"I think if you see her work, you will believe otherwise. Look at the sketch of me she is making now," the Queen said.

Madame de Noailles scowled as she bent to examine Lisette's drawing of the Queen. Amazement quickly replaced her grimace. She looked like she was trying to control herself. "It has merit," she said flatly.

The Queen stood and glided across the room to where Lisette was sitting. Lisette had never seen anyone move so gracefully, not even the Salonnière. It was as if the Queen's feet were hovering above the floor.

"Just look at my eyes...you can see into my soul," Antoinette said as she pointed to the various details of the sketch. The Queen was giddy as she spoke.

"It is an acceptable rendering of your visage." Madame de Noailles remained calm and unemotional, but she could not take her eyes off of the drawing.

"Monsieur Pierre," the usher standing by the door called out in a loud voice.

"Let him in," ordered the Queen.

Lisette glanced up as the door opened. Her heart raced and she felt her palms moisten. *What will he think of my sketch?* she wondered.

Monsieur Pierre walked over to where the Queen was sitting and bowed deeply to her. "Madame, how may I serve you?" Monsieur Pierre shifted his weight from one foot to the other. He seemed to be in a hurry, as if he wanted to finish his duty and leave the room as quickly as possible.

To Lisette, he appeared both bored and annoyed.

"Monsieur Pierre, as Premier Peintre du Roi, I want your official opinion on this sketch," said the Queen.

Monsieur Pierre reached for the sketch and began examining it. "It is very good, Madame. A most remarkable likeness of you. An almost exact likeness, in fact. Who is the artist?"

The Queen smiled, obviously pleased that her initial assessment of Lisette's work had been affirmed. "She is right here." The Queen gestured toward Lisette who was sitting directly across from her.

Monsieur Pierre put down the sketch and stared at Lisette. It was the first time he had looked at her since entering the room. Instead of irritation and boredom, his face now registered wonderment and curiosity. His eyes widened as if he was looking upon something that he had never seen before.

"Go ahead and thumb through the rest of her sketchpad. There is much more that you should see," said the Queen.

Still studying Lisette, he replied, "Indeed." Monsieur Pierre went through Lisette's sketchpad. With enlarged eyes he carefully examined each page. After the first dozen pages, his pace quickened and he hastily flipped through the rest of the sketchbook. As he reached the end, he took his time, lingering on the last few pages. His eyes narrowed. Without glancing up, he said, "I would have hardly suspected that this came from a girl's hands."

Lisette immediately retorted, "I am not like other girls."

"Obviously you have proven that, Mademoiselle. You possess a rare talent," Monsieur Pierre said, still examining her sketches.

"Monsieur Pierre, I believe her work is worthy of the Académie Royale de Peinture et de Sculpture," the Queen said boldly.

The Queen's voice seemed to startle Monsieur Pierre. He closed the sketchbook and looked up at Lisette. His gaze was fixed on her. She saw a look of revulsion and contempt in his squinted eyes.

He turned toward the Queen. "I would hardly go that far. Académie membership is a very serious endeavor, not appropriate for a woman. Women are no longer allowed membership."

"The King did not approve that measure," Antoinette said boldly.

Both Madame de Noailles and Monsieur Pierre stared at the Queen.

Monsieur Pierre scrambled to find his voice, "The old King, may he rest in peace, did not. You are quite right, your Majesty. But I have every confidence that your husband, the King, *will* approve it. We must reserve Académie membership for men."

Madame de Noailles, who had been silent, stood. "Madame, I'm afraid it is time we leave. You are expected by the King."

"Very well. Monsieur Pierre, thank you for offering an official opinion of Mademoiselle Vigée's work. You are excused," said the Queen.

"Your Majesty." He bowed to the Queen and then glared at Lisette. He seemed to be frozen, still holding her sketchpad.

Lisette held out her hand to secure its return.

"Monsieur Pierre, is there something else? I've already excused you," the Queen said.

He shook his head *no*, handed Lisette her sketchpad, bowed once again to the Queen and promptly left the room.

Lisette was glad to see him leave. She didn't understand his conflicting opinion of her work or the disdain he seemed to have for her.

Beaming, the Queen held up her sketch proudly.

The Queen's opinion is much more important, she thought. Lisette couldn't help but smile as the Queen regarded the completed sketch.

"Madame, we must be leaving. The King is waiting." Madame de Noailles stood next to the Queen, looming over her like a hawk about to swoop down on a mouse. She crossed her arms in front of her chest. "I must insist."

The Queen looked at Lisette apologetically. "My enchanting new friend, Lisette, I must go." She reached out her hand to take the sketch. "May I?"

Lisette wanted to keep the drawing to remember her time with Antoinette, but she couldn't refuse a Queen. "Yes, of course, your Majesty."

"I can't wait to show Louis." Antoinette appeared hopeful. "It will be a clever way to win his attention."

"Yes," Lisette agreed.

"I look forward to sitting for you again soon. I will send word." The Queen glanced over at her lady-in-waiting as if to show her that she fully intended on having Lisette return.

Madame de Noailles responded immediately, "Madame, we will consult with the Royal Secretary, but I don't foresee any time for another sitting...not soon."

Lisette saw that Madame de Noailles knew just the words that would rattle the Queen and that Antoinette was trying to suppress the girl inside of her who was easily upset.

"You will return soon to paint my portrait. I will see to it," Antoinette said. There was a tone of finality in her voice. The

Queen glared at Madame de Noailles.

Lisette clearly saw a look of defiance in the Queen's eyes.

I am to paint the Queen! Lisette thought. She was not excited about portraits, but for the Queen of France, she could make an exception.

"Madame, we will discuss this with the Royal Secretary, but for now the King is expecting us in your Majesty's chambers for the Grand Couvert. Mass ended nearly an hour ago."

An hour has passed? she thought. Le Sèvre would be livid, she was sure. Lisette hoped that since the Queen was involved in her disobedience, he would be merciful.

Lisette curtsied.

The Queen smiled at Lisette as Madame de Noailles ushered her out of the chamber.

When they had left the room, Lisette sat and executed a quick copy of her sketch of the Queen. Still fresh in her mind, Lisette could swiftly capture Antoinette's likeness before she returned to her mother and Le Sèvre. *I'm already so late, another few minutes won't matter*, she thought. Lisette wanted a memento of her visit with the Queen of France. As soon as she had finished her copy, Lisette left the room.

She walked as quickly as she could through the vast network of halls without drawing unnecessary attention to herself. Lisette couldn't recall the exact path back to the chapel. She should have paid better attention earlier.

Lisette saw a staircase at the end of the hall that she could use to return to the ground floor. As she reached the lower floor, she peeked in the rooms with open doors. Lisette briefly ducked in each one to make sure she was going in the right direction. The first one had violet damask-covered walls and armchairs, while the next one had forest green drapes covering the windows. She had remembered the distinctive decorative features of each room she had passed. *Good. I'm not lost,* Lisette realized.

She slowed down as she approached the intersection of two corridors. *Does this one lead to the chapel?* she wondered. She turned to the left and followed the corridor all the way down un-til she heard a man's thundering voice. It belonged to Le Sèvre. His voice was not only loud, but also distinctive. Then she saw him. He was standing outside the chapel entrance talking with a noble couple. The nobleman's embroidered silk coat and the wo-man's *robe à la française* easily identified them as courtiers. Li-sette slowed her pace to a saunter.

Le Sèvre's captive audience included her mother. He ges-tured toward Jeanne's necklace. Lisette glanced down at herself. She had to be careful to make sure she was presentable. Lisette checked the front of her dress and then her hands for obvious graphite smudges. Le Sèvre would not be happy with any sign of art-making that he had not approved beforehand. Lisette want-ed the chance to explain herself first.

"Lisette! There you are!" Her mother rushed over to her and whispered in her ear. "We are not happy with your disappear-ance, but right now Le Sèvre is finishing an important sale. Come with me and show them your necklace. Behave yourself until we are finished with this couple. Then we will discuss your atrocious behavior." Her mother pulled her over to where Le Sèvre stood.

"Vicomte and Vicomtesse, you may also be interested in this necklace." Le Sèvre glared at Lisette briefly and then pointed to the emeralds and diamonds around her neck. "Lisette, come clos-er so they can inspect the piece."

The Vicomtesse hesitated and then said, "But I own plenty of emeralds and diamonds." She waved her jewel encrusted fan in front of her face.

Lisette saw several large emeralds and diamonds on it.

"Not in this configuration. Please take a look." Le Sèvre pointed to Lisette's neck again.

The Vicomtesse came up to Lisette and fingered the neck-lace. Only looking at the necklace, she said nothing to Lisette. It was as if Lisette wasn't a person standing before her.

"Exquisite. I want that one," the Vicomtesse said to Le

Sèvre.

"Marvelous." Le Sèvre then went up to Lisette to remove the necklace.

Lisette blocked his access to the necklace and said, "I can do it." Lisette did not want Le Sèvre's hands on her.

"No, it is mine. I will be the one to give it to the Vicomtesse." Le Sèvre pushed her hands away and began fiddling with the clasp.

Lisette moved away from him so that he couldn't touch the necklace.

He followed her and continued to reach for the clasp.

"Stop. I will remove it," Lisette repeated herself.

He ignored her and kept tugging at the necklace.

Lisette jerked away from Le Sèvre. As she took a giant step backward, she felt the necklace come off of her neck...in little pieces.

"You broke it! You stupid girl!" Le Sèvre immediately bent down and began picking up the individual jewels that had scattered everywhere.

The Vicomte took his wife's arm. "Come, let's go. Good day, Monsieur Le Sèvre."

Lisette watched the couple walk away.

Le Sèvre rose and came up close to Lisette. Only the beet red color of his face betrayed his anger. His voice was calm. "I have had enough of your insolence. Sneaking behind my back with Le Brun and Briard was intolerable, but interfering with my business is completely unacceptable. I am finished with you. When we return home, I am sending you to the Saint Ignatius Convent where you will remain for the rest of your days."

The room spun and Lisette could no longer breathe normally. Her heart felt like it was going to beat out of her chest.

Lisette's mother, who had been silent until then, fell to her knees in front of Le Sèvre. "No, please, you cannot send her away. Lisette must be allowed to marry and have her own family ...not be locked in a convent. Couldn't you dole out some other punishment? Like you do for the servants who misbehave?"

Lisette thought about Henri's bleeding hands. She clasped her own hands tightly together. Lisette regarded her mother. Even groveling, Jeanne was beautiful. Her mother was stunning, with her creamy white skin, sparkling blue eyes and dark hair swept off her face.

Le Sèvre looked down at Jeanne. His face softened. Then he beheld Lisette. He was silent for several moments before he spoke. "Lashes on her hands it is. But if she misbehaves like this again, I will have no choice but to send her away. Now pick up the jewels, quickly, I hear people coming. I cannot bear further embarrassment. I have had enough of Versailles for one day." Le Sèvre abruptly turned and strode down the corridor.

Le Sèvre disappeared down the hall, but Lisette stood in place until the clicking of his heels on the marble floor had faded. Lisette could breathe a little easier, but she still felt an enormous pit deep in her stomach. When would Le Sèvre lash her? Would it be as soon as they returned to Paris? How many lashes would he give her?

"Lisette! Help me." Jeanne had already started collecting the gemstones that were all over the floor.

Lisette crouched down and helped her mother finish gathering the loose jewels. Lisette wanted to tell her mother how she had just met the Queen, but she suspected that her mother didn't want to discuss anything that had happened today at Versailles. Lisette knew the only thing that mattered was that she had yet again disobeyed Le Sèvre. She tried to get her mother's attention, but Jeanne would not look at her.

The booming voices of two palace guards broke the quiet. "Clear this space. Move on. The King is expected shortly."

They picked up the last of the scattered stones and left the corridor, making their way back toward the front gate of the palace.

In silence, they reached the gate where Le Sèvre was in the carriage waiting for them. Before stepping into the carriage, Lisette tried once again to catch her mother's eye. This time Jeanne looked back at her sympathetically.

"Can you forgive me, Mother?" Lisette asked.

With almost undetectable movement, Jeanne shook her head *yes*.

Lisette felt some relief, but her insides were still twisted in painful knots.

Then her mother whispered, "But Le Sèvre won't."

Chapter Twenty-Five

Lisette sat at her window looking out at the bright autumn day. The leaves of the trees had begun to change color. Their bursts of brilliant oranges and reds contrasted sharply with the deep blue of the sky. Lisette looked over to her easel. She hadn't painted in several months, since before they had returned from Versailles. The last time she had gone months without painting had been after her papa died.

After the incident at Versailles, Le Sèvre had said that he was no longer interested in having Lisette paint portraits for his clients. He had told her that she would have to earn his trust again and accept her punishment, but he had not yet followed through. It had been an agonizing summer, not knowing when he was going to lash her. Each time she heard footsteps outside her door, she cringed. She glanced down at her hands. *Will it be today?* she wondered.

Without any notice, her bedroom door opened.

"Good morning, Lisette," Le Sèvre said to her, as if it was an uneventful visit on a routine day.

She said nothing and continued staring out of the window. She saw below that the Marquise de Benseval's *fiacre* had just pulled up in front of the house. Lisette watched her exit the carriage. *I am not scheduled to paint her portrait. What is she doing here?* Lisette wondered. Then she remembered hearing Le Sèvre and her mother discussing the Marquise a few days earlier. Apparently, the Marquise was a disgruntled customer who was asking to return jewels that she had bought from Le Sèvre. Lisette had never seen Le Sèvre return anyone's money. She doubted he was going to begin with the Marquise.

"Look at me, Lisette," Le Sèvre said.

She needed Henri. Lisette looked past Le Sèvre and toward the open door. She could hear commotion down in the front foyer. It sounded like the Marquise was reprimanding the servants.

"If you don't look at me, I will not stop at five lashes. And I will not confine them to your hands...and don't bother calling for Henri. He is not here this morning. I have sent him out on errands. He cannot help you. Now stand up." His voice was low and calm.

Lisette slowly turned her head to look at him. He held a switch. She felt tears forming behind her eyes. Her mind instantly returned to the Convent of the Trinité where she had been punished with lashes for drawing during her lessons. She already felt her hands stinging. Lisette fought back the tears. She didn't want to give Le Sèvre the satisfaction of witnessing her fear. She rose from her stool.

"Have you thought about your disobedience? Are you ready to accept your punishment?"

Lisette nodded and faced him.

"Put out your hands, palms up."

Lisette realized that he was going to cut the insides of her hands. It would hurt far worse than on the tops of her hands, where her scarred skin had hardened them. Lisette did exactly as he said. She found it difficult to breathe. Lisette had to remind herself not to hold her breath. She closed her eyes and braced herself for the razor sharp cuts of the switch.

"Monsieur! The Marquise de Benseval is here to see you. You must come now." Lisette opened her eyes and saw Camille, the chambermaid. She had run abruptly into the room from downstairs and was winded as she spoke to Le Sèvre.

Lisette had never been so glad to see Camille. Was this a reprieve from her punishment? Lisette carefully watched Le Sèvre. The switch was still in his hand, but his attention was now on Camille.

"Not now, Camille, I am busy. Tell the Marquise to wait. I will see her shortly," Le Sèvre said to her curtly.

"But Monsieur, she is threatening to destroy the Sèvres plates in the drawing room if you don't come down," Camille said, still standing in the doorway. She was more agitated than Lisette had ever seen her. She fidgeted with her apron and readjusted her cap as she waited. Lisette had seen Le Sèvre punish the servants whenever anything was broken or went missing, even if they had not been responsible.

Le Sèvre had not yet turned away from Camille. The nervous chambermaid had won his attention with the words *Sèvres plates*. Lisette knew how much his collection meant to him. Her mother had mentioned that Le Sèvre's collection of Sèvres porcelain was worth a small fortune. Always wanting the fine porcelain plates and service pieces, but never able to afford them before her marriage to Le Sèvre, her mother had been overjoyed with Le Sèvre's collection. Jeanne proudly displayed them in their drawing room.

"The Marquise specifically said the Sèvres plates?" Le Sèvre asked Camille.

Lisette hoped that Le Sèvre would be distracted enough to

leave and not lash her.

Camille nodded her head, "Yes, Monsieur."

Lisette knew that French Sèvres porcelain was in great demand all over Europe and was exported as far as Russia. In one of her portrait sittings, the Duchesse de Chartres had told Lisette that Catherine the Great of Russia was fond of collecting the fine French porcelain. Since living with him, Lisette had seen that Le Sèvre had a keen eye for expensive items. Her mother had proudly explained that Le Sèvre's instincts for the luxury goods market had led to his success as a jeweler. Lisette thought that it was due more to his ruthlessness and dictatorial need to control.

Camille had one foot out of the door, ready to go back downstairs with Le Sèvre, but he wasn't moving. He focused on Lisette.

"I said tell her to wait for me. Now leave us," Le Sèvre said, without looking at Camille.

Before Camille could say anything else, there was another disturbance downstairs.

"Le Sèvre, you better come here now. If you don't, I will have your business shut down. Don't forget who my husband is!" the Marquise screamed from the first floor.

Lisette watched Le Sèvre as he considered his next actions. He appeared to be torn and unable to make a decision.

"Monsieur! You must go downstairs," Camille pleaded.

Le Sèvre looked resigned. "You have been spared by the Marquise. I must go see her." He hesitated before saying, "I need you to paint for me again. The Baron and Baronne de Michaud have asked for you specifically to paint their portraits. They refuse to buy any more jewels from me until their portraits are completed." Then he added, "I will not hesitate to lash you if you interfere in my business again."

Lisette found it difficult to say anything in response. She had narrowly escaped being lashed...at least for now...*and* she was being allowed to paint again.

"Do you understand?" he asked her.

"Yes." Lisette nodded.

"If you disobey me again, if you miss any sittings...and if you do not finish these portraits, I will not only lash you, but I *will* send you away to the Saint Ignatius Convent. No amount of your mother's begging will stop it."

Lisette couldn't look at him. She nodded again.

"I will bring you the canvases and supplies as they become needed. Camille will deliver pigments for the Baron and Baronne de Michaud's sittings later in the week. Don't forget, you must do exactly as I say, Lisette." He bent down so that he was very close to her. "If you obey me, we will get along magnificently."

Then Lisette heard something break.

"Monsieur! I think she is destroying the Sèvres plates. You must help me stop her," Camille said as she rushed out and back down the stairs.

Le Sèvre turned and hurriedly left the room too, following closely behind Camille.

Chapter Twenty-Six

True to his word, a few days later, Le Sèvre had Camille bring Lisette pigments. After the Baron and Baronne de Michaud's sittings, he had also had Camille take them away. Even with Le Sèvre's strict rules, Lisette felt a newfound sense of determination. She had evaded lashes and had resumed painting. Full of fresh hope, she had begun formulating a plan to escape Le Sèvre's control, but she knew she couldn't accomplish it by herself. Lisette needed Le Brun's help.

Lisette had to wait until Le Sèvre and her mother left for the evening before she could see Le Brun. From behind a column at the top of the front stairs, Lisette listened to her mother and Le Sèvre discussing their evening plans.

"I have told you that I am the one who decides where you go – at any time of day," Le Sèvre said.

"But I thought you would want us to attend the Marquise's supper. She has bought your jewelry in the past."

"No. I did not agree to it. You will send our regrets. We are going to the Opéra tonight," Le Sèvre said.

Then her mother let out a yelp of pain. Lisette knew that he was hurting her.

"Do you wish to discuss it more?" Le Sèvre asked.

Her mother did not protest or say anything else. Lisette heard them put on their outer coats and head out of the house.

Lisette went down the stairs and waited in the front hall until there was complete silence. Now that Le Sèvre and her mother were gone, she didn't want Henri or any of the other servants to see her leave. Lisette knew Le Sèvre would be gone for hours. After the Opéra, they would probably attend a late evening supper of Le Sèvre's choosing. He never missed an opportunity to cultivate new customers.

When she was convinced no one would see her, Lisette opened the front door and left the house. It was nearly dark, but the street lamps had not yet been lit. Lisette glanced up at the early evening sky. It was her favorite shade of indigo blue. She often sat at her window watching the day fade into night. Lisette had tried to capture the fleeting moments of dusk on canvas. It was something she had not yet mastered, but would continue trying until she succeeded. She knew of few painters who could accurately render this magical time of the day.

Lisette watched the sun quickly descend below the horizon. It would be dark soon and she knew what that meant. In the evenings, danger lurked everywhere in Paris. Lisette didn't want to repeat the troubles of her previous late-night visit to Le Brun's. She considered taking a carriage, but the crisp evening air was inviting.

She moved quickly down the Rue Saint-Honoré, careful to stay out of the shadows. Many of the shopkeepers were still open for business, so there were enough pedestrians to put Lisette at ease. She felt safe for now.

As Lisette approached Le Brun's shop, she saw light coming from the front windows. *Good. He's there,* she thought. Lisette pulled open the door. It wasn't yet locked for the evening. She looked around and didn't see anyone. Monsieur Faucher hadn't come out from the back as usual.

"Le Brun?" Lisette called out.

First she heard a rustling coming from behind the curtain in the back of the shop. Then Lisette heard a loud clanking, like something large had tumbled over and possibly caused damage. *Was that a pot that just fell to the floor?* she thought.

"Le Brun?" she called out again.

Lisette watched the curtain shake and then slowly part in the middle.

Le Brun emerged.

Lisette had seen him disarrayed before, but never like this. He looked like he hadn't changed his clothes in days. As he got closer to her, she saw dried blood all down the front of his shirt. His linen *chemise*, originally white, was now a shade of light pink. She looked up at his face. His right eye was nearly swollen shut and his lip was badly cut, like it had been split open just hours ago.

"Lisette." Le Brun could barely speak. His voice was weak and he had a difficult time maintaining his balance. He swayed back and forth trying to steady himself as he stood before her.

"What happened to you?" Lisette took his arm to help him stand. "Let's sit." She guided him over toward two armchairs in the corner of the shop and helped him sit down. Lisette sat too.

"After some rest, I will be the picture of health." Le Brun regarded her with his one good eye. He seemed glad to see her. "It has been many months. To what do I owe the pleasure of your visit this morning?" he asked trying to keep his head upright.

Lisette glanced over to the front window. The sun had set and it was now completely dark.

"I can come back. You should get to your bed." Lisette stood.

"Nonsense. Sit. How can I help you?" Le Brun waved his arm in the air gesturing toward the chair.

Lisette sat back down. "I need a studio." She watched his face as his brow furrowed and his eyes narrowed.

"I don't see how that is possible," Le Brun said. "There are too many obstacles."

Lisette stared directly at Le Brun. She repeated herself, "I need a studio."

Le Brun quickly replied, "You aren't hearing me. There are too many obstacles, not the least of which is that you aren't a member of the Guild or the Académie Royale. How can you get a license to have a studio if you aren't a member of either?"

Lisette was unsure why Le Brun would even mention the Académie Royale. They both knew that membership in the Académie was restricted to a select few who had completed the rigorous vetting process. For women artists, it was even more stringent. After her visit to Versailles, Lisette knew that if Monsieur Pierre was successful influencing the King, the few slots open to women might disappear altogether. The Guild was an entirely different story. Because her papa had been a long-standing member of the Guild, Lisette had believed that Guild membership would be easily attained.

"I've considered that. I will apply to the Guild. Because of Papa, it won't be difficult to gain membership," Lisette said nonchalantly.

"This is serious, Lisette. If you are caught operating an artist's studio without a license, one that the Guild gives only to its members, your studio could be seized, all of its contents taken and you could be jailed."

"Don't be so dramatic. That would never happen. Trust me, Guild membership and the license won't be a problem." Lisette looked at Le Brun like he was talking nonsense.

"If I help you, you must take care of it right away," Le Brun said gravely.

"I will," Lisette said.

"What about money? How will you pay for a studio?" Le Brun's voice grew louder as he spoke. "Have you forgotten that Le Sèvre controls everything in your life, including your money?"

Lisette had spent the past day solving this problem in her head. "He doesn't control everything."

"But he does control any money *you* make from painting. You know we can't sell paintings done by your hand to pay for a studio. He would find out about it and we would both suffer." Le Brun remained skeptical.

Lisette smiled. "Yes, but what if the paintings weren't executed by my hand?"

"Go on," he said.

She saw Le Brun start to smile, but then wince.

He put his hand up to his cut lip and let out a low groan. Le Brun said no more. He sat and carefully listened while Lisette explained her plan.

Chapter Twenty-Seven

*L*isette looked at her palette. *I need to mix more brown for Hermes' belt,* she thought. She had finally returned to her allegory paintings – in her own studio. In the past several weeks, Lisette had made up for lost time.

As she put the finishing touches on the figure of Hermes, she heard her stomach growl. She ignored it and continued painting. Lisette hadn't wanted to put down her brush for a moment. She glanced out of the tiny window in the corner of the room. It was almost dark outside. *What time is it?* she wondered. Lisette's stomach growled again and this time it didn't stop. Lisette set down her brush and palette and pulled out her papa's pocket watch. If she wanted to keep her new studio a secret from Le Sèvre, she would have to leave it for the day. She could return again in the morning.

As Lisette put her palette away and cleaned her brushes, she surveyed her new supplies. A warm feeling came over her. She hadn't felt such contentment for many months. Rosalie, Marguerite and Le Brun had all helped her. She had taken great risks involving so many people in her plan, but it had worked. In exchange for several still life paintings, Rosalie had received an elaborate wedding *coiffure* from Léonard. Marguerite had happily arranged it. Le Brun had sold Rosalie's paintings and used the money to pay for Lisette's supplies and her new studio. It had been enough to cover several months' rent. Because they were operating within the law, Le Brun had agreed to participate. He had no interest in crossing Le Sèvre.

Le Sèvre never has to know, Lisette thought.

Lisette was nearly finished cleaning up when she heard someone lightly tapping on the door. Her heart stopped for a moment and she froze. Le Brun's words of warning echoed in her head, *If you are caught operating an artist's studio without a license, your studio could be seized, all of its contents taken and you could be jailed.* She had meant to apply for Guild membership, but had not yet done it. *I will go to the Guild first thing tomorrow,* she thought. Lisette reassured herself that the likelihood of the police being on the other side of the door was low. No one knew the location of her studio except Le Brun.

She heard the tapping again. *Le Sèvre?* she thought. *He wouldn't bother himself to knock. He would simply enter,* Lisette realized. She was glad the door was bolted. Lisette moved closer to the door. In a commanding manner, she asked, "Who is it?" Her pulse quickened.

"Lisette? May I come in?"

Lisette instantly recognized the woman's voice. *Marguerite,* she thought. Relieved, Lisette exhaled. She felt her heart beat return to normal. Lisette opened the door.

"So this is it." Marguerite glided into the center of the little room and pivoted as she spoke. "This is why you needed me to make the introduction to Léonard. It is small, but all yours. Well done, Lisette." She smiled and nodded approvingly.

Lisette didn't have to ask her how she had discovered the studio. It was well-known that Marguerite knew everything about everyone. She had made it her business to know everything. Marguerite also had a reputation for discretion.

Lisette returned the smile and nod. She checked her papa's watch again. "I'm sorry, but I must be leaving, Marguerite. I'm late."

"Yes, yes. I won't keep you long." She walked around the studio carefully pausing at each canvas.

After only a few weeks, Lisette had begun to run out of room in the small space. She had lined up canvases against each wall. On several of the walls, the canvases were already stacked three and four deep. Le Brun had not yet agreed to sell Lisette's paintings again. He had told her he was loathe to go behind Le Sèvre's back. It was a problem that Lisette needed to solve. For now, she was content to paint allegories and historicals again …and to be in her own studio, out from under Le Sèvre.

"You could use some curtains and a chaise-lounge…or at the very least a pair of stools for your guests." Marguerite pointed to the one empty corner in the studio.

"Can we talk another time?" Lisette glanced at the watch again.

Marguerite moved closer. She inspected Lisette, starting with her hair and moving down to her feet. "No wonder you have caused such a stir. Every time I see you, you grow ever lovelier."

Lisette stared at her. *What is she talking about?* she thought.

Marguerite continued, "Why have you not seen Amante? It has been many, many months – almost a year."

Lisette had thought about Amante in the past months, but she had not been ready to see him again. She wasn't excited to be with a man that gave her orders. Lisette already had Le Sèvre for that.

"I have been very busy," she said flatly.

"You should call on him. He wants to see you," Marguerite said.

"If he wants to see me so badly, why not come himself? Why send you?" Lisette asked.

"He wasn't sure you would agree to see him," Marguerite said. "Lisette, he did not mean to upset you. Quite the contrary, he only wanted to protect you."

"He had an odd way of showing it," Lisette said.

"Please, see him my dear. You won't regret it."

"You are not going to leave until I agree, are you?" Lisette smiled at Marguerite.

"No, I am not." Marguerite grinned back at Lisette.

Resigned, Lisette replied, "I will see him."

Marguerite nodded and said, "I would call on him soon. There is a rumor that his garrison will be sent away any day now...away from France." Marguerite's face revealed her concern.

Lisette had rarely seen Marguerite so serious. "I promise. I will see him soon," Lisette said.

Marguerite appeared only slightly reassured.

They moved to the door. Marguerite kissed Lisette on both cheeks and said, "I will be out of the country for a month or so...I'm going with Monsieur Mondeval to his cousin's estate in Italy." She waved at Lisette and then left.

Lisette stood in the doorway. *Amante,* she thought. She recalled the last time they were together. She immediately saw his full lips. She remembered how they had felt so warm on hers. Her own lips tingled. But she also remembered his harsh tone. Would he speak to her that way again?

Lisette returned to the present when she heard a man howling at his daughter in the hallway. The man sounded like Le Sèvre.

I must get home, she thought. Lisette pulled the studio door shut and quickly locked it from the outside. She descended the four flights of stairs and headed out of the building.

Lisette could think of only one thing as she walked toward Le Sèvre's house: *I have to get home before he does.*

Chapter Twenty-Eight

*L*isette did not know how to make the men understand. She carefully surveyed the faces of each Guild member sitting on the other side of the long table in front of her. They comprised the leadership council of the Guild of the Académie de Saint-Luc and had the final say in who was made a member. Her papa had served on this council for many years before his death.

"Mademoiselle Vigée, the council has decided. There is nothing more to discuss," Monsieur Gervais said.

Lisette explored her mind for a counterargument to convince them. They had voted to reject her application for membership. She was appealing their decision. *Surely, I can change a few minds,* she thought. But as she looked at their faces, not a single one appeared sympathetic. Lisette felt like she was back at the Convent of the Trinité defending herself for drawing. Like the

Guild councilmen before her now, the nuns had not allowed her to appeal then.

Lisette repeated herself, "But I *have* fulfilled the apprentice requirement."

The men remained unmoved. *Why won't they let me in?* Lisette wondered. She had told Le Brun that membership in the Guild would be easily granted to her. She had reassured him several times that it was a certainty. Lisette now knew that was not the case. Le Brun had argued for a certain order: first, gaining Guild membership, then, attaining a license from the Guild, and finally, renting a studio. She had convinced him otherwise. Lisette was realizing that she may have made a mistake.

Monsieur Gervais regarded her sternly. "We have already made ourselves clear. According to our rules, you have *not* met the requirement."

Several of the other men grunted and nodded in agreement.

Lisette stood firm. *I have to convince them*, she thought. She needed to keep her studio and she didn't want to risk going to jail for it. She had believed this process would be seamless. Instead, the ten men sitting before her were proving exceedingly difficult.

"But I was an apprentice to my father, Louis Vigée," Lisette said.

"Mademoiselle, we are well aware of who your father was. His dedication and service to the Guild was unwavering. He is greatly missed. That is beside the point. You were never his apprentice."

"But I was. He taught me the basic techniques of painting when I was a small girl. I worked in his studio. I even painted some of his backgrounds for him...when he got sick."

Lisette watched several of the men's faces soften as she talked about helping her papa. Then they looked at Monsieur Gervais. He shook his head in disapproval and the men's expressions hardened again. Lisette knew that no one councilman was in charge, so she wondered why the other men were deferring to

Monsieur Gervais.

Monsieur Gervais spoke with a defiance in his voice, "That may be so, but it doesn't change the fact that you were never offi-cially apprenticed to him. You were never registered as an apprentice with the Guild."

"I am telling you now. It is after the fact, but it makes my apprenticeship no less valid. Please messieurs, grant me mem-bership in the Guild. You would honor my father's memory."

As Lisette stood before the councilmen begging for member-ship in the Guild, she found herself thinking about her papa. She wondered, *If he were still alive, would they have already granted me membership?* She didn't understand why they weren't helping her.

"I'm sorry, Mademoiselle Vigée, but the council has decided. Your membership has not been approved at this time. If you complete a formal apprenticeship with a master artist, you are welcome to apply again. We would be honored to have another Vigée as a Guild member," Monsieur Gervais said.

Lisette searched the stalwart faces of the ten older, gray-haired men sitting in front of her. Each one appeared resolute. She had known most of them since she was a young child. Many of them had supped with her family. Her papa and mother had often discussed how the other councilmen clung to their rules and regulations, which sometimes hurt younger artists just be-ginning their careers. Today their rules and regulations had hurt her. Lisette realized that she should have known better.

The men rose and began talking with one another. It was over. Lisette knew there was nothing she could do to convince them today.

Resigned, Lisette curtsied and thanked the councilmen, "Good day, messieurs."

Before Lisette could leave the room, she was stopped by one of the men, Monsieur Archambauld.

"Mademoiselle Vigée, I knew your father well. I am not happy with today's decision. I wanted to grant you membership.

Unfortunately there are other forces at work. Please apply again soon. I believe it might turn out very differently."

As Monsieur Archambauld spoke, he moved his head in the direction of Monsieur Gervais.

Lisette looked over and saw Monsieur Gervais speaking with a woman. "Monsieur Archambauld, is that Madame Gervais?" Lisette asked.

"Yes, it is. Why do you ask?"

"No reason in particular. Thank you." Lisette smiled politely at him and then quickly departed.

She left the building with so many thoughts swirling around her head. *Why was Madame Gervais there? How could they not have granted me membership? Is my studio at risk?* She tried to push away such thoughts. Her studio was a small room in a nondescript building on the Rue de Richelieu. No one but Le Brun and Marguerite knew about it. She hadn't even told Rosalie why her still lifes were necessary. Rosalie had been so overjoyed at the thought of having Léonard style her hair, she had agreed with no questions asked. Lisette had realized that the fewer people involved, the better.

As she made her way onto the street, Lisette felt certain that her studio was safe. What bothered her more was seeing Madame Gervais. She couldn't stop thinking about her.

After her meeting with the Guild councilmen, Lisette went directly back to her studio. She was surprised and disappointed that they hadn't granted her membership, but she didn't think it would be her undoing as Le Brun had said.

Lisette entered the building and went quickly to the stairs. Her studio was on the fourth floor, at the top of the building. As she climbed the winding, narrow staircase she saw a male figure standing at the top. She couldn't identify him because the man faced away from her. When the man turned around, she realized it was Amante. Lisette froze. She had told Marguerite that she would see him, but in her own time. She didn't know if she was ready to allow Amante into her life again. Would he try to command her like he had before? She continued to the top of the stairs and moved directly to the door, passing by him.

"I am very busy right now," Lisette said as she put the key in the lock.

"Lisette, please. Can we talk?" Amante came up directly behind her while she turned the knob.

She went inside and he followed.

Lisette removed her cloak and immediately stepped over to her easel. "I already told you, I am very busy today."

"Marguerite was quite right. You have done well for yourself," Amante said, glancing around the room. He was smiling at her.

Lisette noticed his mouth. His full lips were distracting.

He walked closer to her easel. "You are back to allegories. This one appears promising...is that Hermes?"

He was standing so close, Lisette could smell the pomade in his hair. It was sweet like oranges. She wanted him to move away.

Lisette concentrated on her canvas. "Yes, it is. I must get back to work." She picked up her palette.

Amante came closer still.

When Lisette reached over for her brush, Amante gently laid his hand on her forearm.

"I've missed you, Lisette." He moved both of his hands to her face. Amante held Lisette's head and regarded her.

Lisette looked back at him, seeing something new in his eyes. She had never seen him look at her that way. She could feel her resolve melting. Amante closed his eyes and leaned in so that his lips were just barely touching hers. Lisette immediately remembered how his lips felt. She closed her eyes and opened her mouth. She couldn't think clearly any longer.

As they kissed, she felt her spirit move toward the clouds. It was just as Marguerite had once described. Lisette didn't want to come down. She wanted to float with him forever.

"Let's retire over there," he said while kissing her.

She could barely make out his muffled words but she knew he was talking about the chaise-lounge on the other side of the room. Their lips remained locked together when he picked her up and carried her across the room. As Lisette felt her feet leave the floor, her elbow bumped a large pail of water sitting on the window ledge next to her easel.

Splash! Without seeing exactly what had happened, Lisette realized that they were both doused in frigid water. Somehow in their maneuvering from the easel to the chaise-lounge, they had managed to tip over her water pail.

"Oh!" Lisette cried out.

They both stood and surveyed the damage.

"Are you hurt?" Amante asked.

"No." Once Lisette realized that it was only water and not turpentine, she was relieved. She shivered. "Just cold!" Lisette noticed that the front of Amante's *culottes* were dark from the spilled water.

He removed his waistcoat and placed it on Lisette's shoulders. "It isn't a fire, but my coat might help keep you warm."

"It could have been much worse," Lisette said, pulling the coat snug around her.

"Are you sure? Have you seen the front of my *culottes*?" Amante had a sparkle in his eye. "It looks like I couldn't find the chamber pot!"

Lisette tried not to smile, but he was right. He looked ridiculous. She let out a chuckle and then Amante laughed. Soon they were both cackling loudly. The levity was contagious. After several minutes, they stopped laughing, but neither of them could stop smiling. They were quiet for a time as they took in each other.

"Aren't you glad that Le Sèvre can't barge in?" Amante said, breaking the silence.

Lisette felt the smile disappear from her lips. She removed

his top coat from her shoulders and handed it back to him. "I need to clean up and get back to work." Lisette reached down to pick up the pail.

"But aren't you relieved that you have escaped Le Sèvre, at least for short intervals?" Amante asked.

"Can you bring me that mop?" Lisette pointed over to the corner of the room. "I need to collect this water." When Amante didn't move, she went to retrieve it herself. Lisette began sliding the mop back and forth over the puddle.

"But he no longer controls your life. You can't tell me that you aren't elated. Look around you."

Lisette released the mop allowing it to fall to the floor. "But he does still control everything. You don't understand." There was so much that Amante didn't know about Le Sèvre. Amante had been out of her life for many months. He had missed Le Sèvre's threats of lashes and the convent. Lisette stared at the spilled water.

"Nonsense. You have this studio. You are now an independent, licensed artist," Amante said.

Lisette grabbed the mop again and resumed wiping the floor.

"Lisette, look at me." Amante snatched the mop out of her hands. "You are now an independent, licensed artist, right?" he said again.

"Not exactly," Lisette said.

"What do you mean, not exactly?"

"I wasn't granted Guild membership."

"You are operating this studio without membership in the Guild *and* without a license?" He didn't wait for an answer. "But you know what that means. It can be confiscated...everything here...everything you have worked for can be taken away...*and* you could be jailed." His voice grew louder with every word.

"I don't require membership. No one knows about this place," Lisette retorted.

"Yes, you do. You must take care of that immediately." Amante's tone had drastically changed. He sounded like he was ordering one of his soldiers. It was all too familiar.

Lisette backed away from him. She would not be ordered a-round.

"You need to leave. I have to clean up this mess and get back to work." Lisette hurried to the door and opened it.

Amante shook his head and said, "Lisette, please."

Lisette didn't care if he was frustrated with her behavior. He wasn't her commanding officer. She said nothing as she held the door open.

Amante looked at her pleadingly for a moment and then left the studio.

Lisette bolted the door from the inside. She didn't want any more disturbances today. She had considerable work to finish before heading home. Le Sèvre had made it clear that Lisette was expected to spend time painting in her room in his house. In the past few weeks, he had arranged numerous portrait sittings for his jewelry customers. Lisette took out her papa's pocket watch. *I only have two more hours,* she realized. Lisette had a sitting with the Comtesse de Labelle later that afternoon.

She grabbed the mop and swiftly soaked up the remaining water.

Chapter Twenty-Nine

e Sèvre waited by Lisette's bedroom door. She was sure that he didn't trust her to be alone to paint the Comtesse de La-belle. Today was the third sitting with the Comtesse in the past several weeks and Le Sèvre had been present for each one. If Lisette made sufficient progress today, this could be the final sit-ting. Le Sèvre hadn't arranged any additional portrait sittings for the next few days, so Lisette was looking forward to working in her studio. She wanted to return to her latest allegory paint-ing of Hermes and the Infant Dionysius. But Lisette had her doubts about finishing with the Comtesse. Le Sèvre had inter-rupted each sitting, prolonging the process.

"Comtesse, you will be very pleased with these sapphires. They are as big as eyeballs." Le Sèvre hadn't stopped talking since the Comtesse arrived, insisting on describing his latest shipment of jewels.

From the irritated expression on the Comtesse de Labelle's face, Lisette could see that the Comtesse was not interested in jewels today.

"Comtesse, could you relax your brow?" Lisette asked her. "I don't want to capture it furrowed for your portrait."

The Comtesse turned to Le Sèvre. "Monsieur Le Sèvre, would you please leave us? My session will be much more successful if we are left alone." She swiveled to face Lisette before he could answer.

"Yes, of course, Comtesse. Please do not hesitate to have the servants fetch me should the need arise." Le Sèvre bowed deeply to the Comtesse and then left the room, careful to leave the door open.

The Comtesse's face immediately relaxed. "I thought he would never leave! What an oaf that man is. I told him earlier today that I will not be buying any more jewels from him until my cousin's wedding next month." She paused and then added, "He must be terrible to live with."

Lisette knew better than to concur with the Comtesse, but inside she silently agreed. He was an oaf, yes. But he was so much more. The Comtesse de Labelle had no idea how truly terrible it was to live with Le Sèvre. Lisette continued painting.

They sat in silence while Lisette worked. She was about to add the finishing touches to the Comtesse's neck when Lisette noticed that the Comtesse wore a different necklace from the previous two sittings.

"Comtesse, you are wearing a different necklace."

"Yes, the portrait should include the one that I am wearing now."

"But what about the other one….the rubies and diamonds offset your eyes so nicely. It is such an unusual piece with the large, heart-shaped, central ruby," Lisette said.

"I want this one in the portrait. I'm afraid the other one is gone." The Comtesse squinted her eyes and knit her brow again.

"I apologize, Comtesse, I didn't mean to upset you."

"It isn't your fault, Lisette. The necklace was stolen a few days ago...taken from our home...from my bedroom."

"That is despicable!" Lisette said.

"And that isn't all...the thieves plundered three other necklaces and a bag of loose jewels. The Comte is beside himself. He is determined to find the scoundrels and bring them to justice. As we sit here, the Lieutenant Général de Police, Jean-Charles-Pierre Lenoir, is questioning everyone. Those jewels have been in my husband's family for over three hundred years. The Comte will not relent until justice is served."

Lisette shook her head in sympathy for the Comtesse's plight. She began reworking the portrait so that the missing necklace was no longer portrayed on the Comtesse's neck.

Lisette glanced at the window. The sun was already setting. It would take Lisette more time to repaint the necklace. Her painting of Hermes and the Infant Dionysius would have to wait.

The Comtesse held her pose for the remainder of her portrait sitting, but she continued to mutter under her breath, lamenting the loss of the jewelry.

Chapter Thirty

*I*t had been several days since Lisette had last painted in her studio. Le Sèvre had scheduled portrait appointments without giving her much notice. She had been restricted to her room in his house with the sitters for days.

That morning, as soon as Le Sèvre had left the house, Lisette had headed out to her studio. The day held the promise of freedom. She would be free to paint what she liked. Her allegory painting of Hermes and the Infant Dionysius awaited her. The walk to the studio had been liberating as well. Lisette had hurried, but had been careful to dodge the many carriages that had begun to populate the mid-morning streets of the Rue Saint-Honoré and the Rue de Richelieu.

Lisette entered the building and climbed the four flights of stairs. Unlike most Parisians, she preferred the top of the building. There was less light, but there were also fewer apartments and people. Besides being the least expensive rooms to rent, the highest floor boasted quiet. Her neighbors were poor old widows scraping to survive. Today, the entire building was tranquil. As she ascended, Lisette didn't hear the usual noises of families bickering, babies crying and lovers quarreling on the lower floors. *Good. Better for me to focus,* she thought.

Lisette unlocked the door and went inside. She shivered. Lisette yearned for the fireplace in her room in Le Sèvre's house, but she gladly traded warmth for freedom. Lisette kept her cloak around her shoulders and went over to her easel.

Just as she had begun to mix pigments, someone knocked at the door. Over the past month, Lisette had let go of her paranoia. No one was coming to seize her studio or haul her to jail. She had even shared her studio's address with close friends.

Lisette opened the door.

"Rosalie! What a pleasant surprise. Please come in," Lisette said to her.

Rosalie wasted no time coming into the studio and beginning her inspection. "It is quite small, isn't it? I should have thought that my paintings would have commanded more space," Rosalie said with a coy smile. "Yes, I uncovered your motives. You needed my paintings to pay for this studio."

Lisette wasn't sure of Rosalie's opinion.

"Don't fret, my dear friend. I quite approve! It is lovely that you have your own studio."

"Thank you, Rosalie. I wouldn't have it without your help."

Rosalie smiled at Lisette and walked around looking at the canvases piled up around the small room. As soon as Rosalie was finished with her examination, she turned to Lisette. "I'm a married woman!" she blurted out.

Lisette was surprised that Rosalie hadn't mentioned her marriage as soon as Lisette had opened the door. Rosalie had been talking of nothing but her engagement since the first day they had met.

Lisette embraced her. "Congratulations, Rosalie." Lisette was truly happy for her friend.

"I had hoped to see you at the wedding," Rosalie said as she stepped back.

"I am very sorry that I was unable to be there. I know it was a beautiful occasion." Lisette had wanted to attend, but had been confined to Le Sèvre's house on the day of the wedding. It had been at the same time as a portrait sitting for the Comtesse de Briole. Lisette felt horribly, but she knew that Le Sèvre would not have allowed her to miss the sitting. Because Lisette had narrowly evaded lashes and banishment to a convent, she had thought it best not to disobey Le Sèvre again, even for her friend's wedding.

"It was magnificent. My hair was incredible. Léonard's creation was superb. I had never seen such a *pouf* in my life. I daresay the Queen might have been jealous." Rosalie let out a giggle, like she was a little girl. Then Rosalie became serious. "How long have you been a Guild member and had the license for this studio?" Rosalie asked her.

Lisette tried to change the subject. "How is your husband?" she asked Rosalie. Lisette didn't want to appear foolish to her friend.

"You don't have a license, do you?"

Lisette shook her head *no*.

"Honestly, I don't understand why you take such risks, Lisette. How can this little studio be worth it? Painting is a worthwhile endeavor, but you would be much better off getting married. Marriage is much safer!"

"I'm not using the space to exhibit and I have not sold anything without Le Sèvre's involvement. I don't think I have anything to worry about," Lisette said. She truly believed the words she was saying to Rosalie.

"I suppose so. Still, I don't understand why you don't find a husband."

Lisette searched for something other than marriage to talk about with Rosalie. "Have you stayed in contact with Adélaïde? Did she attend your wedding?" Lisette asked.

Before Rosalie could respond, there was a loud pounding on the door.

"Open up, by order of the Lieutenant Général de Police and the Commissaire," a voice bellowed from the hallway.

Lisette headed toward the door. She and Rosalie exchanged glances. Before Lisette could open the door, it flew open with great force. A bailiff with a fierce expression appeared in the doorway.

"Élisabeth Louise Vigée?" the officer asked vociferously.

Lisette faced him and nodded. "Yes."

"This studio is being seized, by order of the Lieutenant Général de Police and the Commissaire." The bailiff motioned to three guards who stood behind him. When they entered the room, the studio seemed to shrink. It felt tiny with so many people in it.

Rosalie gasped as she fanned herself.

Lisette watched as the bailiff ordered his men to seize her art supplies. They snatched everything they could carry. Lisette moved to prevent the men from taking her finished canvases that lined the back wall of the room.

"Why is this happening?" Lisette asked the question, but she already knew the answer.

"You are operating this studio without a license. The studio and *all* of its contents are being seized. Now step aside." The bailiff shoved Lisette so hard that she nearly fell to the floor.

Rosalie ran to Lisette's side, but she was of little help. Rosalie needed steadying herself.

"Monsieur, must you do this now? Could you return after we have prepared for your arrival?" Rosalie asked the bailiff.

He ignored Rosalie and ordered the men to finish collecting the paintings against the back wall.

Rosalie stared at the guards in astonishment. As she stood in the middle of the room watching them, she appeared unable to move.

"Monsieur, what about the large painting on the easel?" one of the guards asked the bailiff.

"Take it too. Monsieur Gervais said to collect everything," the bailiff ordered.

Lisette moved to block the guard. "You cannot do this!"

"I most certainly can...and if you continue to interfere, I will have you arrested and brought to jail." The bailiff ordered one of his men to pick up the allegory painting that was on the easel.

At first the guard struggled with its large and awkward size, but then he began bending it until the stretcher bars snapped and it more easily fit in his arms.

"No! You will ruin it." Lisette lunged forward and tried to wrestle the painting out of the guard's arms.

The bailiff came close to Lisette. "I told you not to interfere. I was given explicit instructions that if you protested at all, I was to arrest you." He restrained Lisette's wrists behind her back and pushed her out of the studio. The bailiff waited in the hall with Lisette while the men carried Lisette's supplies, canvases and even her easel and stool out of the studio and down the stairs of the building.

She wanted to fall down onto the floor and cry, but she didn't. Instead, she stood and watched them remove everything she had worked so hard to accumulate.

When the room was empty, with the exception of Rosalie, who was still inside dumbfounded, the bailiff said, "This studio must be cleared out...completely empty...that means you, madame."

Rosalie came out and the bailiff shut the door behind her. Then he held up a piece of paper with the words: *Seized by order of the Commissaire.* He proceeded to nail it to the back of the closed door. He ordered Lisette down the stairs.

Before Lisette started moving, she turned and looked at the

sign. She thought that if she stared at it long enough, it would make sense. She read all of the words several times but she saw only one: *Seized*.

"Come on, move." The bailiff nudged Lisette down the stairs.

Rosalie followed behind them in silence.

Lisette thought Rosalie might be in shock. She wondered if Rosalie had ever experienced anything so traumatic in her life. Rosalie wore a trancelike expression.

Lisette tried to get her attention. "Rosalie...this is very important...I need you to find Henri, a servant boy at Le Sèvre's house. Tell him that I need my money. He is to bring it to La Salpêtrière."

Rosalie stared past Lisette.

"Rosalie! Do you hear me?" Lisette asked.

Rosalie suddenly appeared awake again. "Yes. Henri. I will fetch him."

When they had reached the front of the building, Lisette watched Rosalie walk away. "Rosalie, please hurry!" she called out after her.

Chapter Thirty-One

The next morning, Lisette and Henri hailed a carriage from La Salpêtrière to the Rue Saint-Honoré. The prison was on the other side of the Seine, located in the Faubourg Saint Victor. It was too far to walk.

As she sat in the carriage, the previous night's events flashed through her mind. Lisette had been uncertain that Rosalie would follow her directions, but Henri had arrived at the prison with her money. Lisette hadn't wanted to involve Henri, but he was the only one who knew where her money was hidden. Henri had come to the jail and secured her release, but not before Lisette had spent all night at La Salpêtrière. In those miserable hours, she considered what had led her to that horrible place. Lisette was certain that Le Sèvre's maneuvering was to blame for her arrest and imprisonment in a dark jail cell with rats, roaches and inmates who smelled of death. Most of the other women in the all-female prison were starved and diseased prostitutes. Lisette had been careful to maintain distance from the other prisoners. She kept to herself the entire time.

All that night she had tried to connect Monsieur Gervais, Madame Gervais and Le Sèvre. The bailiff who had seized her studio had mentioned Monsieur Gervais as the man behind the seizure, but Lisette suspected that Le Sèvre had been involved too, probably to an even greater degree. She thought about how Monsieur Gervais had influenced the other Guild members' votes and about Madame Gervais' presence at the council meeting. She also remembered how Madame Gervais had met Le Sèvre in the Tuileries and then had later come to his house. Lisette was convinced that all of these events were linked. They all somehow led to Le Sèvre.

Lisette paid the carriage driver. She and Henri exited to the street. She told Henri to return to the house. He silently agreed and left her. Standing alone in front of Le Sèvre's shop, Lisette felt her heart racing. Exhausted, Lisette was aware of her fragile state of mind, but she had to confront him. She didn't care about the repercussions. Le Sèvre had already taken so much away from her, including her freedom.

Lisette reached into her pocket and felt around. There was a small brush, her palette knife and a few *livres*. She gripped the palette knife. *He can't do this to me,* she thought. Lisette decided it was best if she concealed the knife under her sleeve until she was close enough to Le Sèvre.

She marched toward the shop door. Just as Lisette was about to go inside, someone burst out, knocking Lisette to the ground. Her palette knife tumbled out of her hand and bounced into the street.

"Mademoiselle, are you hurt? I apologize for my clumsiness."

Lisette peered up and saw a man standing above her extending his hand. Lisette accepted it and stood upright.

"I'm not hurt. You came out of the door so quickly." Lisette searched for her palette knife. She spotted it in a ditch meant for collecting dirty kitchen water and human refuse from the nearby residences scattered along the Rue Saint-Honoré.

"I apologize again, Mademoiselle," the man said and departed.

Lisette brushed herself off and smoothed out her dress. She grabbed her palette knife from the ditch. She didn't care that it was wet from the putrid water. The jolt had brought her back to reality and she considered her impetuousness.

As she watched the man walk away, she felt her heart rate and breathing slow. *I can't go in there and confront him,* she thought. Lisette realized that a direct confrontation would only make things worse for herself. She might not ever get her studio back, or worse, she might be sent to prison or banished forever to a remote convent.

She returned the palette knife to her pocket bag. Lisette inhaled deeply, slowly exhaled and calmed herself further. She felt her pulse slow and her thoughts become more focused. She was coming out of the fog of anger that had developed overnight in the prison and that had clouded her judgment for the past hour since her release. Watching the bailiff and his men cart off her art supplies and then spending the night in La Salpêtrière had pushed Lisette past the point of reason.

Lisette checked her appearance in the reflection of the store window. As she looked at herself, she saw Le Sèvre arguing with someone inside the shop. Careful not to be spotted by Le Sèvre, Lisette moved to the edge of the long horizontal windows. She could barely see over the display of jewels. She looked closer.

Le Sèvre Le Sèvre was fighting with a woman whose back was to Lisette. The woman cowered as he hollered and flapped his arms wildly. *That's not like Le Sèvre to act like that,* Lisette thought. He was always collected, even when he was livid. Lisette saw that he held something in his hands, but the

276

woman's body blocked a clear view of it. Then he raised his other hand high up in the air. *He is going to strike her,* Lisette realized. Not a moment later, Le Sèvre whacked the woman in the face. The blow caused the woman to fall to the floor. *I should help her,* she thought. Lisette stepped closer to the door, but then she saw the woman stand. As the woman slowly rose up off the floor, she faced Lisette. *It is Madame Gervais,* she realized.

Lisette continued watching. Le Sèvre had a particularly foul expression on his face. Lisette shuddered. Le Sèvre had stopped screeching at Madame Gervais and now studied the object in his hands. He brought it close to his face. Lisette squinted so that she could better see the object he held. Le Sèvre was examining a necklace. The large, central ruby was heart-shaped. Lisette gasped. Le Sèvre was holding the Comtesse de Labelle's stolen necklace.

Lisette continued to watch Le Sèvre and Madame Gervais from outside the shop. She saw Le Sèvre, still clutching the Comtesse's necklace, disappear into the rear of the store. When he reappeared, he no longer held the necklace. Madame Gervais exchanged a few more words with Le Sèvre and then headed out of the shop.

Lisette followed Madame Gervais down the street and around a corner before speaking to her.

"Madame Gervais?" Lisette asked. She noticed that today Le Sèvre's collaborator appeared more like the wife of a successful Guild painter and less like a servant. Madame Gervais wore a simple, but newer pleated dress and matching petticoat. Her shoes had bright shiny buckles and looked unworn.

Madame Gervais narrowed her eyes when she saw Lisette. "I know who you are. I have nothing to say to you." She turned to walk away.

Lisette saw that the right side of her face was swollen from where Le Sèvre had hit her. "Please, Madame Gervais, I think we can help each other," Lisette said to her.

"No one can help me. I have to leave," Madame Gervais said as she dashed off. Lisette followed her, but Madame Gervais moved too quickly. Lisette lost her after being delayed by an assertive Auvergnat boy offering his plank. *She must have caught a fiacre,* Lisette realized.

Lisette took her time returning to Le Sèvre's house. She thought about Le Sèvre and Madame Gervais and wondered if she had reacted appropriately. *If I would have gone inside...* Lisette stopped herself. She knew that she would have only caused more problems for herself – and probably for Madame Gervais too. *If I had interfered, I would have never seen Le Sèvre with the Comtesse's necklace.*

As Lisette approached the house, she pondered her options. *I could go to the sergent,* she thought. But why would the *sergent* believe her? She knew he would never accept a girl's word over a man's, let alone the word of a disobedient step-daughter over an established, successful jeweler. *I could tell Mother,* she thought.

Lisette had reached the house, but she hesitated before going inside. *Has Le Sèvre told Mother about my arrest and night in jail? Does Mother know the truth?* Lisette wanted to tell her everything and ask her for advice, but Lisette knew better. There had to be another option.

Before she could do anything, her mother opened the front door. She had lingered too long outside.

"Lisette, what are you doing standing in front of the house? Where were you? I've been worried! Please come inside. Your father was about to send one of the servants to look for you. He is home for the mid-day meal, a rare treat. He arrived a quarter of an hour ago. Go upstairs and change for the meal," Jeanne said as she disappeared back inside.

Le Sèvre never came home in the middle of the day. *He knows I'm out of jail,* Lisette realized. *But how?* He would not be happy about it. Clearly, Le Sèvre had not told her mother anything. Lisette did not want to talk to him. *He is sending me to the convent,* she realized.

Reluctantly, Lisette walked into the house. Before going up the stairs, she peeked into the drawing room. Le Sèvre stood near the fireplace, holding a glass of brandy. When their eyes met, he locked his gaze on Lisette. Le Sèvre took several large strides toward her.

"You have your allies in this house and I have mine," he whispered so that Jeanne couldn't hear him. She was deeper in the drawing room, sitting on the upholstered settee holding her own glass of brandy. "You've crossed me for the final time. And so has that boy, Henri."

Le Sèvre was different somehow. Lisette had never seen such a look of contempt in his eyes before. *He truly wants to hurt me.*

"What are you going to do to him?" Lisette asked without thinking.

Le Sèvre came closer to her. "That is none of your concern."

Lisette stepped back. Her instincts told her to move away from Le Sèvre.

Lisette headed toward the front door, but before she could reach it, Le Sèvre pulled her back toward him.

"You will go when I say you can go," Le Sèvre said as he shoved her. "Get in the drawing room. There is something I want to say to both you and your mother."

When Lisette did not move, Le Sèvre grabbed Lisette with both of his hands and threw her down on the floor. "I said move."

Lisette landed with a thump on the hard marble surface. On her way down, she hit her head on a tall Sèvres porcelain vase sitting on the center table. Her vision blurred and she vaguely heard her mother calling her name. Then the room faded to black.

When Lisette opened her eyes, she saw her mother crouched over her, propping up her head and smoothing her hair. They were both on the floor. "Lisette, how do you feel?"

"Stand up, Lisette." Le Sèvre paced in front of them. "Both of you stand. I have some important news."

Lisette knew that standing was not an option, but with her mother's help, Lisette tried to sit up. The room whirled around her. She closed her eyes again and collapsed on her mother's lap.

"Sit up slowly," Jeanne said as she supported Lisette's back. She had never suffered such injuries. Her head was bleeding and she felt a sharp pain in her wrist.

"François, you've really hurt her. She can't stand," Jeanne said to him as she applied pressure to Lisette's head wound with her linen kerchief.

"Get up," Le Sèvre said. His tone lacked both remorse and sympathy.

Lisette tried to rise, but she couldn't.

"Whatever you need to say, you'll have to say with both of us on the floor. She cannot stand."

Jeanne said these words with more force and conviction than Lisette had ever heard her use when speaking to Le Sèvre.

"Lisette will be leaving for the Saint Ignatius Convent next week," he said flatly.

"You are sending her away?" Jeanne asked. There was panic in her voice.

Le Sèvre ignored Jeanne. "You will be taking none of your current possessions with you. You will be renouncing a life of marriage, children and certainly painting. You will become a nun."

"You cannot do this!" Jeanne shrieked.

Lisette tugged at her mother's arm. "Mother, stop. Let him talk." She didn't want her mother to suffer at Le Sèvre's hands. Lisette knew that he wouldn't hesitate to hurt Jeanne if she continued to scream at him and question his decisions.

"François, I don't understand this decision. Is it final?" Jeanne's voice was calmer.

"The nuns are expecting Lisette in one week," Le Sèvre said

and then he promptly left the foyer.

Lisette looked at her mother. She wanted to ease the pain on her mother's face.

"You know there is nothing that we can do. He has made his decision," Jeanne said. She resumed stroking Lisette's hair.

"Mother...this doesn't have to..." Lisette had to tell her mother about what she had seen earlier at Le Sèvre's shop.

"Shhh. You need your rest," Jeanne said as she put her fingers gently over Lisette's mouth.

"But Mother, we don't have to do what he says. Today, I saw —"

Jeanne interrupted her, "Lisette, you know that is not true. There is no need for any more words. Let's get you into bed."

With her head pulsating, Lisette leaned on her mother and they headed for the stairs. As Jeanne guided her up to her room, Lisette realized that her mother would not be able to help her. Jeanne would always be firmly under Le Sèvre's control.

Lisette needed rest tonight. Tomorrow, she would have a clear mind and could focus on how to free herself from Le Sèvre's control — for good. She had exactly one week.

Chapter Thirty-Two

*I*t was late the next morning when Lisette awoke. Her head no longer ached. Her mother had been right, she had needed the sleep. Lisette could think clearly again. She was not going to spend the rest of her life in a convent, but she didn't know how to stop it from happening. As she searched her mind for answers, Lisette thought of Marguerite. *She can help me,* Lisette realized. She hoped that Marguerite had returned from Italy. It had been over a month since she had visited Lisette's *atelier.* Lisette thought, *Surely she has returned.*

Lisette waited until Le Sèvre left for the day before she departed. She considered hailing a carriage, but decided to walk. Lisette needed the time to plan out what she would say to Marguerite.

As she traversed the Rue Saint-Honoré, Lisette found her

brain moving very quickly. Her mind raced as she considered all of her options. Lisette forced her legs to move as rapidly as her thoughts. How could she prove Le Sèvre's guilt? Could she stop Le Sèvre in just a week? Marguerite would have answers for her. Lisette continued moving briskly. She wanted to reach Marguerite's before the afternoon guests arrived, or at least before her house became overrun with visitors.

Lisette reached the Salonnière's and went directly inside. The footman took her cloak and indicated that Marguerite was in the main drawing room. Before Lisette had fully entered the room, she spotted Amante. He was standing on the far side of the entrance, flirting with several young, attractive women. She hadn't seen him since their disagreement over the studio license, nearly a month ago. Lisette felt like she had behaved badly. She wanted to apologize to him, but she wasn't sure if he wanted to hear it. Lisette would wait until he noticed her. If he acknowledged her, then she would approach him.

Lisette spied him from across the room. He was incredibly dashing in his officer's uniform. His officer's waist coast accentuated his already broad shoulders and made him appear very strong. The deep blue color of the coat stood out against his dark hair and eyes. Lisette knew that it wasn't only his good looks that drew women to him. The confident aura that surrounded him was irresistible. Most women became helpless in his presence. It had happened to her. Lisette watched him bring his cordial to his lips to take a drink. Lisette wanted to touch those lips. *They would feel so ….*

"Lisette!" Marguerite suddenly appeared directly in front of her.

As soon as Marguerite had called out her name, Lisette saw Amante's head swivel in her direction. At first he smiled broadly at her, as if nothing unsavory had ever transpired between them, but then he stopped himself. He turned his back and returned to the women who were hanging on him.

"What a wonderful surprise to see you." Marguerite took Lisette's arm like she was about to guide her out of the room.

"Wait. I don't want to leave before speaking to Amante. He is over there." Lisette pointed to where Amante stood with the young women.

"Yes, I know he is." Marguerite tried to turn Lisette's body so that she faced away from Amante.

"I need to speak with him. I must apologize for my rudeness last month." Lisette pulled her arm out of Marguerite's.

"No, Lisette, he doesn't want to see you. Let's retire to my private chamber." Marguerite grabbed her arm again.

Just as Lisette was about to pull away from her once again, Amante glanced over at Lisette. She recognized the look. It was one of longing. He wanted to be with her. Lisette was certain.

"Yes, he does want to see me." Lisette broke free from Marguerite's hold and strode across the room over to Amante.

Before she could reach him, he extended his hand in front of his body. "Lisette. No, stop there and turn around. I cannot talk to you."

"But I need to apologize. You were right about the license. My studio was seized."

"I know, Lisette. But I really cannot talk to you." Amante walked away.

Lisette followed him. "It was Le Sèvre."

"I know. Why do you think I cannot see you anymore?" Amante looked at her pleadingly. His eyes said that he wanted to be near her. "Good bye, Lisette. It is for the best. Please do not contact me again," he said and left.

Lisette continued to run after him. "But I have a way to get him out of my life...can't we just talk?" Lisette had followed him all the way to the front door, but Amante was much faster.

By the time she had reached the entryway, his carriage had driven away. Lisette stood in the front vestibule looking at the empty forecourt for several minutes.

"Let him go. It is for the best." Marguerite stood next to Lisette. "Come, let's move to my boudoir."

Lisette plunked herself down onto one of the velvet couches in Marguerite's boudoir. She scanned the room. It hadn't changed since her previous visit, when she had first met the Salonnière. Marguerite had given her advice then. Advice was what she needed now.

Marguerite sat on a striped satin *duchesse* directly across from Lisette. She didn't recline, but the piece of furniture, being a combination of an armchair and a daybed, was very well-suited for lounging. On either side of the *duchesse* were delicate rosewood end tables, both of which held silver perfume burners. Lisette remembered their sweet smell from the last time she had visited Marguerite's boudoir. The scents of jasmine and lavender filled the room. Lisette watched the playful smoke wisps emanate from the burners and move up toward the ceiling. They were mesmerizing. Lisette inhaled deeply. The pleasant fragrance instantly relaxed her.

"Don't fret about Amante," Marguerite said as she went around the room lighting more perfume burners.

"But I have offended him. I'm ashamed of the way I acted."

"You shouldn't feel ashamed of anything."

Lisette looked at Marguerite. "But I do."

"Amante is only doing what is best for you. He wants to protect you and so do I." Marguerite had finished lighting the remaining burners. She laid her hand on Lisette's arm as she sat down on the couch beside her.

"I don't need to be protected," Lisette told her.

"My dear, there are forces here at work that are much bigger than you. Be mindful of that."

"Le Sèvre? Are you speaking of him?" Lisette scooted forward to the edge of the sofa.

Marguerite nodded. "I don't know what he has said to Amante." Marguerite shook her head in disgust. "I hope he did not threaten his career in the military. His position is already tenuous."

"What do you mean?" Lisette asked.

"There are some who are working to prevent men like Amante from becoming officers."

"But he is already an officer." Lisette was confused.

"For now, yes. But there are highborn men who don't believe that the lowborn should achieve any rank."

"But Amante isn't lowborn," Lisette said.

"To them, a provincial noble might as well be lowborn. He isn't of their ilk. To make matters worse, he is a graduate of the École Militaire. Even though he is well-trained, the nobles do not like officers like Amante who they consider to be lowborn upstarts. They are threatened and afraid that one might have to actually learn military science to lead a regiment and to engage the enemy in battle."

Lisette thought for a moment. "So Amante is only helping himself...his career. That is why he can't talk to me."

"Oh no, my dear. Amante is trying to protect you from that awful Le Sèvre."

"I don't need protection," Lisette said again.

"Of course you do, don't be silly." Marguerite waved her hand dismissively.

"Right now, I don't need protection, but I do need help. I don't have much time," Lisette said.

"I don't understand," said Marguerite.

"Le Sèvre is sending me to the Saint Ignatius Convent next week," Lisette blurted out.

"A nun? For the rest of your life? He cannot do that." Marguerite covered her mouth with her hand.

Lisette supposed that to Marguerite, a life of abstinence would be worse than death.

"Le Sèvre does seem to have the upper hand, Lisette. We need to find a way to get it back...turn the tables on him."

Lisette knew that Marguerite would be ever hopeful and always resourceful.

"That is why I came here to see you today," Lisette said.

Marguerite's eyes narrowed like she was already strategizing. "But what can we do?"

"I might have a way," Lisette said.

Marguerite's eyes widened and she waited for Lisette to speak again.

"The jeweler may be more than a jeweler," Lisette said.

"Go on," Marguerite said, leaning toward Lisette.

"Le Sèvre is a common thief disguised as a businessman."

"A thief? You are speaking in riddles, Lisette. Please, be plain about it. What do you know?"

"Enough to cause him great harm..." Lisette paused.

"Let's hear it." Marguerite moved so that she was closer to Lisette on the couch.

Lisette told Marguerite what she had seen at Le Sèvre's store the day before. She related every detail about Madame Gervais and the Comtesse's stolen necklace.

Marguerite listened intently.

Lisette felt a burden had lifted after she had shared this information with Marguerite.

After Lisette finished speaking, Marguerite's eyes lit up. "Lisette, you are going to turn him over to the authorities."

"You mean have him arrested?"

"Precisely." Marguerite left the couch and began pacing.

"But wouldn't they execute him?" Lisette asked. She was willing to do just about anything to be free of Le Sèvre, but she didn't think that she could send him to his death.

"No, that very rarely happens to thieves. They are either banished or sent to the galleys to serve their sentence."

Lisette considered banishment. Criminals who received this punishment were sent away from France, never to return. If he was banished, he would be gone forever.

"But how?" Lisette asked her.

"First you need to find Madame Gervais and enlist her help."

"I tried that. She wanted nothing to do with me. She ran away when I tried to talk to her."

"She was scared...scared of Le Sèvre. You need to find her and make sure she listens to you. If you can allay her fears and make it clear that if she works with you, Le Sèvre will be sent away forever, I think she will be agreeable."

"And then?" Lisette asked.

"You leave that up to me, my dear." Marguerite touched Lisette on the shoulder. "You won't have to become a nun."

Chapter Thirty-Three

The next morning, Lisette slipped out of Le Sèvre's house just after dawn. She wanted to find Madame Gervais at her own home before she left for the day. Lisette had stayed late at Marguerite's the night before, learning every detail and nuance of Marguerite's plan. The first step was to talk to Madame Gervais.

The streets of Paris were practically empty at this early hour, so it took her no time to reach the neighborhood of Les Halles, which claimed Paris' largest food market and the Gervais' apartment. Lisette remembered her papa talking about where the Gervais family lived. He had been to their home on the Rue Saint-Denis for suppers.

Lisette walked east down the Rue Saint-Honoré and then headed north on the Rue Saint-Denis. Her papa had also mentioned that they lived above a bric-a-brac shop named *Les Arnaults*, after the Arnaults family that owned it.

Once on the Rue Saint-Denis, she searched for the shop sign. Not knowing exactly where on the Rue Saint-Denis the shop was located, Lisette had to move slower than she would have liked. An hour after she had left Le Sèvre's house, she spotted a dark blue shop sign with the words *Les Arnaults* written in bright gold lettering. She had arrived at the Gervais' apartment building.

Lisette didn't have to wait long before someone came out of the building, leaving the door open so that Lisette could enter. She asked the woman which apartment belonged to Monsieur and Madame Gervais and the woman pointed up to the first door on the second floor. Lisette went up and knocked.

Madame Gervais answered the door. "I told you, I have nothing to say to you. You shouldn't have come here," she said as she started to close the door.

"But Madame Gervais, we can help each other. Please hear me out," Lisette pleaded with her.

Before Madame Gervais was able to close the door, her husband came over and stood next to her. "Mademoiselle Vigée. What do you want with my wife?" Monsieur Gervais had immediately recognized Lisette. He looked confused. "You know the Guild council has spoken. Membership was not granted."

Lisette heard a young child babbling in the background.

"I understand, Monsieur. I have other business with your wife. May I come in?" Lisette asked. "It concerns her safety. I know how she received that black eye." Lisette pointed to Madame Gervais' face. Her right eye was swollen and purple from when Le Sèvre had hit her two days before.

Madame Gervais quickly spoke up, "Husband, I am going to take a walk with Mademoiselle Vigée. I will return shortly. The coffee and rolls are on the table." Before her husband could protest, Madame Gervais darted into the hall, shutting the door behind her.

"Let's go outside," Madame Gervais told Lisette.

When they had reached the street, Madame Gervais motioned for them to walk away from the building. They headed down the Rue Saint-Denis.

"Your husband doesn't know that you work for Le Sèvre," Lisette said to her.

"And he will never know," Madame Gervais said, looking straight ahead.

Wasting no time, Lisette said, "I am certain that you want to be free of Le Sèvre as much as I do."

Madame Gervais stopped and stared at Lisette. "But there is nothing that can be done. I don't know why you came here this morning." Madame Gervais' eyes looked dull, as if any bit of hope had been stolen from her long ago.

"Because I have a way that we can both be rid of him."

"I'll never truly be free of him. Neither will you...your mother is married to him."

"Yes, but some bonds can be broken."

"Not the bonds of blood." Madame Gervais focused on Lisette. "My son...he is not my husband's. He belongs to Le Sèvre. Years ago, we were together. He promised me so many things ...and I believed him."

Lisette was not expecting to hear that Madame Gervais had borne Le Sèvre's child, but as Lisette let her words sink in, Madame Gervais' arrangement with Le Sèvre began to make sense. "Is that why you work for him?"

"Yes, because he has threatened to tell my husband about our tryst. I cannot risk my son living a life of illegitimacy." Madame Gervais had a look of desperation on her face.

Lisette saw that she would do anything to keep her secret safe. "If we turn him over to the authorities, that won't happen."

"But they will never believe two women." Madame Gervais' face was tense. Her eyes constricted as she spoke to Lisette.

"If they can catch him in the act, they will believe it."

"But how?"

"I have a good friend who is close to the Duchesse de Chartres. She will make sure that Le Sèvre is invited to supper at the Duchesse's house. You and I will do the rest."

As she carefully listened to Lisette, the tension in Madame Gervais' face gradually dissipated. She looked skeptical, but also open to considering Lisette's plan.

"Tell me, but hurry. I don't have much time before I need to get back to my son," Madame Gervais said.

Lisette saw hope creeping back into Madame Gervais' eyes. For the first time in a long time, Lisette felt hopeful too.

After Lisette left Madame Gervais, she went directly home. Lisette needed to execute the next step of her plan immediately.

Once back inside Le Sèvre's house, she went quietly up to her room. Lisette didn't want to be spotted by her mother. It was better that her mother not know anything. Lisette was sure that her mother would try to stop her.

Safely in her room, Lisette was careful to lock the door. After prying up the loose floorboards, she reached down and removed several canvases that she had been storing. Having run out of space at her studio weeks ago, Lisette had moved her most important canvases to her room. At the time, Lisette had bemoaned the burden of not having enough storage at her studio, but now, she felt fortunate that they had been transferred before the seizure. Lisette then retrieved her money bag. After spending much of it on her release from jail, there was not much money that remained, maybe 20 *livres*.

What can I use to transport the paintings? she asked herself. Lisette wanted to remove them from Le Sèvre's house for safekeeping. She searched through her *armoire* and found a large satchel. *This will work,* she thought.

She placed her money in the satchel first and then her paintings. There were nearly half a dozen rolled-up canvases. She carefully arranged their placement in the bag so that they would avoid damage in transit. Lisette didn't want any of her works ruined, but she also couldn't take the risk of leaving them at Le Sèvre's house. If her plan failed, he would certainly destroy all of them. *I will make them fit,* she thought.

Lisette replaced the floor boards and the carpet. Then she searched her room. She wanted to be sure she wasn't forgetting anything else.

She went to the *commode* against the far wall and opened each one of its drawers. Lisette removed a hand painted snuffbox and a small portrait of her brother, both gifts from her papa. She placed the keepsakes in the satchel. Once she was satisfied that she had gathered her most important belongings, she left the room. As Lisette turned to shut the door, she heard someone come up behind her.

"Lisette, where you are going?"

Lisette spun around. It was her mother.

"For a walk in the Tuileries gardens."

"With that large satchel? I know that isn't true. What is going on? Is something wrong?"

"Mother, I'm well...or I will be soon. Now, I need to leave."

Jeanne put her arm around Lisette. "My daughter, you must not cross him. You must accept that you are leaving for the convent in a few days. It is too dangerous to disobey him. He is only becoming more violent toward you."

Lisette looked her mother directly in the eye. "And you too." Lisette pointed to new bruises on her mother's neck. *Had he tried to strangle her?* she wondered. Lisette swallowed hard pushing down the lump that had formed in her throat as she inspected her mother's injuries. *I must make this plan work,* she thought.

"Lisette, it's you that I'm worried about." Jeanne hugged Lisette tightly.

"I'll be safe, Mother." Lisette squeezed her mother. "We both will," Lisette said. She withdrew from the embrace, ran down the stairs and out the front door.

Once outside and on the street, she paused for a deep breath. *I hope Mother will be safe until this business is finished,* she thought. Lisette stood up straight and traversed the Rue Saint-Honoré.

Lisette noticed that everyone on the street was gaping at her. She must have been a spectacle trying to carry such a large, heavy satchel herself without the help of a servant or male companion. Lisette didn't want to draw unnecessary attention to herself by struggling with the satchel on foot. She decided to hail a carriage. One pulled up almost immediately. "The Pont Notre-Dame," she told the driver.

When the carriage stopped, she paid the driver and descended slowly, carefully balancing the great size of the satchel. She lumbered toward the front door of Le Brun's shop. Marguerite had been the one to suggest that Lisette trust Le Brun with her paintings. Lisette had protested, but had eventually agreed that Le Brun was the best choice.

Marguerite had left Paris the day before, but not before she had arranged for Le Sèvre's supper invitation from the Comtesse. Monsieur Mondeval had insisted on an encore voyage to Italy. Marguerite had told Lisette that she would oblige him, for fear of losing Monsieur Mondeval's affections. Lisette had not seen Marguerite carry on with a man for longer than a week or two. Monsieur Mondeval must have been a superior lover to have captured Marguerite's attentions for so long.

Lisette struggled, but she managed to open the door and go inside.

Monsieur Faucher came rushing to the front as soon as Lisette had entered. "Mademoiselle Vigée, we are not open. I'm afraid we cannot accept any canvases right now. Monsieur Le Brun is not here." Monsieur Faucher stuck his nose up in the air, as usual.

Lisette ignored him. She strode past Monsieur Faucher and

headed for the back where she knew Le Brun would be hiding. Lisette could hear rustling behind the curtain that separated the back area from the front. Then she saw the curtain move. *Le Brun is here. I knew it,* she thought.

"Mademoiselle Vigée, you can't go back there!" Monsieur Faucher followed closely behind Lisette.

She reached the curtain and then drew it open. "Le Brun! I know you are here. I can hear you," she said. Lisette took a few steps forward so that she was on the other side of the curtain.

The space behind it had been divided into several different areas, all separated by screens to create multiple rooms. Within the partitions, Lisette saw Old Master paintings from Italy, Dutch landscapes, Flemish portraits and French genre paintings. She could only imagine what other paintings Le Brun stored here. She also noticed large wooden crates on the floor containing even more paintings. Lisette heard a male voice whispering behind one of the partitions. She was sure it was Le Brun.

"Le Brun! It is Lisette. I have something for you," she said.

Lisette hoped that he would at least be curious. They hadn't seen each other since before her studio was seized. He had not agreed to sell her paintings, but he had said that he wanted to remain in contact.

There was silence for a moment and then Lisette heard stirring again. She could make out the sounds of buckles clanking like someone was quickly getting dressed. Soon after the noises ceased, Le Brun stepped out from behind a partition.

"Lisette! How good to see you," Le Brun said.

Like the past few times Lisette had seen him, Le Brun's appearance was disorderly. His hair was disheveled, his linen *chemise* was stained, wrinkled and untucked from his *culottes* and he had a smear of red on the left side of his face. *Rouge,* she thought. Lisette rolled her eyes. *Always the same with Le Brun,* she said to herself. Lisette had heard the rumors about Le Brun: the gambling, the debts, the drinking, and the women. As long as it hadn't interfered with their business relationship, Lisette hadn't been concerned about Le Brun's private life.

Lisette held out the satchel in front of her. "These are for you."

"I didn't know that you were painting again...after the studio was seized." Le Brun looked confused.

"I haven't been. These paintings were spared," Lisette explained.

Le Brun raised his hand in protest. "You know I cannot sell your works without involving Le Sèvre. You know we can't work together."

"These aren't for sale. These are for safekeeping."

"Why? Are you leaving? Where are you going?" Le Brun sounded paranoid.

"It doesn't matter. All that matters is keeping these paintings safe. I can't have anything happen to them. I've already lost so much."

"Losing the studio was a shame, but I warned you. I said you needed a license from the Guild first."

Lisette did not want to discuss what had happened with the Guild or with Le Sèvre. She needed Le Brun to take her paintings.

"Keep my paintings safe, please?"

"Does Le Sèvre know about this?"

"Just take the paintings and keep them here. No one has to know about it but you and me," Lisette said.

She heard someone cough. *Faucher,* Lisette thought.

He was standing on the other side of the curtain.

"Don't worry about him. He does what I tell him to do," Le Brun said.

She saw the curtain move and Faucher appeared in front of them.

"Monsieur Le Brun, have you forgotten about the agreement between Monsieur Le Sèvre and Monsieur Voclain? It will be enforced if you fail to comply with Monsieur Le Sèvre's wishes. No more loans for your private affairs," Faucher reminded him.

Lisette had heard that name before. Monsieur Voclain was notorious. He was a well-known lender of money to gamblers. Lisette thought about the bag of money that was in the bottom of her satchel. She decided that it was probably best not to mention it to Le Brun. If he didn't know of its existence, it might still be there when Lisette returned. In all of their business dealings, Le Brun had always given Lisette the money that she was owed. She had no reason to think that he would want to steal from her now. Besides, it wasn't that large of a sum.

Le Brun was silent as he considered Lisette's request.

She asked again, "Then you'll do it? You'll keep my paintings safe?"

"I can't. I'm sorry, Lisette," Le Brun said and then turned around and returned behind the partition.

Lisette moved swiftly through the corridors of the Louvre. *He has to say yes,* she thought. There wasn't anyone else Lisette could trust with her paintings. *Briard has to help me,* Lisette hoped.

As Lisette approached Monsieur Briard's studio, she heard raised voices. The door was open, but she waited before stepping inside. Lisette stood next to the open door and listened from the hall. She didn't want to upset Briard immediately before asking him for a favor. Lisette couldn't see inside the studio, but she could hear every word that was said.

"But Monsieur Pierre, you said you would support her," Lisette heard a woman's voice say.

"I never said any such thing, Comtesse." Lisette heard a man reply, probably Monsieur Pierre. Lisette had previously met the Premier Peintre du Roi, but it had only been once and she didn't immediately recognize his voice.

The woman spoke again, "I distinctly remember when you

gave your explicit support of my daughter for the position of Queen's Painter."

"Monsieur Briard, you were there, do you remember me uttering such a statement about the Comtesse's daughter?" Monsieur Pierre asked.

"Monsieur Pierre, I was there, but not for the entire meeting. If you recall, I had Académie business which required my attention. I left the meeting early."

"Well then, will you give me your support today? There are others I need to speak to about this matter. I must tread carefully with the Queen and your outward support would make this process much smoother," the Comtesse said.

"I have not yet made up my mind, Comtesse. I do not know who I will back for Queen's Painter. Such an official position for the Queen has no precedence. I require more time to consider the choices," Monsieur Pierre said.

"As do I," Briard said.

"But my Adélaïde is the best painter for the position, isn't that right Briard?" the Comtesse asked.

That is Adélaïde's mother, the Comtesse de La Valette! Lisette realized.

"Comtesse, there is no doubt that Adélaïde is a very talented painter." Briard sounded reassuring.

"So then I have your support?" the Comtesse asked.

"You cannot put so much pressure on us. We will both give our decisions when it is time," Monsieur Pierre said, speaking for both himself and Briard.

"Monsieur Pierre is right. I am not yet ready to make a decision," Briard said.

"I cannot wait forever. I expect a response shortly. My daughter *will* be the Queen's Painter. Good day, messieurs," the Comtesse said.

Lisette heard fabric rustling and the light footsteps of a woman. Within moments, the Comtesse de La Valette came out of the studio. Lisette tried to stay out of her way, but the Comtesse moved so quickly, her shoulder brushed Lisette's arm.

"And who is this little spy?" the Comtesse de La Valette asked vituperously.

Lisette stepped back. She immediately recognized the woman. Lisette could never forget the scar on her left cheek. The Comtesse had threatened her at Versailles when Lisette had mistakenly stumbled upon her with her daughter.

Lisette said nothing.

The woman's dark eyes bore into Lisette. The Comtesse de La Valette bent close to her and in a whisper said, "I remember you. The last time we met you were in a similar position – listening to conversations that don't concern you. My dear, I hope I do not see you here or at Versailles again...or anywhere for that matter. I do not care for spies." The Comtesse turned to walk away, but before she left, she said in a glaring voice, "Briard, you have a little eavesdropper. You ought to be more careful."

Lisette watched her stride away.

Briard came over to the door. "Lisette, how pleasant to see you. Never mind the Comtesse de La Valette...please come in."

Lisette stepped into Briard's studio. It had been many months since she had been there last. She immediately relaxed. It felt like she had come home.

"Lisette, let me introduce you to Monsieur Pierre."

"We've met." Pierre barely looked at Lisette as he headed toward the door. "Good day, Monsieur Briard." Pierre nodded slightly to Briard and then left the studio.

"To what do I owe this visit, Lisette?" Briard asked her once they were alone. He glanced at her satchel, noticing it for the first time.

"I need your help with these paintings." She offered him the satchel full of her canvases.

Briard smiled at Lisette and took the satchel from her.

After returning to Le Sèvre's house from Briard's *atelier*, Lisette waited. She patiently anticipated the invitation's delivery.

Finally, as dusk approached, a servant wearing the livery of the Orléans family arrived at the house.

Lisette plucked the invitation out of the servant's hands.

"But Mademoiselle, this letter is intended for Monsieur Le Sèvre. My instructions were to deliver it to *him*," the servant protested.

"I will personally hand it over to my father this evening. You have my word," Lisette said. She held the young boy's gaze until he conceded and departed.

Lisette examined the invitation. It bore the seal of the Duchesse de Chartres. Lisette knew what was inside: an invitation to supper at the Palais-Royal at the request of the Duc and Duchesse de Chartres. *Le Sèvre won't be able to say no,* Lisette thought. *Marguerite has succeeded.*

Lisette threw on her cloak and left the house. She had no desire to see Le Sèvre and had been avoiding him for the past few days, but for her plan to work, she had to deliver the supper invitation in person. She would go to his store and convince him to say *yes* to the supper. Lisette took out her papa's pocket watch. *Good. He'll still be there,* she thought.

As Lisette made her way down the Rue Saint-Honoré, she watched the people and carriages moving in every direction. Great ladies and men rode in carriages on their way to the Opéra or the Comédie-Française. Servants gathered last minute supplies for the suppers that were to take place after their masters returned home from the evening's performances. Lamplighters were just beginning their momentous task of lighting Paris' street lamps for the evening.

Once she had arrived at Le Sèvre's shop, Lisette went up to the front door, but didn't go in immediately. She didn't want to interrupt Le Sèvre if he was with a customer. Lisette peered in the front windows to see what was happening inside.

Le Sèvre moved around behind the back counter. He paced while barking orders at his assistants. Lisette did not see any customers.

She smoothed out the front of her dress and went inside. *Breathe,* she reminded herself. She clenched her fists as she walked in.

It took several moments before Le Sèvre noticed her. One of his assistants saw Lisette first and alerted Le Sèvre to her presence. Le Sèvre was reading papers he held in his hands. He barely looked up at her.

"Lisette, you do not need any more supplies, you are leaving for the convent in a few days. Now, go home. I am very busy." As he returned to his papers, Lisette noticed that his face was relaxed, without any particular expression on it. He neither smiled nor grimaced.

"I thought you would want to know about this immediately. I came right over as soon as it came to the house," Lisette said, holding up the invitation. She tried to maintain a similar neutrality, even though her stomach twisted itself into coils as she spoke. She felt her mid-day meal creep its way back up her throat.

Le Sèvre's face remained unemotional. "Know about what?"

"This," Lisette said as she waved the invitation in the air. *Keep breathing,* she thought. She could feel her fingernails dig into the inside of her hands, her fists were clenched so tightly.

"Lisette, I am a very busy man, I can look at whatever you have when I get home." He dismissed her and then beckoned his other assistant. "Frédéric, I don't see the sapphire necklace on this inventory. Where is it?" His back was now to Lisette. She noticed a distinct look of distress on Frédéric's face. He was scared of Le Sèvre.

Lisette cleared her throat loudly. "It is from the Duc and Duchesse de Chartres."

Immediately, Le Sèvre whipped around to face her. "Give me that." He swiped the invitation out of Lisette's hand.

She stood motionless while she watched him break the seal and read it. Some broth from lunch came into her mouth and she tried not to gag. Lisette swallowed hard.

For the first time since they had been talking, Le Sèvre's face registered emotion. He scowled. "But it says here that *you* are to attend. That must be a mistake." Le Sèvre drew the invitation closer to his face. "Let me read this again," he said.

"Even so, do you want to take the chance that you offend the Duchesse de Chartres? When will you have the opportunity to visit her house again?"

Le Sèvre set down the invitation. The scowl disappeared. He now appeared to be scheming. Lisette had seen that expression on his face many times before.

Lisette wondered if he was thinking about the jewels that he would steal from the Duchesse's house.

"Leave," he said curtly.

She nodded her head and turned toward the door. Lisette didn't want to utter another word to him.

She walked out and quickly made her way to the street corner. She turned the corner and stopped. Leaning against a building, Lisette tried to catch her breath. She took several deep breaths in and out. She repeated the deep breathing until she felt calm again. Lisette stood up straight and then hailed a *fiacre*.

I can do this. This will work, she told herself.

Chapter Thirty-Four

he next day dragged on interminably. The hours had ticked away more slowly than Lisette had ever experienced. The supper at the Palais-Royal was to begin at nine in the evening. By the early afternoon, Lisette was dressed and ready to leave. Now, sitting in the carriage with her mother, she realized the next few hours would determine the rest of her life.

Although they lived directly across from the Palais-Royal and could walk, Le Sèvre had wanted to arrive in a carriage. He insisted it was more respectable. Lisette and her mother were to pick up Le Sèvre at his store just before the supper began. They would all ride in the carriage together to the Palais-Royal.

As they sat in the carriage waiting for Le Sèvre to come out of his jewelry shop, Lisette noticed how sad her mother appeared.

"Lisette, you look lovely this evening," Jeanne said. Her mother was on the brink of tears.

"What is wrong, Mother?" Lisette asked her.

"I'm afraid this will be the last time I will see you look so becoming...dressed in a fine silk gown with matching slippers," Jeanne said. Her voice trailed off as she spoke. Lisette saw tears filling her eyes.

She wanted to tell her mother that if everything went according to plan, they would have many more evenings together. It was Le Sèvre's evenings that were numbered. Instead, she took her mother's hand and squeezed it. Lisette noticed that Jeanne wore her long gloves. *She must have new bruises*, Lisette thought.

"I love you very much, Mother," said Lisette.

Her mother patted her eyes with her handkerchief.

Lisette released her mother's hand and the carriage door opened.

Le Sèvre stepped inside and sat beside her mother. "Driver, to the Palais-Royal," he said gruffly. Le Sèvre said nothing to either of them. As they started moving, he looked out of the side of the carriage.

Lisette turned her head too. She wanted to avoid looking at Le Sèvre. Exhausted, Lisette closed her eyes. The previous night had been a restless one. She had met with Madame Gervais one final time to go over the details of the plan. Once Lisette had returned home and was in bed, she went over the plan in her mind repeatedly. For her *and* her mother's sake, she couldn't afford any missteps. Lisette couldn't bear any harm coming to her mother. She pushed away thoughts of failure. *It will work*, Lisette reassured herself.

She felt certain that after tonight, Le Sèvre would no longer have control over her life or her mother's. Lisette fretted that her mother might not agree with her actions, but she hoped that Jeanne would eventually accept that they were both better off without Le Sèvre.

"François, you seem pensive this evening. Are you well?" Jeanne asked Le Sèvre.

He was still staring out of the side of the carriage. Without turning to look at Jeanne he replied, "Yes, of course."

Lisette knew that Le Sèvre was thinking about the heist that he had planned with Madame Gervais for that evening.

"I don't want to pry...but..." Jeanne wasn't going to relent.

"Then don't pry. You know how I need my privacy, Wife." He glared at her for a brief moment and then turned his head back toward the passing street.

Jeanne immediately stopped talking.

For the next few minutes no one talked. All Lisette heard was the creaking of the carriage wheels over the cobblestones and the clappity-clop of the horses' hooves as they pulled the three of them down the Rue Saint-Honoré toward the Palais-Royal.

Within a few minutes, they had arrived. Their carriage entered the outer gate and proceeded into a large forecourt. There was already another carriage sitting in the courtyard. The driver stood outside of it, kicking the dirt. *He must have already dropped off his passengers,* Lisette thought. She wondered how many people would be there tonight. The more guests that attended the supper, the better for Lisette. They would provide the necessary distraction, making it more difficult for Le Sèvre to uncover her plan.

As soon as the carriage stopped moving, Le Sèvre motioned for Jeanne to exit first. After Jeanne was out of the carriage and a safe distance away, he turned to Lisette, "I trust you will behave yourself tonight...not like at Versailles. I need to conduct some important business this evening."

Lisette nodded and disembarked. They went inside and were immediately greeted by the Duc and Duchesse de Chartres. Lisette tried to listen to what the Duchesse said, but she found herself distracted by the grandness of the house.

The front hall was round-shaped and boasted marble floors

with a tall ceiling. Sitting atop two small, round violet wood tables were Sèvres porcelain vases and white marble statuettes of Greek and Roman figures.

The Duc and Duchesse exchanged pleasantries with Le Sèvre and her mother. Then the Duchesse turned to Lisette. "After the second course," the Duchesse whispered and motioned for Lisette to follow her into the drawing room.

After nearly an hour of conversation in the drawing room, they were invited to enter the dining room for the meal. The dining room was as luxurious as the rest of the house. The delicately tinted chairs set the tone for the room. Painted in the same lilac that matched the varnish on the chairs, the *boiserie* was carved with motifs of pearls, garlands and musical instruments. The tall, wide windows and mirrors interrupted the rhythm of the wooden paneling.

Lisette noticed Madame Gervais. She was dressed as a servant standing near the back wall waiting to serve. Madame Gervais would assist with the supper and then leave after the second course to go upstairs to the Duchesse's bedroom. Lisette was careful not to stare at Madame Gervais or to give Le Sèvre any indication that they were colluding.

Lisette's stomach tightened as she sat down at the long table. Everything was proceeding according to their plan and yet Lisette was nervous.

She distracted herself with the table's *décor*. The plates, silverware, crystal glasses and silver-gilt candlesticks were spectacle enough, but then Lisette saw the great centerpiece. In the middle of the table was an entire land-scape complete with valleys, hills, trees and flowers and even a river, all covered with frost and snow. Lisette noticed that the longer she sat watching it, the more the "snow" started to melt, probably from the warmth of the candles placed throughout the scene. *The snow must be made of starch*, she thought. As the "snow" melted, the trees became greener, the flowers brighter and the river filled with liquid. Lisette couldn't take her eyes off of the spellbinding *tableau*.

For the next hour, Lisette ate with her parents, the Duc and Duchesse and a dozen other supper guests. It seemed to her that everyone was taking more time than usual to eat their first and second courses. Finally, when she saw the third course about to be served, Madame Gervais slipped out. The Duchesse then excused herself, complaining of illness and the need to rest.

As Lisette stood to leave too, her mother placed her hand on Lisette's arm. "Where are you going?" Jeanne asked her.

"Don't worry, Mother. I will return shortly." Lisette tried to pull away from her mother's grip.

"I asked you a question, Lisette. Where are you going?" Jeanne asked her again.

"I'm afraid, like the Duchesse, I do not feel well. I need some air," Lisette said. She noticed Le Sèvre frowning. He didn't look pleased.

Before her mother could respond, the Duc spoke, "You may be excused, Mademoiselle Vigée."

Lisette saw her mother look at Le Sèvre. He nodded his head and Jeanne loosened her hold on Lisette's arm. She walked away from the table and out of the room.

Lisette's entire body tensed as she found the stairs and made her way up toward the Duchesse's private rooms. She was to meet the Duchesse and the inspector in the Duchesse's sitting room, which adjoined the bedroom. *The third door on the left,* Lisette reminded herself. It was critical that she find the sitting room quickly so that she could join the Duchesse and *le mouche* who had already hidden themselves there.

Lisette concentrated to remember exactly what Madame Gervais had told her. Over the past few days, Madame Gervais had become familiar with the layout of the Duc and Duchesse's private rooms. In exchange for her help capturing Le Sèvre, the Duchesse had agreed to spare Madame Gervais punishment. She would not be arrested and no one would discover her criminal history with Le Sèvre or their child together.

When Lisette reached the top of the stairs, she turned and went down the left side of the hallway. *One, Two, Three,* she counted. Lisette noted each door as she passed them. She stopped in front of the third one. It was slightly ajar. Lisette gently pushed it open, just enough to allow her to squeeze through. She went inside and carefully pulled the door closed.

As soon as Lisette entered the room, she saw the Duchesse and the inspector standing near the door that connected the sitting room with the bedroom.

The Duchesse waved at her. "Lisette, come over here with us." The Duchesse pointed to where she should stand. "Lisette, Monsieur Roche will be the inspector arresting Le Sèvre this evening."

"Good evening, Mademoiselle. I am at your service," Monsieur Roche said to Lisette.

She was very familiar with *les mouches*, the vast network of police spies that the Lieutenant Général de Police of Paris relied upon.

"Now we should wait in silence, as we do not know exactly when Le Sèvre will arrive. We do not want him to hear us in here," the Duchesse said gravely.

Lisette agreed. At this point there was no need for any more talking. Lisette had rarely seen the Duchesse so serious. The Duchesse wanted to apprehend Le Sèvre as badly as Lisette. According to Marguerite, years ago, the Duchesse had been robbed of several necklaces and rings. She had always suspected it was a servant, but she was now convinced it had been Le Sèvre. She believed he had accomplished the heist during a supper not unlike the one this evening. To the Duchesse, this was long-awaited justice about to be served.

Lisette took her place behind the Duchesse and the

inspector. The three of them positioned themselves so that they couldn't be seen. The adjoining door remained open just wide enough to see the tulipwood and mahogany secretary's desk in the corner of the Duchesse's bedroom. Lisette's view was partially obstructed by the heads of the Duchesse and Monsieur Roche, but she could still see into the bedroom. Lisette watched as Madame Gervais made herself comfortable in a dark pink upholstered armchair next to the writing desk. Le Sèvre would be joining her soon.

As they stood waiting in silence, Lisette peered around the Duchesse's sitting room. It was exquisite. The elegantly carved *boiserie* displayed flowers and woodland animals. The curtains were made of damask and gathered in the middle with satin ribbons that matched the dark pink stripes of the fabric. The sofas and armchairs were covered in the same fabric. Everything was coordinated, down to the smallest detail.

The bedroom decoration was an extension of the sitting room, full of dark pink upholstered furniture and matching damask curtains. There was a pink taffeta screen, a small painted tin table for washing and a walnut dressing table with a mirror. Even the *chaise percée* had an embroidered seat cover of the same pink hue. Lisette had never seen such an elaborate chamber pot. She thought that such a beautiful piece of furniture almost betrayed its function as a human waste receptacle.

Lisette glanced over to the large window located next to the door. She peeked down to the inner courtyard below. She saw several footmen and lackeys standing near their masters' coaches. They were milling around talking and laughing with each other. There was no other visible activity in the courtyard. All was quiet. *Good. Better that it is still and quiet,* she thought. Lisette continued to watch the courtyard. There was little else to do while they all waited for Le Sèvre.

After a quarter of an hour, the Duchesse broke the silence. "Monsieur, would it be more effective to hide behind the false fireplace?"

"No, Duchesse it would not. It would be too difficult to hear or see the goings-on in the bedroom. We are better off right here," the inspector said.

Suddenly, the Duchesse bent down. "I think I see Le Sèvre!" she said in a hushed voice.

"Madame Gervais! What is taking you so long?" Le Sèvre sounded irritated.

Lisette knew he was trying his best not to scream at Madame Gervais. Lisette stretched her neck so that she could better see around the Duchesse and Monsieur Roche.

"You startled me. I was about to come find you," Madame Gervais said calmly.

"Did you grab it yet?" Le Sèvre asked her.

"No, that is the problem. I can't find it. The necklace isn't where you said it would be. Your sources were wrong."

"Impossible. I'm never wrong. Let me see." Le Sèvre walked over to the corner of the bedroom to where the writing desk stood.

It was an unusual piece, much larger than similar desks. There were several drawers – at least that were visible. Many of these desks had secret drawers where their owners hid their most precious possessions.

Lisette hoped Le Sèvre would believe Madame Gervais' incompetence.

Le Sèvre crouched down on the floor underneath the desk and examined it closely.

"I checked there. I doubt you'll find it," Madame Gervais said to him.

Leave it alone, Lisette thought. She was afraid that if Madame Gervais continued challenging Le Sèvre, he might become suspicious.

He looked over to Madame Gervais and frowned. "Why are you suddenly having problems lifting jewels?"

"I know you'll have much better luck," Madame Gervais said in a sing-song voice.

Lisette worried that she had changed her tone too abruptly, because Le Sèvre's skepticism wasn't subsiding.

He stepped away from the desk and toward the main door of the bedroom.

"Where are you going?" asked Madame Gervais.

"Something doesn't feel right. I'm not sure what, but I think we should abandon it," Le Sèvre said.

"How can you say that? After waiting for so many years for this opportunity to arise again?" Madame Gervais had moved to the door to block him.

"Get out of my way, Woman."

"No. You seem to have a short memory, but I remember....I recall that night well. I nearly died by your hand. You were so upset that we only found a small portion of the Duchesse's jewels."

Le Sèvre was listening. He hadn't tried to push his way out of the room any farther.

"Remember how you swore to me that night that we would return? No matter how many years it took...we would come back...and do it right. We would grab the best of her collection....the ones locked away in there." Madame Gervais pointed to the desk.

Le Sèvre glanced over at it.

"This chance will never come again," Madame Gervais said confidently. "Your scheme is very good, but sooner or later it is bound to fail." She paused and then quickly added, "Take this opportunity now, before it is too late."

"What are you talking about? You and I have a flawless arrangement. It has been working for years." Le Sèvre looked intensely proud of himself, as if he had invented a new medicine that would benefit all of humanity.

He really believes that he is clever, Lisette realized.

Lisette noticed the different reactions of the Duchesse and Monsieur Roche. The Duchesse looked horrified while Monsieur Roche seemed eager to pounce on Le Sèvre.

Madame Gervais repeated herself, "Take this opportunity now. We are here. It might not ever come again."

Le Sèvre returned to the desk and fiddled with the mechanisms on its underside. Lisette heard the clanking of metal knobs. After a few moments of tinkering, nothing happened. No new drawers opened or suddenly appeared.

"That was my problem. I couldn't find the secret drawer," Madame Gervais explained.

"Be quiet and let me think. I know it is in here." Le Sèvre continued to fumble with the desk.

He'll get it very soon, Lisette thought.

"You found the necklace?" Madame Gervais asked Le Sèvre in an uncharacteristically loud voice.

"Shhh. Keep your voice down. No, not yet, but I'm close. I can feel it," Le Sèvre said as he continued to struggle with the desk. He retrieved a small metal tool from his pocket and tried to pry open the hidden compartment. Within a few moments, a drawer popped open.

"Voila!" Le Sèvre exclaimed.

"You found it!" Madame Gervais cried out as she carefully watched the door to the adjoining room where Lisette was waiting with the Duchesse and the inspector.

"Shhh. You stupid wench."

Lisette saw Le Sèvre pocket the necklace.

"You stay up here for another quarter of an hour, then return downstairs. It will arouse suspicion if we are seen together," Le Sèvre said and then turned to leave.

Before Le Sèvre could escape, the inspector pushed open the adjoining door and charged into the room. The Duchesse and Lisette followed closely behind.

"Stop!" The Duchesse pointed to Le Sèvre. "Arrest that man!" the Duchesse said to Monsieur Roche.

Le Sèvre started to run, but the inspector was younger and quicker. He easily caught Le Sèvre and escorted him back into the bedroom. Le Sèvre fought against Monsieur Roche, kicking and spitting at the inspector as he tried to subdue him. After Monsieur Roche had tied Le Sèvre's wrists behind his back, the inspector pushed Le Sèvre directly in front of the Duchesse.

"Give it here. I believe you have something of mine," the Duchesse said as she held out her hand.

"I don't know what you are talking about," Le Sèvre said without flinching.

The Duchesse turned to Lisette and said, "I think we all saw where he put it."

Lisette stepped out from behind the Duchesse and beheld Le Sèvre. She said confidently, "He put the necklace in his right coat pocket."

Until now, Le Sèvre had not noticed Lisette. As soon as she spoke, he stared at her in disbelief. "You?"

The Duchesse motioned to Monsieur Roche who reached into Le Sèvre's pocket and removed the necklace. As he handed it over to the Duchesse, she said, "Take him away."

"You little shrew! I will make sure you pay for this betrayal." Le Sèvre lunged at Lisette, but the inspector quickly pulled him back and gained control of him.

"You are coming with me," Monsieur Roche ordered.

Before Monsieur Roche hauled him out of the room, Lisette approached Le Sèvre. She stood a nose length away from him. "You no longer control me." She swiveled away from him and went to the window. Lisette wanted to see the carriage drive away with Le Sèvre safely shackled inside.

As the inspector dragged Le Sèvre toward the bedroom door, Lisette heard him yell out, "Ask Capitaine de Chaumont about Général Truclot. The Général and I have known each other for many years. He owes me a favor."

Refusing to meet his gaze, Lisette glanced toward the courtyard below. She listened to Le Sèvre scream profanities as he was led down the stairs. Then she heard her mother shrieking. Lisette would have to make her understand that they were better off without him.

After much commotion and carrying on in the foyer, Lisette finally heard the front door slam shut. Madame Gervais and the Duchesse had gone downstairs, leaving Lisette alone in the Duchesse's sitting room, near the window.

A few moments later, she saw Le Sèvre in the courtyard below. Even though he was restrained, he continued to struggle against the inspector's hold as he was forced to enter the carriage. It took two men to subdue Le Sèvre inside the *fiacre*. Lisette remained fixated on Le Sèvre's carriage as it drove out of the courtyard, through the outer gate and onto the Rue Saint-Honoré. Lisette stood by the window watching it become smaller until she could no longer see it at all.

Le Sèvre is gone.

Chapter Thirty-Five

Lisette set down her palette and brush, stood back and assessed her progress. She was nearly finished with her latest allegory painting. *One more glaze of Demeter,* she thought. As Lisette picked up her palette again, she heard a knock at her studio door. *Maybe if I ignore it, they will go away,* she said to herself.

In the month since Le Sèvre went to prison, many friends had come to her studio. Over the past few days, however, the number of well-wishers had dwindled. Almost everyone she knew had already visited.

Lisette gripped her brush and began painting again. Now operating her studio legally, Lisette had been painting furiously, making up for lost time. Madame Gervais had easily convinced her husband to approve Lisette's Guild membership and grant her a license. Rarely leaving the studio, Lisette had completed more paintings in one month than most artists could produce in six. To maximize her painting time, she would often spend the night in the studio. Lisette would stay late painting, take a short rest and then begin again each morning.

Lisette was also working once again with Le Brun. As soon as Le Sèvre had gone to jail, Le Brun had immediately sold the paintings that she had stored with Briard, including the allegories. Le Brun continued to discourage her from creating allegories and historicals, but he was still willing to sell them and pocket his commission. Le Brun had also sold Lisette's most recent portraits...and for copious amounts of money. Even without Le Sèvre, her reputation as a portrait painter was growing among the noble classes. After only a month, Lisette was supporting herself, her mother and her brother, who had returned to school, in a very comfortable manner.

Lisette looked over at the chaise-lounge on the other side of the room. It was cluttered with her nightclothes and a bed sheet. *I should sleep at home tonight*, she thought. Her mother had been asking Lisette to spend more time at home. Jeanne had told Lisette that she was still uncomfortable being alone, but she had grown accustomed to life without an abusive husband. Lisette knew that her mother had endured great trials in the past several years, not only losing two husbands in that time, but also her house and many of her possessions too. As a convicted thief, Le Sèvre forfeited his home and much of his personal property. Lisette was pleased that she could provide her mother with a new house and replace many of the items she had lost when Le Sèvre went to prison. While not on the most fashionable street, the house that Lisette could afford to buy for them was still very posh. It was a stand-alone house with three floors and two servants. Lisette had insisted that Henri and Mademoiselle Tothier remain with their household.

The knocking resumed. *This person is not going away,* she realized.

Lisette opened the door. It was Amante. Lisette had wondered why he had not come to see her immediately after Le Sèvre had been jailed. There was no longer any reason for him to stay away. Lisette had tried not to be hurt by his absence, but it had been difficult. There was so much that she had wanted to say to him. She had so many questions. Maybe today she would get some answers.

"Amante. Come in."

"I heard about Le Sèvre. How are you?" Amante asked.

"Better," Lisette told him.

Amante smiled. "You must have felt such relief when you heard the news of his death."

"Death?" Lisette felt like he had slapped her in the face.

"You didn't know?"

Lisette shook her head. She began to sway.

"Come, let's sit." Amante helped her to the chaise-lounge and sat down next to her. "It happened yesterday in prison. The rumor is that the Duc de Chartres was responsible. The Duc has never taken kindly to people who steal from him, or even attempt to steal from him."

"He is really dead?" Lisette still wasn't sure she had heard Amante correctly.

"Yes, dead," Amante said, nodding his head.

Lisette sat back on the chaise-lounge and closed her eyes. She inhaled and then exhaled deeply. It was finally easy for her to breathe again and her insides were no longer twisted. Le Sèvre was really gone...forever. She opened her eyes and saw Amante. She found it difficult to look away from his dark eyes.

"He didn't have long to rot in jail. About a month, if I'm correct," Amante said.

Lisette thought for a moment about Amante's words. *He knows exactly how long Le Sèvre was in jail?*

Lisette looked right at him. "If you knew Le Sèvre had been arrested and taken to For-l'Évêque why didn't you come to see me?" She stood and moved to the other side of the studio. "Are you still upset with me for not listening to you and taking your advice about the license?"

Amante let out a low laugh and followed her. He reached out and touched her cheek. "No, *ma chérie*. Nothing could be further from the truth. How I have wanted to see you...to touch you...to kiss you." He leaned in and lightly touched his lips to hers.

Lisette wanted to kiss him back, but she controlled herself. "I don't understand. What stopped you?" Lisette asked him.

Amante leaned in again and gently whispered in her ear, "Shhh. All that matters is that I'm here now. My sweet Lisette."

As he kissed her earlobe and moved to her neck, her protestations faded. The more he kissed her, the weaker her resolve to push him away. She could feel her body going limp at his touch. Amante kissed her passionately. A warm feeling shot down the length of her body causing her legs to wobble. His tongue was soft and sweet in her mouth. She found it difficult to concentrate on anything but him.

"I want to make love to you, Lisette," he said softly as he scooped her up in his arms.

She didn't fight him.

Amante carried Lisette over to the chaise-lounge. Once Amante had laid her down on the long chair, he began unfastening the back of her dress. Before he had finished, he leaned down and kissed her again. In between kisses, he whispered, "Lisette, I have missed you." He moved his hand up inside her petticoat and stroked her inner thigh. He finished unfastening her gown and the bodice fell to the floor. He pulled off her linen *chemise* and then his own.

She closed her eyes, but sensed him looking at her nakedness.

"You are so very beautiful, Lisette." He kissed her again and cupped her bare breasts. His hands were warm and strong. "How I have longed for this day...when we could make love. I don't know when it will come again."

As soon as she heard these last words, Lisette bolted

straight up. "What do you mean?"

"Shhh, *ma chérie*, lie back and enjoy my lips on you," Amante said, dismissing her question. He gently moved her down onto the chaise-lounge.

Lisette sat up again. "Are you going away? Is that why you don't know when we'll be together again?"

Amante sat up too. He faced her and was silent.

"Tell me. I have a right to know the truth," Lisette said as she pulled the sheet to cover herself.

"Yes. I have to leave Paris," he paused and then added, "…France."

"Why? When will you be back?"

"You have a lot of questions." Amante leaned in like he was going to kiss her.

Before she could push him away there was a thundering knock at the studio door followed by a booming voice. "Capitaine de Chaumont! It is urgent. You are needed right away, orders of Général Truclot."

"I must leave you, *ma chérie*," Amante said as he threw on his *chemise*.

"Right now?"

"Yes, the army will not wait," he said as he adjusted his waistcoat.

"When will you be back?"

"Whenever Général Truclot gives me orders to return." He smoothed his hair and stood. Amante held both of her hands. "My sweet Lisette."

Lisette pulled her hands out of his. *Général Truclot,* she thought. She remembered what Le Sèvre had said to her just as he was being taken away by Monsieur Roche, *Ask Capitaine de Chaumont about Général Truclot.*

Lisette stood up. "This is Le Sèvre's doing," she exclaimed.

"I have to go," Amante said firmly.

"But he is gone. You don't have to leave," Lisette said, trying to get Amante to understand that the threat no longer existed.

Amante took a step forward and held Lisette tightly in his arms. "*Ma chérie*, I'm afraid I do not have a choice." He leaned down and kissed her forehead and then her lips.

She returned his kiss, locking her lips with his.

The soldier knocked again, this time so violently Lisette thought he might break the door. "Capitaine de Chaumont!"

Amante gently pulled away from Lisette and stepped to the door. He hesitated, turned around and said in a low voice, "I love you, Lisette."

Amante opened the door and left with the soldier.

Lisette went to the threshold and watched them walk down the stairs and out of sight. She stood in the doorway staring at the empty stairwell. *I love you too.*

Lisette stepped back inside the studio and collapsed on the chaise-lounge. Peering out of the room's small window, she saw no clouds, only a hazy, gray, lifeless sky. Lisette turned her head away from the window and toward the other side of the studio. At first, she saw only piles of supplies and empty canvases, but then she noticed it – her old sketchpad. It had been months since she had drawn in it last...not since her visit to Versailles the previous summer.

Pulling herself off the chaise-lounge, Lisette rescued the sketchbook from a stack of papers. She thumbed through it until she saw the sketch of the Queen. *How becoming she is,* Lisette thought. She smiled as she remembered the impromptu sitting with Antoinette and wondered if she would see the Queen again.

Will she have me back to Versailles? Will she have me paint her?

About the Author

Rebecca's experiences organizing art museum exhibitions and teaching college Art History courses motivated her to write historical fiction. She continues to be inspired by the untold stories of women from history. When not writing, Rebecca enjoys discovering new places and foods, especially those that involve France. Rebecca lives outside Washington, D.C., with her husband and three children.

For more information about this book or to contact the author, please visit: rebeccaglenn.com/

Coming Soon!

Don't miss the next two installments of the
Queen's Painter Series:

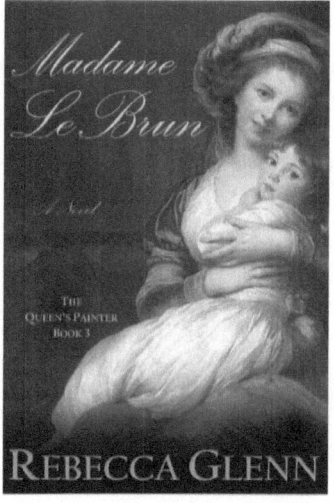